"LOOKING FOR SOMETHING TO READ, CONTESSA?"

Sofia laughed as she caressed the leatherbound books. "The party is rather a bore, Lord Osborne. I was seeking a distraction—and it seems you are of the same frame of mind."

The flicker of the candlelight did not quite reach Deverill's face.

"Perhaps we could make the night a bit more interesting," she added coyly.

"Is that an invitation?" Deverill's voice was as inscrutable as his expression. "I was under the impression that my advances were not welcome."

"A lady must sometimes play hard to get." Hearing voices at the far end of the corridor, she took a step closer. "Most gentlemen are hunters at heart. They find the chase exhilarating."

"And when the quarry is cornered?"

She reached out her hand and touched his jaw, smooth, strong, with just a faint hint of stubbling against her fingertips. "Then I expect the hunter will move in for the coup de grace."

Deverill hesitated for a heartbeat, then caught her up in his arms . . .

"Pickens is a wonde

RAVES FOR *SEDUCED BY A SPY . . .*

"4½ Stars! TOP PICK! Merlin's Maidens make a comeback in a thrilling sequel. But it's more than action that makes this a keeper; it's the emotional depth of Pickens's honorable characters, strong conflict, and superb repartee."

—*Romantic Times BOOKreviews Magazine*

"Excellent . . . A rollicking action adventure full of smoldering romance, historical intrigue [and] dry wit . . . The return of two popular characters from the first book in the series will delight readers who have already discovered Merlin's Maidens, while those who are new to the series will thoroughly enjoy getting to know the spirited and courageous Shannon and the wickedly charming Alexandr. I highly recommend it."

—FreshFiction.com

"Pickens has added the swashbuckling of *The Three Musketeers* and some steamy romance. It's a lot of fun."

—JandysBooks.com

"Action-packed, with passion and romance radiating between Shannon and Alexandr . . . Another wonderful historical."

—BookLoons.com

Also by Andrea Pickens

The Spy Wore Silk
Seduced by a Spy

The
SCARLET
SPY

~

ANDREA PICKENS

FOREVER

NEW YORK   BOSTON

Copyright © 2008 by Andrea DaRif
All rights reserved. Except as permitted under the U.S. Copyright Act of 1976, no part of this publication may be reproduced, distributed, or transmitted in any form or by any means, or stored in a database or retrieval system, without the prior written permission of the publisher.

Cover design by Diane Luger
Cover illustration by John Paul
Handlettering by Ron Zinn

Forever
Hachette Book Group USA
237 Park Avenue
New York, NY 10017
Visit our Web site at www.HachetteBookGroupUSA.com

Forever is an imprint of Grand Central Publishing. The Forever name and logo is a trademark of Hachette Book Group USA, Inc.

Printed in the United States of America

First Printing: October 2008

10 9 8 7 6 5 4 3 2 1

For Frances Jalet-Miller

With many thanks for all your thoughtful insights and comments.
You really helped the Merlins take wing!

Chapter One

Candlelight kissed the cut crystal, the fire-gold sparks dancing in time to the Viennese waltz. The whisper of silk swirled with the scent of roses and jasmine. A lady's laugh, light and lush as the pearls at her throat, twined with the trilling notes of the violins.

"Place your hand a bit lower." Her partner, a dark-haired gentleman with angelic eyes and the devil's own smile, slid her gloved fingers to his hip. "*Si, si.* Now, if only I could ask you to dip into my trousers, *bella.*"

She stifled a laugh as the spinning steps of the dance drew them closer. "Naughty man. I—"

"*Non, non, NON!*" The dancing master rapped his ebony stick against the pianoforte. "That was clumsy as an ox—I saw your hand slip into his coat pocket."

"Sorry." The student known only as Sofia ducked her head in contrition.

"Try again." *Thwack.* "And you, Marco, stop distracting her with your lovemaking."

"Ah, but I cannot help it." Marco's lips twitched. "We Italians have a weakness for heavenly beauty, and signorina is a work of art, an ethereal Venus in velvet. Botticelli himself could not—"

Another sharp smack cut off the florid reply. "If you can't keep your lively appreciation from straying to Sofia's arse, you will be spending the rest of the class time scrubbing the stables."

"These hands were not made for mucking manure," he murmured with a waggle of his well-shaped brow.

"Zees class is not a joke, Monsieur Musto! Sofia must master not only the nuances of ballroom etiquette, but also the fine points of picking a gentleman's pocket. The success of a mission may depend on it."

"It's my fault, Monsieur Lemieux." Sofia spoke up quickly. "I fear I'm far more comfortable dressed in buckskins and boots than satin and slippers. And my grip is far more used to taking hold of a sword than a sliver of gold."

"Would that you'd take hold of *my* sword, *bella*," whispered Marco.

"Put a cork in it." She punctuated the warning with a discreet kick to his shin. "You're going to land us both in deep suds."

Marco composed his expression to a semblance of seriousness. "*Prego, bella*. I don't want you to suffer for my sins."

"Which Lord knows are legion," she muttered as the music struck up again. "Do try to behave, Marco. A black mark on my record is no laughing matter. I can't chance a failing grade."

Discipline. Duty. Mrs. Merlin's Academy for Select Young Ladies held its students to a higher standard than most schools. But then, its mission was not to polish the highborn daughters of the *ton* into Diamonds of the First Water. Rather, it was to mold a ragtag group of orphans—all handpicked from the slums of London for their courage and cleverness—into a secret force of women warriors. Dancing and drawing room manners were part of the curriculum. But so were fencing, shooting, and riding—not to mention the more esoteric arts of war and seduction. And the lessons learned within its classrooms could mean the difference between life and death.

"*Attendez-vous,* musicians. The violins and cellos will begin at the last stanza."

Sofia forced herself to relax. The subtle sleight of hand depended on perfect timing. A twirl, a spin . . .

This time around, her fingers slipped in and out of Marco's coat without stirring a thread. As the melody rose to a final crescendo, she held the gold pocketwatch aloft.

The dancing instructor—a former jewel thief whose exploits had been the toast of Paris until the Terror cut short his career—gave a grudging nod of approval. "Better. But there is still room for improvement."

"That is all we have time for today." Mrs. Merlin, the elderly headmistress of the Academy, rose from her chair. "However, I've scheduled a double session for tomorrow. It's even more important that a document or letter can be removed from a gentleman's coat without anyone being the wiser." Dressed in dove-gray silks that matched the silvery hue of her hair, she looked frail as a feather in the swaying shadows of the potted palms. But the glint from behind her spectacles was still sharp as steel as she surveyed the school ballroom.

Sofia slanted a look around as well. From its polished parquet dance floor to its ornate Adam ceiling, every detail was designed to replicate the splendor of a Mayfair mansion. The headmistress was a firm believer in having her students practice their skills under real-life conditions. Were a rose petal or a velvet swag out of place, it would not escape the lady's eye.

Seemingly satisfied, Mrs. Merlin's gaze turned from the decorative urns flanking the entrance. "It appears you are making good progress, Sofia. You may take a short recess before your next class."

Good. But was it good enough? Sofia bit back a sigh.

"I've ordered refreshments to be served. Do sample the champagne. You ought to become familiar with its taste and how it affects your head." As the headmistress stepped away to confer with the dancing master, a servant approached with a tray of drinks.

"I must say, I am having a hard time deciding which is my favorite extracurricular activity—dancing or art." Giovanni Marco Musto's official duties at the Academy were to serve as assistant riding and fencing instructor. However, the mercenary from Milan—who preferred "Marco" to his other moniker—was often called upon to serve as a model for the advanced drawing class, a position he enjoyed with shameless delight, seeing as it called for posing in the nude. With his dark eyes, sensual mouth, and sable locks that curled in Renaissance ringlets around his collar, he was a picture of masculine beauty.

And well he knew it.

"I would rather be practicing my skills with a saber," muttered Sofia under her breath.

"Si?" Marco cocked his head. "But you have a natural knack for more subtle forms of attack."

"I've had enough practice." She forced a sardonic smile, though the memory of her early life was not something she cared to recall. "Stealing is one of the basic skills for survival when you are living on the streets. You don't last very long if you aren't good at it."

Despite his exaggerated preening and ribald banter, he was sensitive enough not to miss the tautness in her voice. "There is nothing shameful about staying alive, *bella*," he replied softly. "And Signora Merlin obviously feels those early lessons can be put to good use."

"I would rather be working on more martial skills."

"All work and no play makes for a dull existence, *bella*." His swagger returning in the blink of an eye, Marco thrust a glass of champagne into her hands and drew her to the far corner of the ballroom. "Come, let us drink up. After all, part of your education in the ways of Polite Society is to learn an appreciation for fine wine."

"I can't help but wonder why all this is a necessary part of my training. Merlins are meant to fight." Sofia waited until she was sheltered behind one of the marble columns before making a face. "Blades and bullets are far more important subjects to master."

"Beauty can also be a deadly weapon." The Italian grinned as he raised the crystal coupe to his lips. "Indeed, its effect on men can be lethal."

"I'm not looking to slay hearts," she replied somewhat snappishly. Marco's teasing was usually amusing. But of late, her mood had been a bit blue deviled, though she couldn't put a finger on why. Save for the small stumble on the dance floor, she was earning top honors in all of her other studies. And yet, loath though she was to admit it, the daily routine *had* grown a bit dull. "Unlike you, I try to think of more than pleasuring my flesh."

"Well, your thoughts do not appear to be making you very happy. If you would come to my bed tonight, I would tease that scowl into a smile."

Sofia laughed in spite of herself.

"*Va bene*—that's better." He cocked his head. "Is something bothering you, *bella*?"

"No," she lied. "It's just that Siena and Shannon never had to polish their ballroom skills to this extent."

She looked away and smoothed at her skirts, trying not to think too much of her former roommates. The three of them had become as close as sisters during their years at the Academy. Shared adversity was perhaps a more binding tie than blood. They had all managed to survive the savage slums without family, without friends. Without names. On first entering the Academy, all students were placed before an ornate globe, and as it spun, they chose a moniker from the swirl of gold lettering. A new name for a new life. *Siena. Shannon. Sofia.*

And now, suddenly, her comrades were gone. Within the last eight months, they had both been given difficult, dangerous assignments. Not only had they passed with flying colors, but they also had moved on to new lives and new responsibilities in the world outside the Academy walls.

Leaving her as the only one of the tight-knit trio who had not been called upon to test her wings in a real mission.

Sofia fought down a stab of self-pity. She could not help feeling a little lonely, a little lost. Of the three friends, she had always been the voice of reason and restraint, reining in her more reckless roommates to keep them out of disciplinary trouble. Did her superiors think she lacked the mettle to be a Merlin?

Seeing Marco's eyes narrow in concern, she quickly swallowed her doubts with a tiny sip of champagne. "Their victories depended on swashbuckling feats of daring, rather than picking a gentleman's pocket while dancing a waltz," she went on. "My swordplay may not be quite as sharp as theirs, but my riding and shooting skills are bang up to the mark. I daresay I can hold my own in a fight against any opponent." A hint of heat, at odds with her usual cool composure, crept into her voice. "Yet of late, it seems I've been relegated to nothing but drawing room duties."

"Each Merlin is called upon to undertake a different sort of mission, Sofia." As if by magic, the Marquess of Lynsley appeared in one of the archways of the alcoves. Dressed in somber shades of charcoal and gray, he was nearly invisible in the darkness—a choice that was no doubt deliberate, for the marquess spent much of his time in the world of shadows.

"One that is matched to her unique talents," he continued. "Not every enemy can be fought with steel or gunpowder. You have a natural grace and elegance, which are far harder to learn than fencing or marksmanship. Such qualities will allow you to move within the highest circles of Society without drawing undue attention."

She felt her heart flutter. "Does that mean you have something specific in mind, sir?" Not only was Lord Lynsley the founding father and leading benefactor of the Academy, but he was also the commander in chief of the elite force of women warriors who trained within its walls. It was he who personally picked each child and offered her a place at the school. And it was he who decided which member of the Master Class was ready to fight against England's enemies.

"Perhaps." It was hard to read his face in the flickering light. "Much as I enjoy Mrs. Merlin's excellent strawberry tarts, I did not journey here from London simply for tea and cakes."

"Must you leave so soon, my dear, delightful Devil?" Lord Deverill Osborne untangled his legs from the satin sheets and sat up. Squinting, he tried to bring the hazy shapes on the gilt dressing table into focus. *Was that a third bottle of brandy?* Or merely a crystal flask of Collette's expensive French perfume? Judging by the overlush scent clinging to both the bedclothes and his person, it was likely to be as empty as the glass of spirits that had fallen to the carpet.

"It's past noon." His gaze had cleared enough to make out the hands on the ormolu clock.

"Then stay until the morrow. Think of all the sinful things we can do before the next dawn." The courtesan lowered her voice to a smoky murmur. "Have you any idea how many naughty ways there are to use an ostrich plume?"

"I've no doubt a ladybird of your talent can exercise a great deal of creativity." He laughed softly as her fingers glided over his cock. Like the rest of her, they were supple, shapely, sensuous . . . and a little too grasping of late. "But I fear I have quite exhausted my own capacity for pleasure, sweeting."

"With a little rest and a little champagne, I am sure I can coax a little more life into you."

"I've had enough to drink." Osborne tugged his shirt out from beneath the rumpled counterpane. His trousers had suffered a similar fate. "In any case, I must go. I am engaged to meet Lord Harkness at Tattersall's, and it looks as if I will have to make a stop at my town house for a change of clothing." He drew in a deep breath. *And a bath.*

"Will you return tonight?"

He shook his head. "Sorry, but I promised to attend Lady Haverton's ball."

His *cher amie's* lips pursed to a pout. "I don't intend to be a ladybird forever, Deverill. Marriage would make me a respectable lady, and then I could accompany you to the glittering ballrooms of Mayfair." In the sliver of sunlight coming through the draperies, her eyes took on a mercenary gleam. "Just think of it—we could drink and dance until dawn, and you could awake every afternoon with me by your side."

Marriage?

He repressed a shudder. It was time to think of giving La Belle Collette her congé. She had lasted longer than most of his mistresses. Perhaps because it had seemed too great an effort to look for a replacement.

"Come, sweeting, you are a woman of the world." He found his shoes under the bed and slipped them on. "Let us be frank. Our arrangement is one of mutual convenience. It will not culminate in a walk down the aisle of St. George's on Hanover Square."

"But you find me *tres* amusing, *non*?"

"No. Not when you start to sound like a shrew." He looped his limp cravat over his collar, somehow feeling as if a noose were tightening around his neck. The air was suddenly cloying, and his head was beginning to ache abominably. "Wheedling and whining does not become you."

"Why, you ungrateful, uncaring man! After all I've done to please you—how *dare* you accuse me of wheedling!" Her voice was now more of a screech than a whine.

Osborne had heard quite enough. He turned to retrieve his coat, ducking just in time to avoid the Sevres figurine she hurled at his head. Picking his way through the shards of porcelain, he paused just long enough to toss a fistful of banknotes onto her dressing table.

"Choose a parting gift at Rundell and James," he said

quietly before shutting the door on a string of French invectives.

Lud, the ladybird's language would put a bloody pirate to blush. She was no longer speaking of what she would do with a feather. The muffled shrieks were more of a blow-by-blow description of how she would sauté his testicles in garlic and olive oil.

He supposed he should count himself fortunate to have escaped with his limbs, if not his dignity, intact. Running a hand through his tangled hair, he sighed and finished tucking in his shirttails. In the past, he would have found the scene highly diverting. Now it was merely . . . depressing.

Stepping out to the street, Osborne flagged down a passing hackney and settled back against the squabs for the ride back to Grosvenor Square. He was weary to the bone, and not just from a night of torrid sex. The truth was, his rakish life was becoming tiresome. *Was he growing old?* Or merely jaded? Everything seemed to come easily to him.

Too easily, perhaps. He feared he was in danger of becoming careless, contemptuous of everything around him. It was hard to value the things that required little effort to possess. Osborne sighed. Having breezed through his studies at Oxford with the highest academic honors, he ought to be smart enough to figure out the cause of his malaise. But somehow it defied all logic. By any rational measure, he had everything a man could want. Yet something essential seemed missing.

Catching a glimpse of himself in the windowpane, he stared for a moment at the smudged glass. Fair hair, blue eyes, classically chiseled features that many ladies were wont to describe as angelic. He knew he was a great favorite of the *ton*, a sought-after guest at any entertainment. His face was considered highly attractive, his conversation highly amusing, and his manner highly engaging, to both men and women alike. Such qualities, coupled with a perfect pedigree, opened any door in Polite Society.

Handsome. Witty. Charming. Whispering the words aloud left a stale taste in his mouth. It all sounded so shallow. Skin deep, rather than having any real substance.

The vision suddenly dissolved in the pelter of a passing rain shower. What was the true reflection of who he was?

Closing his eyes, Osborne pressed his fingertips to his temples and thought about how he was spending his time. At the moment, the few hours a week that he spent reviewing military documents for Army Intelligence was the most rewarding part of his life. The challenge kept boredom at bay. Perhaps his friend on Burrand's general staff could be persuaded to give him more work.

The idea helped him shake off his melancholy musing. There was a good chance he would encounter Major Fenimore at the ball this evening. If not, he could always stop by White's on the way home.

"This is a rather unusual situation." Mrs. Merlin took a moment to pour a cup of tea before opening her notebook.

. "That is one way of putting it." Lynsley went to stand by the hearth. But despite the blazing fire, he could not dispel the chill in his blood. "The duke approached me on a purely personal basis. We have known each other for years, and though he has no notion of my true duties at Whitehall, he thought that I might be able to advise him off the record on what he should do."

"At first blush, the death of his grandson from an overdose of opium appears to be a personal tragedy and not a matter of government concern."

The marquess nodded. "I thought the same thing,

despite Sterling's insistence that the young man had discovered some sinister forces at work here in London."

"Grief can stir up strange imaginings," said the headmistress softly as she began jotting a few notes. With her mild manners and ruffled silks, she presented a picture of matronly propriety—save for the point of a razor-sharp poniard peeking out from beneath her cuff.

"Indeed," agreed Lynsley. "Still, I made a few informal inquiries, thinking that if I found any evidence of foul play, I could ease a bit of his pain by helping to bring the miscreants to justice."

Mrs. Merlin's pen hovered over the page. "And?"

He blew out his breath. "And I fear there may be some truth to his accusations." Coals crackled in the hearth as he contemplated the flare of flames. "There is an old adage—where there is smoke, there is fire. In this case, a visit to several opium dens favored by the *ton* turned up some very unsettling information. Lord Robert Woolsey was not the first gentleman to die under suspicious circumstances. Seven have perished over the past six months, including a diplomat from Antwerp and an envoy from Venice."

"Unsettling indeed, but still not something that your branch of the government has any authority to handle. It seems more a matter for the local magistrates than our Merlins." She paused for a fraction. "However, if this were simply a sordid story of drugs and debauchery, you would not be here telling it." A tiny smile momentarily softened the pinch of her mouth. "Much as I enjoy your company for tea, Thomas, I am aware that you do not waste your time in social calls."

"You are right—there is a deeper, darker mystery here," answered the marquess. "A web of intrigue that seems to spread from the slums of St. Giles to the mansions of Mayfair. God only knows where it goes from there." Lynsley heaved a sigh. "Opium is only a small part of the mix. My informants have heard rumors of a sophisticated scheme of embezzlement, one that somehow siphons money from legitimate government contracts to a private consortium. Some shipments are diverted and sold for personal gain, while others are made with inferior materials, and the difference is simply pocketed as profit."

There was a small silence as he pressed his palms to the marble mantel. "Unfortunately, I have no other details as to what specifically is involved. But if it is true, essential services and military supplies are being compromised while a small circle of conspirators make a fortune."

"That certainly casts a different light on the duke's personal tragedy." Mrs. Merlin set aside her teacup. "If it is true."

"We can't afford not to follow the thread and see where it leads," he replied. "If there are high government officials tainted by corruption, it could have disastrous repercussions for the country. A scandal at this point in time would seriously weaken our efforts to stop Napoleon's march eastward."

"Yet you seem reluctant to act."

"It is never easy to send one of our students into danger. Especially when the enemy is naught but a swirl of smoke and shadow."

"Of course it's not easy, Thomas," replied Mrs. Merlin. "Keeping England safe from all its enemies is a difficult, dirty business. That is why the Academy exists." Seeing his fingers tighten on the polished stone, she added, "If it's any consolation, the girls understand the risks and accept the challenge. They believe as strongly as we do that our freedoms are worth fighting for."

"An eloquent speech, as usual. So you think I should have a clear conscience?" The marquess glanced up at the gilt-framed portrait of Sir Francis Walsingham, but the stern features of England's first spymaster offered little in the way of sympathy. "Even though I am considering putting one of our Merlins into a nest of vipers with little to go on save for rumor and innuendo?"

"If you are asking for a second opinion, I would say you have no choice but to do so. I take it you do not feel it is a case that can be handled through any normal channels of investigation at Whitehall."

He shook his head. "Given the sensitive nature of the charges, I do not trust involving any of the other departments."

Mrs. Merlin opened one of the document cases on her desk and took out a sheaf of papers. "One of our operatives working on the East India docks recently submitted a report on the trafficking of illegal goods from India and China. It should provide some useful leads. Indeed, one item already comes to mind. There is a new source, as yet unidentified, of extremely potent opium coming in from the East. At the same time, the Levant Company has suffered the loss of a number of shipments, which has driven up the price."

Lynsley frowned. "I shall have one of my men take a closer look at the activity around Mincing Lane, as well as attend the next fortnightly auction at Garraway's Coffee House." He thought for a moment. "I shall also send a sample of the narcotic found next to Lord Robert's body to Lady Sheffield for analysis. She may be able to identify its place of origin."

"Lady Sheffield?" Mrs. Merlin's brow furrowed. "Isn't she the one who was recently accused of poisoning her husband?"

"Malicious gossip," replied Lynsley. "The earl was a brute who drank himself to death. As for the lady, she is a serious scholar, a highly respected member of the Scientific Society, and a brilliant chemist. I've used her before, and her work is impeccable."

"I should have guessed the truth. The *ton* is always quick to attack a female of imagination and intelligence." The headmistress reached for a fresh sheet of foolscap. "Those investigations should turn up some answers. As for the duke's suspicions, did he give you any clue of what we are looking for?"

"There isn't much to go on," replied Lynsley, pursing his mouth. "Based on a diary found in the young man's rooms, Sterling believes his grandson was investigating a group of gentlemen who call themselves the Scarlet Knights—on account of their red waistcoats and wild carousing from dusk to dawn."

"I've heard rumors of their revelries." Mrs. Merlin tapped the pen to the tip of her chin. "Drinking, gambling, and raising hell in the less savory parts of the city is not uncommon behavior for blades of the *ton*, but the Knights are said to carry excess to the extreme."

Lynsley turned from the fire and clasped his hands behind his back. "It would all seem juvenile, if not for the people involved. Lord De Winton is said to be one of its regulars, as are several foreign noblemen. Their names are noted with red ink in Lord Robert's diary." He withdrew a small object from his coat pocket and placed it on the leather blotter. "This was found as well."

The headmistress picked up the gold key and carefully studied the blood-red enameled poppy crowning its end. "What is it for?"

Lynsley's lips thinned to a grim line. "That is what we

need to discover. Unfortunately, Lord Robert left no hint of its significance in his writings. But I have a strong feeling that it will unlock the secrets we seek."

"If we put it in the right hands."

"Yes. The right hands." The marquess's voice was barely audible over the hiss of the glowing embers.

The headmistress took a moment to sharpen her quill. "I think it's time we summon Sofia."

Chapter Two

*B*rushing the grains of gunpowder from her buckskins, Sofia took a seat on the wooden bench outside the head-mistress's private office. With its dark wainscoting and stone floor, the foyer offered few frills to soften a student's anxiety. A summons to report to the headmistress was never a purely social call. It usually signaled serious school infractions—discipline, detention, demerits. Or dismissal for failing to meet the rigorous standards of performance.

Sofia drew a deep breath and touched the tattoo above her left breast. Only a very few students ever made it to the Master Class and received the small black badge of a hawk that marked them as true Merlins. The rest were assigned to less demanding duties, serving as the eyes and ears of England around the globe.

Were Mrs. Merlin and the marquess having second thoughts about her rank? Lord Lynsley's oblique words might have been meant as a kindly warning. Though his austere face rarely revealed any emotion, his blue eyes al-ways held a spark of warmth when regarding any of the students. He had chosen them all—skinny little urchins abandoned in the stews—and monitored their progress over the years. In some sense, he was like the father none of them had ever known.

Had she let him down? Sofia couldn't help but think that the recent emphasis on ladylike manners reflected badly on her martial skills. Her gaze slanted to the window, where the fencing grounds, the stables, the shooting ranges, and the training fields stretched out as far as the eye could see. A Merlin must be the match of any man when it came to weapons or hand-to-hand combat. Perhaps the headmistress and the marquess doubted her steel. Her flesh began to prickle. Perhaps they were about to strip her of her commission.

Sofia stilled her fidgets by fingering the necklace beneath her sweat-dampened shirt. The thin filigree chain was new, purchased on a field trip to the fancy shops on Bond Street, but the gold locket had been in her possession since . . . a long time ago.

The case had the well-worn patina of age. The faint outlines of an initial were unreadable, the engraving crisscrossed with nicks and scratches. She liked to think it was an *S* carved into the precious metal. But whatever the letter, the locket had served as a personal talisman in times of trouble. *A lucky charm.* It had kept her safe in the savage streets; it had seen her through the difficult adjustments to Academy life.

Drawing it out from her shirt, Sofia opened the worn case and peeked at the tiny portrait. The pigment had faded over the years, blurring the features, the smile, the curling strands of raven hair that framed the fine-boned face. But the image was indelibly etched in her memory. She knew every nuance by heart. When she was a child, she had fancied a resemblance between the young lady and herself. *And now?*

Her own sea-green gaze looked away from the painted eyes. It was not wise to dwell on childish dreams. The Academy lessons all stressed that one had to be practical and pragmatic. *Dispassionate.* Emotion had no place in the line of duty. It didn't matter who she was; it only mattered what she had become.

Strange, but her roommates had never given much thought to their heritage. It had not bothered them to know nothing of their past, their parents. Afraid of appearing too sentimental, Sofia had feigned the same devil-may-care attitude. But in private, the picture had seemed to whisper a tantalizing question.

Who am I?

"Sofia. Mrs. Merlin will see you now."

Quickly, tucking the locket back inside the folds of linen, she stood and squared her shoulders. She would *not* show any sign of weakness. She was born to be a Merlin.

"Reporting for duty." Sofia snapped off a salute as she came to a halt in front of the oak desk.

"At ease." The headmistress regarded the martial stance and muddied boots for a long moment before setting aside her pen. The wrinkles on her brow appeared to deepen slightly. "I did not mean for you to march straight here from the stables, my dear." Sofia saw her slant a quick glance at Lord Lynsley, who was standing half hidden by the marble hearth. "Why don't you go back to your quarters and change—to the indigo blue silks, if you please. The marquess and I are in no rush."

Sofia felt her throat constrict. She turned on her heel, then hesitated. *To hell with behaving like a lady.* If she was to be drummed out of the Merlins, she would not go meekly.

"I would rather stay dressed as I am." Her chin took on a mutinous tilt. "With all due respect, I feel it unfair that my mastery of manners appears to have counted as a black mark against me. I may not wield a saber or stiletto quite as well as Siena or Shannon, but I'm a better shot and more skilled when it comes to stealth. It's unfair to demote me to the ranks of a mere observer without giving me a chance to prove myself in a mission."

"You think we are judging you unfit for active duty?" Mrs. Merlin set aside a plate of strawberry tarts and brushed a bit of sugar from her fingertips.

Sofia's martial tone turned more tentative. "Why else would you wish for me to dress in satins and lace? I . . . I assumed you were going to assign me to some menial work, like serving as a lady's maid to some foreign diplomat's wife."

"All of our students go on to do important work, whether as a tavernkeeper or a tweenie," replied the headmistress with a hint of reproach.

Sofia colored. "I meant no disrespect to my fellow students. It's just that I . . . I feared that . . ." She let her voice trail off, unsure of how to explain her misgivings.

"You feared that in comparison to your former roommates, you would be seen as somehow lacking?" It was Lord Lynsley who broke the awkward silence.

She nodded, not daring to meet his eye.

"As I said earlier, each Merlin is meant to have different skills. That is the strength of this school." His lips twitched. "If all our students possessed Shannon's explosive temper, the place would long since have gone up in smoke."

"And Siena shrouded herself in an air of mystery that was unsuitable for many missions," added Mrs. Merlin.

Shannon *did* have a tendency to set off sparks, thought Sofia. But her new husband, a raffish Russian spy by the name of Alexandr Orlov, seemed to have tempered her fire. Together they made a formidable team and at the moment were somewhere in Prussia, working to prevent Napoleon from marching any farther east.

As for Siena, she was also recently married—to an earl, no less—and on a clandestine assignment in Italy. Sofia gave an inward sigh. She had never met Lord Kirtland, but Shannon had said that Byron's poetic heroes paled in comparison to the raven-haired earl. . . .

". . . So, I trust you will have no cause for complaint," finished the headmistress.

"Sorry?" Roused from her momentary musings, Sofia snapped to attention.

"What Mrs. Merlin means is, you will find the situation no less challenging than those faced by your friends." As Lynsley turned, the candlelight caught the deep lines of worry etched at the corners of his eyes. "And no less dangerous. Indeed, to be truthful, I am having second thoughts about asking anyone to undertake the assignment. It may be an impossible one, even for a Merlin."

"Whatever it is, I should like to try, sir." Seeing his brow furrow, Sofia quickly added, "What is there to lose?"

"Your life, to begin with." Lynsley looked more serious than she had ever seen him. "As for the other ramifications, I wish I knew what they all might be. In this particular case, I cannot give you a name or a face of the enemy. I would have to toss you into the heart of London Society—a spider's web, however silken—and expect you to unravel the lies and intrigue by yourself."

"I've managed a number of sticky situations here at the Academy, sir." Sofia tried to appear calm and collected, though her heart was pounding wildly against her ribs. "I am adept at using both my weapons and my wiles. Whatever is called for, I won't let you down."

"It is not myself that I am worried about," replied the marquess softly. "I don't send any Merlin into battle unless I feel she has a decent chance of achieving victory."

Standing her ground, Sofia quickly countered. "We are trained to deal with adversity, are we not? The very reason we exist is to take on a task when the odds seem impossible."

"She has a point, Thomas," said Mrs. Merlin.

Lynsley sighed and allowed the smallest of smiles to appear on his lips. "I see you wield rhetoric as well as a rapier, Sofia. You are right about the Academy's purpose, but that does not make it any easier to send you into mortal danger." Reaching into his pocket, he took out a small packet sealed with a wafer of black wax. "You will need to read over these documents before you come to London."

The feel of the paper set her palms to tingling.

"Unfortunately, I cannot stay to make the detailed explanations. I have a pressing engagement this evening in Town. Mrs. Merlin will go over the basics of the assignment and work with you on refining the skills you will need to masquerade as a lady of noble birth."

"It was not for the sake of preserving my sofas from mud that I requested the change of clothing," said Mrs. Merlin dryly. "Once you change from breeches to blue satin, we will be devoting every waking hour to perfecting your poise and your polish. Lord Lynsley wants you ready to leave for London on the day after tomorrow."

"Unlike most other missions, this one will allow us the

opportunity to meet socially," continued the marquess. "You will, after all, be joining the *ton* at the height of the season, and as the widow of an Italian count, you will quickly be included on everyone's guest list."

"How—" began Sofia.

"I hope to have all the particulars worked out by the time you arrive in Town." Lynsley was already reaching for his ebony walking stick and charcoal-gray gloves. "In the meantime, I trust you will pay close attention to all of Mrs. Merlin's lessons."

Sofia had a headful of questions she wished to ask, but she kept her reply short and simple. "Yes, sir."

"Thank you for the excellent tea and tarts, Charlotte." Lynsley tucked a large leather portfolio under his arm. "And for dispensing a liberal dose of wisdom to go along with them."

"Nice legs . . . well-defined chest . . . good stamina and good wind, wouldn't you say so?"

"A bit *too* good." Osborne winced. "Lud, I daresay her shrieks could be heard all the way to Kew Gardens."

"I am talking about the *horse*, Dev." Lord Nicolas Harkness gave a low snort. "Damn it, do try to pay attention. This is an expensive proposition."

"So was Collette," he quipped. "Cost me an arm and leg to sever the relationship."

"You're lucky it didn't cost you your prick in the bargain." Harkness chuckled as he stepped away from the stallion and propped a boot on the fence rail. "From what you said, she was looking to sever more than her services."

"Escaped by the skin of my . . . teeth." He grinned, then winced again as the big bay let out a sharp whinny. His mouth felt dry as straw, and the cacophony of harried hooves and high-stakes haggling echoing through the yards was exacerbating the pounding in his head. Not to speak of the pungent smells. The auctions of prime horseflesh at Tattersall's always drew a crowd of gentlemen looking to buy or sell.

Taking a seat on a bale of hay, Osborne began massaging at his temples. "Sorry to be such dull company, Nick. Give me a moment to collect my wits and I'll take a better look at the animal."

"It's worth the wait. I trust your judgment." Harkness lit up a cheroot. "Even when your brain is half pickled in brandy."

In his present mood, he wasn't quite so sanguine as his friend. His judgment had been sadly lacking of late. The scene with his mistress was just the latest in a series of embarrassing little incidents. At Lady Haverstick's musicale, he had been a bit too vocal in voicing the limericks he had composed about a rotund peer of the realm. The rhymes *had* been clever, and people had laughed. But he had embarrassed an acquaintance and had woken the next morning feeling ashamed of himself.

"I'm not sure I'm in any shape to find flaws in your stallion, seeing as I've been acting like an ass recently."

Harkness cocked a brow. "Is that a black cloud hanging over little Lord Sunshine's head?"

Osborne swore, loud enough to startle an elderly gentleman who was examining a pair of matched carriage grays nearby. "Call me that again and you will be digging your teeth out of yon pile of horse droppings." A number of ladies had given him the moniker on account of his fair hair and ebullient manner. He usually laughed off any teasing from other men, but at the moment it was not remotely amusing.

"A show of temper?"

Osborne muttered another oath.

"Any particular reason for the foul mood?" His friend blew out a smoke ring. "Aside from losing your place in La Colette's bed."

He merely shrugged, happy to encourage the idea that his malaise was on account of sex—or the impending lack of it.

"Not that you won't have a host of ardent admirers willing to assuage your loss. I hear Lady Pierson arrived from Yorkshire yesterday, leaving the old earl to rusticate with his horses and hounds."

"Luscious Lucinda?" Osborne gave a mock shudder. "I have no desire to jump from the proverbial frying pan into the fire. Her ample physical endowments are matched by a penchant for emotional excess."

"Lady Wellton has always appeared to have her eye on you—you lucky dog." Harkness coughed slightly. "But then, you may already be intimately aware of her interest."

"If I was, I would not be so ungentlemanly as to talk about it."

"Quite right, quite right." His friend ground the butt of tobacco beneath his boot heel. "Perhaps a night away from female company would clear that black scowl from your brow. There are several new gaming hells in the stews that I've heard are worth a visit, and you always have the devil's own luck at cards." Harkness lowered his voice. "The place in Seven Dials is said to be quite unusual."

Osborne shook his head. "Tempting. But I have promised to show my phiz at Lady Haverton's ball. She is counting on me to keep Silliman and Morse from coming to blows."

"Lud, are they still threatening to spill each other's claret over the pattern of a waistcoat?"

"They both take matters of fashion very seriously. But I believe I've thought of a way to stitch together a truce."

Harkness rolled his eyes. "Well, if anyone can mend frayed feelings, it's you."

Would that he could feel comfortable in his own skin.

"Now, about the horse, Dev."

"Right. Let's have a look . . ."

"I can't thank you enough." Light from the glittering chandeliers caught the curve of the lady's smile as she twirled through the last figures of the waltz. "Without your help, those two might well have declared a duel right here on the dance floor. It would have ruined the evening."

"Nothing could have marred such an enchanting entertainment." Osborne glanced around the crowded ballroom. "The musicians are marvelous, and the flower arrangements are exquisite."

Lady Haverton turned as pink as the peonies. "You like them?"

"Stunning," he murmured, knowing full well that the lady, a bluestocking botanist, had designed them herself.

Her blush deepened. "You are too kind—"

"La, Osborne!" As the final notes of the dance ended, a buxom blonde turned from her partner and tapped his shoulder. "You simply must call on me tomorrow and give your opinion on which shade of blue I should choose for the drawing room draperies."

He inclined a bow. "I should be delighted to."

"Osborne!" The hail was from a group of gentlemen by the punch bowl.

"As always, you are in great demand." His hostess

smiled as she took her glove from his arm. "Let me release you to your friends."

"I shall be back. I've put my name on your card for the supper dance."

"Much to the dismay of every other lady in the room." Lady Haverton patted his sleeve. "Go on."

"Osborne!"

"Osborne!"

He slowly made his way through the crowd, stopping every few steps to exchange pleasantries. When finally he managed to slip behind a screen of potted orange trees, he let out a sigh and took a sip of his champagne.

"A popular fellow, I see."

Osborne looked around to find Lord Lynsley by his shoulder. "I seem to have a knack for keeping them amused," he replied lightly, though to his own ears the words had a slight edge to them.

The marquess regarded him thoughtfully before replying. "Major Fenimore thinks your talents merit a more serious adjective than *amusing*. He said your analysis of French cavalry tactics at the battle of Marengo will prove invaluable for our Eastern allies."

"I am gratified to hear it." Osborne quaffed another swallow of his wine, unsure of how else to respond.

Lynsley's official position at Whitehall was not overly important, but Osborne was aware that his real government responsibilities were a closely guarded secret. The vague rumors about the marquess's early exploits abroad were enough to make a man's hair stand on end. And though Lynsley now spent most of his time behind a desk, Osborne imagined he was involved in more than pushing papers around on his blotter.

"I wonder . . . might you be interested in helping out in

another matter?" In the play of light and shadow, it was hard to make out the marquess's expression. "This one would not require any military expertise."

"Perhaps," he replied, keeping his own face neutral. "I would, of course, have to hear what you have in mind."

"A diplomatic reply." There was no mistaking the twitch of Lynsley's lips. "It's a very a simple matter, really, especially for a gentleman of your standing in Town. You would do me a great favor if you would agree to introduce an Italian countess to Society. The lady is a wealthy young widow who knows no one here in London."

"And you wish to see her established among the *ton*," said Osborne slowly. "Invited to all the evening entertainments, included in the rounds of morning calls."

"Precisely. My upcoming duties do not allow me the time to take on the obligation myself."

"It seems a simple request." *Far too simple.* Given the aura of intrigue surrounding the marquess, Osborne suspected that Lynsley was leaving a great deal unsaid. But despite the swirl of questions suddenly spinning in his head, he merely asked, "Is she pretty?"

"Very," replied Lynsley.

"That should make the task even easier. I will—"

"Ah, Osborne, there you are." Two gentlemen in regimentals waved for him to join them. "Come help settle this argument about who makes the better pistol—Manton or that upstart Purdey."

"Forgive me, but Captain Tolliver won't take no for an answer," said Osborne softly. "I had better go before they go off half cocked and ruin Lady Haverton's evening."

"Perhaps you should consider taking up a position in the Foreign Service," murmured the marquess. "In the meantime, think it over—"

"No need." He finished his drink and set the glass aside. "When would you like me to meet her?"

"The day after tomorrow. I'll come for you at White's around two, if that is convenient."

"Perfectly." A change in his daily routine might be just what he needed to shake off his odd mood.

Chapter Three

*S*horten your stride, my dear." Mrs. Merlin murmured a low reminder. "A lady never appears to be in a rush."

"Sorry." Sofia swallowed a sigh as she took another turn around the Academy drawing room. "I shall try not to trip up again."

The headmistress smiled. "You are doing very well."

"*Si, si, bella.*" Marco eyed her with obvious approval. "Lift your chin a touch higher, add a curl of condescension to your smile—yes, that's it. Now you are the very picture of a regal *contessa.*"

"You are looking rather respectable yourself," she shot back. The starched cravat was a perfect counterpoint to his olive complexion, and the tailored fit of the elegant evening coat accentuated his broad shoulders and slim waist. Even his hair had been trimmed, though it still fell nearly to his shoulders. She had to admit that the effect was impressive. "Indeed, I think you are an even better impostor than I am."

"What makes you think I am merely playing a role?" he asked, sweeping low in a courtly bow.

Sofia's laugh ended on a note of uncertainty. The school instructors included a former courtesan to King Carlos, a convicted cardsharp, a Negro pugilist, and an Indian yoga *guru*. It was not beyond the stretch of imagination that the Milanese swordsman could be . . .

"Watch your step, Sofia," cautioned Mrs. Merlin.

Watch your step. Those words would be her mantra for the coming months.

"You must always appear cool, calm, and collected," added the headmistress.

Sofia nodded, though her insides were aflutter. Her traveling trunks were already in the entrance hall, packed with the costly silks and glittering jewels that would turn a nobody into a noble lady. Her fingers felt the plain gold locket under her lace fichu. Unlike in a fairy tale, there was no golden wand to help with the transformation.

They would all have to hope that Mrs. Merlin's magic was enough.

"Excellent." The headmistress removed her spectacles and pinched at the bridge of her nose. "I think we've finished with the lessons. Come have some tea before the coach arrives."

Sofia assumed a seat on the sofa and smoothed her silks into place. "Thank you," she said with a hint of hauteur. "You have no idea how difficult it is to get decent tea in Rome. It is only when I am at my summer *calle* near Venice that my cook can purchase a proper oolong blend from Ceylon."

"The accent is perfect," said Marco. "You have a good ear for Italian, *bella*."

She grinned. "I've been listening to you whisper sweet

nothings for long enough. Something was bound to rub off."

"A pity it was not my hands doing the caressing."

"Behave yourself," she muttered under her breath.

"Ah, yes, I almost forgot—I must act like a gentleman. How very . . ." He mouthed the word *boring,* then winked.

Sofia bit back a grin. "Not for much longer."

Steam swirled though the air as Mrs. Merlin poured hot water over the tea leaves. "Actually, Marco will also be traveling to London. Lord Lynsley is arranging for you to have an English escort to ease your way into Society. But given the complexities of this mission, we decided it would do no harm to have an ally on hand. Besides, his amorous attention will also serve to spark the interest of the other gentlemen."

Marco flashed a wicked smile.

"I trust I don't have to remind you not to overplay the role," added the headmistress with a warning wag of her finger.

"*Non, non.* When I put my mind to it, Signora Merlin, I can recall all the rules of proper etiquette."

Sofia arched a skeptical brow. "I shudder to think of where you might have picked up such knowledge."

He exaggerated a look of reproach. "My family is one of the oldest and most respected names in all of Lombardy."

Skeptical, she looked to Mrs. Merlin, only to see the headmistress nod. "I think it is about time we cleared up any misconceptions regarding our assistant fencing master. Marco's full name is Giovanni Marco Musto della Ghiradelli. Heir to the Conte of Como's title and fortune."

"A bloody *conte*?" Sofia could not contain her shock.

"Ladies must never swear, *bella*," he murmured.

"On second thought, I'll strangle you with my bare

hands." Shaken by the revelation, Sofia felt somehow betrayed. She had seen Marco as a kindred soul—a rascal with no place in the world, save for what he could carve out for himself with his blade. To learn his august bloodlines ran back for centuries made her feel even more alone.

"Damn it, you *lied* to me."

His look of amusement was gone in a flash. "Never. I may have omitted some parts of my background, but I never told you anything that was not true."

"It comes down to the same thing," she snapped. "You deliberately deceived me."

"Deception is one of the basic teachings of the Academy. It must fit as easily as a second skin if we are to serve our purpose." Mrs. Merlin was observing her through hooded eyes. "Marco's true identity was something that Lord Lynsley wished to keep a secret. But as he is acquainted with one of our suspects from their school days in Geneva, it was decided that his presence could prove useful in making your mission successful. If you have any problems with that, Sofia, please voice them now."

Drawing a deep breath, Sofia willed the heat to cool from her cheeks. "I've no problem at all," she replied. "You are right, of course. It simply took me by surprise that a friend . . . It won't happen again."

"There is no such thing as friendship in our world," said Mrs. Merlin. "The only emotion allowed is a dispassionate devotion to duty."

"I won't make that mistake again."

For a moment, the only sound in the room was the ticking of the tall case clock. Sofia sat very still, spine rigid, wondering if her slip had just cost her dearly. Perhaps Mrs. Merlin was recalling all the times she had bent the Academy rules to help keep her roommates out of trouble.

Personal loyalty would no doubt be seen as a weakness, not a strength.

The crackle of papers seemed loud as cannon fire. The headmistress edged forward, light flashing off the lenses of her spectacles. "Let this be a last lesson before you go— you must never lower your guard, Sofia."

Her muscles relaxed ever so slightly, allowing her to nod. "I won't fail you or Lord Lynsley."

Mrs. Merlin skimmed over her notes, then looked up. "It won't hurt to use the last few minutes here to review the assignment. The first order of business is to establish your welcome with the highest circles of Society. You are . . ."

"I am Contessa Sofia Constanza Bingham della Silveri," recited Sofia. "My father, a younger son of Lord Whalley, was an English expatriate living in Rome who married an Italian *barone*. My husband was an elderly Venetian noble-man who passed away a little over a year ago. I am just coming out of mourning and wished to visit the country of my father's birth." She paused. "I take it all these people are real, seeing as there are several Italians among the group you wish me to infiltrate."

"Of course," replied Mrs. Merlin. "Mr. Bingham and his wife passed away years ago. Their only daughter—who, by the by, is living in a nunnery in Sicily—has never met her English relatives. As for your late husband, he was a no-torious recluse and sheltered his young bride from Vene-tian society for the few months of their marriage. She then slipped away to Greece with her head gardener. You should encounter no awkward inquiries concerning your identity, but if you do—"

"If I do, I shall improvise," said Sofia.

"Excellent. And, of course, Marco will lend credence to your story. He will appear in London a day or two after your arrival and will take up residence at the Pulteney Hotel." Mrs. Merlin turned a page. "Once you are accepted in London Society, you are to cultivate a friendship with a group of gentlemen who fashion themselves as the Scarlet Knights."

The headmistress glanced at Marco. "Again, the *conte* will help with the necessary introductions."

Sofia avoided his eye. "Have we a name for the Englishman who is providing an entrée into the *ton*?"

"Not as yet."

"Not that it matters. I don't imagine I will be seeing much of him after the first round of parties." She quickly continued with the review of her orders. "The plan calls for me to hint that life as a proper young widow is a bit boring and that I am not averse to experiencing a little adventure."

"Exactly. From there, however, you will have to script your own moves. You have read over the pages from Lord Robert Woolsey's diary. Lord Lynsley not only wishes to learn whether the Duke of Sterling's grandson was the victim of foul play, but also whether the hints of government corruption have any merit."

The headmistress meditated for a moment on the dregs of her tea, as if some last bit of advice might be hidden in the leaves. "Make no mistake, my dear—it is a daunting, dangerous task. I regret that we can give you no more specific information as to what you are looking for. Lord Lynsley will have a few more details to add once you arrive in Town. After that, you will simply have to go by your own instincts."

Another oblique hint that the only one she could trust was herself?

"I understand."

A brusque knock on the door announced the school porter. "The carriage is loaded and ready, ma'am."

Sofia rose. "Time to go."

Finding Lynsley awaiting him in the foyer of White's, Osborne did not bother removing his overcoat. The marquess was punctual—a pity, seeing as the club had some of the finest port in Town.

"Thank you for keeping the appointment, Osborne," said the marquess. "My carriage is right outside."

Osborne waited until they both were settled back against the squabs before asking, "I confess to being curious, Lynsley. Why me?"

The marquess took a moment to answer. "London can be daunting for one unfamiliar with its manners and cliques. You move with ease through all the circles within circles of Society, while a stranger would likely find it hard to navigate through the hidden shoals and currents. I am hoping that your charm and your connections will help smooth the way for Lady Sofia."

Sofia. It was a pretty name.

"Your own stature in Society would surely guarantee invitations to any soiree worth attending," observed Osborne.

"My current duties will not permit me to spend much time in Society during the next few months. The contessa cannot appear unescorted without giving rise to unpleasant gossip."

"I fear you may be overestimating my influence in Society. I am sure you know others with more power and prestige. After all, I'm only a mere younger son of a marquess."

"That is true. But power and prestige tend to create enemies." The marquess slanted a sidelong glance at him. "From what I hear, you have none to speak of."

Osborne felt himself color slightly. Though Lynsley was by no means an elderly gentleman—the marquess's age appeared to be just a shade over forty—he felt a bit like a grubby schoolboy being examined by a demanding schoolmaster.

"I see. So, then, tell me a bit about the lady," he said, anxious to change the subject.

"As I mentioned before, she is the widow of an Italian count," answered Lynsley. "Her father was, however, English, and she is anxious to spend some time in the country of her heritage."

Osborne frowned slightly. "Why aren't her relatives handling her introduction into Society?"

Lynsley didn't hesitate a fraction. "Her father was estranged from his family. She has never had any contact with them and has no desire to attempt a reconciliation."

"And how, may I ask, are you acquainted with the lady?"

Again, the marquess's response came without a hitch. "I have known the young lady since she was a child. My diplomatic travels have allowed me to keep in contact over the years, and, indeed, I recommended the school she attended. It was natural that she looked to me for advice."

The explanation was perfectly reasonable, yet Osborne could not help feeling an odd prickling along his spine. His closest friend, the Earl of Kirtland, had briefly crossed paths with Lynsley eight months ago, only to be caught up in a swirl of mystery and murder at a remote Devonshire castle. Not to speak of the strangest rumors regarding a tattooed woman . . .

Damn Kirtland for being so tight-lipped about his expe-

rience. And his new bride. The couple had left soon after their marriage to make the Grand Tour of Italy, so he could not press the earl for more details. There were a great many questions he would have liked to ask.

But seeing the faintly quizzical curl of Lynsley's mouth, he set aside his musings. "Ah, that explains the connection," he said politely. Crossing his legs, he went on. "As you mentioned before that she was attractive, I assume that she doesn't have a squint or a limp to impede her acceptance into Society. You know the tabbies can be quick to seize on a weakness, and their teeth are unmercifully sharp. It is not that I would refuse to help, I simply would like to be warned in advance."

"I assure you, Lady Sofia's physical appearance leaves nothing to be desired. Nor do her manners. She is poised, polished, and well-educated." Lynsley's smile grew a touch more pronounced. "She can converse on art, music, and literature in several languages, she plays the pianoforte with exceptional skill, and she is a picture of grace on the dance floor."

"She sounds like a paragon of perfection," replied Osborne. "A patterncard of propriety. Everything should go smoothly as silk. Indeed, I cannot imagine what could stand in our way."

"Let me have one last look, milady."

Sofia turned slowly, her skirts brushing lightly over the Axminster carpet.

"Very good." Her lady's maid gave a gruff nod. "Let me just add another hairpin to your topknot, and then we are done."

"You are very skilled with your hands, Rose." Sofia watched in the looking glass as the agile fingers gave a deft twist to the curls. "You appear to have a good deal of practice in dressing a lady."

"Yes, madam." Rose smoothed a hair ribbon and stepped back from the dressing table.

"Have you worked with Lord Lynsley before?"

"Yes, madam."

Sofia did not try to prolong the conversation. Like all the servants staffing the London town house, Rose was highly efficient at performing her duties but seemed to have little inclination for discussing anything of a personal nature.

A tacit reminder that they were not here to become friends.

"Thank you," she murmured, observing the final effect with a wry smile. "I don't even recognize myself."

"I daresay you will have all the gentlemen asking for an introduction, once you begin appearing in public."

Sofia was unsure how much Rose knew about her mission. Quite a lot, she would guess, seeing as the maid had not batted an eye on seeing a case of swords and assorted weaponry among the bandboxes and dress trunks.

"Will you be going out tonight, milady?"

"I—I am not sure." Sofia moved to the windows and peered down to the street below. It was still strange to see the parade of fashionable carriages and phaetons rolling by, rather than the spartan training fields and bridle paths of the Academy. The noise, the dirt, the gallimaufry of colors—it was all a bit overwhelming.

"I shall lay out the emerald silk with the ruched bodice. The color will set off your eyes very nicely." Rose tapped her chin. "And the pearls, rather than any fancier jewels. I believe the marquess wishes the first impression to be one of understated elegance."

Understated? Sofia regarded the gold and ruby ring on

her finger. Lynsley had provided a king's ransom in jewelry to go along with the trunkfuls of stylish clothing. She had never seen such a rich assortment of costly gems. A single earbob would have fed and clothed her and her ragtag urchin friends for several years in the stews.

The marquess had also provided ready blunt—a good deal of it, according to the accounting of the majordomo in charge of her town house. Her orders were to spend it freely in the shops along Bond Street. It was her wealth as well as her looks that would attract the attention of the Scarlet Knights. Their sort of pleasure did not come cheap.

Neither did the vast assortment of sumptuous ballgowns and elegant day dresses. Sofia looked longingly at the dressing room where her breeches and boots lay tucked away in a bandbox. *Curse corsets and petticoats.* Such feminine finery felt terribly constricting after the freedom of her academy uniform.

"The ivory gloves and fringed India shawl . . ." Rose was surveying the armoire full of accessories. "And the sea-green reticule, to match the silk flowers I will thread through your hair."

A knock at the door interrupted the maid's murmuring. "Lord Lynsley has arrived," announced the footman. "He and his companion are waiting in the drawing room."

Sofia felt a flutter of nerves. *Had she mastered the mannerisms of a real lady?* Or would a stranger see her for what she was—a nameless urchin, a nobody?

Steeling her spine, she reminded herself that she was no longer a frightened little orphan, alone in the streets. She was a Merlin. And Merlins were meant to fly.

"This way, madam." The footman inclined a bow before leading the way down the curved staircase.

Chapter Four

$\mathcal{A}$h, Contessa." The marquess turned from his study of the Canaletto painting above the side table and came to meet her. "How delightful to see you in London. I trust your journey was not too arduous?"

"Not at all, thanks to all your arrangements." Sofia extended a hand for Lynsley to lift to his lips. "You are too kind, my dear sir. I should have been quite lost without you."

"It is always a pleasure to be of assistance to you, Lady Sofia." Smiling, the marquess kept hold of her fingers. "I had, of course, also planned on providing the proper entrée into London Society. But alas, my duties at the ministry are going to require a great deal of my time over the next few weeks, and I may be called on to do some traveling." He looked to his companion, a fair-haired gentleman who had remained standing by the gilt-framed canvas. "So I have enlisted a friend to help guide you through all the subtleties of the *beau monde*. Allow me to introduce Lord Deverill Osborne."

"*Buongiorno*, Lord Osborne," she murmured as the gentleman stepped forward and bowed.

"Osborne, let me present the Contessa Sofia Constanza Bingham della Silveri."

"Is a mouthful, no?" she said, regarding him through a fringe of lowered lashes.

"The sound is like honey on the tongue—a sweetness to savor," he replied smoothly as his lips grazed her glove. "It is a pleasure indeed to make your acquaintance, Contessa. I am greatly honored that Lord Lynsley thinks I may be of assistance to you."

"La, and they say that Italian men are the masters of flowery compliments." *Did the touch of a foreign accent sound a little too forced?* "Lynsley, you did not warn me that the English reputation for reserve has been greatly exaggerated."

"It appears that no words could exaggerate the beauty of Italian women," said Osborne.

Talk about a honeyed tongue. No wonder Lynsley's dossier on Lord Osborne indicated he was a great favorite with the *ton*. Allowing just a hint of a smile to play on her mouth, Sofia angled her gaze to meet his.

She found herself looking into a pair of luminous aquamarine eyes, their color as cool and clear as the painted ocean behind him. The dappled light from the bowfront windows seemed to add a shimmering warmth. And yet beneath the surface, there were hints of an intriguing depth, a darker intensity to his air of sunny charm.

A sudden shiver of awareness washed over her. Confused, she quickly looked away.

"Are all your friends so dashing, Lynsley?" Sofia touched the marquess's sleeve. "I confess, I have been extremely nervous about venturing into English Society—"

"Don't be," murmured Osborne.

"Yes, my dear, I am sure you have nothing to worry about," assured Lynsley.

"But there are still so very many things I do not know about the customs and the correct way things are done."

"I'm sure it is not so different from what you are used to," replied Osborne.

Hah!

Sofia allowed a wry twitch of her mouth. "Oh, I fear there is much I must get used to." Taking up a silver bell from the escritoire, she rang for a servant. "Beginning with the offer of tea and cakes to any caller. Is that not right, Lynsley?"

"Correct, my dear." The marquess smiled.

"There, you see! I have already been rude." Appearing a bit nervous was proving easier than she imagined. "Please come have a seat on the sofa, gentlemen."

Moving with a lithe grace, Osborne crossed the carpet. He was slender and sleek as a cat, with a narrow waist and long legs—not at all an overpowering impression at first glance. But Sofia imagined that the lack of bulging muscle and broad shoulders was not what most people noticed first about Lord Deverill Osborne.

Framed by an artful tumble of long, fair hair, his face was the very portrait of classical male beauty. The fine-boned features, chiseled to the smoothness of Carrara marble, possessed a perfect symmetry—wide oval eyes, sculpted cheekbones, and a straight nose. The shapely, sensuous curl of his mouth might have been considered effeminate, save for a certain hint of steel beneath its pliant curves.

Hard and soft. A man of contrasts and contradictions. No wonder women found him fascinating.

Sofia forced her gaze away, surprised to feel a faint heat stealing up to her cheeks.

"I do hope you will not think me impertinent, Contessa, but I took the liberty of bringing you a welcoming gift." Osborne walked past the sofa to retrieve a small package from the sideboard. "A lady is not usually supposed to accept presents from a strange gentleman, but in this case, I hope we may be allowed to bend the rules."

Sofia hesitated, but seeing Lynsley nod, she slowly slipped off the wrapping paper to reveal a leatherbound book. *"A Guide to London and Its Sights."* She read aloud the title stamped upon the cover. "Why, how very thoughtful, Lord Osborne. Thank you."

"I hope you will allow me to show you a great many of them," he replied with a smile. "Though I imagine I will quickly have competition for the privilege of serving as your escort."

"Speaking of which . . ." The marquess waited for the parlor maid to set down the tea tray before going on. "Are you planning to attend Lady Jersey's ball tonight, Osborne?"

"Silence would never let me hear the end of it were I not to appear." He turned to Sofia, his smile taking on a more pronounced curl. "Sally Jersey is the undisputed queen of London Society. Many think her cold and haughty, but I have always found her to enjoy a good joke—almost as much as she enjoys talking. Which, by the by, explains her nickname of 'Silence.'"

"I, too, have an invitation," continued the marquess. "I planned on taking Lady Sofia and thought that it would be the perfect opportunity for you to begin her introductions to the *ton*."

"Indeed. The other six Patronesses of Almack's are all

sure to be there as well." Osborne once again fixed Sofia with a flash of pearly teeth. "As the self-appointed arbiters of style and propriety, they are a force to be reckoned with. Lady Sefton is the most easygoing of the group, while Mrs. Drummond-Burrell is the highest stickler—"

Sofia's face must have betrayed her dismay, for he stopped with a short laugh. "I will not overwhelm you with such meaningless descriptions. You will soon have faces to put with all the names, for Lady Jersey's entertainments are always a crush."

"It *does* sound rather intimidating. I am used to being somewhat of a recluse."

"Ah, but now that you are here in London, it would be a shame for you not to sample the feast of experiences that the city offers." His gold-fringed lashes gave his gaze a cherubic look—a fact he appeared to know full well, for he let them flutter half closed for a moment before going on. "And from a purely selfish perspective, I would think it most unfair if you chose to deprive us of your lovely company."

Something in his eyes sparked Sofia to a rather sharp reply. "Do you always flirt so outrageously with every lady you meet, Lord Osborne?"

His well-shaped brows arched in amusement. "I am afraid so. But I assure you, I am quite harmless."

That was not the word that came suddenly to mind. *Dangerous.* Sofia could not quite explain why she felt a tingling of heat in her hands as she poured the tea. The wisps of steam seemed to whisper a warning. . . .

Lynsley's voice quickly drowned out any such fanciful feelings. "Yes, I will vouch for the fact that Lord Osborne has a reputation for being a perfect gentleman."

"If I promise to behave, might I be permitted to take

you for a drive in the park later this afternoon?" His glance was at the marquess rather than her. "It wouldn't hurt to stir a bit of speculation concerning a lovely new stranger." He added a splash of cream to his tea. "You know how Society loves to gossip. The ballroom will be abuzz with the news, and everyone will be anxious to make the contessa's acquaintance."

"An excellent suggestion." Lynsley cleared his throat. "Do you feel up to the rigors of such a long day, Lady Sofia?"

She took a dainty sip of oolong before replying. "Oh, I assure you, sir, I am tougher than I look."

"Then I may call on you a little later?" asked Osborne. "Five is the fashionable hour for promenading in the park."

"I shall be ready, sir."

"Excellent. I will return then." Osborne finished his tea and rose. "Right now, I am sure the two of you would like some time alone to catch up."

She waited until he had left the room before letting out her breath. "I may have overplayed the accent, sir. I shall do better next time." The first performance of her new role would have been trying under any circumstances, but to have Lynsley as her audience had added an extra measure of pressure.

"You did very well, Sofia." The marquess flashed a fatherly smile. "My advice is to relax and trust in yourself."

"Yes, sir." She essayed a note of ironic humor. "I suppose it helps that I have no idea who I really am. It makes being a chameleon quite easy."

A frown furrowed his brow for an instant, but he moved on smoothly to other matters. "What was your first impression of Lord Osborne?"

Dangerous. But as she would have felt foolish voicing such sentiment aloud, she kept her answer a bit more circumspect. "He was not quite what I expected," she replied.

A twinkle came to his eye. "No doubt you assumed I would choose an elderly fellow like myself."

"No! That is . . ." Sofia stammered as color rushed to her cheeks. "You are hardly in your dotage, sir. Marco says you still best all of our times on the equestrian obstacle course."

Lynsley chuckled. "He knows who pays his salary."

"It does not sound as if the rascal has need of the Academy's money."

"Conte della Ghiradelli was under my strict orders to keep his identity a secret."

Sofia dropped her gaze. "I was not questioning your authority, sir. All of the Merlins know that our usefulness to our country depends on discretion and deception."

"Among other things," he murmured.

"But you were asking about Lord Osborne, not Lord Marco," she went on quickly. "My comment only meant that he seems very attentive to ladies. I hope that will not prove a distraction from the duties you wish him to perform."

"Ah, you fear his amorous attention might interfere with our plans?" Lynsley laced his hands together and looked up at the ceiling rosette. "All my information indicates that Osborne makes a point of favoring everyone with his charms. He has assiduously avoided any serious involvement with a lady, so that should not be a problem."

Her blush grew warmer. "I was not implying that the gentleman would find me irresistible. It's clear his flirtations are just a game. I . . ." She hesitated, unsure of what she meant to say. "I realize that I know nothing of Polite Society. So if you are satisfied that Osborne will do, I most certainly defer to your judgment, sir."

"It's merely for a matter of a fortnight or so. You will soon be established in your own right. The ladies won't welcome a new beauty to their ranks, but they will not dare withhold their invitations, fearing that another hostess will have you—and all the gentlemen under sixty—gracing her ballroom." The marquess paused, his expression taking a more serious slant as he dropped his gaze from the decorative detailing. "Do not underestimate your own charms, Sofia. Men *will* find your beauty irresistible. And as a widow, you will be considered fair game. It will take a good deal of prowess to play along and turn their lust to your own advantage. The mission depends on your skill."

"The class in seduction came right before self-defense," she quipped. "I can handle myself in a duel of wits or steel."

"If I did not sincerely believe that, you would not be here."

"Thank you, sir." The marquess was right. She wasn't going to need Osborne for very long. Which was probably for the best in light of her odd reaction to his presence. "Mrs. Merlin mentioned you might have a few more things to add to her explanations."

"Just one key element." He took a handkerchief from his pocket and slowly unrolled its folds. "This was found hidden in the binding of Lord Robert's diary."

Sofia studied the details of the key and its distinctive scarlet poppy for several moments before speaking. "The goldwork and enameling look to have been crafted in Venice," she said slowly, glad to discover that the long hours of art history classes could be put to practical use. "Have you any idea what it's for?"

"That's part of your assignment, Sofia. I suspect it is part of a set, but it's up to you to discover what it's for and who else might possess similar ones."

She was beginning to understand why the marquess considered this such a difficult mission.

The shadows beneath his eyes seemed deeper, darker than just a few days ago. "Having second thoughts?" he said softly.

"Not at all, sir. A Merlin rises to any challenge."

Her bravado brought a ghost of a smile to his face. "I appreciate your courage, but be careful how you unfold your wings, Sofia. London is home to many dangerous predators." Rising, he tucked the silk square back in his coat but handed her the key. "It might prove useful, so you keep it."

Its ornate teeth looked rather menacing against her palm.

"After tonight, we will not be seen together in public. The Scarlet Knights must think the connnection between us is a distant one at best. I won't really be traveling, but neither will I be making any appearance in Society. You may send word to me through Rose when you have something substantive to report. Otherwise, you are on your own."

"Don't worry, sir. If I have to probe every lock in London, I will discover what secrets this pretty poppy guards."

"Rotten Row? What a very odd name."

"It's said to derive from from the French *Route de Roi*, or King's Road. King William III had the avenue built in 1690, in order to have a safe way to travel between St. James's Palace and his new court at Kensington Palace." Osborne shifted the reins of his phaeton to return a greeting from the dowager Duchess of Canfield and her party. "At night, it was lit by three hundred oil lamps—"

"Osborne!" A wave of lace fluttered up from a quartet of ladies strolling beside the crush of carriages. "You must *promise* to attend my musicale. The tenor is from Milan and is said to have the voice of an angel. But as your taste in music is divine, I must of course hear *your* opinion."

"You may count on my presence, Lady Caroline." He drew his team to a halt. "However, I imagine Contessa della Silveri, who has just this week arrived from the Continent, would have a more expert opinion on Italian singers. Allow me to introduce you and your friends."

The lady did not look overly enthusiastic at the prospect. Her smile froze, and she greeted Sofia with a chilly politeness and ice in her eyes. It took several more pointed hints before an invitation to the musicale was grudgingly given.

As for Lady Caroline's companions . . . Osborne allowed a harried inward chuckle. He did not know how females managed to defy the laws of physics by appearing to be looking down their noses when observing someone high above their heads.

His gentlemen acquaintances showed a decidedly warmer response to the presence of a new face in the crowd. The high-perch phaeton was quickly surrounded by riders eager to get a closer glimpse of the features beneath the poke brim bonnet.

"You seem to know a great many people, Lord Osborne," said Sofia as the crowd of well-wishers finally thinned.

"It may seem as if all of London takes a turn down this pathway, but in truth, the *ton* is a very small world." He guided his team around a lumbering barouche. "Surely you must be acquainted with some people in Town."

"No, not a soul, save Lord Lynsley."

"The marquess mentioned your father was English. Will you not seek some contact with this family?"

"No." Her voice was clipped, cold.

"The expatriate community in Rome is quite large, though. No doubt some friends of your parents would be delighted to hear you are in London."

"My parents did not socialize much."

Clearing his throat, Osborne tried another topic of conversation. "Your English is impeccable, Contessa. Lynsley mentioned having recommended the school you attended—it appears you were subject to a rigorous training in the language."

"The Academy's curriculum demanded that its students become proficient in a number of disciplines."

"It sounds awfully strict." He smiled, hoping to encourage her to relax a little.

"Yes, it was," she replied with rigid correctness.

"All work and no play? And here I thought Eton was tough on its charges." He gave a light laugh. "What was the name of this institution of learning?"

"I am sure you have never heard of it, Lord Osborne." Her tone signaled an end to the subject.

Leaving off his questions, Osborne manuevered through the crush of carriages and turned homeward, using the stretch of silence to regroup his thoughts. He was rarely at a loss for words, especially with women, but the contessa was proving devilishly difficult to converse with. Clearly her past was an uncomfortable subject.

It was strange, but he sensed a tenseness to her that seemed more than mere shyness. Her gaze was wary, watchful of everything around her.

There was definitely more to all this than met the eye.

His sidelong glance lingered for a moment on her profile. Not that he minded the view. Lynsley's description had not done the lady justice. She was not merely lovely—she was absolutely stunning. Raven-dark hair, thick and lustrous as polished ebony, curled around her face. Unlike English ladies, she had allowed the sun to color her complexion to a light tan. Unfashionable perhaps, but the effect was entrancing. The green of her eyes seemed even more intense, and the kiss of bronze seemed to make all her features come gloriously alive. The angled slant of her cheekbones, the pert tilt of her nose, the lushness of her lips—everything about her was sculpted in strong relief.

Maybe too strong by conventional standards. Yet, next to Contessa Sofia Constanza Bigham della Silveri, the milk-and-water London beauties paled in comparison. Osborne felt his mouth quirk. He wouldn't be at all surprised if tanned cheeks became all the rage for the coming season.

Seeing that her eyes were intent on something up ahead, he reluctantly let his own gaze follow hers.

"Are you interested in horses, Contessa?" he asked, noting that she was studying a sleek silver-gray stallion being put through his paces along the Serpentine. "Grafton's mount is a splendid animal, is it not?"

"Well-muscled, but there is a slight hitch to his gait." She watched until horse and rider disappeared around the bend. "Are ladies allowed to ride in the park?"

Ah, finally, a slight unbending of her spine. "In a manner of speaking. You are permitted a sedate walk, but a gallop is frowned upon."

Sofia looked slightly disappointed. "London Society certainly has a great many rules governing what a female can and cannot do. Still, it will be pleasant to get a bit of fresh air and exercise."

"Have you arranged for a saddle horse while you are here? I should be happy to have a look at Tattersall's for you. Unfortunately, it is yet another rule that ladies are not allowed to attend the auctions. However, I am accorded to be a good judge of horseflesh. You have only to tell me what qualities you are looking for and I'll find you a prime animal."

"Thank you, sir." She resumed her expression of formal politeness. "That won't be necessary. Lord Lynsley has already taken care of the matter."

"Then perhaps you would allow me to show you the best bridle paths. Some parts of the park are a bit rough for a lady."

"I tend to ride quite early, sir. As for the paths, I've ridden under far rougher conditions than these."

Damn, the lady seemed determined to keep him at a distance.

Though his jaw tightened, Osborne maintained a smile in the face of the obvious rebuff. He was not so vain as to think that every female in Christendom was longing to throw herself at his feet. But nor did he expect to have his pleasantries hurled back in his face. Did she think him naught but a flirt and a fribble?

Fisting the reins, he silently guided his team through several tight turns. It was only when the Stanhope Gate came into view that he spoke. "Is there a reason you have taken a dislike to me, Contessa?"

He saw a flare of emotion in her eyes before she looked away. "I fear, sir, that you misunderstand my English."

Both in word and inflection, her English was perfectly clear. It was her motives that were cause for question.

"Please forgive me if I have given you the wrong impression," she continued. "Lord Lynsley and I are extremely grateful for your willingness to introduce a complete stranger into your circle of friends. I should be greatly upset if you should think otherwise."

It was a handsome apology, and yet her spine remained stiff, her gaze guarded.

"It is I who must apologize for distressing you," he said softly. "The last thing I shall say on the subject is that if I have unwittingly offended you, I hope you will allow me to make amends."

After an awkward silence, Sofia asked him to identify several of the buildings along Half Moon Street. The rest of the ride passed in pleasantries; however, as he helped her down from the high perch, Osborne sensed she was anxious to escape his presence.

Lud, he didn't have the plague or a paunch. His irritation increased as he watched her hurry up the marble steps and let the door fall closed without a backward glance. Perhaps his feelings were still on edge from his recent mistakes, but the fact that a complete stranger had snubbed his offer of friendship piqued his pride.

Still staring at the dark green portal, he flexed his gloved fingers. For whatever reason, Lady Sofia Constanza Bingham della Silveri had thrown down a gauntlet. *Was he up to the challenge?*

The corners of his mouth curled. The duel would at least keep boredom at bay. It would be interesting to see which proved stronger—his reputed charm or her inexplicable disdain.

Turning away, he walked back to his vehicle with a spring in his step. His friend Kirtland, a decorated veteran of the Peninsular War, had a name for such a confrontation.

Mano a mano.

He gave the horses a light flick of the whip.

Mano a mano, he repeated to himself. Well, may the best man win.

Chapter Five

$\mathcal{T}$he scent of sweet perfumes and spicy colognes mingled with the smoke from the blazing torchieres flanking the front door. The evening was cool, but the heat inside the crowded entrance hall was already oppressive.

Sofia looked around, taking care to mask her amazement over the sights, the sounds, the smells of her first London ball. She was now a fine lady, she reminded herself. No one must guess she was not at home in the sumptuous splendor of Mayfair's mansions.

A lady must always be in control of her emotions. For an instant, the echo of Mrs. Merlin's words rose up over the trilling voices and velvety swoosh of the evening finery. She could feel the curious stares upon her as the marquess handed her cloak to one of the porters.

From now on, she would have to do a much better job at hiding her feelings. That Lord Osborne had seen through her show of politeness so quickly was something of a shock. Given his golden looks and great popularity, she had assumed that he would be more interested in himself than anyone else. She would take greater care not to underestimate his powers of observation again.

"A dreadful crush, is it not?" The marquess surveyed the line of guests trying to make their way up the curved stairway. "That is, of course, the highest accolade for any evening entertainment."

"A crush indeed." Sofia swept her skirts from the paths of two young gentlemen, who nearly collided with each other as they turned to ogle her bosom. "Cabbage heads," she said under her breath, watching them fuss with the voluminous folds of their cravats. "If their shirtpoints were any higher, they would be in danger of poking out their eyes."

"As you see, many of the *ton* are slaves to fashion," said Lynsley dryly. "Take a moment to look around and familiarize yourself with the beau monde. Once we pass through the receiving line and enter the ballroom, things will begin moving quite fast."

"I will stay on my toes, sir." She had not made mention of her pointed exchange with Osborne. She would give the marquess no further cause for complaint.

"Just Lynsley," he reminded her. "I am no longer your superior, merely a friend."

Yes, sir. Quelling the urge to snap a salute, Sofia assumed an air of nonchalance and began a slow survey of her surroundings.

The vast stretch of black and white marble floor tiles were barely visible beneath the sea of ruffled silks and polished pumps. The effect was still impressive, as was the glossy white paneling, trimmed in a tone of deep claret. Several large gilt-framed portraits peered down in grim-faced silence at the milling guests. Judging by the starched white ruffs and richly embroidered velvet doublets, they had witnessed several centuries of frivolity without cracking a smile.

Their old-fashioned sartorial splendor was more than matched by the feathered finery of the present day.

Lud, were those really pink ostrich plumes crowning a billowing purple turban? Sofia stilled the flutter of her lips as her gaze moved on. The ballgowns ranged from demure pastel confections to daring jewel tone designs that bared a goodly amount of flesh. Highlighting the soft shimmer of the fabrics was the hard-edged sparkle of gold and precious stones. Lace fichus, gold-threaded overskirts, fringed shawls, painted fans . . . Sofia felt her head spinning at the flamboyant show of au courant styles.

The gentlemen were strutting around like peacocks as well. Though some were, like Lynsley, dressed in stark black and white, there was plenty of colorful plumage to be seen. Her eye lingered on a swallowtail coat of canary yellow pressed shoulder to shoulder with a sky-blue wasp-waisted jacket. Even more colorful were the waistcoats, which came in a dizzying assortment of stripes and patterns. The accessories were no less extravagant. Brass buttons the size of saucers festooned the superfine wool, ruby stickpins held knotted cravats in place, and the thick gold watchchains hung heavy with ornate fobs.

Privilege, power, pedigree. Wealth had a language of its own.

"If you are ready, my dear, I think we can begin making our way up to greet our hostess." Lynsley's words roused her from her study.

"Yes, of course."

The line snaking up the ornately carved staircase did not appear to have thinned much, but Sofia followed Lynsley's lead. She felt the brush of wool against her bare arms and heard whispers stir behind her back. Lifting her chin, she pretended to take no notice.

She was an actress playing a role, she reminded herself. Now that the curtain had risen and she had stepped onto the grand stage, she must get used to being the subject of scrutiny.

As they made the last turn to the upper floor, the light from the massive chandelier seemed to take on an even more glittering intensity.

"My dear Thomas! To what do we owe this rare honor? It isn't often that we can coax you out of the warrens of Whitehall."

"To the daughter of an old friend, Sally. Allow me to introduce Lady Sofia della Silveri—"

"Ah, yes, I've heard all about the contessa." Lady Jersey waggled a plump finger. "You've stirred up quite a gaggle of gossip, my dear, by convincing the devilishly handsome Lord Osborne to ask you to ride in his phaeton." The countess lowered her voice, though to Sofia it still sounded like a stentorian shout. "Caro Culverton has been trying for *years* to wheedle her way to such lofty heights. But Osborne is known for never sharing the seat of that particular vehicle. You must tell me what hold you have over the man."

"None at all, I'm afraid." Sofia matched the other lady's light laugh. "Lord Osborne was simply being exceedingly kind, in response to Lord Lynsley asking a favor of him."

Lady Jersey arched a brow at the marquess. "I didn't realize the two of you were friends. It's true he shows great loyalty to his friends. He stood by Lord Kirtland, despite all the ugly rumors swirling around the earl's name."

"Osborne is a gentleman of great integrity," agreed Lynsley. "I am fortunate he is free to escort Lady Sofia around Town until she is settled into Society."

"How very kind of you, Thomas." The countess tapped his sleeve with her fan and winked. "Not many gentlemen would be so gracious as to cede that task to someone else."

"Alas, I have little choice in the matter. Work is a harder mistress than any female."

Lady Jersey gave a snort of laughter.

"Besides, Lady Sofia will have a much gayer time with someone who is not old enough to be her father."

The countess made a show of examining the marquess through her quizzing glass.

Sofia, too, ventured a surreptitious look, aware she was seeing him in a whole new light. A whole new world. The glittering Mayfair ballroom, aswirl in silks, champagne, and crystal-edged laughter, was so utterly unlike the simple, spartan Academy classrooms.

Though Lynsley's neatly trimmed hair was showing a touch of silver at the temples, it was still thick and a rich, burnished brown. His face, while not precisely handsome, was austerely aristocratic. Lines crinkled the corners of his ice-blue eyes, but age had not softened the strength of his chiseled features. And though his somber dress—devoid of any color or ornament that might draw the eye—seemed deliberately designed to blend in with the crowd, there was a subtle air of authority about him.

Sofia blinked. Anyone who looked carefully would see he was a very attractive man.

Lady Jersey seemed to agree. "You don't appear to be doddering into your dotage quite yet. I've several ladies I would like you to meet—"

"Perhaps later." Lynsley smoothly lifted the lady's hand to his lips. "But for now, we ought to let you get back to greeting your other guests. I already feel the daggered looks at my back."

"Not on account of *me*." The countess shot a speaking look at Sofia. "Very well, I'll let the two of you go." A last waggle of her fingers shooed them off. "But be warned—I shall catch up with you later, Thomas."

"Now you know why Lady Jersey is known as 'Silence'—she does like to talk," murmured Lynsley as he took two glasses of champagne from the tray of a passing footman.

Sofia sipped slowly, already feeling a bit light-headed from the effervescence of the crowd. The first notes of a waltz struck up, and the couples on the polished parquet began to spin through the elegant figures of the dance.

Focus, she told herself. Amidst the blur of sound and color, she must concentrate on picking out the members of the Scarlet Knights. She had memorized the names from the files passed on by Lynsley. It shouldn't be hard to spot the telltale blaze of red—

"Ah, here is Osborne," observed the marquess.

Biting back a sigh of frustration, she schooled her expression to a polite smile. He was *not* the gentleman she wished to see at the moment, but she must go through the motions of greeting him.

"Lady Sofia, you look like a Botticelli painting come to life." Osborne bent low over her hand.

Recalling her resolve to appear more friendly, she replied with a coy smile. "Thank you for not saying Rubens. I should have been forced to give up my favorite strawberry tarts."

"Rubens is French, and we all know their cuisine calls for a surfeit of butter and cream."

To his credit, the man had a quick sense of humor.

"We Italians have our vices as well."

"Whatever they are, be assured that they are far outweighed by the virtues of beauty and wit." Osborne finished his bow with a graceful flourish, catching the pristine square of pasteboard dangling from her wrist. "I see you have saved the first waltz on your dance card for me." He scribbled his initials on the blank line. Then, to her dismay, put them down for the supper dance as well.

Damn. The prospect of lobster patties and Russian caviar no longer seemed so appetizing.

It was not that she disliked the man. Oddly enough, she was a little afraid of him. A tiny frown thinned her lips. Well, not precisely *afraid*—she was not intimidated by any man. It was more an apprehension, a worry stirred by the strange sensation that came over her when his lazy gaze met hers. Deverill Osborne was a . . . distraction.

The mission was going to be difficult enough without anything drawing her attention from duty.

Sofia was suddenly aware of his glove grazing lightly over her bare arm. A tingle of heat, a shiver of ice.

"Shall we dance, Lady Sofia?"

Just as Lynsley had promised, the contessa was a marvelous dancer, her slim body following his lead with an effortless grace. Her steps were light, lilting, like a love sonnet of Dante . . .

A wry grimace pinched at Osborne's mouth. Where had *that* thought come from? He wasn't in a particularly poetic frame of mind. And love was certainly not the sentiment that came to mind in regard to Lady Sofia. She had responded with a light laugh to his banter, but her smile had not touched her eyes. There was still a coolness there, and despite her fluid movements, he sensed a stiffness in her spine.

Like an angry cat, its back arched, its claws barely sheathed. *Or rather a panther.* Beneath her soft silks, he was aware of an intriguing hint of muscle.

He wondered what he had done to draw her displeasure. Most ladies enjoyed a bit of flirtation. But from the start, she had made it clear she found his attentions annoying.

Even now, with their bodies only inches apart, he sensed she was determined to keep her distance. Her thoughts certainly seemed elsewhere, and her gaze was riveted to a spot over his left shoulder.

"Who is that gentleman?"

He glanced around. "Adam De Winton. But Lord Lynsley would not want me to introduce you to him."

"Why not?"

"He has a rather nasty reputation for wildness."

The dance drew them away from the balcony doors, yet as Osborne led her through a series of twirls, he was aware that Lady Sofia's eyes kept drifting back to De Winton.

Perhaps she simply preferred dark-haired men to blonds, he told himself. Or perhaps she was not quite as prim and proper as she wished to appear.

Women were fascinated by sinners rather than saints. They seemed to find shadow and darkness more interesting than sweetness and light.

Quickening his tempo to the cresecendoing music, he shrugged off such musings. Why the devil did he give a damn what sort of man Lady Sofia cared for? Whether she liked him or not was of no consequence. He was simply doing a personal favor for the marquess. After he discharged his duty, the cold contessa could go to hell.

As the last strains of the violins died away, Osborne led

her toward a knot of gentlemen who had gathered by the punch bowl. *Hillhouse, Whalley, York, Howe.* All were prominent peers, men of influence in Society.

"Lady Sofia, allow me to introduce you to some of my friends."

There was a clinking of cut glass as the gentlemen hurriedly set aside their cups. The claret appeared untasted, for they had all been drinking in the sight of the lovely stranger.

"Enchanted, Contessa."

"Italy has just lost one of its artistic treasures."

"It is a pleasure to meet you."

The fellows were nearly tripping over their feet to make their bows to the lady. He stepped back and watched in sardonic amusement as her dance card was quickly filled in a flurry of scribbles.

Lord Hillhouse had won the honors of leading her out for the next set, a lively country gavotte.

Seeing that she was in good hands for the next little while, Osborne turned away and quickly found a glass of champagne. His throat was dry and prickly from his exertions, but even though he quaffed it in one long swallow, its sweetness did not quite wash the sour taste from his mouth. He reached for another, sipping more slowly this time as he observed Lady Sofia and Hillhouse sharing a merry laugh. It shouldn't rankle that the contessa had given *him* the cold shoulder, yet his hand gripped the glass so tightly that the cut crystal pattern was imprinted on his palm.

He tried to temper his irritation by telling himself it was based on principle rather than personal pique. The lady ought to have a reason for treating him with ill-disguised contempt.

"Osborne." A rice-paper fan slapped softly against his sleeve. "I find you free at least."

"Lady Caro." He kept his eyes on the capering couples.

"The contessa appears to have made a number of conquests."

His only answer was a brusque shrug.

"Why, even *you* seem smitten by her charms." Lady Caroline's tone was playful, but her eyes sharpened to a slitted gaze. "Everyone has remarked on the promenade in the park."

"For God's sake, I am merely doing Lord Lynsley a small favor," he snapped. "I don't know why it should stir such a fuss."

Lady Caroline paled.

"Forgive me." He sighed and pressed his fingertips to his temples. "I am feeling a bit out of sorts . . . a headache."

Her expression softened into a look of concern. "I thought you looked unwell. You should not be straining your strength by staying out until all hours. Return home at once and seek your bed. I will send one of my servants around with the recipe for a soothing posset."

More likely she would bring it around herself.

He and Lady Caroline had had a brief affair some months ago—another of his recent lapses in judgment. She was very pretty, but very possessive, despite the fact that she had a husband. The elderly baron hated Town life, while Caroline loved the pleasures of London. Now that she was back from the country, she had been dropping obvious hints about her desire to resume the arrangement.

"It's merely a trifling bother. And besides, I promised the marquess that I would help introduce the contessa into Society."

"She does not look as if she needs any assistance," replied Lady Caroline. Her voice was waspish.

Women. Osborne gave an inward wince. The ache in his head was beginning to feel as if someone was pounding a spike through his skull.

"Osborne!"

Seeing Henry Griswold's wave, he excused himself from Lady Caroline and made his escape. The fellow, a noted authority on Roman antiquities, could be a bit garrulous at times. But he would gladly listen to the whole of Caesar's Commentaries on the Gallic Wars in return for such a fortuitous rescue.

"Osborne, I must tell you all about the bust of Dionysius I just purchased at auction. You, of all people, will appreciate its artistic merits. . . ."

The lecture lasted until the supper dance. Osborne felt a little guilty about listening with only half an ear, but his occasional murmurs and nods seemed to satisfy his friend.

"How fascinating, Griz. But alas, I am promised for the upcoming waltz." He was finally forced to put an end to the detailed description of orgies in the second century. "Can't keep a lady waiting."

"Er . . ." The scholar blinked. "Oh, right."

"A toast to merriment and revelry." Osborne raised his glass and winked before walking back to the dance floor.

It was not hard to find the contessa. She was surrounded by a bevy of admirers anxious to make her formal acquaintance. "Forgive me, gentlemen, but I am afraid I must claim the lady for the next dance."

The announcement elicited a chorus of sighs.

"Be a good fellow and introduce me," asked Lord Westford in a low voice as he stepped aside. "We all know *you* have no interest in donning a legshackle, but the contessa's beauty might tempt me to make an offer."

"Not to speak of her wealth." Osborne paused for a fraction. "It's well known you need to marry for money, Fitz. But don't get your hopes up. The marquess will be sure to warn the widow away from fortune hunters."

And if Lynsley didn't, he would. The lady, for all her faults, deserved better than a dissolute drunk like the Earl of Westford.

Taking Lady Sofia's hand, he drew her onto the dance floor. "Are you enjoying your first foray into London Society?"

"Very much, thank you."

"By the look of it, you will have no trouble fitting in."

"Everyone has been very kind." Her eyes kept moving around the ballroom. "Perhaps I shall not have to impose on your hospitality for too much longer."

His mouth curled in irony at the suggestion. "Don't worry, Lady Sofia. You won't have to endure my obnoxious presence for more than another week or so."

"Th-that is not precisely what I meant, sir," she stammered. "My English—"

"Your English is perfectly clear," he said lightly. "No need to blush. We are out of earshot from Lord Lynsley. However, as the marquess has asked me to be responsible for seeing you set within the right circles, we shall have to spin along together for a little longer."

The silence between them stretched on for several twirls before she spoke. "You take your responsibilities seriously?"

"Yes," he replied, more sharply than he intended. "I do."

On that note, it was time to turn their steps for the supper room.

After filling their plates from the sumptuous array of delicacies, Osborne found them seats in a corner by the mullioned windows.

"I could not help but notice, sir"—Lady Sofia took a tiny nibble of a lobster patty, then set it aside—"there are several gentlemen wearing waistcoats of a similar shade of bright red. Is there any significance to their dress?"

"Yes. But I won't disturb you with the details."

Her jaw tightened. "Dear me, are you one of those men who feel that talk of the weather and the latest fashions are the only subjects fit for a lady's virginal ears?" For an instant, it looked like her knife was poised to spear his liver rather than the morsel of sautéed foie gras. "Be advised that I am not a virgin. Nor am I a child."

"No one would ever mistake you for a child, Contessa," he drawled, hoping that humor might help dispel the tension between them.

The set of her mouth relaxed. *A twitch of amusement?* Or merely a flicker of candlelight? "No comment on the other assertion?"

"None that a gentleman would dream of making."

This time there was no mistaking her chuckle. It was lush and liquid, like cool water running over smooth stones. "I wonder, sir, why it is that you seem to go out of your way to appear—"

"Frivolous?" he finished. "Ah, well, I suppose beauty is in the eye of the beholder."

"You clearly have a sharp intelligence lurking beneath your frivolous flirtations."

She seemed to be challenging him. "I wonder, madam, why it is you seem to go out of your way to appear cold and condescending," he replied calmly. "For you clearly have a sly sense of humor lurking beneath your imperious scowl."

"Touché."

"I didn't realize we were at daggers drawn."

She sliced off a small piece of roast beef. "About the red waistcoats, Lord Osborne."

Damn. He had hoped to steer the conversation away from De Winton and his friends. The Scarlet Knights were likely not the sort of men Lynsley had in mind for Lady Sofia. If there was any truth to the rumors he had been hearing lately, their exploits went far beyond the usual vices of drinking, wenching, and gambling.

"A vulgar color, don't you think?" He exaggerated his teasing tone. "I am crushed that you have yet to comment on *my* waistcoat. I would have thought that a lady from the country of the Renaissance would find this subtle shade of seafoam blue far more intriguing. Indeed, my tailor assures me that it is a work of art."

A spark of annoyance flared from beneath her sable lashes. But when she looked up, her gaze had darkened to a deep smoky green. "It suits your coloring to perfection—as I am sure you know well."

"I was not fishing for compliments, Contessa."

"And yet I rose to the bait," she said tartly.

Her humor was quick, cutting. To his surprise, Osborne found himself enjoying the verbal thrusts and parries. It was stimulating, in a way that was difficult to describe. "Would that you were hooked on my company. But alas, it appears you can't wait to wriggle away from me."

Lady Sofia stilled her fidgeting. Yet her eyes kept darting over the supper crowd. "Perhaps if you would speak to me as if my brain were as well-developed as other parts of my anatomy, I would find our time together a more comfortable experience."

Osborne nearly choked on a swallow of champagne. "From that barb, am I to assume you prefer plain speaking?"

"Yes."

"Most ladies would rather hear sweet nothings."

There was a hint of hesitation. "I am not like most ladies, sir."

He was fast becoming aware of that. Everything about her—the intense emerald gaze, the sultry dark beauty, the sleek stretch of muscle—was exotic. Unexpected.

Before he could answer, she turned slightly, her eyes following a figure near the ballroom archway. "However, if you do not care to answer my questions, I can always ask the gentleman himself."

"Lady Sofia," he began.

"Lady Sofia!" Lord Webster approached, accompanied by none other than Adam De Winton.

Osborne tried to warn his friend off with his eyes, but the baron was oblivious to the daggered look.

"Allow me to introduce you to another admirer, Contessa." He winked at Osborne. "Sorry, Dev. I tried to keep her to ourselves, but De Winton would not take no for an answer."

When it came to pleasures of the flesh, the word was likely not part of the man's vocabulary, thought Osborne rather acidly.

"Indeed, the lady is far too lovely to keep sequestered in this corner. I beg you will permit me the honor of making your acquaintance." De Winton held her hand a fraction too long at his lips. "I have a confession to make, Contessa—I have been watching you from afar all evening, hoping for the opportunity to approach and pay my respects."

Lady Sofia favored him with a smile. "I, too, could not help noticing you, sir—or rather your waistcoat."

Osborne gritted his teeth to keep from grimacing.

"Do you like bold colors?" asked De Winton.

"That depends."

Osborne saw De Winton's smile stretch a touch wider. "On what, madam?"

Lady Sofia batted her lashes. "On a great many things."

Damn. Was she actually *flirting* with the man?

"As for your choice, sir, that is a very distinctive shade of scarlet. I was just asking if there was a story to it."

"Oh, yes. I would be most happy to tell it to you during one of the upcoming dances."

"Alas, I am afraid that my card is full, sir."

"What a pity."

Up close, De Winton's gaze mirrored the reddish cast of his waistcoat. *Was the lady blind to the telltale signs of dissolution?*

"You must promise to save a waltz for me next time we meet."

"I shall indeed."

The crowd was beginning to drift back to the ballroom. Already the musicians were tuning their instruments.

Osborne welcomed the chance to put an end to the exchange. "Lady Sofia, I believe Woodbridge is written in for this set."

If looks could kill. The contessa did not look at all happy at his interruption. "Please excuse me, Lord De Winton. It seems as if I must not miss a note of this opening gavotte."

"Ciao." De Winton mouthed the word as if he were biting into a ripe peach.

He felt Sofia turn for a last little look. "If I were you, I would say *arrivederci*," he muttered. "De Winton is a dissolute scoundrel. And his taste in clothing is execrable."

She kept her eyes averted from his. "As you said earlier, Lord Osborne, beauty is in the eye of the beholder."

Chapter Six

Sofia finished writing up her daily report and set down her pen. Lady Mooreworth's tidbit on De Winton's favorite gaming haunts—served up with sugared lemon cakes and tea in the lady's overheated parlor—was an interesting bit of gossip. As was Mrs. Wentworth's dark hint of drug use among his friends. However, as she thumbed back through the pages of the notebook, a sigh of frustration slipped from her lips. True, she was beginning to compile some useful information on the members of the Scarlet Knights. Still, it felt as if her mission was proceeding at an excruciatingly slow pace.

As opposed to her social life, which rarely allowed her a moment to breathe. She made a wry face. The last few days had passed in a whirl. Dress fittings, morning calls, shopping for baubles on Bond Street—the life of a pampered aristocrat was more demanding than she had imagined.

Stifling a yawn, Sofia massaged the back of her neck. The hours were certainly more grueling than her Academy schedule. The *ton* danced every night until the wee hours of the morning, so it was no wonder that the pampered ladies of privilege rarely rose before noon. She, on the other hand, was usually up at the crack of dawn. Riding, yoga, an hour of fencing exercises in the ballroom to keep her skills sharp. The household staff, all carefully selected by Lord Lynsley, did not question such strange activities. But as the threat of someone spying her secret exercises always hovered over her head, she took every precaution to keep them well hidden.

Thrust, spin, parry. No amount of strenuous physical activity could dispel the nagging worry that things were not going as fast as they should. Lynsley had given no deadline, but it was understood that in any mission assigned to a Merlin, time was of the essence.

Patience, princessa—like your sword, it can be used as a weapon. Her fencing master's exhortations echoed in her ears. *Il Lupino* was a lecherous old wolf, but he was a master strategist when it came to the art of war. His teaching stressed that victory was as much a matter of mental discipline as it was of physical strength.

Sofia studied her reflection in the looking glass. Of the three roommates, she was considered the most refined. Siena and Shannon both had a swashbuckling athleticism, a certain bold spirit that seemed to give a fire to their eyes. She leaned in a bit closer. Her own spark was perhaps a bit more subtle. *Ladylike.* Her fingers tightened and slid down to the locket at her throat. Did that mean she was any less of a warrior than her sisters-in-arms?

Such questions seemed to trouble her more than they did the others. Siena and Shannon never gave much thought to who they were and where they had come from. They were Merlins, and that was all that mattered. Sofia took a quick peek at the tiny portrait nestled within the gold case, then snapped it shut. She, too, was a Merlin. And she would prove her mettle in this mission.

Tucking the filigree chain back inside her dressing gown, she turned her focus back to the challenge at hand. Lord De Winton was becoming increasingly attentive. Now it was time to encourage a more intimate acquaintance. One of her dance partners had mentioned that Lady Serena Sommers sometimes played hostess to special soirees for the Scarlet Knights. It should not be too difficult to coax De Winton into offering an invitation.

Lord Osborne would, of course, disapprove.

He was taking his role of White Knight rather too seriously. Sofia frowned. His protectiveness was surprising, given his own dalliances with married ladies and widows. But then, the man was an odd mix of contradictions. Most of the time, he seemed naught but a charming flirt. But there were moments when he showed an unexpected depth of character.

Who was the real Deverill Osborne?

Sofia took up her brush and began combing out a snarl in her hair. It didn't matter. Osborne could be the Angel Gabriel or Lucifer Incarnate for all she cared. His role in her mission was over—a fact for which she should be grateful. She had enough mysteries to unravel without getting entangled in any further musings on the man.

The bristles snagged in a knot. "Damn," she muttered, angry at herself for letting Osborne get under her skin. *Hot and cold—the shivers were conflicting, confusing.* That her reaction to him defied reason made her more determined to ignore him in the future.

Rising abruptly, Sofia took her notebook and locked it back in the secret compartment hidden beneath the parquet floor of her dressing room. The click of the cunningly designed latch was an audible reminder of how she must never let her guard down. The slightest slip could betray her charade . . .

"You had best start dressing for Lord and Lady Gervin's ball, milady." Rose entered the bedchamber after a discreet knock. "Shall it be the apricot velvet and gold-threaded overskirt?"

"No, let us choose something a bit more . . . daring." Sofia returned to her chair and resumed a careful study of her own reflection. *Deception must fit like a second skin.* Smoothing a hand over her bosom, she said, "The new gown from Madame Fournier arrived this afternoon, did it not?"

She had ordered a special design from the most fashionable modiste in Town. Not only was the neckline cut to show a provocative amount of cleavage, but also the color was a deep, luscious shade of scarlet.

"Yes, ma'am."

"Excellent." Sofia turned from the looking glass. "I think it's time to take the bull by the horns, so to speak. Tonight we shall wave a red flag in front of Lord Adam De Winton."

Rose nodded. "Shall you wear the rubies as well?"

She shrugged. "If I am to appear as a scarlet lady, I might as well dress to the hilt." The earbobs were large, teardrop jewels dripping from a chain of tiny seed pearls. The matching necklace featured a massive pendant that dangled just above the curves of her cleavage.

"Aye. And with a string of seed pearls setting off the ebony luster of your hair . . ." The maid began to dress the strands in a stylish topknot. "The man will come running."

Sofia watched the nimble movements of her maid's fingers. She, too, would have to exercise exquisite skill in handling De Winton. One slip could destroy her chances of unlocking the secret of the golden key and its mysterious crown—

Looking up abruptly, she asked, "Have we any poppies to use as hair ornaments?"

"No, milady."

"Send one of the footmen to find some. I don't care if he has to go all the way to Kew Gardens." A smile blossomed on her lips. "There is an old adage about gilding the lily. . . ."

Red was fast becoming his least favorite color. Bypassing the claret punch, Osborne took up two glasses of champagne. Lady Sofia seemed intent on ignoring his warnings about the Scarlet Knights. Not only had she danced two sets with De Winton at this evening's festivities, but she had also allowed several other members of the group to take their turn as her partner.

Slanting a sidelong look at her profile, he repressed a scowl. By the look of it, she was fascinated by the devilish color. Not that the deep red ballgown didn't look divine on her. The bold hue brought out every sleek, sensuous curve of her body.

Bloody hell.

Osborne's eyes narrowed even more as he turned from the punch table. Yet another gentleman was sauntering up to the contessa. This one was not wearing red, but his appearance was still cause for concern. He looked to be a Continental coxcomb, for the velvet cutaway coat and snug-fitting pantaloons had not been fashioned by any English tailor.

As he returned to Lady Sofia's side, Osborne found his impression was confirmed by her greeting to the stranger.

"*Ciao*, Marco! How delightful to discover you have come to England!" She allowed him to kiss her cheek instead of her hand.

"The pleasure is all mine, *bella*."

A fellow countryman? That would explain the prancing entrance and flamboyant dress—Italians were, after all, famous for their love of operatic spectacle.

"Will you be in London long?" asked Sofia.

"Is hard to say." Her friend emphasized his words with a lift of his elegant shoulders. As he did so, Osborne noted the subtle ripple of muscle beneath the soft wool and ruffled linen. So, the fellow was no mere fop, despite the pretty face and flowing curls of shoulder-length hair.

"I have some business to attend to before returning to Milano."

Osborne cleared his throat, causing Sofia to give an embarrassed laugh. "*Santa Cielo*, I am forgetting my English manners again." She turned. "Lord Osborne, allow me to present Conte della Ghiradelli." To her countryman, she added, "Papa's old friend, Lord Lynsley, has kindly arranged for Osborne to escort me through my first few weeks in London Society."

"Lucky devil," murmured the *conte* with a broad wink.

Taking an instant dislike to the jackanape, Osborne fixed him with a cool stare and inclined his head just a fraction.

Sofia's brow winged up for an instant before the *conte* leaned in to whisper something in her ear. They both laughed.

Restraining the urge to plant his foot in the Italian's well-shaped arse, Osborne took a long swallow of champagne. But the explosion of tiny bubbles on his tongue only exacerbated his prickly mood.

"Lord Osborne."

Welcoming the excuse to turn away, he smiled. "Lady Serena."

"I have not yet had a chance to thank you for recommending Repton's book on landscape design."

Like the contessa, Serena Sommers was a young, wealthy widow. However, the similarities ended there. In contrast to Lady Sofia's dark coloring and willowy height, Lady Serena had a pale, finespun fairy appearance. Silvery blond curls framed delicate features, and her porcelain complexion accentuated the deep topaz hue of her eyes. *A Pocket Venus.* Pretty, polished, petite. And possessed of a lively wit, which was something he had only recently discovered.

His smile broadened. "I trust that you found some interesting ideas for your terrace."

"Very interesting," she replied. "His ideas on nature and maintaining a certain wildness are very provocative. I have begun making some sketches of what I have in mind."

Catching the flash of pasteboard at her wrist, he seized the chance to leave the contessa to her Milanese macaroni. "If you are free for the next set, I would be delighted to hear more about it."

"I did not mean to interrupt . . ." She slanted a look at Lady Sofia and the *conte.*

"Not at all. The contessa would no doubt welcome the opportunity for a private chat with her compatriot." Good manners demanded that he make introductions all around, a task he performed with deliberate brevity after setting the drinks aside.

"I feel I am the last lady in London to make your acquaintance, Contessa." Lady Serena flashed a dimpled smile. "Please accept my belated welcome to Town. You have an excellent guide in Lord Osborne. He is so very knowledgeable about a great many subjects."

"How very kind of you, Lady Sommers." Sofia did not so much as glance his way. "I am indeed fortunate that Lord Osborne sacrifices so much of his time to a complete stranger."

"I doubt you shall remain a stranger in Society for long," replied the widow. "Indeed, if you do not find discussions of art and literature too dull, you must come to one of my soirees—"

Osborne cut her off with a touch to her arm. "The music is starting, Lady Serena."

"If you are sure . . ." The widow hesitated, still looking a trifle embarrassed at having interrupted.

Taking her hand, Osborne stepped smoothly for the dance floor. "Very sure," he added once they had assumed their position for the first steps. "Indeed, you have done me a favor."

She looked surprised. "From what I have heard, you occupy the most enviable position in Town. The lady *is* very beautiful."

"There is an old adage about beauty being only skin deep."

A spark of amusement lit in Lady Serena's eyes. "Dear me, how very cruel of you to reveal just how easily you see through the rice powder and rouge."

"Ah, but seeing as you have no need to resort to such artifice, you have no need to worry."

Lady Serena was quick with an answering quip. "Think what you will, sir. You will not trick me into giving away my secrets for keeping the ravages of age at bay."

Osborne gave an appreciative chuckle. The lady had just the tart sort of humor he enjoyed. "You have a few years to go before you sink into permanent decline."

"I am greatly relieved to hear that Lord Sunshine does not yet think I am cast in the shade," she said dryly.

His smile turned a bit pinched at the corners. "Speaking of light and dark, tell me more about your designs for a city garden. If I recall, the height of your garden walls will block . . ."

Sofia lost sight of the dark navy coat amidst the sea of swirling couples. Would that she could lose the recollection of Osborne's sardonic smile as he had turned away. *What was ailing the dratted man?* His manners tonight had been brusque to the point of rudeness.

Her mouth pursed. That was rather like the pot calling the kettle black, she supposed. She had been deliberately cool over the past week, so perhaps it was not so surprising that he had responded with a cold shoulder.

"Something wrong, *bella*?" Marco was trying to follow her gaze.

"No . . . just thinking." She touched his sleeve. "Come, let us take a stroll on the terrace. We'll have more privacy to talk."

"Not to speak of stirring up a bit of gossip." He lowered his voice and leaned in a touch closer. "People are already staring."

"All the better."

The brass torchieres cast a flickering glow over the stone balusters and slate tiles. A light breeze set the flames to dancing, their movements matching the melody drifting out from the ballroom. Marco took her arm, and after promenading the length of the walkway, he chose a prominent position at the railing, in full view of the French doors.

"How are things progressing?" he asked softly.

"A good deal slower than I would like," she replied. "I have met several members of the Scarlet Knights but have yet to manage a more intimate acquaintance." Staring out at the shadowed garden, she expelled a sharp sigh. "I wish Lord Lynsley had given me more than vague hints and suspicions. I feel as if I am fencing with specters."

"Don't be too hard on yourself, *bella*. Things will shape up soon enough. You have done well to establish yourself in Society so quickly."

"You think so?" She was not so certain. For some reason, she was feeling unsettled this evening, even though the introduction to Lady Sommers was a step forward.

Noting the edge to her voice, Marco cocked his head. "You are sure you do not have anything else that is troubling you?"

"No." Even if she wished to confide in her friend, she was not quite sure how to express the strange flutterings inside her. A Merlin did not allow any distractions from her duty. The mission was all that mattered, not her own personal puzzlings over Lord Osborne.

Marco did not press her. "*Bueno.* Then let us get down to business. I have learned that Lorenzo Sforza, my old acquaintance from Lombardy, was joined here last week by Guiliano Familligi—who is even more of a rapacious rogue than Sforza. Word has it—" He fell silent, allowing a bejeweled matron and her elderly escort to stroll by before continuing. "Word has it they have rented rooms in Town for the entire Season." He paused. "A dangerous combination, those two. The last time they were in league together, the Duca of Spoleto—who just happened to be a business rival—and his wife were found murdered aboard their pleasure yacht in Portofino harbor."

Sofia felt a ripple of unease. *Yet more pieces to fit into the puzzle?*

"I've also confirmed that they are on intimate terms with the Scarlet Knights."

"Are they here tonight?" she asked.

"No, but they will both be at the Theatre Royal tomorrow evening. I will introduce you."

She frowned slightly. "Lord Osborne has accepted an invitation to a musicale."

"Cry off." Marco flashed a grin. "It is a lady's prerogative."

"Yes, of course." The man already thought her cold and unfeeling. The rudeness would not surprise him.

"The two gentlemen are from noble families that have powerful interests in banking," her friend went on. "Sforza is also involved in trade with Constantinople."

"I see," she replied, though at the moment, she had not a clue as to how the connections tied in with Lord Lynsley's information. But that was her job—to discover if there was indeed a web of intrigue spreading out from the heart of London.

Sofia repressed a shiver, aware of goose bumps prickling like dagger points along her bare arms.

"Shall we go back in?"

"Yes—no." Turning, she caught a glimpse of Adam De Winton and his fellow Knight Charles Lexington at the far end of the terrace. The two men were lounging in the shadows of a massive stone urn, savoring a smoke and their snifters of brandy.

Tired of all the waiting, she made a quick decision. "I

have an idea. Let us show De Winton that I am a real scarlet lady."

Marco followed her lead along the railing. "What do you have in mind, *bella*?"

Sofia waited until they were close to the urn before drawing his hand to her waist and whispering, "Kiss me."

Marco did not need any further encouragement. Spinning with a low laugh, he pressed her back up against the weathered stone and brought his lips down upon hers.

"Naughty man," she scolded, after allowing the lush kiss to go on for a lengthy interlude. "I ought to slap you." However, she took care not to sound the least outraged.

"*Sí,* but I can't resist your charms, *cara*. It's been far too long since we have had the chance to be together."

"Ssshhhhh. You will ruin my reputation."

"As what? A lady of straightlaced propriety?" Marco nuzzled her neck and gave a husky laugh. "We both know better."

"My dear Marco, unlike men, we ladies cannot afford to be too blatant in our behavior. I do not want to be shunned by Polite Society, so I must appear to play by the rules. At least in public."

"Ah, very well." He exaggerated a sigh, then quirked his brows in silent question.

Sofia gave a tiny nod. *Enough. Now it was time to withdraw.*

The charade should tempt Adam De Winton into seeking a more intimate acquaintance.

"Why the stormy face, Lord Sunshine?"

"Stubble the chatter, Nick. Unless you wish to have your deadlights darkened."

"Really, Dev." Harkness rolled his eyes. "You've had an awfully thin skin of late."

"Perhaps my patience has been worn thin by the company I've been keeping these days," snapped Osborne.

"I wouldn't be complaining if I were you," drawled his friend. "You are the envy of every gentleman in London between the ages of eight and eighty."

"Trust me, it has not been quite so edifying an assignment as everyone seems to think."

"Ah, you mean to say that for once you haven't managed to charm a female out of her stockings—"

"Nick . . ." warned Osborne.

"Metaphorically speaking, of course," replied Harkness. "I know you would never be so ungentlemanly as to discuss the luscious details."

"Let us drop the subject, if you please."

Harkness gave a shrug. "There doesn't seem to be anything else interesting to talk about here. I'm heading on to White's. Care to accompany me?"

"Not tonight," he answered brusquely. "I am obliged to stay with the lady until the end of the evening."

"She does not appear to be lacking in male companions to keep an eye on her," quipped his friend.

"Nevertheless, I promised Lynsley to serve as her escort."

Harkness finished his wine. "Suit yourself. But you really ought to save a night soon for a trip to Seven Dials. The Puff of Paradise is a most fascinating place. The Oriental motif is exotic—and so are the women within the private gaming rooms." He lowered his voice. "Those serving the drinks are usually buck naked."

"Sounds interesting," replied Osborne without much enthusiasm.

"Lud, are you sure you aren't ill? You don't sound at all like your usual self."

His usual self?

And what was that? wondered Osborne. A sunny but essentially superficial fellow? An amusing supper partner, but not someone to be taken seriously? Perhaps his irritation with the contessa's character was due in part to his own dissatisfaction with himself.

Her cold courtesy seemed to say that style was no substitute for substance. And while such scorn stung, he could not argue.

"I am fine," he replied. "Just a trifle tired of Polite Society."

"A night out in the stews would relieve the boredom. What say you to tomorrow?"

Osborne shook his head. "I am engaged for a musicale. Maybe later in the week."

"You know the saying about all work and no play making for a very dull boy. Take care you do not lose your edge, Dev."

His life at the moment was not only dull but also depressing.

As his friend walked away, Osborne turned for the terrace, hoping to soothe his sulky mood with one of his host's spiced cheroots. The breeze had freshened, and its coolness ruffling through his hair was a welcome antidote to the stuffiness of the overcrowded ballroom. Seeking to avoid any company, he slipped behind a grouping of marble statuary—Lord Gervin was a noted collector of Greek antiquities—and found a secluded spot in the shadows.

Muted laughter mingled with scented smoke as several more gentlemen stepped out for a break from the indoor festivities. Leaning back against the railing, Osborne lit the tip of his tobacco from one of the torchieres, glad that he was hidden from view. He drew in a mouthful of the pungent sweetness . . . and nearly choked on looking up.

From his vantage point, he had a clear view across the boxwood plantings to the large Athenian urn on the other side of the terrace. The angle afforded not only a lovely view of the sculptural details, but also of the couple engaged in a passionate kiss.

Damn.

What the devil was the contessa thinking? A widow was permitted to have an affair, but only if she was very discreet about it. Lady Sofia ought to know better than to flaunt her preferences so shamelessly. It was almost as if she *wished* to be thought a trifle risqué.

The taste of the smoke suddenly bitter on his tongue, Osborne tossed down the unfinished cheroot and ground it out under his heel. Lynsley had asked him to be an escort, not a nursemaid. It was not his responsibility to lecture the lady on proper behavior. Besides, she had already shown how little stock she put in his advice.

He glanced around, but no one else seemed to have witnessed her indiscretion. The lady had been lucky to escape without suffering any serious consequences. However, Luck was notoriously fickle. She might not be so fortunate next time.

Chapter Seven

Osborne added another splash of brandy to his glass. Yet neither the warmth of the spirits nor the banked fire in his bedchamber hearth had eased the tautness of his temper.

"Absurd," he growled aloud, smoothing the silk of his dressing gown against his bare skin. He had returned home over an hour ago, and yet here he was, acting like an adolescent schoolboy, mooning over a lady who could barely tolerate his presence. Was it the challenge that had him too restless to seek sleep? Her disdain was tantamount to a taunt.

And he was vain enough to believe that his charm could disarm any female.

Yet, so far, Sofia Constanza Bingham della Silveri had parried his pleasantries with ruthless ripostes. With cold steel.

Damn. The recollection of her kissing the Italian sent a frisson of fire through his limbs.

Shrugging off the silk, Osborne stalked to the window and pressed his brow and palms to the leaded panes. The patter of a passing rain seeped through the glass, cool against his naked flesh and tensed muscles. If only it could drown the devils in his head.

"I'm a bloody, bloody fool," he cursed, hoping to counter the seductive demon whispers concerning the arch of her neck, the curve of her breasts.

If anything, the voices grew louder. He stared balefully at his growing erection. The sinful words were like pitchforks to his prick.

He swore again, his breath misting the glass. Air—he suddenly needed to escape the stifling confines of his room, of his own overheated imagination. Dressing quickly, he grabbed up his boots and hurried for the back stairs.

It was barely light as he eased open the doors of the mews and rode out toward the Cumberland Gate of Hyde Park. The snorts of his stallion formed puffs of vapor with every step, ghostly white against the rain-gray dawn. Fog hung heavy over the cobblestones, muffling the sounds of the waking city. He passed a drowsy scullery maid struggling with a coal scuttle and a costermonger wheeling his barrow through the puddles.

At this early hour, the bridle paths should be deserted, he mused. The perfect time for a hell-for-leather gallop. Though as he shifted in the saddle, Osborne realized that riding was perhaps not the best activity at the moment. The feel of his stallion's flexing muscles and sleek hide against his legs was an uncomfortable reminder that his discontent was as much physical as mental.

He needed to find another mistress, and fast. Someone sultry and sexy enough to cause his mind and body to forget all about Lady Sofia.

Spurring to an easy canter, Osborne slowly relaxed into the rhythm of the ride. The question was, who among the available ladies might suit his fancy. No old flame could hold a candle to the contessa. It would have to be someone new, someone unexpected—

Through the mists and shadows, he suddenly spotted a ripple of motion up ahead. An instant later, the blur took shape as a stallion galloping at breakneck speed between the trees. Amidst the flailing hooves and flying clods of earth, a slim figure was just visible, crouched low and clinging to the saddle.

"Bloody hell." Osborne watched in horror as a boot kicked loose from the stirrup, and the rider tumbled toward the ground. But by some miracle, both feet hit the earth, and the lucky devil managed to bounce back up and gain a tenuous grip on the wet pommel.

Despite the timely acrobatics, the young groom had clearly lost control of the horse and was in danger of being trampled. Osborne urged his own mount forward, ducking the overhanging branches as they gathered speed and raced along the narrow bridle path.

Thundering through a break in the trees, Osborne's big bay gained enough ground to pull abreast of the runaway stallion. Fisting his reins in one hand, he angled in closer— a dangerous move, for one tiny slip could break both of their necks.

Just another inch or two . . . Daring a low lunge, Osborne grasped the runaway rider around the waist and yanked him to safety. But instead of holding a tearful lad, limp with relief, he found himself fighting a twisting and tossing of tensed muscle.

"For God's sake, stop squirming like an eel."

The boy had the ballocks to answer with an oath. Another kick grazed his horse's flanks. The bay snorted and shied away, nearly unseating them both.

"Bloody little bastard," he growled, trying to control the ungrateful imp's sharp elbows.

In the tussle, the lad's floppy cap came loose, revealing a tumble of raven tresses.

"L-lady Sofia?" Osborne blinked, wondering whether he had taken complete leave of his senses. For unless he was crazy, it was the contessa in his arms, dressed as a boy in breeches and a moleskin jacket.

"Yes, dammit. Now let me go," she demanded.

As he drew to a skittish halt, she wrenched free of his hold and dropped lightly to the turf. Turning without a word, she stalked away to snatch up the reins of her own mount.

He slid down from the saddle and hurried after her. "Are you all right, milady?"

"I am quite fine," she snapped.

"But . . ."

"But what?" She whirled around, eyes ablaze, cheeks flushed, ringlets in wild disarray around her face.

Osborne couldn't tear his eyes away from her—and the curves set off by the snug buckskins.

"Hell, you ride like a Hussar," he said admiringly.

"A fact I hope you will keep to yourself." It was no longer merely anger but trepidation he saw on her face. "*Prego*, Lord Osborne," she added after drawing a deep breath. "I beg you will not speak of this to anyone. I am aware that the rules governing a lady's behavior are very strict here in England. Many people might consider me too . . . fast."

"Dangerously fast, Lady Sofia." Osborne stepped closer. They were both still a bit breathless from the exertion, and he could feel the whisper of warmth cut through the damp mists swirling around them. Gentlemanly scruples demanded that he honor her request. But at the moment, a far more devilish desire seemed to overpower any notion of honor.

"In our country, it is customary that one who asks a favor is willing to grant one in return."

Her eyes widened slightly. Whether it was shock or a spark of some other emotion was difficult to discern in the shifting shadows. "What sort of favor, Lord Osborne?"

Despite the chill, her skin glistened with tiny beads of sweat, and the pulse at her throat mirrored the thud of his own racing heart. His lips lowered and covered the quivering spot.

A moan resonated somewhere deep in her throat, but she didn't push him away.

Emboldened, Osborne skimmed a kiss along the line of her jaw, inhaling the sublime sweetness of her scent. *Heather and honey.* He couldn't help himself—he simply *had* to have a deeper taste. Crushing his mouth to hers, he drew her lower lip between his teeth.

Gently, gently. But his body was not listening to his mind. His stubble scraped against her delicate flesh as he forced her head back. His hands threaded through her windblown hair; his tongue thrust deep inside her, drinking in her warmth.

Dear God, he was drowning in pure, primal desire.

What a spectacle he was making of himself. The debonair Deverill Osborne, desperate for a fleeting kiss.

He didn't care. His hands found the opening of her jacket, and then the swell of flesh beneath the scrunch of linen. Cupping her breasts, he stroked upward.

Her response was fiercely feminine. The tips of her nipples hardened against his palms.

"Please . . ." She twisted back and forth, rubbing the

front of her breeches against his hardening cock. "Please, this really must stop."

Osborne's simmering frustrations were on the verge of exploding. "If you are begging for release, you are going about it all wrong."

She stilled in his arms.

"Why are you so warm to that preening peacock of a conte and so cold to me?" he demanded.

"I . . . he . . ." she stammered. "Marco is an old friend."

"An old lover?"

She looked away, her loosened hair falling across her face, a shimmering black curtain between them.

"I'm sorry. That was unspeakably rude," he said with a ragged sigh. "I don't know what comes over me when I am around you. My manners seem to go up in smoke."

"Please let me go, Lord Osborne."

He drew his hands away, but not before brushing an errant curl from her cheek. She flinched as if singed by his touch. And yet, for a fleeting moment, her mouth had been molten with desire. He had kissed enough women to know that without a doubt.

"And now that you have taken your pleasure, sir, I trust I can count on your silence in return."

Stung by the scorn in her voice, he couldn't keep from retorting in kind. "The pleasure was not all one-sided, Contessa. Admit it, you wanted me just as much as I wanted you."

Her cheeks flushed red as her kiss-roughened lips. "Why, you arrogant ass."

"You haughty hellion."

They stood toe-to-toe, glaring at each other through the tendrils of dawn mist. Much as he wished to turn his back on the lady and stalk away, Osborne felt held in thrall by some mysterious spell. *Black magic.* The breeze stirred her loosened hair, setting the raven strands to dancing along the line of her shapely shoulders. Her eyes, aswirl with anger, had an alchemy all their own. Emeralds on fire.

He found it difficult to breathe.

A dog barked, breaking the dark enchantment. Swearing softly, Sofia snatched up her hat and tucked her tresses out of view. Several quick strides brought her abreast of her stallion. Without waiting for any assistance, she caught up the reins and vaulted lightly into the saddle, her boot barely touching the stirrup.

Whatever else her faults, the lady looked magnificent on her mount. Like Minerva, the ancient Roman goddess of war. A bellicose beauty.

"*Andiamo,* Jupiter," she said.

The horse whinnied, his hooves kicking up clods of the damp earth. A flick of her heels and they were gone.

A close call.

Sofia slumped back against the stall door and pressed her palms to her sweat-slicked brow. Another few inches and Osborne's roving hands would have hit upon the small turn-off pocket pistol hidden in her waistband. He was already asking enough uncomfortable questions without wondering why she was carrying a firearm.

She bit her lip—a definite mistake, as it was yet another reminder of how badly she had let her guard slip.

Her tongue flicked over the raw flesh, tasting the lingering traces of his brandy and her own egregious folly. What madness had come over her? The man possessed a potent charm. And a sinful, sensuous smile. When his mouth had come close, hovering a hair's breadth from hers in the morning mists, she had been powerless to resist.

Passion. While she grasped the intellectual concept, the Academy lectures had not quite prepared her for the full brunt of its physical force.

She shivered at the memory of his probing caresses, his tongue sliding so smoothly through her defenses. Hard yet soft. Sweet yet spiced with a hot, masculine need. The effect had been intoxicating. She had surrendered to his demands without a fight.

No wonder the devilish Deverill Osborne had seduced half the ladies of London.

Her sigh sharpened to an oath. Forewarned was forearmed. She would *not* let the man beat her so easily again. He might be a master of sexual swordplay, but he would soon discover that he was not the only one who could wield a sliver of steel. Any future advances on his part would be parried with better skill, she resolved.

She was no fledging chick—she was a Merlin. Woe to any man who got too close to her talons.

Osborne marched down the corridors of Whitehall, outpacing the young lieutenant who had been assigned to show him the back stairwell that led to the marquess's office.

"Sir!" wheezed the officer. "I ought to announce your presence—"

Ignoring the call, he barged past a startled copy clerk and entered the room.

"Osborne." Lynsley looked up over the gold-rimmed lenses of his reading glasses, his brows arching in inquiry.

"Forgive the intrusion." All of a sudden, he felt rather silly interrupting affairs of state to pass on a bit of tittle-tattle. But retreat would appear even more foolish. "Might I have a word with you? In private."

The marquess dismissed his secretary with a tiny nod.

"You may go ahead and draft the memorandum to the Swedish ambassador, Jenkins. I will review it later."

The young man gathered up a sheaf of documents and withdrew from the room.

"Would you care for a drink?" Lynsley gestured to the tray of decanters on the sideboard.

"Thank you, but no. I shall not take up any more of your time than necessary to . . ." *To what?* Grass on a lady's indiscretions? Osborne felt his cheeks turn a trifle warm as he finished by saying, "To mention my concerns in regard to the contessa."

"Concerns?" Lynsley's brows rose a touch higher.

"I fear she may be falling in with a rather disreputable crowd," he said stiffly. "I have tried to warn her off, but my opinion seems to carry little weight with her."

"Indeed?"

"To be frank, the lady doesn't like me much. However, I thought that you might have some influence over her."

"Lady Sofia is of age," replied the marquess dryly. "She is free to choose her own company, regardless of what either you or I have to say about it." He picked up a pile of reports and resumed his reading. "I appreciate your telling me this, but I wouldn't worry about the lady. I have great confidence in her judgment."

Osborne made a face. "Even though she encourages a hellhound like Adam De Winton to come sniffing around her skirts?"

Lynsley calmly turned a page. "De Winton's pedigree allows him entrée into the highest circles of the *ton*. If the leading hostesses of London do not object to his presence, I don't see how we can argue."

The marquess's offhand manner was beginning to set his teeth on edge. "It is not his pedigree but his purse that is cause for concern. It's common knowledge in the gaming hells around Town that his finances are precarious at best."

"A fortune hunter? Be assured that Lady Sofia is familiar with that breed of gentleman. She isn't likely to be fooled by false flatteries."

"Perhaps you would be a tad more concerned if I mentioned her early morning habits," said Osborne.

Lynsley finally looked up.

"I happened to spot her alone in the park around dawn," he growled. "She was galloping hell for leather astride a great black stallion. Did you know she rides like the wind?"

"Seeing as I arranged for her equestrian instructor, I am aware of her skills in the saddle," replied the marquess.

Osborne fell silent for a moment. He ought to leave it at that, but stubbornness overcame sense. "If she doesn't slow down a bit, she may find her reputation in tatters. The tabbies are quick to pounce if a lady strays from the confines of conformity."

"A widow is allowed a little more latitude, as I'm sure you well know." The marquess took up a pen and began making a notation in the margin of the paper. "Consider that you have done your duty, Osborne. You have opened the right doors, which is all that I asked of you. In good conscience, you may now stand aside. If Lady Sofia wishes to go on from here on her own, we must respect her wishes."

"Bloody hell." The force of his fist hitting the desk blotter nearly knocked over the inkwell. "There is something damn peculiar about all this, Lynsley."

"How do you mean?" asked the marquess.

"Well . . ." Nonplussed, Osborne realized he was not quite sure how to word his misgivings. Like the morning mists, they were no more than vague swirls. Ghostly vapors with no real form or substance. He blew out a harried huff of air. "I can't help but wonder if this has anything to do with your . . . government duties."

Lynsley's mouth quirked. "Ah, you think the lady is a secret agent from the kingdom of Naples? Or perhaps an assassin, sent by the Prince of Venice?"

Said aloud, such suspicions did sound patently absurd.

"Did one of your lady friends lend you a copy of *The Duchess of the Dark Dagger*?" went on Lynsley, a hint of humor shading his voice. "I hear it is a highly entertaining novel—even better than *The Curse of the Velvet Glove*."

Osborne swore under his breath. "Truth is sometimes stranger than fiction," he said defensively. "Take the recent events at Marquand Castle—two peers end up dead, and my friend Kirtland returns with a mysterious bride. How the devil do you account for *that*?"

"Art auctions can be a cutthroat business from what I hear," replied the marquess with a straight face. "As for the particulars of Lord Kirtland's love life, you would have to ask the earl himself. I was not among the guests invited to his nuptials."

"Yet you were investigating him."

"My job requires that I investigate a great many people. Most, like the earl, are proved innocent of any treasonous activities." Lynsley cocked his head. "In any case, I fail to see the connection between Kirtland and the contessa . . . other than the fact that the earl and his bride took a wedding trip to Italy."

Put that way, Osborne had to admit that his misgivings did sound like a plot straight out of a horrid novel. The *Cabal of the Killer Contessas*. Mayhap he deserved to be their first victim for having such a lurid imagination.

"Forget it," he muttered. There was no point in prolonging the conversation. Even if there was some deep, dark secret to Lady Sofia's presence in London, the marquess was far too clever to let it slip by mistake. "I won't keep you from your work any longer."

"Osborne."

He turned, expecting a last little quip.

However, Lynsley's expression was deadly serious. "Thank you again for the warning. Allow me to return the favor. It would be a mistake on your part to become too involved with Lady Sofia. She is . . ."

"Dangerous?" The word came unbidden to his lips.

"In a manner of speaking. Though the word I was about to use was *complex*."

"How very kind of you to mention it now," replied Osborne with a sarcastic sneer. "I wonder why you chose to honor me with the task in the first place?"

"For the very reason that your detachment from romantic entanglements is well known throughout the *ton*." The marquess set down his pen and folded his hands. "It's said that you bestow your favors quite freely. But your heart is wholly your own."

Osborne could think of nothing to say in answer.

"It is a wise strategy," finished Lynsley. "Especially in this case."

"You fear that I may lose my heart to the contessa?" He took hold of the brass door latch. "Ha. If I were ever foolish enough to fall in love, it would not be with a high-flying spitfire with a taste for vulgar red."

Chapter Eight

*G*rateful that duty provided a distraction from the early morning encounter, Sofia sat down at her dressing table and opened the portfolio of files provided by Lynsley. *No more mental mistakes*, she chided herself. It had been careless of her to assume that no gentleman of the *ton* would be up and about at dawn.

She frowned, wondering just what Osborne had been doing at that hour in the park. *Returning from a late-night tryst?* Quite likely. The background information on him included a rather lengthy list of lovers. And no wonder. He was an incorrigible flirt, handsome, witty, and engaging enough to charm the scales off a dragon.

As for his kisses, they were certainly practiced enough—

Thinning her lips, she quickly thumbed through the folders to a different set of pages. Enough of Deverill Osborne. She must concentrate on the coming challenge.

In truth, it offered a welcome change of pace from the overcrowded ballrooms and simpering suitors. She was slated to attend an afternoon lecture at the Society of Caesarian Antiquities. The gathering would provide an opportunity to meet the Duke of Sterling.

Lynsley had made it clear that she was to seek an acquaintance with the man, though the duke must, of course, remain in the dark about her real identity and her real purpose. She wasn't certain as to why the marquess thought a meeting important. Surely there was nothing more Sterling could tell them about the suspicious death of his grandson. But perhaps Lynsley felt the duke would be an unwitting ally in learning more about Lord Robert's circle of friends and their favored haunts.

Not that she expected any great revelations. However, she couldn't afford to leave any stone unturned. The looking glass reflected her wry grimace. Even if that meant memorizing several chapters on the sculptural techniques of ancient artists. Sterling was a noted connoisseur of classical coins and portrait medallions. Pretending to share his passion would provide a perfect excuse to cultivate a friendship.

Lies and deception.

"Shall you wear the forest-green daydress, milady?" Rose entered the room, a stack of freshly ironed handkerchiefs in her hands.

Sofia looked up from her reading. "Yes." Its conservative cut—long sleeves, high neck, full folds—would help create the illusion of a prim widow, interested in furthering her knowledge of serious scholarship. "And a plain wool shawl."

"Very good, milady. We had best begin dressing, if you are not to be late."

Time to don yet another disguise.

As her maid turned away, Sofia fingered the locket beneath her silk wrapper. *A stranger in her own skin.* It was yet another kinship she felt with the mystery lady portrayed in the miniature. The faded features reflected her own blurred identity. They were both nameless, with no discernible past. This foray into London Society, where every minute detail of family, rank, and relationships was scrutinized, had made her even more aware of her own isolation. Her own unanswered questions.

Lady Nobody.

"A simple hairstyle would be fitting, don't you agree?" Rose gathered the loosened tumble of raven hair and coiled it in a tight bun.

Sofia pulled her thoughts back to the present. "Yes, yes, that looks just right."

However, she remained somewhat distracted through the rest of her dressing. Picking up the book on Roman history, she reviewed the chapter on the Pantheon as her maid set about making the finishing touches.

"Would that the duke had an interest in Florence or Siena," she murmured. "I at least have a rudimentary knowledge of Renaissance art."

Her maid fumbled a hairpin, and it fell to the carpet.

"It's my fault." The bobble brought a rueful smile to Sofia's lips. Rose was normally so sure-handed. "I fear that my fidgets are making things harder for you."

"No, milady." But Rose wore an odd expression as she reached for another pin.

"Is something wrong, Rose?"

"No, milady." There was a pause as she anchored the loose strand in place. "It was simply the mention of the city—Siena. It reminded me of something else."

Sofia turned in her chair, nearly undoing her maid's handiwork. "You know . . . Siena?"

Rose's gaze turned more shuttered. "I have not had the opportunity to travel in Italy."

"That was not what I meant." Sofia decided to press the point. The world of polite society was all so new and disorienting. It would be nice to have someone in whom she could confide some of her secrets. Lynsley had assured her that the woman was completely trustworthy. "I was speaking of . . ." Sofia hesitated for a fraction. "My sister. My sister-in-arms, that is. Siena and I trained together for years."

The announcement finally elicited a crack in the maid's stony stoicism. "The resemblances between the two of you are striking," murmured Rose, allowing just a hint of a smile.

Sofia studied her own reflection for a moment. "Would that I can show the same skill and courage in the face of danger as she did."

Looping the last strands of hair into place, Rose set the pins in a precise row. "From what I have seen, milady, you have no need to worry."

"Why, thank you, Rose." The compliment, however oblique, was a boost to her confidence.

The maid's answer was a rustling within the armoire. "The burgundy shawl will add just the right touch of coloring to your ensemble. Elegant, yet sober and sensible." The fringe feathered over Sofia's arms, and though it might only have been her imagination, it seemed as if Rose's workmanlike hands lingered a touch longer than usual.

"Excellent." The maid stepped back to judge the effect. "Now, you had better be on your way. The carriage is waiting, and it would not be wise to make a late entrance to the lecture."

Accepting her reticule, Sofia smiled. "I am not quite

sure what to expect. Let us hope I shall not find myself thrown to the lions of the Coliseum."

"More likely they will put you in a place of honor so that they may feast their eyes on you."

The words proved to be no joke, for a short while later, Sofia found herself being escorted to a front-row seat by the head of the Society, a portly, middle-aged baron who, despite his advancing years and receding hairline, wore his locks in the latest *a la Brutus* style.

"What a pleasure to have you join our little group this afternoon, Contessa," he announced.

"I do hope I was not too forward in asking if I might attend one of your lectures."

"Not at all, not at all. We are always anxious to have those with a serious interest in scholarship join our ranks."

Sofia hoped that Lynsley had not started a rumor regarding her expertise in some arcane area of ancient study. She was still struggling to tell the difference between Aurelian and Octavian stylistic elements. "I confess, I am merely a neophyte, but I am anxious to learn more." She paused and heaved an audible sigh. "My late husband was a connoisseur of Roman sculpture, and he passed on his passion to me. I wish to become more conversant with his collection."

The baron's smile turned positively Dionysian. "That is very commendable of you. I would be delighted to provide a private tutorial whenever you might wish."

"How kind." She fixed him with a stony stare that quickly sobered his expression.

"And then, of course, our series of talks on the—"

"Ahem." Clearing his throat, the gentleman at the lectern glared and shuffled his papers. "If you would all take your seats, I would like to begin with a few words on the early years of Augustus. . . ."

The talk prosed on for nearly an hour. Sofia struggled to keep up with the detailed explanation of stylistic nuances, yet she found her attention wandering. The elderly lady dressed in flowing white silks and a golden headdress of artificial laurel leaves must be the eccentric Dowager Marchioness of Muirfield, a lady who claimed to commune with the ghost of Cleopatra. That oddity was overlooked because of her generous financial contributions to the Society, and because her essays on Roman garden design were considered quite lucid.

Seated to her left was an effete-looking young man in high shirtpoints and an elaborate cravat. The frothing folds of the Waterfall knot matched the artful curl of his long hair—surely he was the *enfant terrible* poet Bryce Beecham, whose translation of Virgil's *Aeneid* had made him the newest sensation of the literary world.

Sofia's gaze slid sideways, trying to match faces with the names and descriptions in her files. Fat and florid Lord Rockham penned sonnets in classical Latin, rail-thin Mr. Jervis had authored several scholarly treatises on the ancient aqueduct system, and the copper-curled Miss Pennington-Pryce was an authority on Roman sculpture . . .

Her eyes nearly missed the Duke of Sterling, who was seated in the far corner, deep in the lengthening shadows of a large statue of Jupiter. Even half obscured, he exuded an aura of authority, with a sculpted strength to his profile that matched the regal Roman stone. The angular planes and chiseled lines had weathered over the years to a harsh edge in places. But at the age of five and sixty, the duke was still a handsome man, with a leonine mane of white hair crowning a high forehead and prominent aquiline nose.

He looked austere, aloof and aristocratic, as befitting his august lineage. And sad.

The death of his grandson must still be sharp in his memory, mused Sofia. She also seemed to recall mention of another family tragedy buried in the past, something about an estrangement from his only daughter, a great favorite, who had eloped in defiance to his wishes. By all accounts, the young lady had died before any reconciliation had taken place.

Sofia gave an inward sigh. *Family.* Life was so fragile, so fleeting. How could any quarrel sever the bonds of love?

After staring a moment longer, she looked away. The Academy's classes on the beau monde had taught that love had little to do with the lives of titled families. Marriages were based on pragmatic considerations like land, power, and money, rather than any flutter of the heart. Duty came before desire.

A rueful smile played on her lips. In many ways, it was not so very different from the rules governing her own world.

"And so that covers the sculpture of the Flavian period. In the coming weeks, I shall be talking about the later years of the Empire, but for now, I will be happy to answer any questions."

Several people raised stylistic queries; then the meeting was adjourned for refreshments. Sofia allowed the baron to introduce her to a circle of his friends, but after a few polite pleasantries, she managed to excuse herself from the conversation. Eluding eye contact with the two ladies, she made her way to the glass display cabinets in the arched alcove.

"You appear to have a keen interest in coins, madam." A deep voice, gruff and gravelly, sounded close by after she had been studying the artifacts for some time.

She looked up. "Very much so. I find the faces fascinating."

Up close, the Duke of Sterling did not look so intimidating, perhaps because his lively gray-green eyes suddenly lit with a certain spark of amusement. "Indeed, one can see the full range of human emotion," he replied. "Greed, pride, avarice, lust."

"As well as courage, nobility, and compassion," she added softly.

"That, too." He pressed his broad palms to the glass. "I suppose I have become a trifle cynical in my old age."

"Not nearly as cynical as Tiberius." Sofia pointed to the pronounced sneer of the ancient emperor. "I sometimes like to imagine stories to go with the faces—who they really were, what their lives were like. Not very scholarly, I fear, but it makes history very human."

Sterling chuckled. "I confess that I do much the same when studying my own collection. Some of the likenesses are haunting." His gaze narrowed for an instant; then he shook his head slightly. "Of course, it's naught but flights of fancy, yet as you say, it does make the past come alive."

"By all accounts, your private collection would inspire more than a few stories, Your Grace. I have heard that it is one of the finest in England."

"It does not compare to some of the collections in your country." His smile had returned. "Permit me to make your formal acquaintance, Contessa, though it seems we have no need of exchanging names."

"Indeed not, sir. It is an honor to meet such an august personage."

He gave a wry grimace. "Good heavens. You make me sound as if I, too, should be under glass."

She feigned a show of embarrassment. "Forgive me—my English is not as polished as I would like."

"Your English is delightful, Contessa." He patted her arm. "Though I daresay you ought to be conversing with the younger gentlemen, rather than an ancient artifact like me."

"I much prefer intelligent discourse to false flatteries, Your Grace."

He gave a short, sardonic growl of laughter. "You, too, find toadeaters tiresome? Then allow me to spirit you away to the other galleries and show you the rest of the Society's collection."

"I should like that very much."

Sofia followed the duke through the other display cabinets, hoping that her occasional comments did not betray her unfamiliarity with antiquities. *False flatteries, indeed.* She felt a little guilty for leading him on. Clearly the subject was one that was dear to his heart. The set of his mouth softened as he described the exquisite workmanship on a series of bronze castings, and the shading beneath his eyes seemed to lighten.

Turning into the Sculpture Room, Sterling paused before a bust of Ovid. "My grandson was a great admirer of rhetoric and logic." He sighed. "Perhaps too much so."

"Forgive me if I stir painful memories, but I would like to offer my condolences. I am only recently arrived in Town, but I have heard mention of your recent loss."

"Yes, I have no doubt that Robert's death was grist for the gossip mills." His jaw tightened. "London loves a scandal. And the more lurid the details, the better."

"Unfortunately, the penchant for sordid speculation is universal, Your Grace. Rumors and innuendo tend to take on a life of their own."

"You are wise beyond your years, Contessa." His expression turned bleak, brooding. "I thank you for offering such words of comfort."

They appeared to be of cold comfort. The duke's face was as pale and lifeless as the carved marble.

"Did your grandson share your love of antiquities?" she asked. Though loath to pry into painful memories, it was her duty to learn all she could about the young man.

"Yes. Robert had a lively interest in a great many things. He was an extraordinary fellow. . . ."

Osborne stalked past the display of botanical books, seeking the section of shelves devoted to Italian history and culture. There must be a Mediterranean version of Debrett's, a volume that listed the titled nobility of the various principalities and city states.

Count della Ghiradelli. Contessa della Silveri. He would begin by seeing whether they were fact or fiction. Lynsley's teasing had rubbed his already-sensitive nerves raw.

It took some searching but he finally found what he was looking for. That it was in Italian didn't matter, for all he needed was to page through the alphabetical listings on Milan and Venice.

Ghirabella, Ghiracetti . . . damn. He felt a tiny twinge of disappointment at discovering an entry for Giovanni Marco Musto della Ghiradelli. The age looked to be right. As did all the information on Conte de Silveri, who had indeed passed away several years ago. A marriage date was there, but the name was left blank.

"I was not aware of your genealogical interest in Italy, Lord Osborne." The voice of Lady Serena Sommers floated over his shoulder.

He snapped the book shut and shoved it back in place.

"I—I was merely checking on something for a friend." Turning quickly, he slouched against the gilded spines to hide the titles. "Did you see that the new collection of Repton's essays has arrived?"

Lady Serena held up a small leatherbound book. "Yes. I have already picked up a copy."

"I think you will find them of interest." Osborne took her arm and drew her down a different aisle. "You might also find the portfolio of Verrochini's villa designs fascinating."

"I shall have the clerk add this to my purchases," she said after perusing the first few prints. "Thank you for the recommendation."

"My pleasure, Lady Serena."

A becoming blush suffused her cheeks. "Speaking of pleasures, Lord Osborne . . ."

"Yes?" he encouraged.

"I do not wish to appear forward. But as you are a man of discerning sensibilities, I was wondering whether you might like to attend a small party I am giving on Thursday evening. It will be a small affair, and much more informal than the usual Society soirees."

She hesitated a fraction, her coloring deepening as she lowered her voice to a whisper. "I ought to warn you that I invite people who I feel are interesting, though they may not be welcome in the highest circles of Society. And we do not always follow the rigid rules of propriety. I am of the opinion that women should have a bit of freedom to discuss subjects that are normally forbidden to their sex. But you may not agree."

In other words, did Lord Sunshine only smile on conformity?

Osborne curled his lips and answered in the same low murmur. "It sounds quite intriguing."

She let out a soft breath. "Excellent. Come around at eight."

"I look forward to it."

"It sounds as if your grandson was an unusually gifted young man, Your Grace," said Sofia. "No wonder you miss him terribly."

"It is painful to lose family—but then, you are aware of that." The duke made a face. "Here I am, an old man boring you with selfish reminiscences while you have suffered your own tragedies."

Sofia sought to assuage his guilt. "Please do not apologize, sir. I enjoyed hearing you speak of your grandson." In truth, she had learned a number of new facts from the conversation, including the names of Lord Robert's closest friends and the locations of his favorite antique galleries. "Indeed, I wish that I could have met him."

The duke looked rather wistful. "He would have liked you very much. What a pity that . . ."

Allowing his words to trail off, Sterling squared his sagging shoulders. He was a tall man, and by the way his spine snapped to a ramrod stiffness, it was evident that he did not often allow himself a moment of weakness. *Unbending steel.* He would not be easy to live with. Sofia could well imagine the clash of wills when his daughter dared defy his wishes. And yet, beneath the show of armor, she sensed . . . regret? Recrimination?

She liked him all the more for it.

"But enough of such maudlin talk," he went on. "What particular aspect of Roman art are you most interested in, Contessa?"

"Please call me Lady Sofia, Your Grace. As for my interests, I am quite partial to coins, though I still have so much to learn on the subject."

The answer seemed to please him. "You must come view my collection sometime. The majority of it is housed in the Ingot—"

"The Ingot?" she interrupted.

He laughed. "It is the nickname for the ancestral castle in Kent. A past duke took it into his head to cast the front door out of solid silver—earning not only the moniker but also the curses of countless footmen who have had to polish the deuced thing."

"It sounds as if your forebearer had a shining sense of humor," she said dryly.

"Actually, he had a tarnished reputation, both personally and politically. The door was more a monument to overweening pride."

"We cannot choose our family."

The duke allowed a ghost of a smile. "No. We must simply live with them."

If we are lucky. Sofia stifled a sigh. Perhaps she was fortunate to be unfettered by the past. There was no burden of hereditary sins, no weight of family expectations, no memories of wicked ancestors.

"In any case," he went on. "I rarely entertain at the Ingot these days, but a selection of my medallions are here in London."

"I would love to view them."

"I will be out of Town for several days, but when I return, I shall send a servant to inquire when it would be convenient for you to come by."

"That is very kind of you, sir."

"No, actually it's very selfish. At my age, I have to use

every possible ploy to be in the company of a lovely young lady." The duke slanted a look at the refreshment room and waggled a silvery brow. "Sir Stephen looks as if he would like to throw me to the gladiators for keeping you from the others. I had better allow you to mingle with the crowd."

Sofia acknowledged the compliment with a gracious smile. The fact was, she had enjoyed Sterling's company. Despite his exalted rank and intimidating reputation, he had shown himself to possess a kind heart and self-deprecating wit during their brief tour. Strangely enough, she also had the impression that for all his wealth and retinue of retainers, he was rather lonely. Of all the men she must cozen up to for this mission, the duke was promising to prove a pleasant assignment.

"I would prefer to give a thumbs-down to the idea, but that would be unconscionably rude," she replied.

Sterling offered his arm. "Duty can often be a cursed nuisance." He gave her a conspiratorial wink. "A quarter hour is sufficient. After that, you may feel free to take your leave."

"Thank you for the advice, sir. I fear I have yet to learn all the steps in making my way through London society and will unwittingly tread on sensitive toes."

"If you make a misstep, just do as you would on the dance floor, Lady Sofia. Simply shuffle your slippers and spin by with a regal smile. No one will dare take offense."

She chuckled. "What very wise counsel, Your Grace."

"I am sure you will receive equally sage advice from Lord Lynsley. He is, I hear, your sponsor in Town."

"Yes, the marquess is an old family friend," she replied. "Alas, I fear his government duties do not leave him much time for leisure. I already feel that I have imposed on his goodwill, so I shall take care not to bother him with mere trifles."

"Allow me to offer myself in his stead."

"How kind. You truly wouldn't mind me seeking your advice if I have further questions on protocol or propriety?" *A damsel in distress*. It provided yet another excuse for seeking his company.

"Indeed not. Please feel free to turn to me if you have any trouble," he replied with a fatherly pat to her hand.

Trouble. In his wildest dreams, the Duke of Sterling could not begin to imagine what sort of trouble she was likely to encounter. Not that she was about to enlighten him.

Instead she simply lowered her lashes. "How very reassuring, Your Grace. A lady never knows when she may have need of a knight in shining armor to ride to her rescue."

Chapter Nine

*O*sborne stepped into the entrance hall of Lady Serena's town house, curious as to what the evening entertainment was going to offer. Perhaps his hostess had built a secret temple to Bacchus among her bower of climbing roses. Leering satyrs, fountains of wine, naked . . .

Granted, he *had* purchased the latest horrid novel at Hatchard's, but *The Pagan Princess* was for the ailing octogenarian Lady Hawthorne, who was currently confined to her bed with a head cold.

He, on the other hand, had no such excuse for his feverish imagination. Or his brooding sulks. That Lady Sofia had cried off from last night's musicale ought to have been a relief, rather than a further irritation. After all, Lady Serena thought him interesting enough to include in her soiree.

"This way, milord." A footman—dressed in ordinary livery rather than a Greek toga—escorted him past the marble staircase to a corridor leading to the rear of the house. "The Garden Room is straight ahead."

Osborne entered a large, airy space with cream white walls and a frescoed ceiling. A glance up showed that the painting did indeed depict fauns and females frolicking in a pastoral setting, but the nudity was really quite tame and tasteful. The soft blues and pastel greens were reflected in the decorative trim and the draperies. Dropping his gaze, he saw that the far wall was a series of arched French doors that opened onto a slate terrace. In afternoon, with the sun slanting in through the glass panes, the room would be bathed in light.

"Do you approve of the architectural changes I've made so far? I had the brick wall replaced by the glass." Lady Serena rose from the sofa and brought him a coupe of champagne. "I copied the design of the doors from a sketch I found in a book on the châteaux of the Loire Valley."

"Very original," he replied. "The classic style and symmetry fit the space very well." Another look around showed that the furnishings were equally elegant. There was a spare simplicity to the room, but each piece was obviously chosen with care to complement the others. The effect was one of understated grace and harmony.

"You don't think it *de trop*?"

"On the contrary, Lady Serena. It shows great restraint and an eye for detail."

"I consider that a great compliment, coming from one of the leading arbiters of taste in Town."

"How kind of you to say so." Raising his glass, Osborne took a moment to observe who else had been included in the gathering.

Slouched on the sofa was a young man he recognized as Bryce Beecham, the *enfant terrible* of literary London. Next to him was Graham Andover, a prominent art dealer whose gallery on Bond Street was known for its exotic treasures and extravagant prices. Slim and short, with showy ginger side-whiskers framing an otherwise ordinary face, the man looked to be wearing a king's ransom worth of his wares. The sapphire stickpin centered in his snowy cravat was as large as a robin's egg.

Rings flashing in a kaleidoscope blur of gold and jewel-tone colors, the art dealer was showing a portfolio of botanical prints to Lady Cordelia Guilford, the recent bride of an elderly baron, and her younger sister.

The ladies looked up and smiled, though the elder's expression was a tad cool.

Osborne pretended not to notice and let his eyes move on to where Adam De Winton, resplendent in a ruby silk waistcoat spangled with silver stars, was standing by the sideboard, pouring drinks for a pair of dark-haired strangers.

"I don't believe you are acquainted with Signor Sforza or Signor Familligi, who are visiting from Milan," murmured Lady Serena.

What was it about the cursed climate of Italy that was driving its denizens to England? Osborne bit back the urge to make an acid retort and simply shook his head.

"I think you will find them quite interesting company." Lady Serena hooked his arm and led him across the Turkey carpet.

"Osborne." De Winton acknowledged his arrival with a lift of his brow. "It seems you are straying outside your usual circle of sunshine." To the Italians, he added, "Lord Osborne is known for his sweetness and light, while some of us find the hours of darkness more intriguing."

"You think the difference between us is night and day?" Osborne matched the other man's half-mocking tone. "Perhaps the shading is not so great as you imagine."

"The sun and the moon have their own worlds," replied De Winton.

> *"The clear Moon, and the glory of the heavens.*
> *There, in a black-blue vault she sails along,*
> *Followed by multitudes of stars, that, small*
> *And sharp, and bright, along the dark abyss*
> *Drive as she drives: how fast they wheel away,*
> *Yet vanish not!"*

Beecham shook off his artistic ennui enough to quote from Wordsworth.

"How *very* handsome a sentiment," said the baroness's sister. As an unmarried young miss, she ought not be attending such a gathering. But both ladies had a reputation for wildness, and though their beauty blinded many to their lack of restraint, they were not invited within the highest circles of Society. "You pen the most marvelous words, sir."

Beecham ran a hand through his curling hair and shrugged.

"Lord Osborne is right to imply that he's not such an angel." Lady Cordelia shot him a pointed look. "Indeed, to hear tell, he's a bit of a devil, especially when it comes to ladies."

Reminded of their last meeting—a party at Vauxhall Gardens that had included a rather intimate stroll down the Dark Walk—Osborne had a feeling the baroness was piqued that he hadn't pursued the opportunity to have a dalliance. She had been blatant about her availability, but once the sizzle of the arrack punch and the fireworks overhead had died down, the prospect hadn't been overly attractive. The lady was undeniably lovely, and exhibited some talent as a painter. But there had been a predatory edge to her need that did not bode well for an amiable affair.

"Ah, but to be honest, what lady does not like just a hint of Lucifer in a lordly smile." Lady Serena quickly extinguished any spark of trouble with her droll rejoinder.

Osborne tipped his glass in silent salute as everyone laughed.

"*Si, si*, Adam." Sforza snickered. "Like your namesake, you, too, have succumbed to temptation when it comes to pleasures of the flesh, eh?"

Fire glinted off the goblet as De Winton raised his brandy to his lips. "To Temptation."

Taking a seat on the divan, Osborne wasn't sure whether to feel annoyed or amused by the evening so far. The present company didn't promise much in the way of stimulating conversation. Beecham and Andover were too pompous, Lady Cordelia too rapacious, and her sister too gauche to excite any real interest.

But he had to admit that Lady Serena was intriguing. Their paths had not crossed much in the past. However, now that she had decided to take up residence in Town, they were bound to meet far more often.

The champagne tickled against his tongue. The possibilities were tantalizing. Enough so to offset the sour taste bought on by the presence of De Winton and his friends.

Catching a scarlet flash of the man's reflection in the glass door, Osborne found himself wondering again what attraction he held for a lady of obvious intelligence. Granted, he was handsome and possessed a certain rakish charm, but surely any female with half a brain knew better than to think there was a knight in shining armor hidden beneath the roguish red silk.

But perhaps ladies were not always looking for a chivalrous hero. He thought for a moment of his own forays into the darker side of London life. Without an occasional taste of spice, Society could be bland and boring. Who could blame females for having the same cravings?

"Are you having second thoughts on the design of the doors?" Lady Serena arched a brow as she settled herself by his side. "Please don't hesitate to give me your honest opinion."

"A lady who prefers the truth to flatteries?" he teased. "How very unique."

"I'm not sure I should consider that a compliment. Most men prefer women to be patterncards of propriety," she said in a throaty murmur. "But as you see, I am not as conventional as many other ladies of the *ton*."

Osborne eyed the curved moldings and panes of glass for an instant before replying. "Be assured that I think your style shows a commendable imagination." He was flirting quite shamelessly, curious to see how she would respond.

"Thank goodness you did not call me an Original. That would put me in league with bluestockings or the eccentric old ladies who have miniature palaces built for their cats."

Her sly humor provoked a grin. "Did I not catch a glimpse of cerulean peeking out from beneath your petticoat?"

"How very ungentlemanly to mention it if you did." She shifted her skirts to show a touch of ankle. "There—you see you are mistaken."

Osborne decided that the evening was going to be enjoyable after all.

But alas, that illusion was quickly shattered by the footman's announcement of the latest arrivals.

"Conte della Ghiradelli and Contessa della Silveri, madam."

"*Pardone. Pardone.* I trust we are not unfashionably

late." Lady Sofia's escort did not look in the least contrite. "Fifi had not yet seen the Serpentine by moonlight."

Fifi? Osborne felt his teeth set on edge.

"Izz very romantic, you know."

Was it his imagination, or did the contessa's cheeks looked kissed by more than the evening breeze? Osborne looked away quickly.

"Yes, but do have a care about venturing into the park at night, sir," said Lady Serena. "There is always the danger of footpads."

The conte cut a zigzagging flourish through the air. "I am very skilled with a sword, *cara*."

Bloody buffoon.

The ladies, however, seemed to find the man's antics amusing. All of them were smiling. Especially Lady Cordelia, whose lips parted to reveal a flash of teeth.

Osborne bit back a smirk. Let the Italian snake seek to slither into her bed. He would soon find that his fangs were no match for those of the baroness. She would fight like a cobra to keep him away from other women.

"I believe you know the others, Lady Sofia," went on their hostess. "But are you acquainted with your fellow countrymen, Signor Sforza and Signor Familligi?"

"Yes, we met last night at the theater."

Osborne's grip on his glass tightened. So, her excuse of fatigue had simply meant she was tired of *his* company. He knew he ought to ignore the provocation, and yet he could not refrain from comment.

"Did you enjoy the play, Contessa? Do remind me what was playing—was it *The Taming of the Shrew*?"

Sofia met his slitted gaze without batting an eye. "No, it was *The Merchant of Venice*. Marco thought I might enjoy a reminder of home."

She made the conte's name sound as if it were melted toffee on her tongue.

"Speaking of home, Marco, word has it you have been absent from Milan for quite some time now," said Sforza. "What have you been doing with yourself?"

The conte flicked a mote of dust from his sleeve. "Oh, a little of this, a little of that. For the most part, though, I have been teaching at a school for select young ladies."

It took several moments for Sforza to control his laughter. "Pray, what subjects?" he sputtered.

"Art. The fine points of fencing. Ballistics."

"You do have an explosive effect on females." Familligi chortled. "I seem to recall two *puttanescas* from Pisa who fought a duel for your favors. *Diavolo*, the curses were flying like bullets."

"I heard the weapons were whips at two paces," said Sforza. "And that poor Lucrezia bore the marks on her bum for weeks afterward."

"Might I remind you gentlemen that there are ladies present?" muttered Osborne.

"Oh, come, sir, we are all worldly people here." The baroness tossed off the last of her wine and signaled Sforza for more. "There is no need to pretend we don't know that bawdy houses exist."

"What Lady Cordelia means is that among select friends, we have a more relaxed attitude in regard to expressing ourselves," explained Lady Serena. "Females included."

"A more sophisticated view of the world and its workings," said De Winton softly. "But then, if you are not open to new ideas, you might want to take your leave now, Osborne. I've brought along a special treat for the group—however, it may not be to your taste."

"*Sí*. For the most part, the English seem to favor burned

toast and boiled beef." Familligi gave a dismissive wave. "While we Italians, whose heritage mixes East and West, appreciate much more exotic fare. We are open to new flavors, new delicacies."

"Being half English and half Italian, I suppose that leaves me somewhere in the middle." Sofia strolled away from the *conte* and went to stand on her own by the japanned curio cabinet.

The silver candelabra, ablaze with a tiered glow of flickering flames, illuminated every detail of her attire. She was wearing a deep plum velvet gown, a simple but striking design that accentuated her willowy height and cascade of ebony curls. The bodice was embroidered with shimmering gold thread. As if any glitter was needed to draw the eye to her magnificent bosom. The lush fabric clung like a second skin to her curves.

Osborne meant to ignore her presence, but he found he could not tear his eyes away. There was something so very different about her. As yet, it was impossible to define. There was something in the lithe, feline grace of her movements, the low, smoky lilt of her accent, and the way her eyes cut like steel against his flesh.

Dangerous.

No question about it. His peace of mind had suffered several serious blows. Lynsley's advice to make a strategic retreat made sense, especially as he had not quite hit on an effective way to defend himself.

But he was not the only man who was drawn, like a moth to a flame, to the sight of her fire-kissed profile.

Indeed, the baroness and her sister were starting to pout, when Marco sauntered over to them and began flirting.

Fool. The fellow was a brainless fribble to prefer women

who offered themselves on a platter over the darker, more distant allure of the contessa.

"Now that all of the guests have arrived, let us move into the Grotto Room," said Lady Serena. "I've had a special table set up, and my chef has prepared a selection of *amuse-bouches* that I think you will find quite titillating."

Appetite teasers? Osborne rose, wondering what sort of games Lady Serena had in mind.

"Keep the ladies amused." Sofia managed a whisper to Marco as they made their way down the corridor.

"What about Osborne?"

The dratted man's presence did present an unexpected complication, but she would deal with it as before. "Don't worry, I will simply ignore him," she replied.

Marco's expression was eloquent in its skepticism, but he shrugged and quickened his steps to catch up with the sisters.

"Might I escort you to your place, Lady Sofia?"

She caught a flicker of red as the gentleman extended his arm. "Ah, how lovely of you to ask, Lord De Winton. As you see, that rascal Marco is extremely fickle in his attentions."

"Does that distress you?"

"La, not at all." Sofia met his inquiring gaze with a light laugh. "If you are asking whether the *conte* and I have any understanding between us, the answer is no," she added. "We are simply casual friends."

"I am delighted to hear it."

She lifted her chin in challenge. "Would it have stopped you from seeking a closer acquaintance, sir? I have heard you are a man who is not afraid to take what he wants."

De Winton allowed a flash of teeth. "Some ladies might find that reputation frightening."

Her answer was a coquettish smile.

After everyone was seated at the table, Lady Serena rang the gilded bell by her place. Two servants dressed in saffron silks and bulbous red turbans pinned with peacock feathers paraded into the room, each bearing a large silver platter of sweetmeats.

"Turkish delight," announced Lady Serena as she helped herself to several pieces. "For those of you who are unfamiliar with the treat, it is a confection of dates, walnuts, sugar, cinnamon—"

"Spiced with a liberal sprinkling of high-quality cannabis," finished De Winton.

Familligi enhaled deeply over his helping, setting off puffs of the powdered sugar. "Very fine, indeed."

"These are my favorites." The baroness nibbled on one of her squares. "Do have a taste, Osborne. They are reputed to be a potent aphrodisiac, you know."

Sofia sensed there was a history between the two of them, though the lady's name was not on the list of his past lovers. *Food for thought.* But not now, she reminded herself. Breaking off a piece of sticky sweet, she popped it into her mouth. "Mmmm. Unusual."

"I assure you, the taste will grow on you," said Familligi, much to the hilarity of his friends. Marco joined in the male laughter while making eyes at the baroness.

Diverted from her surreptitious study of Osborne, Lady Cordelia looked more than happy to strike up a new flirtation.

The platters were served up again, accompanied by cups of sweetened tea. Out of the corner of her eye, Sofia saw that the servants extinguished a number of the candles on their way out, leaving only the wall sconces lit. The Murano glass shades, a spiraling mix of translucent red and white patterns, cast a warm pinkish glow over the table. The illusion was soft, sensuous, like bathing in rose petals.

The laughter took on a languid note as well. Sofia flicked open her fan, using the move to secret the rest of the sweetmeat into her reticule. She wished to keep her head clear, yet the others seemed to be enjoying the effect of the narcotic. Even Osborne seemed more relaxed. His attention had shifted from her to Lady Serena.

All the better. Yet oddly enough, she felt her insides clench at seeing his face light with a smile. Their hostess touched his sleeve, then leaned in to whisper in his ear. Highlighted against the dark wood paneling, the two heads, with their finespun flaxen hair, appeared nearly as one. Ducking away, Sofia shook off the tautness with another flutter of her fan. Her rebuffs had been purposefully rude. Of course the man would seek more congenial company.

It must be the cannabis affecting her senses. She must not allow it to dull her sense of duty.

Duty.

She forced her flirtations to be more blatant with De Winton. "Do tell me about some of the interesting attractions of London, sir." Lifting the screen of painted silk, she fanned her lashes. "And I don't mean the museums or the Tower menagerie."

He responded with a predatory flash of teeth. "There are, to be sure, more exotic places and creatures than a cage of mangy lions. Assuming a lady is willing to be adventurous and explore what lies outside the gilded confines of Mayfair."

"Boundaries are so boring." Her breathy laugh stirred the folds of his cravat.

"My sentiments exactly." Edging his chair a touch closer, he asked, "Do you like to gamble, Contessa?"

"That depends on what I stand to gain."

He laughed softly. "Oh, I know of some places where the risk is worth the reward . . . ." He began to describe several gaming hells in the slums of Seven Dials.

Sofia was soon rewarded for her efforts. Under the table, De Winton's thigh was pressing hers, and as he spoke, he inched his chair in far closer than was proper.

She fingered the scarlet silk of his waistcoat, egging him on. "How fascinating. What other pleasures can be found in the stews?"

"Most anything you can imagine."

"Indeed?" She arched her brows suggestively. "I have a very vivid imagination."

He wet his lips with a swallow of wine.

Deciding not to overplay her interest in the slums, Sofia turned her hand to matching his physical flirtations. "You, too, appear to have a bold sense of style." She touched his watchchain, then fell to toying with the fobs. "This is an unusual design." The gold serpent had huge ruby eyes.

"It is Ottoman. I purchased it from Andover. His gallery has many unique offerings."

"I shall have to pay him a visit." Sofia playfully pulled the pocketwatch from his waistcoat pocket. There was, she saw, a slight bulge beside the oval shape. Another fob?

Sure enough, a last little tug revealed a gold key, crowned with a red poppy.

The discovery dispelled all thought of Osborne. Senses sharpened, Sofia let her fingers linger on the smooth enamel. Now, finally, there was something tangible to go on.

She peeked up to see De Winton staring at her. For an

instant, a wolflike wariness clouded his expression. Then he laughed and casually tucked the key back in his pocket.

"What a very pretty fob," she murmured. "I've seen one just like it in Italy."

Would he take the bait?

"You must be mistaken, Lady Sofia," he said softly. "This particular key was specially made and is not for sale in any shop."

"Oh, I am aware of that," she replied in the same dulcet tone. "Just as I am aware that it is not handed out indiscriminately. It's only for a discreet group of people who appreciate the finer things in life and are willing to pay for the privileges it unlocks."

"Ah, so you *are* familiar with *la bella papavero*. Tell me, whose did you see?"

Sofia decided to play it a bit coy. "What makes you think I don't have one of my own?"

His eyes betrayed a flicker of surprise. "Do you?"

"Perhaps." She must take care not to let the game of cat and mouse get out of hand tonight. The trick was to tease more information out of him while not giving herself away.

Switching tactics, she let her fingers tickle over the back of his knuckles as she reached for a sweetmeat.

"Won't you have another treat, De Winton?" She held the confection teasingly close to his lips. "One can never have too much of a good thing."

"Indeed not." He leaned in closer to take it with his teeth. She felt the hot rush of his breath on her skin as his tongue flicked out over his lower lip. "Do call me Adam. My friends do not stand on formality."

"You missed a bit, Adam." Sofia brushed a crumb of crystalized sugar from the corner of his mouth.

"Mmm, wouldn't want it to go to waste." He caught her hand and licked the tip of her thumb.

A shiver ran through her, but as she maintained a seductive smile, he seemed to mistake it for one of pleasure.

"Westover is having a gathering at his town house on Monday evening. A very private affair that won't be mentioned in polite circles. But I promise, it will be far more entertaining than the poetry to be recited at Lady Kennington's literary soiree."

"Naughty man." Sofia tapped her fan to his cheek. "You are suggesting I change my schedule? The baroness would be most disappointed."

He winked. "The same could not be said for you, Lady Sofia."

"How can I resist?"

"At ten, then. And I suggest you come in an unmarked carriage. You wouldn't want to risk your reputation by having someone spot your arrival at a rake's private residence."

Sofia peeked over the painted silk. "A soupçon of risk adds a certain spice to life, Adam. Count on it. I will be there."

"Excellent." A smile stretched on his lips. "Oh, and if you do have a key, be sure to bring it with you. If it's a fit with mine, I promise you it will unlock some special treats here in London."

Chapter Ten

*P*ushing up from the parquet floor, Sofia arched her back into the cobra position of her yoga routine. The stretching and sweating had helped dispel the muzziness lingering from the previous evening. Still, the noxious taste of the drugs and drink clung to her tongue, an unpleasant reminder of the revelries, which had lasted into the early morning hours.

She and Marco had left before Osborne. Had he spent the night with Lady Serena? It was, of course, none of her business. His private life, his personal pleasures, were not of prurient interest. She was merely curious, in case his choices affected her mission.

A flex of muscle and she moved to the lotus position. The previous evening had left no doubt that within the stately world of Mayfair mansions dwelled a nest of vipers. Just how far their poison spread was what she must discern—without drawing a venomous strike. Lord Robert had come too close to whatever sordid secrets they were hiding.

Was De Winton the head of the serpentine coil? Sofia

held the stretch a moment longer, then expelled her breath and lowered herself to the canvas mat. He had the scruples of a snake, that was for sure. Hopefully the discovery of the key, and the coming meeting, would begin to open the way to the truth—

A soft knock on the door was followed by the equally discreet voice of her maid. "There is a Conte della Ghiradelli to see you, milady. He insists you will not mind the interruption, despite the early hour."

Sofia stood up and toweled the sweat from her face. "Please show him in, Rose," she murmured, quickly unlocking the door. Catching the maid's questioning look at her short cotton tunic and drawstring trousers, she added, "It is quite all right. He's a trusted member of Lord Lynsley's network."

Marco did not appear to be suffering any ill effects from the party. "*Ciao, bella*. Keeping up your strength, I see." He picked up one of the thin wooden cudgels and cut a *swoosh* through the air. "Care to test your steel against mine?" He gave the tip a suggestive waggle. "Winner take all."

She made a rude sound. "I'm in no mood for games, if you don't mind." Looking a bit more closely, she saw his face was not quite so fresh as she had first thought. Beneath the fringe of dark lashes, his eyes were red with lack of sleep, and the cocksure smile was a bit ragged at the edges. "Anyway, it looks as if you played hard last night."

He shrugged. "I'm no angel."

Sofia realized that she knew very little about his past life. His disappointments, his desires. What needs would drive a man of pampered privilege to become a blade for hire?

"Is there a smudge of the ladybird's lip paint on my chin?" He stroked the dark stubbling shading his jaw and exaggerated a leer. However, the banter sounded a bit brittle. "I met up with Sforza and Familligi at a gaming hell near Jermyn Street. The barmaids were all Swedish."

"Go to bed, Marco."

"With you, *bella*?" He clasped his hands to his chest. "Be still, my fluttering heart."

"Be still, your twittering tongue." Sofia took his arm and urged him toward the door. "Let us have a seat in the study. I'll have Rose bring some tea and toast."

He dropped the role of bawdy jester long enough to sigh. "*Grazie*. Coffee would be even more welcome than sex."

"I take it this is not a purely social call," she said once the order for refreshments had been given.

"Much as I longed to see you again, your guess is correct." Marco dropped into the leather chair by the hearth and propped his boots on the fender. "A message from Lynsley was waiting at my rooms when I returned this morning. I've just come from meeting him—though he might have had the grace to choose a more comfortable spot than an unmarked carriage jostling over the rutted byways of Regent Park."

Sofia felt her spine stiffen as she perched on the arm of the facing chair. "I imagine the marquess had more on his mind than ministering to your physical well-being."

A grin quirked at the corners of his mouth. Then for once, Marco looked dead serious. "Correct again, *bella*. A naval courier sloop from Bombay docked at Isle of Dogs last night. It brought word of an East India Company scandal. One of their high officials, the man in charge of trade with the Moghul princes, was found murdered in his own house." He paused as Rose entered with the coffee and gratefully accepted a cup.

Sofia shook her head. Her throat was suddenly too tight to swallow.

Marco took a long sip before continuing. "Along with the official dispatch came a confidential report from the chatelaine in charge of the company residence—a former Merlin. It included a mention that among the man's personal effects was found a gold key topped with a red enamel poppy."

Another key. But to what?

"Of course, the marquess does not think it a coincidence. But he did not offer any speculation on what it might mean to your investigation."

"No, he would not." Lynsley struck her as a most meticulous man. He would follow every lead before coming to a conclusion. She was determined to do the same. But as she watched Marco wolf down a piece of buttered toast, she wished she had a clearer idea of which way to turn.

What, exactly, was she looking for?

Even Lynsley seemed unsure. Which did little to loosen the knot in her stomach. Despite the hour of rigorous stretching, she felt her muscles begin to tighten.

The obvious path was to discover who else here in London possessed a gold key. Did all of the Scarlet Knights carry one? It seemed doubtful. Whatever privileges the key unlocked were likely shared by only a select few.

Still, she could not afford to guess.

"It seems a little callous to leave you without a clue to go on," said Marco between bites. "You are not a magician or a seer who can divine the truth from a crystal ball."

"No, I am a Merlin. And Merlins are trained to fly on their own. If the marquess had wished to be a mother hen, he would have hatched a very different sort of school than our Academy."

Marco refilled his cup. "The *Inglieze* are lucky to have your beauty, your brains, and your bravery."

"You may leave off dispensing with flatteries, Marco. Let's get down to work." She kneaded the back of her neck. "I made a discovery of my own last night. De Winton also possesses a key. He wears it on his watchchain. I hinted that I might have one too."

"Dangerous." Marco frowned. "Seeing as you don't have a clue as to its significance."

"A calculated risk," admitted Sofia. "But in a mission like this one, I doubt we will get anywhere by being conservative. In thinking over all the information at hand, I came to the conclusion that the secret circle of keyholders likely stretches from London to the Far East. Which leaves just enough room for doubt as to whether I am part of it."

"Perhaps," he conceded. "In any case, you will have to handle the next meeting with extreme care."

"That goes without saying." She shrugged and changed the subject. "Did you learn anything from your long-lost friends?"

"Aside from the fact that their company is even more boring than it was in the days of our misspent youth?" Marco pursed his lips. "So far, I got little more out of them than a detailed description of the bordellos favored by the rakes of the *ton*. The only information that sounded halfway interesting was a mention of a club in Seven Dials that caters to more exotic tastes."

"In what way?"

Turning his palms up, he made a face. "We were interrupted."

Still puzzling over the connection between countries, between continents, Sofia took another turn around the room. "I confess, I have yet to see how these pieces of the puzzle fit together," she muttered. "Any suggestions?"

Marco shook his head. "You have the brains, *bella*. I am merely the brawn."

She certainly wasn't feeling very smart at the moment. Mayhap it was a residue of the drugs. Her mind was sluggish, her thoughts clouded. Lynsley's new information tickled like a tendril of smoke against her consciousness. *Damn*. What was it she was missing?

Pausing by a window overlooking the garden, she watched a sparrow flit from tree to tree, wings flapping hard against the freshening breeze to keep from being blown off course.

"Shipping," she suddenly said aloud. "What cargo does Sforza's family fleet bring to England? And do the Familligi banking interests help finance the endeavor?"

Marco smacked a palm to his brow. "You see, *bella*. You *are* the clever one. I shall look into it."

"Do."

Another question occurred to her. How did De Winton support his vices? On paper, his family fortune had been reduced to naught but a scribble of red ink. The unentailed land had been sold off long ago, and the rest of the estate had been mortgaged to the hilt. More recently, a collection of art had been put up for auction. But other than the proceeds from the sale, the man had no discernible source of income.

Tracing a random pattern on the glass, she said as much.

Marco took his time in considering the statement. "Perhaps he is lucky at cards. I know of some men who live on their wits alone."

"Perhaps." However, De Winton did not strike her as

having the discipline or diligence to win at the gaming tables. She made a mental note to ask Rose to send Lynsley a request for more information on the man's finances.

A clear picture had yet to take shape, but Sofia had a feeling she was beginning to sketch in the first faint outlines. It would, however, take a number of bold strokes to fill the blank canvas.

"Go home and get a few hours of sleep, Marco. Then I'd like you to take me to Bond Street this afternoon."

"Shopping?"

"Yes, but not just for any old bauble."

"Lord Osborne! How lovely that the weather allowed us to keep our rendezvous." Lady Serena looked up at the cloudless sky with a mischievous smile. "Have you a certain sway with heavenly bodies?"

He chuckled. "I'm afraid my reach does not extend past the divine shapes here on Earth." Rotten Row was already beginning to crowd with the crush of fashionable ladies and gentlemen out for their daily promenade. "Shall we avoid the herd and ride toward the Serpentine?"

Lady Serena reined in her mount and motioned for her groom to make way for Osborne's bay. "Your reputation precedes you, sir. Mayhap I ought to be careful just how close I allow you to come."

"Oh, I promise to behave like a perfect gentleman." He winked. "For now."

Seated on her petite mare, the lady was a picture of elegance and grace in the saddle. A stark contrast to Sofia and her daredevil skill on a muscled stallion. *Heaven and Hades.* Sweetness and shadows.

Determined to take Lynsley's advice to heart, Osborne jerked his thoughts from that wild dawn gallop, that hellfire kiss. It was high time for tamer pursuits. Let Sofia flirt with the red devils of the Scarlet Knights. Or that vagabond in velvet, Conte della Ghiradelli. Despite her protestations, he had a feeling they were more than just friends.

"I do hope you did not disapprove of my soiree. Such diversions are not to everyone's taste."

"On the contrary, I found it quite stimulating. A constant diet of the same bland entertainments leaves one starved for a bit of spice."

"I am relieved to hear it," she replied. "I feared you might think me too . . . naughty."

"Are you?"

The bridle path skirted close to a row of stately elms, forcing his horse closer to hers. A whisper-soft *swoosh* of merino wool brushed against his boot, light as her little laugh. "You must promise not to tell, but I think I am somewhere between naughty and nice."

"Your secret is safe with me, Lady Serena."

"I had a feeling I could count on your discretion in that."

Flirtatous flatteries. He knew the game well. However, his vanity did not object to a bit of stroking. Ducking the dancing leaves, he returned the favor by touching a quick caress to her knee. "I should like for you to trust in confiding any matter with me, whether naughty or nice."

They rode out of the trees and close to the water's edge. Sunlight shimmered off the flat calm, its brilliance nearly blinding.

"Well, then . . . There is to be another party early next week." Was she testing his daring? "At Lord Concord's house."

"Is that an invitation?"

"Would you care to come?" she countered. Coy, but not cloyingly so.

"Very much so."

Lady Serena smiled. "I will let you know the time and direction." A light pressure on her reins turned the mare back toward the Cumberland gate. "I read the first of Repton's essays on nature, and I am curious as to your opinion on the subject. . . ."

The door to Andover's antique shop was polished to the patina of aged sherry. It swung open at the touch of Marco's gloved hand, setting off a melodious chiming of bells.

"Tibetan," he murmured, glancing up at the cluster of carved silver. "Very old, very valuable."

"The same can be said about everything here," said Sofia dryly.

The main gallery was a long, narrow space paneled in dark wood. The multitude of nooks and wall niches were crammed with all manner of exotic treasures. They looked to be mostly Eastern in origin—Ottoman, Persian, Mogul, Chinese. Brass figurines, exquisite porcelains, colorful carpets, gold and silver jewelry glittering with precious stones. And, as Marco had remarked, everything looked extremely ancient and extremely costly. It was as if one of the legendary Silk Road caravans had by some mysterious magic transported its booty from the Khyber Pass to the middle of London.

"Speaking of which," she said after making her survey, "how do you know that the bells are Tibetan?"

"I am an art instructor, remember?"

"And pigs may fly."

The whisper drew a low snort from Marco. *"Porca—"*

he began, but the sound of a door opening silenced his retort.

Sofia edged a step sideways in time to see the shop owner come out of a side room, accompanied by another gentleman she had never seen before. Blocked by a life-size statue of Buddha, Andover did not spot the two of them until Marco called out a greeting.

"*Ciao*, Signor."

He seemed surprised—and, to her eye, a little nervous—at finding them inside his gallery, but he quickly assumed an ingratiating smile. "Lady Sofia. Lord della Ghiradelli. What an unexpected pleasure."

"We had the afternoon free and thought we would come have a look around. If you don't mind, that is." Marco was already inspecting a small bronze statue of Shiva, the Indian destroyer god. "Or would you prefer that we make an appointment?"

"Not at all, not at all. Please, make yourselves at home. My assistant is running an errand, but I will be with you in just a moment." He did not look inclined to introduce his companion. However, the man took matters into his own hands.

"Don't rush me away, my dear Andover. Granted, you've shown me a number of the rare treasures reserved for your special clients, but none are half so lovely as the Contessa della Silveri." He bowed low over Sofia's hand. "Allow me to make your acquaintance, milady. I have heard much about you."

"Mr. Stanton Roxbury, Lady Sofia," said Andover.

Again, Sofia had the impression that he was reluctant to perform the social niceties.

"Are you an avid collector, Mr. Roxbury?" she asked after he finished his string of effusive compliments.

"I make the occasional purchase," he replied. "Alas, a gentleman in my humble position cannot afford more than that."

Raising his ribboned quizzing glass, Marco subjected the man to an ogling scrutiny. Magnified by the gold-rimmed lens, his eye appeared as large as a cricket ball. "And pray, sir, what position is that?"

No wonder Osborne had looked tempted to bat the Italian's ballocks through a wicket, thought Sofia. Marco could be insufferably obnoxious without exerting much effort.

"I am employed by the Ministry of War."

Mention of Whitehall snapped her senses into full alert. "How very impressive, sir, given England's importance in defending the world from Napoleon's onslaught."

Roxbury's chest immediately swelled. *So, the man had an inflated sense of his own worth*, she thought. The added bulk did not quite hide the fact that his large body was going to seed. His face was still handsome enough, despite a weak chin and florid complexion. But another few years of excess food and drink and he would be fat as the Prince Regent.

Oblivious of her critical eye, he preened like a peacock. "As Associate Minister for Military Transport, I do play a rather significant role in seeing that our armies are supplied with ordnance and supplies in all the far-flung corners of the globe."

"Bravo." Marco contrived to look extremely bored by the mention of war.

"Is not Lord Lynsley your sponsor in London Society, milady?" asked the minister, as her friend wandered away to inspect a display of Persian jambiyahs from the time of the First Crusade.

"He was an acquaintance of my father, from a long time

ago." Sofia thought it wise to distance herself from any real relationship with the marquess. "And, yes, he was kind enough to arrange my entrée into the *ton*. But I've only met him on several occasions since arriving in Town. His work does not permit him much time for entertainment, or so he claims." She lowered her voice to a conspiratorial whisper. "In truth, he strikes me as rather . . . dull."

"Dull as dishwater." Roxbury gave a sharp laugh. "His Lordship is always so very sober and straightlaced. And by all accounts, a stickler for detail. Thank God my department has very little contact with his."

"How fortunate for you," she replied.

"Indeed, indeed." As a Damascene clock struck the hour, Roxbury's smile faded. "Alas, duty does demand that I return to the Ministry. No matter that your company is far more alluring than a desk full of documents."

"We must not keep you from your work." Sofia favored him with a flutter of lashes as he passed by. "Perhaps we will meet again soon."

"Oh, I shall make sure that Andover arranges a social engagement without delay."

The gallery owner escorted Roxbury to the front door, where they exchanged a few private words before the minister hurried off after a passing hackney.

"Do forgive me," said Andover as he rejoined them.

"Rather it is for us to apologize, for barging in unannounced," said Sofia.

"You are, of course, welcome anytime." Seeing Marco casually hold a piece of Ming Dynasty porcelain up to the light, he added, "May I show you anything in particular, milord?"

"Just looking." After spinning the bowl on the tip of his finger, Marco put it back in its place.

"This is quite fascinating." She chose a Byzantine brooch at random. "What lovely filigree work, and the stones look to be of excellent quality." After studying the lapis and carnelian inlays a bit longer, she asked, "Have you any others?"

Andover found another on a nearby shelf. "These are the only two I have at the moment."

"I don't like the colors." She made a moue of disappointment. "You are sure that you do not have one in the private rooms reserved for your special clients?"

"Roxbury was jesting, milady. I assure you that everything I have is out on display."

"The two of you *were* locked away—"

"In a storage room, Lady Sofia," said Andover quickly. "I was merely showing him a sketch of an icon that I sold to Lord Hillhouse last month."

She surrendered with a pout and a sigh. "Oh, very well. Then let me have a look at some of the other jewelry."

"I have a very nice selection of Persian pendants just over here. The shades of turquoise are sublime."

Seeing Marco edge around a group of terra-cotta Chinese warriors and signal her to keep Andover occupied, Sofia quickly accepted the offer. "I'll have a look. And then I would also like to see that jade dragon by the set of Turkish scimitars."

"Of course, milady." Andover still appeared a bit edgy as he opened the display case and took out a velvet-covered tray of ornaments.

She took her time in examining each piece, which was not difficult. They were, as promised, exceptionally beautiful, the rich blue stones complemented by the superb craftsmanship of the carved goldwork. "Where on earth do you find such magnificent treasures? Have you discovered

Aladdin's secret cave? Or a genie in a brass lamp who conjures a wealth of riches out of smoke and fire?"

"A flying carpet appears every full moon, loaded with every imaginable prize from the Orient," said Andover, matching her tone of light teasing.

The bells rang out, amplifying her peal of laughter. Looking up, Sofia saw a young man enter the shop, two large packages wrapped in oilskin in his arms. He looked about to speak, but then seeing there was a customer, he ducked his head and quickly slipped into the far aisle. Hurried footsteps echoed in the momentary silence, heading for the far end of the gallery.

A flutter of coattails, and she saw him disappear behind a door set into the paneling.

"My clerk," said Andover, eyeing the clock. "He is late."

"Anything interesting?" she teased.

"Packing supplies," came the curt reply.

Twine and pasteboard seemed an unlikely source of agitation. But perhaps he had an important purchase waiting to be delivered. Sofia dropped the subject and asked him to explain the artistic style of a hammered gold disc set with amethysts.

All smiles again, Andover was quick to reply.

She browsed through a few more trays of jewelry before picking out a simple aquamarine ring for purchase. Marco should have had time to check inside the private room by now.

"A lovely choice," said Andover, then added the price.

She nearly choked, but Marco didn't bat an eye as he sauntered around the corner of the shelves. "Send the bill around to my hotel, signor," he announced. An airy wave cut short her protest. "A belated birthday gift, *bella*."

"*Grazie*," she stammered.

Andover's mouth curled to a scimitar smile. "A bauble is the best way to a lady's heart, milord." His tone implied a rather different part of a female's anatomy.

"*Si, si.*" Marco winked. "I hope to be a regular customer. So save a selection of your prime pieces."

Both men exchanged knowing looks.

Out on the street, Sofia drew in a deep breath and muttered, "Bloody hell, that amount of blunt would feed and clothe an army of orphans for a year in St. Giles."

"*Si.*" Her friend was no longer leering. "But the money is also being spent for a good cause, *bella.*"

"Assuming Lord Lynsley does not succumb to a fit of apoplexy when he sees the bill."

"He can afford it. As can I."

His soft words reminded Sofia once again how little she really knew about the Italian. Save that beneath the braggadocio and blatant flirtations, he was a stalwart friend.

"Don't look so blue-deviled," said Marco after slanting a sidelong look at her face. "Or are you wishing you had chosen the set of diamond earbobs?"

"Don't be daft," she muttered, not about to admit she had picked the ring because its color was the exact shade of Deverill Osborne's eyes. "What about the private room?"

"Locked," he replied.

There was nothing suspicious about that. Records and receipts would naturally be guarded.

"But I will, of course, need more trinkets for my many mistresses." He took her arm and started down the street.

"Don't fritter away the family jewels all in one place."

Grinning, Marco waggled his brows. "The della Ghiradelli fortune is enormous."

She laughed in spite of her vague sense of unease. "I shall take your word for it. And as you say, I suppose the money was well spent. From what we saw just now, I think that both Mr. Andover and Mr. Roxbury are worth further scrutiny."

As they strolled past the other fancy shops along Bond Street, Sofia could not quite shake off the sense that there was something strange about the gallery. It had a cold, creepy feel to it . . .

Lud, she must not start acting like a heroine in a novel, imagining mad monks or a cabal of killers lurking among the antique treasures.

"Hopefully they will be among the guests at the upcoming party that De Winton mentioned." She needed something more substantial than feelings to act upon. "But no matter who is there, it's time to start seeing through the haze of smoke and lies."

Chapter Eleven

*I*n contrast to the previous night's risque revelries, the Harpworth soiree promised to be a staid affair. *Too staid*, thought Osborne with an inward grimace. Though the evening's program of violin and cello concertos had barely begun, the music was already beginning to grate on his ear.

Seeing that Sofia had chosen a seat between Miss Pennington-Pryce and the dowager Countess of Kenshire without so much as a look in his direction, he slipped from his place in the back of the room and into the corridor. Several other gentlemen were milling about, clearly bored by the proceedings. Lady Harpworth's musicales were noted for their lengthy recitals. But as her husband was noted for the quality of his cellars, the evenings always drew a crowd.

When one of the men suggested the refreshment room, the others were quick to follow. Osborne, however, hung back and then headed the opposite way. Another turn brought him to a darkened stretch of corridor at the back of the town house. The trilling of the violins had faded to a faint buzz, and grateful for an interlude of silence, he loosened his cravat and peeked into the first room he came to. It was a study—a masculine one by the look of the chess sets and backgammon boards on the worktable. Several comfortable armchairs flanked the hearth, and an excellent selection of brandies and ports lined the sideboard.

Osborne struck a flint and lit a brace of candles. The scent of tobacco and leather was in the air. It seemed unlikely that anyone would mind if he enjoyed a cheroot in peace and quiet.

Sofia was having an unnerving effect on him, despite his determination to ignore her. Clasping his hands behind his back, he started to wander the perimeter of the room, looking at the sporting prints while trying to dispel the thrum of restless energy that was tingling through his body.

Damn. He would definitely have to do something about arranging a new mistress. And soon. The sense of frustration was threatening to explode.

He was just about to turn in search of the cigar box when his gaze fell on a brass-rimmed dartboard hanging on the wall, its surface intricately painted in a series of concentric circles. As he moved closer, he saw that they were further divided into quadrants of varying widths and colors.

On impulse, Osborne plucked the trio of feathered darts from the cork. Stepping back as far as the gaming table allowed, he tossed them in quick succession at the target.

Thwack. Thwack. Thwack.

Each hit just outside the small bull's-eye.

"Not bad."

Osborne whirled around to find Sofia framed in the doorway.

"I suppose you think you could do better," he snapped.

"Without a doubt."

Don't react, said his brain. It could only lead to another quarrel. Or worse. But the curl of her lip, supremely sensuous in its claim, silenced reason.

"Care to test that assumption?" he challenged.

She walked into the room, her silken skirts whispering against the soft Persian carpet. Stopping before the game table, she slowly stripped the elbow-length gloves from her arms.

The leather slapped softly against the waxed wood.

Osborne swallowed hard, aware his throat had gone a bit dry. If she was trying to distract him, she was doing a damn good job of it.

Next came her shawl, leaving her shoulders bare. "What are the rules of engagement?"

"Fire at will," he said, flexing his right fist. Indicating a medallion on the carpet, he added, "And you must stand there. No foul allowed."

She rubbed her palms together. "Sounds simple enough."

He retrieved the darts and handed them over with a mocking bow. "Ladies first."

One by one, Sofia tested their balance on her two forefingers.

"You hold them point first," he said with deliberate sarcasm. "In case you were wondering."

"You don't say?" All of a sudden, she tossed one straight up, plucked it out of midair, and in the same smooth motion flung it at the board. The point bit into the outer edge of center circle.

"Beginner's luck," he growled.

She shrugged and threw the next two with equal precision.

Osborne removed his coat and rolled up his sleeves.

Several French soldiers lay dead in the dusty plains of Spain on account of his prowess with a throwing knife. He was not about to be bested by a show of circus tricks.

Sofia went to the cabinet and dusted off a second set of darts. She placed them on the table and set a hand on her hip. "Your turn, sir."

Stepping to the line, he gauged the distance to the target with a little more care this time around. She had been right to test the heft of the darts as well. He fingered the brass grips, smoothed the tailfeathers.

"You are stalling," she muttered.

"A seasoned soldier always studies the field of battle before making the first charge." His eyes were still on her as he launched the darts in rapid-fire succession at the target.

Thwack. Thwack. Thwack.

From that distance, it was impossible to see who had won. Sofia picked up the candlestick and moved closer. He followed.

"It appears the round is yours." Her nose was nearly touching the cork. "By a hair."

Caught up in a simple topknot, her curls spilled in soft ringlets to the ridge of her shoulders. Black velvet kissing white satin. Why was it that metaphors of dark and light always seemed to come to mind? *Sofia of Sparks. Sofia of Shadows.*

He inhaled a breath, the mysterious scent of her perfume sweetening the masculine traces of cigars and cognac. "Yours are close. But not close enough."

"I think it's only fair you allow me a rematch," she declared. "One where I set the parameters."

"Very well." Osborne allowed himself a well-deserved smile. Having drawn first blood, as it were, the advantage lay with him. He could afford to be generous. Besides, a gentleman could hardly say no to a lady's request.

A gentleman could, however, in good conscience employ a bit of teasing to rattle her composure. "If you are quite sure you wish to subject yourself to such a trial. The ability to perform under pressure is an art in itself. I know many men whose hands begin to tremble when put on the line."

"As always, an eloquent warning, Lord Osborne." Sofia rolled her shoulders—a movement that caused her bosom to rise and fall beneath the snug silk. "But I'll take my chances."

Damn the minx. His palms prickled and began to perspire.

She was facing the unlit hearth, her back to the target. Setting her hip to the game table, she cleared a bit more space. "Let us add some distance to the toss. We will start from here." Her slipper indicated a swirl of indigo on the carpet. "Winner goes first."

Spinning the first dart between his fingers, Osborne stepped to the spot and assumed his stance. A few paltry yards were nothing. He was about to take aim when she interrupted. "Wait. I haven't finished spelling out the rules."

He straightened.

"You must remain facing the mantel, like so." Her body was squared to the carved marble. "And then throw over your left shoulder."

"Without looking at the target?"

"Correct."

"That's hardly fair," he murmured. Seeing her lips creep up at the corners, he quickly continued. "For you, I mean. I served as an officer in the Peninsular War, Lady Sofia. We soldiers spent hours in the practice of throwing a knife. Our lives depended on such prowess."

The candlelight caught the flicker of her ebony lashes. For an instant, they hid her eyes.

"I thought it only sporting to warn you," he continued. "I wouldn't want to win by foul means, so feel free to choose another position." Osborne couldn't help savoring the moment. "Or to surrender. Be assured, there is no dishonor in conceding the field to a superior opponent."

Her expression remained inscrutable. "As I said, sir. I'll take my chances."

"Very well." He resumed his position, adding an extra flex to his knees as he glanced at the target over his shoulder. The dart's tip nicked the cork near dead center but didn't hold and fell to the floor.

"Sorry." Sofia smiled. "Doesn't count."

"Blast," he muttered. "A bit out of practice." Altering his stance, he made his second throw. This one stuck, but in the outer ring.

"Hmmm. I think you'll have to do better than that, sir."

"You do? Hah! We'll soon see your prowess on the line." Irked by her teasing, Osborne rushed his last try. The needled steel struck home, but only within the middle ring. Not an overpowering display of skill. However, he doubted she could top it.

"Now it's your turn." He perched a hip on the edge of the table and folded his arms across his chest.

Sofia smoothed her skirts, her lithe hands skimming the curve of her derriere. He turned his gaze to the target with an inward smile. In warfare, timing was everything. Her diversion was a touch too late.

"Clothing a tad too tight?" he asked. "Whalebone stays must be deucedly uncomfortable."

"I wouldn't know," she shot back. "I don't wear a corset."

"Ah." Osborne couldn't resist the opening. "What *do* you wear beneath that lovely gown?"

"State secret. I could tell you, sir. But then I would have to kill you." As she spoke, she whipped her hand across her body. The dart flew over her shoulder, as straight as a hawk honing in on its prey.

Bloody hell. Osborne could not quite believe his eyes. The quivering point had hit smack in the center of the bull's-eye.

"This round appears mine." She tossed the two other tiny missiles on the table. "No need for these."

"How the devil did you do that?" he blurted out.

"We had archery classes in school."

Osborne made a face. "It sounds as if Italian classes for young ladies are far more permissive than those here in England."

"To be sure, we were not taught a traditional course of study," answered Sofia.

He suddenly found himself curious to know more about her upbringing. Lynsley had mentioned the hell-for-leather riding instructor. What other martial skills did she possess? "It sounds unusual. What else were you taught?"

"Oh, hand-to-hand combat. Our headmistress believed that a lady should know how to defend herself."

Osborne went to the sideboard and poured himself a drink. "Now I know you are bamming me. Archery? Hand-to-hand combat? Next you will be telling me you studied ballistics and marksmanship."

"I am a crack shot," she replied with just the tiniest hint of a smile.

"Then you won't object to a third round. To break the tie."

"I'm game. Name your challenge, sir."

"Care to make the competition even more interesting?" he asked after a moment of hesitation.

Sofia watched him draw in a mouthful of his whisky. The cut crystal cast a fire-gold pattern of winking light across his face. Like diamonds, sharp-edged and alight with a brilliant glitter. "What do you have in mind?" she asked.

"A wager." He refilled his drink from one of the decanters.

How many glasses of spirits had he drunk? One? Two? Enough to bring a dangerous glint to his eye. "Perhaps we should simply call it a draw, Lord Osborne."

"Afraid of losing? Surely a lady who rides like a hellfire hussar is not about to shy away from a hurdle simply because it's a touch higher than any she's tried before?"

She smoothed at the folds of her skirts. "I have nothing to prove."

"No." His voice dropped to a husky murmur. "But where's your sense of daring now, Lady Sofia?"

"Why is it you feel so compelled to raise the stakes, sir?" she countered.

"All men like to gamble," he replied. "Didn't they teach you that in your fancy school?"

Sofia shook her head.

"They should have." Osborne approached with a slow, stalking step. "After all, whatever the curriculum, those expensive academies are simply preparing you young ladies for matrimony. You should not be innocent of men's baser urges."

Up close, his gold-tipped lashes seemed alight with sparks. The rest of his face was shaded in shadows. She drew a small breath, trying to ignore the spicy scent of his cologne. "Trust me, sir, we were taught enough about the realities of life."

"Indeed?" Osborne laughed softly. "Then I assume that one of the first lessons was that the prospect of risk and reward adds a certain edge to any endeavor."

"Rather, our instructors trained us to react with reason rather than emotion when faced with a challenge," replied Sofia.

"What a pity." He took another swallow of spirits. "I was looking forward to the duel. But then, I should have suspected that a lady would only go so far before retreating behind the skirts of maidenly excuses."

Sofia knew he was simply baiting her. She had proved her point. Her fencing instructor had often said that knowing when to withdraw was as important as knowing when to engage. *Risk and reward*.

"I was going to let you retreat with your dignity intact, Lord Osborne," she answered. "But if you insist—name the stakes."

"The loser must pay a forfeit," he replied.

"Of what?"

"Oh, as to that." He drew out his words. "The winner may name what he wants."

"Or she," countered Sofia. "And the game?"

"Alternate shots, each from a different position in the room." A grin curled the corners of his mouth. "We'll pick the spots as we go along. The winner of each toss shall make the choice." He retrieved the darts from the board, along with a wooden case from the bookshelf. Inside it were four more of the feathered missiles. "We'll each take five. That should ensure that the match does not end in a draw." Light winked off the steel as he separated the weapons into two piles. "By virtue of your last victory, you may call the first shot."

Sofia looked around. Spotting the heavy brass fender around the hearth, she fisted her darts and marched to its far edge. "Very well. We'll shoot from here—balanced on one foot atop the rail." She kicked off a slipper and set her silk-clad toes on the polished metal. "Shoes are optional."

Her throw hit home close to dead center.

"You are good," he said grudgingly as she slipped her footwear back on. He stepped up to the bar and whipped a sidearm toss at the target.

His dart kissed up against hers.

"So are you." Sofia grinned back at him. "Your call, sir."

They traded shots, each winning one.

On her next choice, Sofia turned around and slowly untied his cravat, pulling the length of snowy linen free of his shirtpoints. "This one we'll do blindfolded." She looped it around her eyes and was at once intimately aware of the lingering scent of his shaving soap and bay rum cologne. For an instant, she felt a little dizzy but managed to keep her equilibrium and make a decent strike in the middle circle.

"You have left me an opening, Contessa." Osborne reached out, his fingers grazing her flesh as he unknotted the cloth. "I shall have to see if I can take advantage of it." He cracked his knuckles, then let fly. But his dart only hit the band of blue as well.

"Still tied," she murmured.

"This way." As the choice was his, Osborne drew her to the far corner of the room.

There wasn't much space to maneuver, and the carved

molding forced them shoulder to shoulder. Sofia could feel the heat from his thigh. His profile showed a spark in his eye as well.

Osborne was right. Risk did add a frisson of fire to a competition.

She felt the blood thrumming through her veins. Her fingertips were tingling.

"Last shot. To decide the winner." His lips were tantalizingly close to her cheek. His breath was redolent of whisky. Sharp, sweet.

She turned, just enough to gulp in a bit of fresh air. "You have the honors, sir."

His laugh was light as a feather against her skin. "There is nothing honorable about me right now. Indeed, if we were caught in this compromising position, I would be called a cad. Or worse."

"A widow—" she began.

"A widow ought to be even more aware of the consequences of surrendering to the heat of the moment," said Osborne.

"Then luck must be on my side," countered Sofia. "For there is no one around to witness the transgression."

Some perverse magic must have been in the air, for there suddenly came the scuff of footsteps at the head of the corridor and the murmur of masculine voices.

"Damn," muttered Osborne. Grabbing up his coat and cravat from the table, he moved quickly to a side door, which led to the adjoining room, and eased it open. "Take my glass and have a seat," he called in a whisper. "A widow is permitted to indulge in a discreet nip of spirits. I'll find a way back to the festivities without being spotted."

The latch closed with a soft *snick*.

Sofia had just enough time to grab up his drink and

settle herself on the sofa. After quickly rearranging several pieces on the chessboard, she assumed an air of studious interest as her host, accompanied by two gentlemen companions, entered the room.

"Light the fire, Fitz, while I fetch those Turkish cigars I was telling you about. We have at least a half hour to enjoy a smoke and a bit of peace and quiet before my wife notices that we have scarpered—" Lord Harpworth stopped in dismay as he caught sight of a telltale ruffle of silk curled atop the patterned carpet.

"I'm afraid I've scarpered too, sir." Sofia straightened and fixed the trio with a guilty smile. "I hope you gentlemen will be kind enough not to give away my naughty secrets."

Harpworth eyed the glass of whisky. "Er, you may count on our discretion, Lady Sofia." He gave an embarrassed chuckle. "After all, we are being a bit naughty ourselves."

"Just so," chimed in Mr. Kepton. He, too, seemed to be staring at the whisky, though he quickly shifted his gaze to the chessboard. "Uh, it seems that your king is in danger of checkmate, milady."

Sofia gave a casual shrug. "Someone must have left a game unfinished. Perhaps he—or she—sensed the imminent danger." She slowly replaced the figures to their starting positions. "Let us do the players a favor and allow them a fresh start."

"How very sporting of you, Lady Sofia." Sir Taft cleared his throat. "Well, gentlemen, we ought to withdraw and allow the Contessa to finish her, er, libation—"

"No need. I was just about to return for the Mozart concerto." Sofia rose. "Having heard so much about your Scottish malt, I could not resist trying a sip," she went on. "However, I find it a bit too fiery for my taste." Retrieving her shawl, she draped the Kashmir weave around her shoulders. "I shall stick to champagne in the future."

"A wise choice, Contessa," agreed her host. "Highland whisky is much too rough for a refined lady."

She winked. "Live and learn."

Chapter Twelve

*H*er nerves winding tighter with every turn of the carriage wheels, Sofia watched the glitter of the Mayfair streets fade to a more haphazard swirl of light and shadow. *Would tonight bring her one step closer to the grim truth?* It was, perhaps, waxing overly dramatic, but given what she had learned over the past few days, she couldn't help but feel that this evening's party at Lord Concord's retreat would mark a turning point in her search—she was sure of it.

The last few days had passed quietly, for other than several routine morning calls and an appearance at the Theatre Royal, she had cried off from her other social engagements. Lying low had allowed her to sift through the file of notes that had suddenly arrived from the marquess.

Following up on her request, Lynsley's agents had uncovered a number of interesting leads on De Winton's source of income and Roxbury's ties to Sforza's shipping company in Venice. That all three men—along with a prominent government official in Bombay—were partners in a private banking account was the most intriguing information. Marco had spent the last two nights poking around the East India docks at Blackwall, east of the Isle of Dogs. He would be there this evening as well, instead of joining her here. They had decided his talents were better put to use in picking locks than in serving as her escort.

As she stepped down from the unmarked carriage and moved up the slate walkway, Sofia reminded herself to relax. She must appear a lady interested in a taste of illicit pleasures, nothing more.

It was Lord Concord himself who answered her knock. "Welcome, Contessa. I thought you would prefer to make a discreet entrance, rather than be greeted by strangers." He pressed a kiss to her hand. "A lady can't be too careful of her reputation."

De Winton, who was standing at his friend's shoulder, was quick to offer his own effusive greeting. "Indeed, indeed. Be assured that there are just a few trusted servants around to serve our needs. So your naughty secret is quite safe here."

"Thank you, Adam." She allowed him to take her cloak before adding, "Have I been naughty?"

"Simply by virtue of joining this gathering, you would stir a bit of scandal among the sticklers of the *ton*." His gaze lingered on the satin trim of her bodice, which cut a deep V between her breasts. "As for anything else, I suppose that is up to you."

De Winton's look made it clear he expected to bed her. The idea was not appealing, but if duty demanded it . . .

"Allow me to show you to the drawing room." Concord stepped forward and took her arm. "I believe you are acquainted with some of the other guests, but there are new faces as well."

Perhaps having the two men vie for her favors could be

turned to her advantage. "I always look forward to new experiences, including making new friends," replied Sofia. "It makes life so much more interesting than staying within the same old circle."

"I couldn't agree more, Lady Sofia," said Concord.

Accepting a glass of champagne from the servant stationed by the door, she took a long sip in order to survey the room. She recognized Andover and Roxbury, along with Sforza and Lord Neville, another of the Scarlet Knights. They were by the hearth conversing with a trio of females who, despite their costly silks and jewels, appeared to be . . . not quite ladies.

Cyprians, guessed Sofia. Curious at her first glimpse of the demimonde, she allowed her gaze to linger a moment longer before moving on to the sofa and settee, where Lady Serena was presiding over a group of gentlemen that included Roxbury and Familligi. Osborne had not yet arrived.

Or perhaps he had chosen to stay away.

"Champagne seems such a tame choice for a lady of adventurous tastes." De Winton sidled close. His glass was filled with a liquid nearly as red as his waistcoat. "The punch is a mix of pomegranate juice, brandy, and grappa."

"I am merely whetting my palate," she replied.

"Speaking of treats, Lady Sofia, did you bring your gold key?" The overbright glitter in his eyes looked to be lit by more than the spirits. "Or were you merely pretending to know about the secret language of flowers?"

Thrust and parry. Sofia couldn't afford the slightest slip in this verbal duel. "I will let you be the judge," she countered. Moving into the shadows cast by a japanned screen, she plucked the sliver of gold from a hidden pocket sewn into her sash.

He studied it for a long moment before asking, "Did you get it from Della Croce in Venice?"

Not wanting to fall into a trap, Sofia batted her lashes. "What do you think, *cara*?"

"Beauty and blunt—Vittorio has a weakness for both." De Winton laughed. "No wonder he was willing to share in his part of the business." He fingered the silk of his waistcoat. "Like Venice, there is a special place here in London. You put the key in the lock, and it opens the door to pleasure. And, of course, profit."

Sofia hid her excitement beneath a sly smile. "So I have been told. Just how—"

"How delightful to see you again, contessa." Roxbury's greeting interrupted her question. "I was hoping you would be among the invited guests."

"I wasn't aware that the two of you had met," said De Winton.

"Lady Sofia and her Italian friend happened to stop by for a look around Andover's shop while I was there," replied Roxbury. "Did anything catch your eye?"

"A great many things. He has quite a unique selection of treasures." Sofia held up her hand. "But for the moment, my only purchase was this charming little ring."

"Charming, indeed." But his gaze was on the key. "Andover does not keep *those* out on display."

"I came by mine in Venice," she murmured.

"Ah." Andover joined them, leaving the three Cyprians to Lord Neville. "Might I have a look at the workmanship?"

Sofia could think of no reason to refuse.

The gallery owner studied the enameling from several angles, then handed it back. "Verchiotto's work is unmistakable," he murmured with a tiny nod at De Winton.

"Welcome to our circle, Contessa," said Roxbury before the other men could speak.

"You possess a key, too, Mr. Roxbury?" she asked.

"Indeed, like De Winton and Andover, I am one of the Select Six here in London. I act as quartermaster, coordinating the lists of suppliers, and the logistics—"

Andover nudged him to silence. "Really, Roxbury, you know better than to discuss the details of our business outside the monthly meetings."

"But we are among friends," he said rather sulkily.

Much as she wished to hear more about any lists, Sofia was quick to agree with Andover. "*Si.* We are equally careful in Venice."

"Castillo is said to run a tight ship," said De Winton.

She played it coy, avoiding a direct answer. "Of course, we don't mention names either."

Andover nodded. "Of course."

So far, so good. None of the others called her bluff.

Still smiling, the gallery owner drew De Winton aside. "Adam, do let me show you one of Concord's Chinese porcelains. I have a similar one you might be interested in purchasing . . ."

The two men moved away, leaving her alone with Roxbury. The opportunity was enticing—given the man's vanity, she had no doubt she could tease further indiscretions out of him. But she dared not seem too curious about the workings of the group. Not yet.

"Come, you must introduce me to the man who just joined Lord Neville," she said. "And to their female companions."

Roxbury looked loath to agree, but after several florid flatteries earned him no reprieve, he reluctantly led the way to join the others. As the conversation began anew, Sofia smiled and managed to appear attentive, although in truth her thoughts were engaged on what she had heard earlier.

De Winton, Roxbury, Andover—they each possessed a key. And according to Roxbury's slip of the tongue, there were three more. *Concord?* Given his role as host, he was certainly a prime suspect. As for the other two, it was a pity that Marco had not succeeded in having a look inside Andover's storeroom. The hint of incriminating lists had her fingers itching to put her lock-picking skills to work.

A late-night foray to Bond Street? Too risky without a proper surveillance of the premises.

Sofia made another surreptitious look around. De Winton and Andover were still engaged in a private talk by the curio cabinet, while Lady Serena was keeping the Italian and several other men amused—including Osborne, who had lost no time in joining the ranks of her admirers. The laughter from that end of the room was growing more animated, and to augment the array of champagne bottles, a servant appeared with a tray of jade pipes.

Improvise. The echo of her fencing master's exhortations drowned out the chatter of the Cyprians. Bond Street was out of bounds, but Concord's private study was just a short stroll away, down a deserted corridor.

No one would give it a second thought if she excused herself to find the withdrawing room.

Osborne sipped his brandy, trying to ignore the sight of Sofia flirting with Lord Neville and a man from the ministry whose name he had forgotten. She looked incredibly seductive in the smoky light. The deep green velvet bodice was cut low and spangled with gold. As if the lush curves of her breasts needed any enhancement.

He told himself to concentrate his attention on the *other* Lady S. The fair-haired widow was far more accessible.

Sensing his sidelong glance, Lady Serena turned and offered him a Turkish confection of dates and nuts. "Would you care for a sweetmeat, Osborne?"

He gave a half-hearted chuckle. "Am I looking sour-faced?"

"Your expression is black as a storm cloud—as opposed to your usual sunny humor." She rose, drawing him up along with her. "Come take a turn with me around the display of Indian bronzes. I wish to hear your opinion on their artistic merit."

Osborne followed along. "I'm afraid my knowledge of Eastern art is woefully lacking," he murmured as they approached the teakwood table.

"So is mine," she replied with a light laugh. "However, you looked as if you needed a respite from the crowd."

"Thank you."

"You are welcome." Running a finger over the elephant profile of a Hindu deity, Lady Serena continued on with a few pithy comments on the stylistic details before adroitly changing the subject. "Speaking of long faces . . . You are so popular with the *ton*, I would assume you know everyone, even so gruff a man as George Hartwick."

"Yes, reasonably well, in fact." Osborne was puzzled as to why she would have any interest in the curmudgeonly head of a family that controlled most of the cotton plantations along the coast of the Carolinas. Aside from cotton, Hartwick's other passion was landscape painting, and they had met a number of times at art exhibits. "Is there a reason you ask?"

"In fact, there is. I have a friend who is interested in

doing a bit of business with him. Is it true that Hartwick is a stickler for following the rules?"

Osborne found himself frowning. "What do you mean?"

She gave an airy wave. "You know, some people will not take advantage of certain loopholes in the law, even when a clever business manager can find a way to do it legally."

There was something unsettling in her making light of the matter. But then, a lady would not be expected to understand all the nuances of business ethics. "Hartwick won't seek any special favors," he said firmly.

"Not even if *you* were to speak to him?"

"Actually, I find his refusal to do so commendable," replied Osborne. "Given the war, one should not profit from loopholes simply to pocket personal gain."

"Most men find that money is an irresistible lure," murmured Lady Serena.

He leaned back against the windowsill. "Not to me. I have enough."

She laughed. "Does anyone ever have enough?" The question hung in the air for an instant, and then she softened the cynicsm with a brief smile. "Obviously you have a noble heart, Osborne. How very admirable. Not many men possess your principles."

Strange, but it was almost as if she was mocking him. He shrugged off the sensation and replied with the same teasing tone. "Trust me, I am far from perfect."

"I am glad to hear it—for a moment I was worried about you." A tilt of her chin set her face in flawless profile. "Perhaps you would care to come by my town house after the party, where we have a bit more privacy to discuss the subject of right and wrong."

Spend the night with the lovely widow? Osborne knew

he should be salivating at the offer. But suddenly, for some odd reason, the prospect of a torrid tumble in her bed held little appeal.

He feigned a grimace. "Alas, I promised Harkness I would meet him sometime after midnight in Southwark. He has been anxious to show me a new gaming hell, and it would be shabby of me not to show." He kept his reponse deliberately vague. "Perhaps another time."

Lady Serena's eyes narrowed slightly, and between the glare of the glass and the flicker of the candles, it seemed that a blaze of anger flamed in her gaze.

However, it was gone in a flash, and he felt a little foolish having imagined it, for when she spoke, it was with her usual calm.

"Of course, a gentleman cannot leave his friends in the lurch."

"You are more understanding than I deserve." He ran a hand through his hair, unable to explain his odd mood. "Forgive me. I seem to be poor company for anyone this evening."

As she was about to answer, one of Concord's servants approached and cleared his throat. "Your pardon, milady, but a message has come for you."

"Please excuse me, Osborne." She hurried off to confer with Concord, then returned after several minutes to retrieve her reticule. "I, too, find that I am obliged to attend to another matter this evening. I must take an early leave."

"I trust it is nothing serious?"

"No, merely an ailing relative who needs my attention. There does not appear to be any immediate danger, but I ought not ignore the note." Her tone was quite calm, but Osborne noted a ripple of emotion in her gaze. "You know how trifling things can take a turn for the worse if left unattended."

Seeing her concern made him feel even more foolish for his unkind thoughts. "Your compassion is commendable," he murmured. "I will call on you soon."

"Yes, do."

Osborne could hardly blame her for sounding a bit cool. If she had taken offense at his behavior, it was what he deserved. He ought to go home and brood alone over his brandy.

And yet, he couldn't quite keep his eyes from straying to find the contessa.

Sofia edged along the corridor, keeping to the shadows. The door to Concord's study was unlocked—no need yet for the steel pick hidden among her hairpins. Slipping inside, she hurried to the desk. The drapes were drawn, so she ventured to strike a light to the candle by the inkwell. She would give herself five minutes, no more, to search the drawers. Though the gentlemen seemed engrossed in their pleasures, there was no point in taking chances.

A riffling through the top two revealed little more than bills from a wine merchant and gaming vowels. The bottom one was locked, but it proved no match for her steel. At first glance, she saw nothing of interest, but on probing under a sheaf of estate papers, her hand brushed up against something hard and smooth. Drawing it into the light, she saw it was a gold snuffbox decorated with the same enameled poppy that crowned her key.

Inside was a folded note . . .

The rattle of the door latch gave her just enough warning. Shoving the box into her sash, Sofia quickly relocked the drawer and was just spinning away from the desk when a figure entered the room.

She thought fast and tugged loose the silken ribbons of her bodice, allowing a tantalizing peek of her décolletage. Whoever it was, she trusted that the sight of rosy flesh would distract him from asking what she was doing alone, in her host's private quarters.

"Looking for something to read, Contessa?"

Sofia laughed as she caressed the leatherbound books. "The party is rather a bore, Lord Osborne. I was seeking a distraction—and it seems you are of the same frame of mind."

The flicker of candlelight did not quite reach his face.

"Perhaps we could make the night a bit more interesting," she added coyly.

"Is that an invitation?" His voice was as inscrutable as his expression. "I was under the impression that my advances were not welcome."

"A lady must sometimes play hard to get." Hearing voices at the far end of the corridor, she took a step closer. "Most gentlemen are hunters at heart. They find the chase exhilarating."

"And when the quarry is cornered?"

She reached out her hand and touched his jaw, smooth, strong, with just a faint hint of stubbling against her fingertips. "Then I expect the hunter will move in for the coup de grâce."

Osborne hesitated for a heartbeat, then caught her up in his arms. His kiss was searing and sweet with the taste of brandy. She opened her mouth, allowing the heat to flood over her tongue.

The trail of his lips slid to the hollow of her throat, the ridge of her collarbone. A moment later, his hands tugged the silk down across her skin, and he sucked in the tip of her breast. Fire tingled through her as he teased the sensitive flesh with his tongue.

And then with his teeth.

With a wordless moan, Sofia slid her hand inside his shirt, reveling in the smooth, slabbed muscle, the frizz of curls, fine as spun gold beneath her fingertips. A stud popped loose as she pulled at the tails of his cravat. Stumbling, they fell against the desk.

Osborne lifted her, pushing away the pens and inkwell, and perched her derriere on the burled walnut.

Sofia pulled her skirts up around her thighs and opened her legs, drawing him into the froth of lace and satin. The voices outside were closer now. She could hear the scuff of leather against the parquet floor.

"Deverill!" Her knees clenched around his sword-slim hips. His arousal was hot, heavy against her.

As the door to the study swung open, De Winton and Concord stopped short, their surprise limned in the light of the hallway sconces. After an instant, it turned to leers.

"Oh, dear!" Sofia made a halfhearted attempt to sit up. "It looks as though we've been caught in the act, my dear Deverill. How very naughty of us."

De Winton laughed.

Osborne looked around. "Do you gentlemen mind finding another spot to enjoy your brandy and cheroots?"

"But no other room offers quite such an interesting view," drawled De Winton.

"Indeed." Concord smacked his lips. "Can't we watch?"

"Sorry," said Osborne. "I don't perform before an audience."

"Lud, if I were mounted on such a prime filly, I'd be happy to show off my skill in the saddle."

De Winton added his own lewd remark. But the ribaldry did not quite veil the look of malice in his eyes. Had she made an enemy by appearing to favor Osborne over him? There had been no choice.

"Nonetheless, gentlemen, the lady and I would prefer a bit of privacy," replied Osborne. "If you please."

With a last snigger, they backed off and shut the door.

Sofia smiled, though her heart was pounding so furiously that she feared it might shatter a rib. "Now, where were we, *cara*?"

Osborne was still looking at the doorway.

She tried kissing the corner of his mouth, hoping to arouse his passion again.

He didn't bite. "They're gone. What was that you slipped into your sash?"

"La, you are imagining things, Osborne," she teased.

"I saw the flash of gold as you hid it away, Contessa," he insisted.

"Your eyes deceived you, Osborne." She threaded her hands through his hair. "It was merely the glint of my rings."

"Who the devil are you?" In the flickering shadows, his eyes were as dark as a storm-tossed sea.

"What a strange question, sir." She drew in a tiny gulp of air and tried to soften the shrillness of her voice with a light laugh. "Have you forgotten already which of your legion of admiring ladies you hold in your arms?" She nibbled at his ear. "Here, allow me to refresh your memory, Osborne. I am Sofia Constanza Bingham—"

"I know what names you go by, Signora della Silveri,"

interrupted Osborne. "The far more pressing question is what lurks beneath those silken lies."

"You are calling me a liar, sir?" She tried to sound outraged.

"And a thief." Without warning, his hand shot out and snagged the snuffbox from the sash of her gown.

Sofia tried to grab it back, but he was too quick.

Stepping back, Osborne held it up to the candlelight. "A pretty enough bauble, but there are more valuable pieces in the curio cabinet. Perhaps what is inside it is what interests you." He started to open the lid. . . .

Damn. She had to make a split-second decision.

Spin, step, lunge—in a blur of lashing limbs, she closed the short distance between them. A sharp blow to the jaw momentarily stunned him, allowing her hand to find his carotid artery. Her fingertips pressed against his pulse.

Without so much as a sound, Osborne slumped to the carpet.

"Sorry," she muttered, straightening his unconscious form to a more comfortable position. Looking around, she quickly knocked a small bronze statue of a satyr from its marble plinth. When he came to, the evidence would indicate that he had suffered an accidental slip.

"Sweet dreams, sir," she added before retrieving the fallen snuffbox and hurrying from the room.

Chapter Thirteen

Bloody hell.

Osborne lifted his head from the carpet and winced. *Lud, what the devil had hit him?* Still groggy, he propped himself up on his elbows and looked around. His gaze locked on a squat bronze satyr lying close by. Was he really so clumsy? The recollections were awfully hazy. He had been holding a snuffbox but couldn't quite recall what had happened next.

After studying the marble plinth from several angles, he frowned. The geometry made no sense at all. He would have had to fall face-first into the damn thing, dislodge the statue, then spin around in the opposite direction. And yet, there was no other explanation, unless . . .

No. Impossible.

He rubbed gingerly at his jaw. In any case, the contessa had a great many questions to answer.

Osborne got to his feet and dusted his trousers. She might have won this skirmish, but she was greatly mistaken if she thought he would slink from the field without a further fight. Warfare often called for feints and diversions. He would retreat tonight and let her imagine the battle was over.

For a female, she possessed an unusual array of martial skills. However, a lady unschooled in the art of actual combat was likely to underestimate the enemy. Let them meet again, *mano a mano,* and then they would see who came out on top.

Sofia backtracked from her first hiding place in the kitchen pantries and took up a position in the servant stairwell, watching and waiting for Osborne to leave the study. She flexed her fist, hoping that she hadn't hit him *too* hard.

She frowned. *What if he was truly hurt?* But after a moment of misgiving, she forced herself to squelch her sympathies. Duty came first. Osborne would have to take care of himself.

Finally, he emerged from the room, moving with a slight limp. It served him right for interfering, she told herself. And yet, Osborne *had* served as an unwitting ally in distracting De Winton and Concord. Things might have turned a good deal hotter had he not obliged with his passionate kisses.

Biting her lip, she looked around. *Damn, it was risky.* But she had to replace the snuffbox. Reading over the paper hidden inside had made the task even more imperative. The keyholders must not guess that she knew about this list. On it were the names of some suppliers, which Lynsley could begin to investigate. But what she needed was the names of the conspirators. *And proof of their perfidy.* Until then, she must give no hint that their operation was under suspicion.

Sofia saw no shiver of movement in the corridor, save for the flicker of the wall scones. No sound stirred from within any of the rooms. She waited a heartbeat longer, and then satisfied that she was alone, Sofia eased the paneled door open.

It took only a few moments to replace the gold box at the bottom of the drawer. As the steel pick teased the lock back in place, she lifted her skirts and hurried to retrace her steps.

In and out. Just as the former jewel thief had demonstrated in the Academy classes.

But in her haste to be gone, Sofia did not notice the silk sweep a scrap of paper under the desk.

For some reason, Osborne lingered on the sidewalk rather than heading for the corner where he might flag down a passing hackney. The fog had thickened, its clammy touch like a chill finger at the back of his neck. Teasing a sense of prickling unease.

But then, any thoughts about Lady Sofia stirred the sensation of dagger points dancing across his flesh.

He turned and began walking, but after several strides, he realized what was amiss. The lady's carriage was nowhere to be seen. And yet, he had distinctly heard her taking leave of the group in the drawing room as he had let himself out through one of the side entrances. He hesitated, then reversed directions, moving lightly across the cobbles. The street was dark, deserted. Frowning, he took up position in the gated archway to the adjoining garden.

Perhaps she had other plans—an amorous assignation, another clandestine bit of thievery. It was none of his business, but curiosity kept him in place.

He had not long to wait. The town house door soon opened, and Lady Sofia—unmistakable in her stylish scarlet-trimmed hooded cloak—came down the marble steps. She was alone, and as she reached the curb and looked both ways, it seemed clear that the absence of her horses and driver was unexpected.

She waited a moment or two, a slim silhouette in the mizzle of moonlight, then turned for the alleyway leading back to the mews. Keeping close to the garden wall, Osborne shadowed her steps. The contessa was just disappearing into the gloom when out of the corner of his eye, he caught a sudden ripple of movement from up the side street.

A pack of men materialized from the mists, running swiftly, silently over the slick cobbles.

Footpads.

Calling a warning, he raced into the alleyway and shoved Sofia against the wall. "Stay back," he ordered, squaring himself to meet the attack. *Four against one.* Not the best of odds, especially as he was unarmed. He tightened his grip on his walking stick and dropped to a defensive crouch. Like them, he had no intention of fighting fair.

"Run, Lady Sofia," he muttered. "To the mews or out to Queen Street." Surrounded as they were by walled gardens on either side, there was little chance of anyone hearing a cry for help.

On spotting him, the lead footpad slowed to a walk. "Get out of the way, lest ye want yer fancy throat slit from ear te ear."

"And leave the lady alone with you filth?" replied Osborne. "I think not."

The footpad's cohorts closed ranks to block any escape. "Filth?" snarled one of them. "It's yer golden locks that will soon be soaking up the muck."

Osborne saw a glint of a knife.

"Jem, you and 'arry see to the bitch. Me and Bill will take care of this toff." The leader flicked a menacing slash.

"Use yer blades rather than yer barking irons. No need to risk waking the street with a shot."

Likely not, thought Osborne grimly. But perhaps he could hold them off long enough for the contessa to raise the alarm. He fell back a step and let his hands drop, feigning a look of fear.

Damn. Why wasn't the lady running for her life?

He shifted sideways, hoping to give her an extra second to slip away, but as the leader lunged out with a vicious slash, he had no more time for reflection. The sharpened steel was only inches from his chest when Osborne jerked up his stick and swung it down hard. Wood cracked against bone, sending the weapon flying. He ducked under the outstretched arm and smashed his knee hard into the other man's groin.

A scream shattered the silence, and the leader dropped like a stone.

Osborne hit the ground as well, rolling to avoid a flailing kick. As his hand closed over the fallen knife, he saw a flash of red.

"Run, dammit!"

Sofia had flung off her cape and wrapped the thick wool around her arm. Using the makeshift shield, she was fending off the feints and slashes of her two assailants. Osborne swore again. Was she mad? Pitted against the two hulking brutes armed with cudgels and knives, she had as much chance of survival as a lamb being led to slaughter. In another instant . . .

Before he could make a move, Sofia suddenly spun forward in a blur of whirling limbs and flaring skirts. One elbow caught the nearest man flush on the throat. He staggered back with a gurgling gasp, only to have a stiff-armed jab send him careening into the brick wall. Dazed, he slid down to his knees, blood spurting from his broken nose.

"Poxy slut!" The other man flung himself at her, but his snarl segued into a howl of pain. A flick of her wrist, a twist of her hip, and he was jerked off his feet and thrown head over heels to the ground.

Osborne scrambled to his feet, just in time to parry the attack from the fourth footpad. Steel clashed against steel as their knives crossed. He countered with a swift slice that nearly struck home. But then a fist clipped his cheek, and the man scrambled back, circling warily to his right.

Osborne edged along with him, eyes intent on the razored blade.

"Osborne!" Sofia called a warning.

He looked around to see that the leader had recovered his footing and was pulling a pistol from his coat.

At the same time, Sofia snatched up the fallen cudgel and lashed out at the man's head. He managed to dodge the blow, but the stumble threw off his aim. The bullet exploded against the bricks high overhead, sending down a harmless shower of shards.

"Shoot the bloody she-devil," he bellowed.

Osborne had already flattened Broken Nose with a right cross to the jaw. As for the others . . .

Whipping around, he saw that Sofia had followed up her first slash with a lightning flurry of sword strokes. *Giroste, cavazione, contrapostura.* His jaw dropped slightly. By God, the lady wielded her weapon like a Death's Head hussar. Had the stick been a saber, the men would have been chopped into mincemeat. As it was, their upraised arms were likely purpling with bruises as they were forced to retreat in the face of her onslaught.

A light suddenly lit in one of the town houses across the street. Then another.

"The Charleys will soon be here," snarled the leader. "Let's be off." Grabbing the collar of their fallen comrade, the two others hauled him to his feet. Hurling a last volley of curses, they fled back into the night.

"Sticks and stones may break my bones," muttered Osborne. He flexed his aching fist, then turned to Sofia. Both of them were breathless and bleeding from a number of small cuts. "Are you injured, Contessa?"

Sofia shook her head and dropped the cudgel. "What about you?" Stepping to his side, she reached up and touched a fingertip to the corner of his mouth.

"Nothing to speak of." Looking down, he saw her gown was ripped in several places. "You are sure you are not hurt? In the heat of battle, injuries often go unnoticed. . . ." As he smoothed at the silk, a ruffle slipped, baring her left breast.

Osborne stared at the tiny tattoo of a hawk in flight, not quite believing his eyes. Its jet-black wings stirred a sudden recollection of strange rumors that had floated through General Burrand's headquarters a year ago. Rumors that, at the time, he had dismissed as preposterous flights of fancy.

Feeling a bit dizzy, he lifted his gaze to Sofia's face.

Her lashes fluttered, blurring her expression.

"That mark," he whispered. "I have heard stories about—"

Swearing softly, Sofia hurriedly fixed her bodice. "Before you fly to any conclusions, we must talk, sir." She darted a look around. "But not now. We must be gone from here, and quickly, to avoid being caught up in any scandal."

"When?"

"Tomorrow at—"

"No, it must be tonight," he countered, determined that this time she would not evade him so easily. "I'll slip into your garden through the back gate. Leave your conservatory door unlocked."

The distant shout of a night watchman drew a reluctant nod from her. "Very well."

Not daring to linger any longer, Osborne cut through the mews and led the way out into the adjoining side street, where he quickly flagged down a hackney to take her home.

"Until later," he murmured.

"Give me an hour to dismiss my servants for the night," she replied. "Then we shall have a . . . council of war."

Chapter Fourteen

Sofia paced along the perimeter of the leaded glass walls, her soft slippers noiseless upon the slate tiles. Her thoughts, however, were a babel of curses and consternation.

Bloody hell. Deverill Osborne was coming way too close for comfort. But the question was, what she was going to do about it?

During the ride back to her town house, she had reviewed her options, none of which offered an easy way out.

She stared at the fogged panes, the blur reflecting her own misgivings. Osborne was not only courageous, but also clever. He would not be fobbed off with farrididdles.

Heaving a sigh, she pressed a hand to her breast. How much did he really know about the Merlins? And how much was just wild rumor or speculation that he had overheard?

The latch clicked and a sudden swirl of night air stirred the moist warmth of the conservatory. Sofia turned to see Osborne slip in and shake the rain from his caped overcoat.

"I wondered whether you would keep your word." He stomped the water from his boots. "At least it is a step in the right direction. But we still have a long way to go, Contessa."

"You don't trust me?" she asked.

"Should I?"

Rather than answer, Sofia moved closer and feathered a hand against his cheek. His skin was still chilled from the night air, but the throbbing pulse at the base of his jaw sent a tingle of heat through her fingertips. *Fire and ice.* Both could be dangerous.

"You *are* hurt," she whispered, the scrapes rough against her palm. "There's a cut on your chin."

"It's naught but a scratch." Osborne touched the corner of her mouth. "There's blood on your lip."

"It's naught but a drop."

"This time, yes. But what of the next?" His thumb gently traced the curve of her lip. "Sofia, enough of secrets and lies. Why are you taking such terrible risks? Explain this devilish mystery that surrounds you, and what—"

She stopped his halting questions with a long and lush kiss.

Her Academy training had taught that sex was the most powerful weapon she could wield against a man. *An act of desperation?* Perhaps. But duty demanded she use every means at her disposal to avoid discovery. *Deception, distraction.* She told herself that she had no choice but to use her body to seduce him from asking further questions.

Easing the coat from his shoulders, Sofia let it fall away. Osborne started to pull back, but she tugged open the fastenings of his shirt and slipped her hand beneath the sweat-dampened fabric. "You are also cut here, *cara.*" The chiseled contours of his chest were solid, sculpted planes of whipcord muscle. The finespun curls of hair, glimmering gold in the starlight, tickled against her palm. "And here."

He stood still as a statue as she continued to explore his body. In stark contrast to his fair skin, his flat nipples were intriguingly dark and textured. They pebbled beneath her stroking.

A groan—or was it a growl—slipped from his lips.

Emboldened, Sofia leaned in and flicked her tongue over one taut nubbin and then the other. He tasted of salt and some mysterious male essence. The effect was . . . intoxicating.

"God help me." His voice was hardly more than a stirring of air. In contrast, the stiffening of his arousal was hard against her thigh.

She licked again at his ruddy flesh.

"Did you save me from the footpads just to slay me with your own hand?" he rasped.

"There is a question as to who saved whom." Sofia teased a trail of nipping kisses to the base of his throat. "I haven't yet properly thanked you for risking your neck."

"It is not my neck that is in danger; it's my sanity." His eyes fell half-closed, but through the fringe of lashes, she caught a glimmer of naked desire. "Keep going—you are becoming more eloquent by the moment."

Duty. Did that explain the tingling heat in her hands as she pulled the torn linen up over his head?

The shirt slithered down to join the coat on the slate floor, leaving him bare to the waist.

Osborne leaned down and drew aside the tattered remnants of her bodice. He kissed the hollow of her throat. Then his lips strayed lower, covering the tiny tattoo. A moment later, he was suckling her left nipple.

Heat flared deep within her. Breathing in, she felt herself enveloped in the musky, masculine scent of bay rum, brandy, and an earthier note that was all his own.

"Osborne."

In answer, his mouth moved to her other breast, lapping liquid kisses over her taut, tingling tip. The warm weight of him against her belly teased an aching need inside her.

Sofia moaned, hardly recognizing the husky pitch of her voice.

It seemed inevitable that she would give up her virginity somewhere along in this mission. Suddenly she wanted her first experience at lovemaking to be with Osborne, rather than any other man.

He had risked his life for her, showing courage and honor, despite the shabby treatment he received from her. From the first, she had sensed there were hidden depths to his character. Lord Sunshine was far more than a fair-weather friend. He was a man worthy of respect, worthy of—

No, she could not afford to let herself think in those terms. He was a useful ally, that was all. One who must, at this moment, be distracted from her true mission.

"Sofia?" The word feathered against her cheek, leaving the rest of the question unspoken.

In answer, she found the top button of his trousers. His arousal pressed hard against the placket, steel sheathed in soft merino wool. One by one, the fastenings slipped from their slots. Her fingers tugged at his drawers, allowing his erection to spring free.

What a beautiful man he was, she marveled. Like a classical deity, a pale, perfect form of masculine grace. She traced the flared crest of his manhood before circling his shaft. He was smooth as marble, yet throbbing with life. His breathing hitched up a notch as she stroked its length. From within the crumpled linen flashed a tantalizing gleam of golden curls. She fumbled at the fabric, wanting to see him in all his glory.

Slowly, silently, they stripped each other naked.

Kicking open the folds of his fallen coat, Osborne took her in his arms.

Dizzy with desire, Sofia was hardly aware of him lowering her to the floor. Then her hips lay hard against the unyielding stone, and the press of his body was atop her. She gave a keening cry as his hands ran a little roughly up her thighs and coaxed her legs apart. The intimate awareness of her own feminine heat was overpowering. As was the unyielding fire of his male arousal against her skin. She was too amazed to feel embarrassment.

Osborne slipped his fingers through her Venus curls, finding the pearl hidden within the folds of flesh. Pleasure pulsed through her with each slow, circling stroke. She felt as if every bone in her body were melting into a pool of warm honey.

The sensations were so strange, so seductive. So wildly, wildly wonderful.

Sex was, of course, a part of the Academy curriculum. The Spanish courtesan had matter-of-factly described primal passion and how it could be used as a potent weapon. But words did not begin to describe the raw sensuality of flesh against flesh. Of limbs entwined, hands caressing, tongues tasting the smoky sweetness of intimate kisses.

Suckling her lower lip between his teeth, Osborne bit down as he quickened his caresses between her thighs. Sofia cried out against his mouth. A searing, spiraling fire was taking control of her body. The heat was almost unbearable.

"Deverill," she pleaded, uncertain just what it was she wanted.

He seemed to have no doubts.

"Lift your hips, sweeting." Osborne slid his strong, capable hands beneath her. "*Tesoro*, you are a vision of beauty," he groaned as the head of his cock grazed her feminine flesh. "Lethal, lethal beauty."

Sofia meant to reply, but the words seemed to die in her throat. Coherent speech yielded to a whispery sigh as he pressed closer and positioned himself at the entrance to her passage. He moved with a fluid grace, gentle, yet urgent. Demanding.

"Open yourself to me." His voice was rough with need as he pushed her legs apart.

The throb of him was hot and heavy as he rocked himself against her wet flesh. *So good, so right.* She shifted in response, an instinctive arch that drove him deep inside her.

A soft yelp slipped from her lips.

The sound was echoed by his fuzzed oath. She felt his whole body tense, his muscles knotting as he braced his arms and wrenched his weight upward.

"Bloody hell." As he fell to one side, the soft sheen of light caught the look of shock and surprise on his face. "You—you are a virgin."

"Not anymore." She tried to smile.

"But how . . . that is, you were married for several years," he stammered.

"My husband was . . . incapable of consummating our marriage." That was not a total lie, she told herself. She did not like deceiving Osborne any more than was necessary.

"Why didn't you tell me?" He sounded angry.

"I don't know," answered Sofia. "It didn't seem . . . important."

"Important?" he repeated. "My honor—and yours—is not something I take lightly, Sofia." The fringed shadows

of the potted palms did not soften the rigid line of his jaw.
"I am not in the habit of deflowering innocents."

It was not only anger she heard, but regret. She felt her
insides clench. Deverill Osborne's dismay was sincere—
she saw the fine lines of self-loathing etched around his
eyes and in the pinch of his mouth. She liked him even
more for his vulnerability to pain, to recrimination.

"I am sorry. Forgive me for being selfish." Clasping his
hand, she pressed it to her cheek. "But I—I wanted it to be
you."

"And I—I am vain enough and weak enough to take you
at your word." His fingers slid up and twined in her tangled
hair. "Though at heart, I suspect that your sweet whispers
are naught but another bewitching brew of half-truths
and lies."

Rain pattered against the glass, and the rumble of distant thunder seemed to echo the warning thud of her racing heart. *Dangerous.* A physical coupling with this man
would be more than a fleeting joining of flesh. Did she dare
let him that close?

There was still time to pull back.

A flash of lightning illuminated the curve of his cheek,
the fringe of his flame-gold lashes. The sliver of space between them crackled with sparks. Then Sofia leaned across
the divide. Up close, his stubbling of whiskers looked like
a thousand points of fire.

"I have been less than honest with you about some
things, Deverill. But not about this. I swear it."

"Damn me for a fool, but I'll believe you," he rasped.
His skin was rough yet warm to the touch as he slanted a
kiss over her upturned lips. "At least for the moment."

As he touched her breast, she caressed the ridges of his
ribs, reveling in the masculine lines of his body, the flat

belly, the jutting hip bones, the finespun curls, lustrous as burnished bronze in the lamplight . . .

He groaned as her hand touched his cock, and came instantly erect.

"Make love to me, Deverill," whispered Sofia. "Here. Now."

Love. Osborne had no illusions that her plea was based on any emotional need. Why she was offering herself to him was a mystery. But not one he was going to puzzle out anytime soon. His rational mind wasn't working too clearly at the moment. As for other parts of his anatomy . . .

The air leached from his lungs as she feathered a delicate stroke along the length of his shaft. She was an intriguing mix of innocence and experience. There was nothing virginal about her caresses. Nothing innocent about her kisses. No maidenly blushes, no tremulous tears—it was almost as if she had been schooled in the art of pleasuring a man.

What an addlepated notion, of course. She was a well-born lady. *Or was she?* The tattoo seemed to say otherwise. Its winged shape, stark black against the creamy coloring of her flesh, was a vivid reminder of how little he knew about her, save for a name. And even that was suspect.

The Contessa of Conundrums.

She was a puzzle, a provocation. A penance for his past sins? If she wasn't a real lady, the alternative was even more shocking. The more he tried to make sense of it, the more he felt lost. All he knew was that he wanted her passionately, no matter who or what she was.

"Deverill?" Her smile was sweetly tentative. Seductive. "Am I doing this right?"

He gave a hoarse laugh. "You are an expert in swordplay, sweeting. Indeed, you handle a blade with consummate skill."

She looked away quickly, the silky strands of her hair falling to obscure her expression. "Please, let us not talk about what happened earlier."

"No," he agreed. "I've no intention of engaging in a verbal duel with you, Sofia. Your thrusts and parries have kept me at arm's length for too long. Tonight let us declare a truce of sorts."

"Lay aside our weapons?"

Osborne pulled her closer, skimming the flat of his palms along her legs. "Oh, yes. I shall sheath my sword," he murmured.

Her cheeks turned a beguiling shade of pink. "I fear there are certain maneuvers in which I may prove clumsy. As you discovered, I have no experience in lovemaking."

"You appear to be a quick study, sweeting." Rolling onto his back, he pulled her atop him. "Riding astride allows you to start out slowly and set your own pace." Osborne eased her legs apart until she was straddling his hips. Her thighs were warm and wet, the scent of her essence swirling up to meld with the humid perfume of the potted flowers. The effect was earthy, erotic.

"I—"

"Relax, I won't let you fall, Sofia." His fingers found her warmth and stroked gently through her feminine folds. He watched as her eyes widened and turned a luminous, liquid green.

"Hold me, Deverill."

"Yes, sweeting," he whispered as she pressed up against his cupped hand. He slipped a finger into her honeyed passage, groaning again as she clenched around him. It was all he could do to rein in his desire. *Slowly, slowly,* he told himself. Whatever else happened between them, he wanted this moment, this memory to be right.

Sofia arched and cried out softly.

"Look at me, Sofia," he whispered. "Did your husband never touch you like this?"

"N-no. Never."

"Selfish oaf," he said through gritted teeth, though a part of him was fiercely glad of it. "Lovemaking is meant to be pleasurable for both man and woman." He left off his caressing to slide his palms over the rounded curves of her derriere.

"Don't stop," she whimpered.

"Not if the devil himself demanded I do so," he replied, lifting her up a fraction.

Purring like a hungry kitten, she twisted against his grasp.

His hands fell away and then he was inside her.

Sweet Jesus.

Sofia stilled for a moment, then her hips began to rise and fall. Holding back a grunt of triumph, Osborne willed his body to match her rhythm. He felt her breasts grow aroused, the tips like points of fire against his fevered hands. She cried out again as he teased them with slow, circling caresses. How perfectly she fit in his palms, as if made for him.

It was all he could do to keep from coming completely undone. There was a sinuous, sensuous beauty to the sleek stretch of rippling muscle, the hint of callus on her fingertips. A Goddess of War, leaving a trail of sparks in the misted moonlight.

Osborne shivered, awash in her liquid heat. He had experienced a good many sexual trysts, but nothing quite like this. The connection seemed more than fleshly, the need more than casual lust. Something about her strength, her spirit, touched him in a place he had always kept private.

As the tempo increased, their bodies seemed innately in tune. He was acutely aware of her wonder—and his own—at what was happening between them. A poet might describe it in a lilting ode to love.

That word again.

Closing his eyes, Osborne willed himself not to think of such things. Friendship he gave freely to his lovers—it was, he knew, a part of his charm. Up until now, he had never felt the need for anything more. Need was rather frightening.

For an instant, a wild, desperate laugh rumbled deep in his throat. He used laughter to guard against the unknown. To give himself completely seemed daunting. Perhaps because it required him to look deeply into his own soul, and he wasn't sure he liked what he saw. Everyone else did, because they saw the surface, the good humor, the bon mots.

He had never shared the darker side, the doubts.

"Deverill!" Sofia's smoky plea roused him from his mordant reveries. Her voice sounded stretched to the breaking point.

Time enough later for introspection. *A truce.* With his own demons, his own doubts. For now, he would surrender himself wholeheartedly to the strange alchemy that Fate had forged between them.

Perhaps it was only fool's gold. But for the moment, it was exquisitely real.

"Ohhh, I feel I am about to shatter into a thousand shards," she cried, her eyes aglitter in the flickering candle flame.

"Hold on to me, Sofia," he rasped. "I will keep you safe and whole."

She clutched at his shoulders, her hair falling over his

chest like a shower of silky soft midnight rain. His hips surged up from the stone, meeting her need with his own. She was riding him hard and fast now. Whipped to a frenzy, his heart was pounding at a furious pace.

A last rise and fall, and Osborne felt the tension within her crescendo into a shuddering release. He heard her wordless wonder and his own voice joining in hoarse exultation.

Somehow, a small vestige of reason remained, allowing him to pull her off of him in the nick of time. He rolled on his side, his body spent, his lungs heaving as his climax spilled onto the rumpled wool of his coat.

For a lingering instant, a single drop of his seed clung to the tip of his manhood, a pale, perfect reminder of what they had shared. Two bodies, coming together as one.

"*Cara*." Sofia was touching him, stroking his shoulders, his neck, the length of his spine.

Osborne turned back and kissed her lightly on the forehead before gathering her into his arms. Moonlight danced over their sweat-sheened limbs. Closing his eyes, he was suddenly aware that he hadn't ever felt such profound peace in his life.

It was exhilarating—and frightening.

Her whisper, a teasing, tantalizing mix of English and Italian, tickled against his ear.

Truth and lies. Who was she, this lady who was stealing not only expensive baubles but also his heart?

So many questions. But mystery could wait until morning. For the moment, he would savor the quicksilver magic of these midnight hours.

Chapter Fifteen

Sofia awoke to the sound of rain pattering against the glass. Or was it simply the lingering thrum of her heart, beating a soft tattoo against her ribs? She shifted on the coat, only to find the curve of her spine nestled against Osborne's chest.

The intimacy felt oddly comforting. As if that made any sense. In truth, she wasn't sure she was thinking all that clearly. Had everything changed? Or nothing at all? Every inch of her body felt somehow different. She was no longer a maiden, but a . . .

She was a Merlin, she reminded herself. With a difficult, daunting mission to complete. She flexed her bruised knuckles. Not that she needed a mental scold to remind her of the dangers she faced.

"Awake, are you?" Dawn was just beginning to tinge the night sky, so Osborne's expression was impossible to discern as she turned in his arms.

"Yes," replied Sofia, grateful that the shadows hid her own face. "And we had best dress quickly and be gone from here. The servants will soon be up and about their daily chores."

"Not so fast." He shifted his body to block her escape. "We have yet to talk, Sofia."

"There is no time—" she began.

"There's time enough for certain explanations." He touched the tiny black hawk above her breast. "Beginning with this."

Sofia parried with a question of her own. "How much do you know about my tattoo?"

"Ah, are we back to being at daggers drawn?"

Was the edge in his voice disappointment? She let out a sigh. "I— I don't want to fight you, Deverill."

"But you don't want to trust me either." The curve of his lips hardened. She wished to reach out and soften the sardonic twist.

"It's not a matter of trust," she replied. "I don't want to draw you into danger. You were forced to risk your life because of me tonight."

He hesitated, looking uncertain of what to say. When finally he spoke, it was half question, half statement. "You are involved in a ring of thieves."

"Yes," she admitted, deciding there was no point in denying it. "I've been sent to steal some valuables."

"By whom?"

"That is not important," she said quickly. "What does matter is that it is a difficult, dangerous job."

The rain had stopped, and for an instant the only echo off the glass was of silence. Then his gaze locked with hers. "Perhaps I can help."

Osborne kept surprising her. But much as the idea was intriguing, she forced a shake of her head. "The golden Lord Osborne seized by Bow Street Runners for robbing the mansions of Mayfair? Think what a scandal such head-lines would stir."

He shrugged. "I would not be around to read them. I would be on a transport ship to Botany Bay."

"It's no joking matter," she said, seeing the tiny twitch of his mouth. "I am deadly serious. "

"As am I." He laced his hands behind his head. "Think of it—I am intimately acquainted with the *ton*. I know their habits, their homes, and in the case of some, their most intimate hiding places."

"Don't be daft." Sofia watched the play of rain-washed light, pale and pearlescent, limn his profile. Its softness seemed to bring out the subtle strength of his features. He was no longer just a handsome face, a smoothly sculpted Adonis, perfectly polished but devoid of real character.

She forced her eyes away. "Why would you hazard your reputation for a share of ill-gotten gains? You have no need of money."

Osborne leaned in closer. "Oh, something tells me you are not doing this simply for money, Sofia."

"W-what makes you say that?"

"I consider myself a good judge of character." A flicker of moonlight glinted off his lashes. "It is not greed that that makes you so passionate about your pursuit."

"My reasons are mine alone." His probings were coming far too close for comfort. She must find a way to deflect him. "You haven't thought about the risks."

"You think me too devoted to my creature comforts to chance a bit of danger? Too settled in my drawing-room manners?" His voice had a rasp of roughness to it.

"I am not questioning your courage, Osborne." Sofia sighed. "Merely your sanity. You would be a bloody fool to involve yourself in this affair."

He turned slightly, fixing her with a storm-blue stare. "I already am." His tangled locks shadowed his expression. "It is Osborne now? That seems rather distant, seeing the intimacies we have shared."

The space between their bodies was mere inches, but Sofia knew that there was a chasm he could not be allowed to cross. Duty demanded she keep him from coming too close. "That was . . . nothing personal. As you said, the heat of battle does strange things to the blood."

"Nothing personal?" he repeated. "So I was merely a convenient means of cooling your fire?" His face froze in a sardonic smile. "Dear me, I feel you have taken unfair advantage of me, Contessa."

Sofia felt a dull heat flush her cheeks. "Th-that's not precisely what I meant."

"What, precisely, *did* you mean? For I confess, I am having trouble discerning your true sentiments from all the tangle of lies."

"I work alone." She shivered, suddenly aware of being naked beneath his gaze. Groping among the discarded clothing, she found her chemise and clutched it to her breast. "Let us leave it at that."

Osborne caught her wrist. "I don't intend to be dismissed so easily. You promised some answers, and I mean to hold you to that."

She tried to break away, but he held fast. "That black bird on your breast—what the devil does it signify? Are you part of some secret army? Some force of . . . of . . ."

"Of trained killers?" Sofia finished his faltering words with a scoff. "Good Lord, Osborne, perhaps you should turn your hand to writing novels. You have a lurid enough imagination for the job." Seeing his anger flicker to uncertainty, she went on the offensive. "What will you accuse me of next—being a foreign assassin sent to cut Prinny's throat?"

He had the grace to flush.

"Now please let me go." The rattle of a coal scuttle in the main corridor punctuated her demand.

His grip fell away. "You are sharp as steel—that is for sure, Sofia. Again I shall retreat, so as not to sully your name. But don't be so sure you have seen the true test of my mettle."

Ignoring the raised eyebrows of document clerks, Osborne stormed through the copyroom and turned into Lynsley's office.

This time, the secretary managed to intercept him in the anteroom. "His Lordship is not available," said the young man, moving with great agility to block the path to the closed door.

Osborne stopped just short of bowling him over. "Is he away, or is he simply refusing to see me?"

The answer was fittingly evasive. "The marquess is not at his desk."

He glared at the young man, who did not flinch. "Tell him I called," he said, deciding that it was unfair to vent his spleen on someone who was simply doing his job. Tossing his card on the side table, he added, "It is a most urgent matter."

"I will give His Lordship the message when he returns."

"Let us hope he is not on a slow boat to China," muttered Osborne under his breath.

The secretary kept a straight face. "I think I can safely say that the marquess is not currently engaged in any diplomatic dealings with the Forbidden City."

"But of course you are not allowed to tell me his whereabouts."

The young man gathered up an armload of files. "Is there anything else I can assist you with, Lord Osborne?"

"Good day," he growled.

Quitting the warrens of Whitehall, he made his way to White's. But several glasses of the club's best brandy did nothing to quench the fire in his belly. Indeed, his anger had risen from a slow simmer to a point perilously close to a boil.

Explosive might be a more apt description, he fumed as he took another gulp of the spirits. It was ironic, seeing as he was known for his calm demeanor, his dispassionate view of the Polite World. However, he was anything but detached these days.

What had prompted the odd offer of helping the contessa? She was right. It was absurd to think of him as a cracksman—though in truth he did know a number of flash houses, where stolen merchandise was fenced, on account of having friends among the lower circles of Society as well as at the top.

Why did he care so passionately about Sofia? It was hard to explain, even to himself. She had an unwavering courage and a sense of conviction he found immensely admirable. Opposed to his own recent sense of aimlessness. Of drifting, with no real purpose besides casual amusement to his life.

Shifting uncomfortably in the reading room armchair, Osborne tried to concentrate on the latest war dispatches from the Eastern front. Finally, he tossed back the last swallow of his drink and slapped down the newspaper.

"Aye, the news is grim enough to drive a man to strong drink." Colonel Edwards, an adjutant on General Burrand's staff, looked up from his magazine. "Kutusov appears to be as spineless as the rest of the Russian officers. Bonaparte is now taking supper in the Kremlin. In another month, he'll be skating on the canals of St. Petersburg."

His own mood was on thin ice, so Osborne simply nodded, hoping to avoid a lengthy discussion on military tactics.

"What the Tsar needs is some officers who are unafraid to match wits with the Little Corsican."

"True." Osborne silently signaled to the porter for his gloves and walking stick.

"Someone with the boldness and bravery of, say, your friend Lord Kirtland." Edwards pursed his lips. "Has he returned yet from his wedding trip to Italy? I have some reports from the Peninsula that I wouldn't mind asking him to read over."

"No, he has not." He was halfway out of his chair but sat back down. "Tell me, Edwards, do you recall the name of Kirtland's bride?" He had been in Scotland at the time of his friend's sudden wedding and knew precious little about any of the details. Kirtland was a very private man to begin with, and his letters were even less revealing. The only message the earl had left before departing for the Continent had been a maddeningly short missive dropped off at Osborne's residence—*Married. Will explain when I return from Italy.*

"Er . . ." The colonel tapped at his chin. "Some city name . . . ah, yes, Siena, it was."

Siena. Osborne nodded. "Family name?"

"Haven't a clue. Don't think it was ever mentioned."

"No matter." This time, he rose in earnest. "One last thing, I've been given a message to pass on to Lord Lynsley. I don't see him here tonight. Any idea where he resides? The family town house on Grosvenor Square does not look to be in use."

The colonel slanted a look around before answering. "The marquess prefers quieter quarters while in London. I know you've been working with Fenimore on the Prussian problem, so I daresay you can be trusted with the information." Lowering his voice even more, he murmured an address on a quiet side street off Dorset Square.

"Thank you."

A short while later, Osborne shouldered past the startled footman. "I don't care if he's taking tea with the Prince Regent or sleeping with the Queen of Sheba, tell Lynsley I want to see him." He tossed his hat on the sideboard. "NOW."

"No need to shout, Osborne." The marquess appeared at the head of the stairs. "Do come up."

Osborne shrugged out of his overcoat and took the carpeted treads two at a time.

Lynsley ushered him into a small study.

The room had a comfortable coziness to it. A large pearwood desk was piled high with books and official-looking document cases, but the silver penholder was a dragon, which looked rather whimsical with the ebony shafts bristling from its jaws. The same juxtaposition was evident in the mahogany bookcases lining the walls. Softening the hard-edged planes was an eclectic mix of mementos from faraway places—Cossack daggers, Saracen jambiyas, African masks, Etruscan artifacts. The sideboard held an assortment of ruby ports and tawny sherries, their rich colors mellowed by the glow of the fire blazing in the hearth.

The marquess mirrored the informality of the room. His collar was open, his shirtsleeves were rolled up to the elbows, his feet encased in Moroccan slippers. Stepping over the sheaf of documents that lay on the carpet, he resumed his place in one of the leather armchairs by the fire and gestured for Osborne to do the same.

"Help yourself to a glass of spirits." Lynsley's voice betrayed no surprise or surliness at having his private retreat invaded.

Did nothing disturb the dratted fellow's sangfroid?

"No. Thank you." Osborne remained on his feet.

"Is something amiss?" To his irritation, the marquess picked up a packet of notes and began perusing the pages.

"Other than the fact that the contessa is a jewel thief?" he shot back sarcastically. "And nearly had her throat cut by four footpads last night?"

The marquess didn't look up. "As I told you before, the contessa is an independent lady. She is not subject to your censure or mine. If I were you, I would not involve myself in her private life. It seems that she can take care of herself."

"Don't patronize me. I'm not some snotty-nosed schoolboy." Osborne stalked to the fire and set a boot on the brass fender. "I'll not be fobbed off with a little lecture and sent on my way."

"Then let me phrase it a bit differently," said Lynsley. "You have done what I asked. Now please leave the lady alone."

"I'm bloody tired of being used by you—and by her." He was now perilously close to shouting. "I want some answers, Lynsley."

A sigh. "What are your questions?"

"Tell me all about a group of women who bear a small tattoo of a black hawk above their left breast. Who are they?"

Lynsley set aside his papers and took a long sip of his sherry.

Osborne's temper, already frayed to a thread, suddenly snapped. He fisted a small jade carving from the mantel and flung it at the empty chair. "Goddamn it, man, do they work for you?"

"Sit down, Osborne." The marquess was no longer looking so affable.

The jut of his jaw hardened, but after drawing a deep breath, Osbone did as he was told.

"And please remove my Buddha from beneath your arse," added Lynsley. "It's a rare Ming Dynasty piece, and aside from its monetary worth, it has a certain sentimental value."

Osborne rather sheepishly placed the statue on the lamp table by his elbow.

"Dare I hope that a touch of the Great One's calmness has rubbed off?" added the marquess.

He folded his hands in his lap. "I am ready to be enlightened."

A flash of amusement lit in Lynsley's eyes, but he turned, and his face was quickly wreathed in shadows. "I regret that I am not at liberty to reveal more than a glimmer. Indeed, I would ask that you be satisfied with my word that it is a matter of grave importance that you leave Lady Sofia alone."

The dismissal, though somewhat softened, still struck a raw nerve. "So you think me a superficial fribble, a cabbage-headed coxcomb who can't be trusted with a secret?"

"On the contrary, your intelligence and discretion were the reasons I asked for your help in the first place." Lynsley paused. "As was your ability to avoid emotional attachments."

Osborne shifted uncomfortably in his chair, aware that a slight flush was staining his cheeks.

"I am aware of the work you do with Major Fenimore," went on the marquess. "He speaks highly of your logic and your analytical powers."

"Then why must I be kept in the dark?"

"Touché." Steepling his fingers, Lynsley touched the point to his chin. "But first, I have a question of my own—how did you learn about the tattooed ladies?"

"There was a rumor running through general staff head-quarters about a secret cadre of women warriors. We all dismissed it as a wild flight of fancy, a figment of a foxed imagination." Osborne made a face. "But then, when Kirt-land mentioned a mysterious courtesan bearing a winged mark, I began to wonder if there might be some truth to the talk. You were investigating him at the time. And now, the fact that Lady Sofia has the same sort of tattoo seems to be more than mere coincidence."

Lynsley pursed his lips and sighed. "I won't ask how you came to see such a mark."

"Her dress was torn during the attack."

"Ah." The marquess rose and moved to the hearth, where he carefully put the Buddha back in its place. "Lady Sofia is in a difficult position here in London. Any distrac-tions could put her in danger."

"Such as me?" said Osborne softly. He imagined that Lynsley would consider a bout of passionate lovemaking to qualify as "distracting."

"Such as you."

"I see." Though in fact, so many things were spinning in his head that nothing appeared in very sharp focus. Press-ing his fingertips to his brow, he tried to bring some order to his thoughts. A myriad of questions were flying around, but somehow the first was the most basic. "Is Sofia Constanza Bingham della Silveri her real name?"

"I can't tell you that."

"Does she work for you?"

"I can't tell you that."

"In other words, you can't tell me aught but to mind my own bloody business."

Lynsley cracked a smile. "Correct."

Osborne thought for a moment. "Why can't I help?"

"She prefers to work alone."

He didn't really expect any other answer. Still, the rebuff rankled. "Well, if I had not been around last night, you might have had a dead bird on your hands."

"I wouldn't bet on it. For all her pretty feathers, the lady has a formidable set of talons."

"A regal raptor, a huntress," he murmured. "Which begs the question of what she is after." They regarded each other in silence for some seconds before Osborne rose. "But as it's clear I'll get no further answers, I won't take up any more of your time."

He was at the door when the marquess called softly. "So, what do you intend to do?"

Osborne's gaze fell on the jade Buddha, whose serene stare seemed to mock his own inner turmoil. "Sorry, Lynsley. I can't tell you that."

Chapter Sixteen

Sofia stifled a yawn and tried to pay attention to the visiting professor from the University of Rome, an expert on classical architecture. Lady Wilberton had arranged the special soiree—a scholarly lecture, followed by an early evening supper—at the last moment. And though Sofia would have preferred an evening of rest after the tempestuous events of the last twenty-four hours, she had accepted the invitation after learning that the Duke of Sterling would also be present.

She had grabbed a few hours of sleep during the afternoon after writing up an urgent report for both Lynsley and Marco. With the information in hand, the marquess could set his agents to investigating the companies mentioned in the snuffbox list, while Marco could take a closer look at their warehouses.

As for her own efforts to further the mission, she had sent off a scented missive to De Winton, begging forgiveness for her behavior. Hopefully the man was as susceptible to flattery as she imagined he was. The appeal to his vanity ought to get her back in his good graces—she had all but begged him to take her for a drive in the park at his convenience.

In person, Sofia meant to press her desire to attend the next meeting of the keyholders. She did not intend to take no for an answer. Though now, more than ever, the thought of him touching her intimately sent a shiver of revulsion spiraling through her core.

As opposed to the memory of Osborne's caresses, which brought a rush of color to her cheeks.

"It *is* rather warm in here," murmured Miss Pennington-Pryce with a wave of her fan. "Let us hope the professor does not go on to discuss the reign of Marcus Aurelius."

Sofia smiled, but the flutter of a breeze stirred yet another warning in her head. She must use all of her considerable training in mental discipline to keep her mind on her mission, not on Osborne. Or what had occurred between them last night.

Focus. The Academy yoga instructor had taught her the art of channeling her energy to a single purpose.

Her gaze sought Sterling, who was seated in the front row of chairs, next to the hostess. The duke was the reason she was here. She was hoping that he might help her follow up on a hunch that had occurred to her earlier that afternoon.

"And with that," announced the professor, "I shall conclude my thoughts on the design principles handed down to us by the ancient Romans. If anyone has questions, I shall be happy to answer them—"

"Over refreshments," finished Lady Wilberton in a stentorian voice that would have done Caesar proud. "I am sure you would welcome some tea or sherry. As would the audience."

"Thank goodness." Miss Pennington-Pryce rose and, before Sofia could demur, linked arms and led the way to the main drawing room, where a cold collation and a selection of beverages had been laid out for the guests.

"I must say, I do not agree with his assessment of the Coliseum's proportions," continued Miss Pennington-Pryce. "I have studied the measurements made by Brighton on his visit in 1763 and have my own ideas on the matter."

"I'm sure the professor would be delighted to hear them," said Sofia as she nibbled on a bit of shaved ham.

Thus encouraged, the spinster headed off with a determined step toward the tea table, leaving Sofia free to begin making her way across the room. Sterling was standing by the display of architectural engravings, having what looked to be a spirited discussion with Reverand Tilden.

Sofia was slowed by the demand to exchange pleasantries with several of her new acquaintances. She turned away from Sir Pierson to find the duke looking at her rather oddly.

Catching her gaze, he made a wry face and came to bow over her hand. "Do forgive me for staring. It's just that . . . well, you remind me of someone."

Sofia felt a bit guilty on regarding his pinched expression. Was she stirring up memories of old conflicts, old regrets? "I do hope it is not an unpleasant recollection," she said gently. The last thing she wished was to cause him pain. But duty was duty.

As Sterling looked away, she thought she detected a slight sag of his shoulders. His voice was suspiciously muffled. "No, no. Not at all."

It was, of course, absurd for a nameless orphan to feel a welling of sympathy for a wealthy duke. He had every luxury, every privilege that money could buy, while she had nothing but her wits, her weapons, and her will to complete her mission.

And yet, she did.

But aware that personal musing must yield to pragmatism, she placed her hand in the crook of his arm. "Might we take a stroll to a less crowded corner of the room?" she asked. Loath though she was to speak of his grandson, she had several important queries concerning Lord Robert's last days. Only the duke might have the information she sought.

"You had mentioned that you would be willing to answer any questions I might have," she began.

His lined face wreathed in a kindly smile. "With pleasure, Contessa."

She repressed a sigh, knowing it would be anything but pleasurable. "I was wondering whether you know anything about an antique shop on Bond Street, owned by a Mr. Andover." No mention of it had appeared in the young man's diary, but she was acting on intuition. "Was it, perchance, a place that your grandson frequented?"

He fixed her with a searching look. "Why do you ask?"

Sofia had anticipated his reaction. Coming from a veritable stranger, the interest in the young man's personal habits must appear odd at best. The reply she gave must be compelling—something that would strike a chord with his desire for justice, yet not give away too much.

Truth and lies. Osborne seemed to think she was good at twining the two.

Sofia hoped he was right.

Drawing the duke deeper into the privacy of an alcoved display of Roman artifacts, she allowed a small sigh. "I had a friend—a good friend—in Venice who also died of drugs while in the company of several Englishmen." She hesitated, then dropped her voice to a whisper. "I know this may sound melodramatic, but I have reason to suspect foul play."

The duke paled. "Does Lord Lynsley know of your concern?"

"Yes, he does," she admitted.

He took down one of the leatherbound books and pretended to study the pages. "Don't you think you should leave the matter to him?"

Sofia was ready for the objection. "His government duties are most pressing at the moment, leaving him little time to pursue any leads. And besides, he cannot take any official action unless there is solid evidence of a crime."

"Your courage is commendable, Contessa. But have you any idea how dangerous it might be for you to go around asking questions? A lady ought not take such risks."

"I assure you, sir, I have no intention of taking any risks. All I want to do is gather a few facts before going back to the marquess."

Sterling thought for a moment before asking, "What about Lord Osborne? Have you spoken to him about this?"

The question was one she didn't expect. "N-no." Drawing a quick breath, she added, "Why would I?"

"I am aware that many people consider him naught but a charming fribble, but I've heard from those I trust that he's a good man in a pinch. A fellow who has substance as well as style."

"As you say, sir, it is best to keep this quiet. The fewer people who are aware of my suspicions, the better. There is really no need to involve Lord Osborne."

"I suppose you are right," muttered Sterling, but he did not look entirely convinced.

Seeing he was about to speak again, Sofia raised her eyes, knowing full well that the nearby candelabra would reflect the beads of moisture clinging to her lashes. Given the recent events, it was not all that difficult to summon a show of emotion. "Please, Your Grace. I would be very grateful for your help."

The duke coughed and hemmed. "Dash it all, please don't cry, Lady Sofia. Of course I want to help. But not if there's a chance you could be hurt."

"I won't do anything rash," she promised. She rather doubted the duke would agree with her definition of the word, but that was splitting hairs.

He hesitated, but a last little flutter moved him to speech. "I have your pledge to be discreet?"

She crossed her heart.

"Very well, then." He expelled a breath. "In fact, Robert seemed to have taken a special interest in Andover's gallery during the weeks before his death. And though he had never really expressed interest in Eastern artifacts before, he mentioned making several expensive purchases. A brass statue of some elephant-headed god from India and a Byzantine icon, painted on wood, of St. George and the Dragon."

"Do you still have the items?" asked Sofia.

He nodded.

"Might I come around to see them on the morrow?"

"Yes. If you think it would be of help."

"I do," she replied.

Osborne sealed the letter and tossed it onto the post tray. It was likely a waste of ink. Heaven only knew if or when it would ever reach Italy and find its way into the hands of Lord Kirtland.

Damn Julian. Once again he cursed his friend for being so bloody laconic. One would think a man would have more to say about his nuptials than a few laconic lines. He would wax poetic about his bride, detailing her looks, her charms. Everything about her.

All Osborne knew about the new Countess of Kirtland was that her given name was Siena. He wasn't even sure if she was the sultry courtesan who had sported the tattoo of a hawk above her left breast. Aside from the newlyweds, only Lynsley might know for sure. And the marquess had made it clear that he was not going to be forthcoming with *that* bit of information.

If he was to unlock the secrets of this mystery, he would have to do it on his own.

Staring at the banked coals, Osborne picked up his pen-knife and spun it in his fingers. His friend Kirtland was a decorated war hero, an expert in military intelligence. Whatever intrigue he had been caught up in, the earl had managed to work it out for himself.

His grip tightened on the sliver of steel. In truth, he had laughed off Julian's initial suspicions. Now, the feeling of dueling with naught but specters and shadows was not nearly so humorous.

Bloody hell. Though he might not be as experienced as Kirtland in the art of clandestine activities, he could make a stab at learning what the contessa was up to. She and Lynsley might think him a lackwit, but he had no intention of playing the fool. For the moment, he would heed the marquess's warning and appear to keep his distance. In truth, he would simply slip into the shadows.

It was not merely a matter of pride, but also of personal honor. Lady Sofia might insist that their lovemaking had changed nothing between them. But the look in her eyes during that fleeting intimacy, the thrumming need in every fiber of her body, had belied her words. *Trust.* She had trusted in him, a fact that caused his throat to constrict. He was not vain enough to imagine she had fallen head over heels in love with him. And yet, she must feel something, if only the mysterious force that seemed to draw them together from the very first.

He felt it too. How to describe the powerful attraction? His gaze skimmed over the orderly rows of leatherbound books on the shelves. It seemed to elude both prose and poetry. Was that love—a jumble of conflicting, confounding emotions? Having no experience in aught but lighthearted dalliances, he didn't dare hazard a guess.

All he knew was that he couldn't just walk away, leaving Lady Sofia—or whoever she was—to face danger on her own. Her courage and convictions were unquestioned, but he had rigid notions of honor as well.

Up to now, she had dictated the rules of engagement. It was time for him to take matters into his own hands.

Tossing the knife back on the blotter, Osborne took up his hat and walking stick and turned for the door.

Growing more impatient by the hour, Sofia passed much of the morning watching the clock, silently cursing the silly strictures of Society that prevented her from paying a call on Sterling until well after noon. The waiting set her nerves on edge, more so as she was forced to mull over her machinations of the previous evening. She did not like deceiving the duke, but she simply could not reveal her real identity or her real mission. With luck, Lynsley would be able to tell him the truth at some point in the future.

For now, he would have to be kept in the dark.

Like Osborne.

She drew her shawl a bit tighter around her shoulders. She had been relieved when he had made no objection to her note canceling their engagements for the rest of the week. The Antiquity lecture, a poetry reading at the Literary Ladies Club, a meeting with her mantua maker—the list of excuses was all perfectly legitimate. Yet a small part of her was disappointed that he had accepted the rebuff without argument.

But perhaps one ended a casual dalliance by pretending it had never happened. After all, Osborne was the expert on such protocol. And she should be grateful for it. Neither of them wanted any emotional entanglements.

"Your carriage is ready, milady."

Steeling her spine, Sofia gathered her reticule and marched for the door.

The duke's town house was an imposing building of white Portland stone overlooking Grosvenor Square. Mounting the marble stairs, Sofia felt more like an impostor than ever. The knocker—a lion's head crafted out of gleaming silver—seemed to be looking down its nose at seeing a guttersnipe about to enter the hallowed halls it guarded.

Lifting her chin, Sofia grasped the ring and rapped on the polished wood. She might not be a princess or a duchess, but she was a Merlin, and she would hold her head high.

Sterling appeared in the entrance hall before the servant could send in her calling card. "Come in, come in, Contessa." Waving away the butler, the duke offered his arm and led her down a long parquet corridor toward the rear of the house.

"I've brought the items you wish to see into one of the

galleries." He indicated a large writing table set between the display cabinets.

"Thank you." Setting her reticule aside, Sofia studied the antiques for a moment or two before choosing the icon and lifting it to the light. The wood panel was thick and blackened with age, though the paint pigments and gilding still had a luminous richness. *St. George and the Dragon.* Murmuring a silent prayer that she, too, could slay an evil threat, she carefully turned it over.

Her fingers ran over the rough oak, feeling along the edges of the framing. She wasn't exactly sure what she was looking for. Perhaps Lord Robert had merely been drawn by the art—

Snick.

A tiny lever moved, revealing a small compartment. Inside was a piece of folded paper. Edging a step closer to the leaded glass, Sofia turned slightly, just enough to hide her hand from the duke's brooding gaze.

"Anything of import?" he asked, noting her movement.

It took only an instant to slip the hidden paper into her sleeve. She had decided beforehand to keep any discovery to herself. Not only would the knowledge distress the duke, but it might also put him in danger.

"There is a crack in the edge, but on closer inspection, it looks to be quite old." Sofia set the icon back on the table and reached for the statue.

Clasping his hands behind his back, Sterling wandered to the far end of the casement and stared out at the gardens.

An examination of the carved bronze revealed a similar hiding place. It was empty, but Sofia was satisfied that her hunch was correct. Robert had figured out how messages were passed from abroad to the London group of conspirators. It was a deviously clever plan. Not only was it safe from prying eyes, but also the means of transport was yet another way of making money. Andover would receive a handsome cut for his cooperation, but still, the business in expensive antiquities likely turned a profit for everyone involved.

"Have you found any clues?" asked Sterling.

Sofia shook her head. "Not that I can say. But thank you for the chance to see the items for myself."

Sterling nodded, then indicated the glass display cases. "Now that you are here, would you care to see my coin collection?"

"Very much so, sir."

Sofia did not have to feign her enthusiasm as they made their way around the perimeter of the room. "It is a most fascinating collection, Your Grace." The duke's knowledgeable commentary and his obvious love of the subject had excited her own interest. Each face did possess its own individual character, each expression told a poignant story about the artist as well as the person portrayed in precious metal or clay.

For a moment, she forgot about her own dilemmas while taking in the history of the past centuries. "Have you special friends among all these faces, sir?" she asked, staring in fascination at a set of golden sesterce depicting Julius Caesar.

The duke led her through an alcove, which opened into an adjoining room. Like the larger gallery, it was paneled in sherry-colored wood and lit by a bank of large leaded windows. The afternoon light warmed the acanthus-leaf carvings and beaded molding to a mellow glow.

"There is just one case of coins in here—my personal favorites," said Sterling. "The rest of the art is simply family portraits." His eyes strayed to the gilt-framed paintings on the far wall. "But I prefer this space to the formal splendor of the main library or drawing room. It is here that I come here to read. And to reflect."

"I can understand why." Sofia touched the decorative detailing. A tip of the wooden leaf had been broken off, but judging by the smooth patina of the grain, the damage must have occurred a long time ago. "Even to a stranger, it feels welcoming." She hesitated, loath to intrude on his privacy. Yet a sidelong glance at his lined face prompted her to add, "You must have many fond memories to think about."

He, too, reached out to finger the chipped leaf. "My daughter broke that with her brother's cricket ball when she was ten. Her governess paddled her for the offense, but she said it was worth every stroke to have bowled over the lad at his own game."

Sofia smiled. "It sounds like she had an arm to be reckoned with."

"Aye." As a slow sigh leaked from his lips, the duke seemed to deflate before her eyes. "And a will to match. She did not back down from a challenge. A fault, I fear, she learned from me."

"I think we all have flaws that we would alter, if that were possible," said Sofia. "But we are human, sir, and far from perfect."

"You are most kind to offer such words of comfort. But looking back from the vantage point of my advanced years, it is the flaws that take on a sharper focus." He gave a wry grimace. "Overweening pride, to begin with. Be glad you have no such sin to be ashamed of."

Lies and deceptions. Sofia was not proud of the fact that duty demanded she use false pretenses to cultivate a friendship with the duke. "I, too, have things I regret."

"None so unforgivable as hubris."

Avoiding his eye, she looked around the room again. "Let us not dwell on the dark side of life when there is so much light and beauty here. I should like very much to see more of the things that are dear to your heart."

"Yes, I am surrounded by the things I love," he murmured. "Come, let me show you." He offered his arm and crossed the carpet. "This is Robert, my grandson, done when he was ten."

The painting showed a winsome young boy mounted on a large pony. Though his boots did not quite reach the stirrups, he gripped the reins with a dogged determination.

"I see a great deal of you in him," she said after studying the shape of the boyish chin and the squint of the sky-blue eyes.

"My son George's child," he mused. "He was a young man of passion and principle. I find it impossible to believe he frittered away his talents in drugs and dissipation."

Sofia remained silent.

Sterling sighed, then moved on past several other portraits—twin granddaughters frolicking with a pair of pug puppies, a young man in his Eton robes with a cricket bat on his shoulder. Stepping around a set of Tudor bookcases, he led Sofia to another part of the room.

"And here are my children. John is my eldest son and heir." His gesture indicated a solemn face, its austere planes softened only slightly by a fringe of fair hair. "Next to him you see George, the adventurer of the family, who is currently the Governor-General in Jaipur."

The duke shuffled a step. "And Elizabeth . . ."

The rest of his words were drowned out by a sudden roaring in her ears. Overcome by a wave of dizziness, Sofia swayed slightly, feeling like a thousand little dagger points were prickling against her flesh. Then there was only a chilling numbness, save for the hammering of her heart against her chest.

"Lady Sofia."

She was only dimly aware of the duke's agitated voice.

"Lady Sofia!" He steadied her buckling knees. "Dear Lord, what's wrong? You look as if you have seen a ghost."

Though still in the grip of shock, she managed to loosen her tongue enough to speak. "Forgive me, I . . . I don't know what's come over me. I feel a trifle unwell."

The duke helped her to the sofa and rang for a servant. "Fetch a maid and some hartshorn, Givens," he called to the footman who answered the summons. "Quickly!"

"Thank you, but I don't need any vinaigrette, Your Grace. It was just a fleeting faintness. The moment has passed."

"Don't try to rise yet." He pressed her shoulders back against the damask pillows, then rose and threw open the casement. "Perhaps a breath of fresh air will help."

"Yes," she murmured. "It is a trifle warm in here."

Sterling returned with a glass of sherry. "Drink this," he commanded, thrusting the glass into her hands.

Sofia sipped gratefully at the fortified wine. Falling into a dead faint only happened in the pages of a horrid novel. She was *not* a peagoose heroine but a full-fledged Merlin.

And yet the plot was beginning to rival the gothic twists and turns of Mrs. Radcliffe's wildly popular books. A mysterious locket, a foundling child, a wealthy duke . . .

A kindly grandfather?

"Feeling better, my dear?"

"Yes, much," she lied.

"Perhaps I should summon a physician. You are still looking awfully pale."

"Please, there is really no need for that. I am merely overtired. I fear I am still not quite accustomed to the late hours of London life." Taking a deep breath, she rose and smoothed out her skirts. "Again, I apologize for such a silly show of weakness. I shall take my leave and return home for the rest of the day. A hot posset and a nap are the only medicines I require."

"The swirl of London Society can be dizzying, even to those accustomed to a fast pace." His lined face wreathed in concern as he offered the support of his arm. "You must promise me that you will cancel any social engagements for the evening, else I shall be forced to come stand guard on your doorstep."

"You have my word of honor, Your Grace. The only activities I will indulge in are sipping hot chocolate and reading."

"I am relieved to hear it. Still, perhaps I ought to escort you home, just to make sure—"

"No!" The last thing Sofia wanted was to prolong the encounter. "That is, my carriage is right outside, sir. I feel badly enough about my show of weakness without putting you to any further trouble."

"It is no trouble at all. As if you should feel compelled to apologize. Good heavens, my dear, you are a woman, not a warrior." However, sensing her agitation, Sterling relented with a sigh. "But I shall respect your wishes."

Accepting his arm, Sofia somehow managed to maintain her poise and make polite conversation, though she had no recollection of passing from the duke's private study to the entrance hall.

It wasn't until the carriage door fell closed and the wheels started over the cobbles that she allowed her resolve to waver.

"God help me," she groaned, pressing a fist to her lips. Everything about this mission seemed to be spinning out of control.

But after a moment or two, she blinked the tears from her lashes. She couldn't look for divine intervention.

A Merlin must overcome adversity on her own.

Chapter Seventeen

$\mathcal{T}$attooed women?" Major Fenimore stretched out his legs and signaled the club porter to bring more claret. "I take it this is some sort of joke."

"No, I'm deadly serious," replied Osborne. He shifted uncomfortably in his chair. Within the atmosphere of White's—a decidedly masculine mix of cigar smoke, leather, and gruff laughter—the suggestion did sound absurdly fanciful. However, he refused to be silenced by his friend's wagging brow. "Look, it's rather important."

"Very well, I'll ask around," said the major. "But you will owe me a rather big favor, seeing as I'll likely end up the butt of ridicule."

"Agreed." Slanting a glance around the reading room, Osborne muttered, "Anyone else I might approach?"

"Without thinking you ought to be hauled off to Bedlam?" Fenimore rubbed at his jaw. "I suppose you could search out Porter and see what he knows on the subject. There was an incident in Antwerp a year ago involving a female that was all very hush-hush."

"Does he still favor that gaming hell off St. James's?"

"As far as I know."

Osborne rose abruptly.

"You haven't finished your wine."

"Sorry. I'm in a bit of a rush tonight. Put the bottle on my bill." Leaving his friend looking a bit miffed, he hurried out to the street and flagged down a passing hackney.

It took several stops, but Osborne finally tracked Captain Joshua Porter to a place in Seven Dials favored by the House Guards. The officer was engaged in a heated game of dice, but a few whispered words convinced him to relinquish the ivories for a short while.

"This had better be important," groused Porter. "I was on a winning streak."

"A matter of life and death," assured Osborne, thinking of the street thugs and their flashing blades. "And a certain lady . . ."

A family resemblance? Sofia stared at the looking glass, wishing for some tangible proof of her suspicions. A black tattoo marked her as a Merlin—if only there was some equally indelible badge of birthright.

Sighing, she dropped her eyes to the locket, musing on vagaries of fortune and family. It could be mere coincidence rather than any real proof of her parentage. There were a myriad of explanations for how the aging prostitute who had sheltered her as a child might have come by the bauble. As for her resemblance to the portrait . . .

Sofia smoothed down the lace ruffle of her nightrail and took another long look at her own reflection. No question that the raven-dark hair and green eyes were similar, but other than that, it was impossible to say for sure. Was there a shade of Elizabeth Woolsey's smile in her own lips? A similar slant in the cheekbones? The truth was already blurred by an artist's interpretation, the passage of time, the fading of memory.

Even the duke might see only what he wanted to see.

As for the story of how she had come to the run-down bawdy house, Sofia had no idea of how much was fact and how much was fiction. Sally Edwards, the lightskirt in question, had a romantic streak, as evidenced by her taking responsibility for a child, despite the hardships of her profession.

Sally had always claimed that her sister Mary had arrived one night, bearing a baby and a tale straight out of a penny-sheet novel. Her employers—a highborn young couple cast out by their families for eloping—had succumbed to a sudden epidemic of influenza. On her deathbed, the mother had passed the locket to Mary, along with a name. But as chance would have it, Mary had sickened, too, and by the time she had made her way to the alleyways of St. Giles, she was too ill, too rambling to recall what it was.

Sally's sister had not survived the night, but the story had taken on a life of its own. Sofia felt her lips quirk up at the corners. The other lightskirts had all called her "Princess" and loved to talk about how someday a handsome prince would ride up to rescue her from the sordid streets of the slums.

Sofia sighed. Perhaps she really *was* a highborn lady. And perhaps the prostitute had merely woven a fanciful fairy tale around a locket she had found in the muck.

The truth might never be known. She, of all people, knew how elusive absolutes could be. Her training had taught that often one had to be pragmatic and accept that life was not always so clearly defined.

Her two roommates had been tough enough never to brood over their unknown bloodlines. Maybe because they had never possessed any tantalizing link to their past. Sofia wasn't sure whether her talisman was a blessing or a curse. Sometimes the painted portrait only mirrored the sense of elemental loss and pain she felt at having been abandoned—not once, but twice. Sally Edwards had been a kind yet casual guardian. When the chance arose to retire and return to her native Yorkshire, the lightskirt had been frank about the fact that a child could not fit into such a future.

Well, she was just as tough as her fellow Merlins. She had survived by making herself strong in both body and spirit.

Snapping the gold case shut, Sofia carefully coiled the chain and tucked the locket back into her jewel case. She could not afford to become entangled in personal questions when there were so many other conundrums and conjectures to sort out.

Don't think of the past or the future. Only the present.

Tomorrow would certainly test her skills. After reading over the paper discovered in Lord Robert's antique, she had decided to break the normal chain of communication and request a face-to-face meeting with Lord Lynsley. He would not take the change lightly—her instincts had better be right about the urgency of the matter.

But however intimidating, the marquess was not her most formidable challenge. Later in the day, she was also due to promenade in the park with De Winton. So, rather than expend her strength fretting over her heritage, she must harden her heart and sharpen her steel for the coming confrontations. The duke was wrong—she was a woman *and* a warrior.

And as a well-trained soldier, she knew it was best to fight one battle at a time.

"I can't tell you more than that."

"Can't or won't?" snapped Osborne, who was growing tired of being held at arm's length by everyone around him.

Porter made a face. "Don't bite my head off. I am as much in the dark as you are about what really happened in the alleyway. Our operative swears it was a lady who appeared out of nowhere to save his life. A lady who looked like an angel and fought like a devil."

The description certainly sounded familiar.

"But you know Whitehall," continued the captain. "Everyone in that warren of weasels seems to keep his activities a closely guarded secret, even from the other departments. You would think that General Burrand's staff was the enemy, the way they withhold vital information from us."

"I know exactly how you feel," murmured Osborne. "Though I suppose that intelligence is a tricky business. They must be careful about who knows what."

"What they should be careful about is sticking their heads too far up their arses," replied Porter with some sarcasm. "By the by, you have not yet said exactly why Lord Lynsley sent you to ask about Antwerp."

"Something to do with smuggling and a foreign princess in distress, I believe," replied Osborne, the half-lies slipping smoothly from his tongue. He flashed a self-deprecating smile. "But then, I'm just the errand boy. He doesn't tell me much."

Porter gave a bark of laughter. "To hell with him, then." The rattle and roll of the dice grew more rapid. The captain flexed his fingers, clearly itching to rejoin the game. "Care to stay and try your hand? Maybe Lady Luck will treat you better."

"Perhaps some other time. I have a few more inquiries I wish to make." Osborne turned to go. "Just one last question. Did your operative happen to mention whether his guardian angel had a tattoo of a hawk in flight above her left breast?"

Through the scrim of cigar smoke, he saw the captain's eyes widen.

"Bloody hell, no. And trust me, I would not soon forget *that* bit of information." Porter fingered his chin. "But come to think of it, I once heard a rumor . . ." His words trailed off.

"No doubt it's just that—a rumor," said Osborne after it became obvious that the captain had nothing more to add. "Thank you for your time. Good luck in your games."

Suddenly weary of chasing in circles, he returned to the waiting hackney and gave the orders to return home. He had learned precious little from the experts.

Come morning, he would have to come up with a new strategy.

Rose tapped lightly on the door. "He is here and waiting in the kitchen, madam."

Sofia turned away from the window, leaving a palm print on the misty mullioned glass. Fog still shrouded the garden, silver gray in the cold dawn light. Lord Lynsley must have risen well before sunrise to make such an early meeting. He would expect a compelling reason as to why.

Had emotion clouded her judgment? She took a deep breath and marshaled her thoughts before hurrying downstairs. Duty was not always sharply defined. Hazed by ever-shifting shadows, the lines often blurred.

It took her a moment to recognize the marquess. In contrast to his usual sartorial elegance, Lynsley was clad in tattered moleskin and soot-streaked canvas. He appeared every inch the coalmonger come to collect the monthly bill—right down to the filthy rags he was unwrapping from around his fingertips.

She didn't care to speculate what substances were embedded beneath his normally pristine nails.

"Sorry to put you to such trouble, sir," began Sofia, then stopped short with a strangled cough. "Er, on second thought, maybe I should keep my distance—and not simply because I am in awe of your air of lordly authority." She sniffed again. "What *is* that disgusting smell?"

"You do not find L'eau de Rotten Cabbage to your taste?" said Lynsley with a straight face. "It has taken my valet considerable effort to perfume my person with such a distinctive scent."

Suddenly worried that he might think her remark impertinent, Sofia stammered another apology. "Forgive me, I didn't mean—"

"No apology is necessary. I am not so starchy that I can't be tweaked by my agents in the field," he went on. "You are quite right—the smell is disgusting. But it encourages my fellow pedestrians to hurry by without a passing glance."

"Yes, sir—no, sir," she mumbled. Despite his self-deprecating smile, it was hard to view the marquess as anything other than a commanding presence. Though he no longer took an active role in clandestine missions, the stories of his youthful exploits had become the stuff of legend at the Academy.

"At ease, Sofia. You are a full-fledged Merlin, and as such, there is no need to stand on ceremony." He gestured for her to sit down at the worktable. The cook and the kitchen maid had withdrawn to the scullery, giving them plenty of privacy. "I presume from Rose's message that you have something urgent to pass on."

"Yes, sir." This time she said it with more authority. Determined to show herself worthy of his assessment, Sofia quickly passed over the paper she had discovered in Lord Robert's antique and launched into her well-rehearsed explanation for the meeting. "I would have sent this along through the usual channel, but given your schedule at Whitehall, I feared you might not receive it in time. You see, though it's mostly in code, there appears to be a date." She pointed out the penciled numerals. "Which is the day after the morrow. It may be some sort of delivery or shipment, so I decided that you would want to know about it as soon as possible."

The marquess studied the writing for what seemed like an age.

Perhaps she had overreacted. In which case, Lynsley would have good reason to regret his choice of agents.

Looking up, Lynsley slowly tucked the paper inside his coat. "Good thinking."

She released a pent-up breath.

"The code seems to be based on a Vigenère Square rather than a Caesar shift," he continued. "Still, it should be rather simple to break. Our official cryptographer is away from London at the moment, but I work informally with a small circle of very learned ladies—including a real Italian contessa, by the by—who are very good at this sort of thing. They will have it transcribed in a matter of hours."

Encouraged by his praise, Sofia ventured a question. "Any luck with uncovering incriminating evidence against the list of suppliers I found in the snuffbox?"

"Not as yet," responded marquess. "But based on what

you have discovered so far, we have been able to trace just how far their web of corruption has spread." The lines etched around his ice-blue eyes grew more pronounced. "From phantom shipments of woolen blankets to faulty munitions and spoiled beef, this group is making obscene profits by providing our military with substandard or non-existent essentials. Your work has been invaluable in providing specific names, both of the key conspirators and the companies they do business with. I have no doubt that it is simply a matter of time before we have the proof we need to make them pay for their perfidy."

"I know that learning the identity of the ringleader is imperative to putting a stop to the conspiracy, sir," said Sofia. "And I have reason to think I shall have it for you very soon."

"It would be a great help to know who is the head of the operation," he agreed. "But not at any cost, Sofia. These men are extremely clever—and extremely ruthless. Be very careful how you go on from here. I would rather you didn't take any undue risk to learn the information."

"Don't worry, sir. Unlike my former roommates, I am ruled by reason and restraint. I won't do anything rash."

Lynsley fixed her with a pensive stare.

Sofia couldn't help wondering what he saw. A Merlin who could not quite match the fight and fire of her comrades?

His fingers drummed softly upon the scarred wood for several long moments before he went on. "And then there is the matter of Osborne."

The sudden shift in subject took her by surprise. Still, she managed to keep her composure. "Yes?"

Again there was a pause. "What are your impressions of the man?"

Lynsley was asking *her*?

She shifted uncomfortably in her chair. Was this some sort of test? Did the marquess expect her to confess her tryst? A glance at his profile revealed naught but a lopsided streak of grease across his cheekbone. He was a master of hiding his emotions—a skill she decided to emulate.

As he had reminded her, she was not a callow schoolgirl anymore but an agent who had been given the responsibility of making life-and-death decisions in the field. She wouldn't lie. But nor would she volunteer her methods.

"I would say he is a man of honor and integrity," she answered.

"Trustworthy?"

Her gaze locked with his. "Beyond a doubt."

"Yes, I had come to the same conclusion before I enlisted his help." Lynsley rubbed at his unshaven jaw. "It isn't often that I call in an outsider to be part of a Merlin's mission, but in this case, the situation was unique." A wry sigh punctuated the sound of the kettle boiling on the stove. "However, it seems I underestimated Osborne's tenacity. And his personal passions."

A flush started to steal over her cheeks. "Osborne's actions are not really personal, sir. He has a stubborn notion of chivalry, though I've assured him that I am capable of looking out for myself."

"So I have noticed," murmured Lynsley. "My ears are still blistered from the peal he rang over my head."

To her chagrin, her skin grew warmer. "If you are wondering whether he will be a distraction, don't worry. I can deal with both Osborne and the Scarlet Knights."

"I'm not questioning your competence, Sofia. But a wise general knows that fighting on two fronts is always a risky division of resources." He tapped his fingertips together.

"I would, of course, greatly prefer to keep this mission a secret between ourselves. But given how much Osborne knows already, and how much damage could be caused by misunderstandings, I leave the decision of what to tell him to you, Sofia."

"I . . . I will do my best to make the right decision, sir."

No amount of street grime could dull the intensity of Lynsley's sapphirine gaze. "I am counting on it." He rose and reached for his hat. "Now, if that's all, I shall return home for breakfast." A drizzle of coal dust and decayed cabbage fell from its brim. "And a bath."

As the hour for her ride with De Winton drew closer, Sofia was still brooding over the early morning meeting. There were a number of unanswered questions. . . .

Rose added a last hairpin and stepped back. "Shall you wear the shako or the chip straw bonnet with the emerald ribbon?"

"You go ahead and choose," she replied, averting her gaze from the looking glass. Lynsley's trust was both flattering and frightening. Decisions, decisions—she couldn't afford to make the tiniest error in judgment.

The maid eyed her with some concern. "Did you not sleep well, milady? You are looking a trifle peaked."

"Lord Lynsley is anxious to have this mission resolved as soon as possible," she replied obliquely, unwilling to admit to any weakness of body or spirit. Rose was likely asked to report on any wavering.

"He wants every mission completed without delay. But not at the risk of an agent pushing herself too hard. That is how mistakes are made. Perhaps you ought to delay your outings for a day or two—"

"No." Sofia shook her head. "I dare not put off Lord De

Winton. In many ways, he holds the key to my success."
She did not elaborate. Nor did Rose expect her to do so. "I
must whet his appetite, make him think that he is close to
tasting my charms."

"Then let us ensure that you are a feast for the eyes." The
maid made a few adjustments to the tumble of curls, then
chose the shako and set it at a jaunty angle.

The curling ostrich feathers kissed Sofia's cheek, creating a look that was both saucy and seductive. "You are a
magician," she murmured as Rose added a touch of color
to her lips.

Would that she could work her own magic on De Winton. Putting aside her other thoughts, she made herself concentrate on the task at hand. It was imperative that she coax
her way back into his good graces. The coming meeting
with the keyholders could unlock the last little secret of the
clandestine consortium. Armed with the names of the prin-
cipals and the lists she had discovered in the antiquities,
Lynsley would be in a position to shut down the operation
and bring the miscreants to justice.

All she needed was to learn the identity of the leader.

Rose arranged a lush pink Kashmir shawl over the
shoulders of her azure carriage dress. "There—that ought
to make the man's mouth water."

"The trick will be to stay just out of reach of his teeth,"
murmured Sofia.

"Trust in yourself, milady, and you will be more than a
match for any predator," said her maid.

"Right." Sofia hefted her velvet reticule as if it were a
weapon. "Time to go."

"Her ladyship is not at home, milord."

Aware of Sofia's afternoon date with a mantua maker,

Osborne was ready for the butler's response. "Yes, she did mention she had an earlier appointment in Bond Street." He made a show of consulting his pocketwatch. "Ah, it appears I'm a touch early. I'll wait, if you don't mind."

The man blinked but slowly stepped aside and gestured for him to enter the town house. "Very good, sir."

"The parlor will be fine." Osborne started across the marble tiles before the butler could direct him to the drawing room. "The lady and I do not stand on ceremony."

"A glass of port or sherry, sir?" asked the man, following on his heels. "Or tea?"

Osborne picked up a book on Roman antiquities and began thumbing through the pages. "No, thank you. Her Ladyship has been asking for my opinion of these engravings, so I'll just take a seat and have a quiet study until she returns."

Taking the hint, the butler nodded gravely and drew the door silently shut behind him.

Osborne waited for several minutes before setting the volume aside and easing the latch open. The hall was deserted, and through the curve of carved balusters, the stairs looked clear as well. He slipped out and hurried up the carpeted treads. From casual conversation, he knew that Sofia's bedchamber was at the back of the town house, overlooking the garden. At this time of day, the tweenies would be done with their charwork.

As for her lady's maid . . .

Luck remained on his side. The quarters were empty. He would, however, have to work quickly to avoid the embarrassment of being caught in her rooms. His lips thinned to a wry grimace. He could claim an amorous assignation, which might satisfy a servant. The lady, however, was more likely to throw a punch to his jaw than invite him to slide between her sheets.

He cast a long look at the carved tester bed. Beneath the eiderdown coverlet and plump pillows was a tantalizing peek of creamy white linen, the delicate scalloped edges threaded with gossamer silk.

Tempting though it was to imagine Sofia's long limbs stretched out among the folds, the rattle of a coal scuttle reminded him he had no time to waste in idle daydreams.

He was, after all, a man on a mission.

Moving on to the escritoire by the window, he checked the blotter and her lettercase, then opened the top drawer and began a methodical search of its contents. *How strange*, he thought after riffling through the last little compartment. No passionate billet-doux, no miniature of her late husband, no diary, no . . . nothing. For a lady who had friends and family abroad, she had no correspondence, no estate documents, no mementos from home.

It was as if her previous life had not existed.

Frowning, he circled around to the dressing tables. Other than a pair of scent bottles and a plain hairbrush and comb, the top was bare of the copious pots and potions he was used to seeing in a lady's boudoir. *Simple, spartan.* A pin box and two leather jewel cases sat aligned in military precision along the edge of the gilt wood.

Osborne opened the first case. Glittering emeralds, rich rubies, lustrous pearls—it was no surprise that a contessa possessed a wealth of expensive necklaces and bracelets. Carefully smoothing the velvet flaps back in place, he refastened the clasp.

The second box held an equally impressive selection of earbobs and jeweled pendants. He was just about to close the lid when his hand brushed up against a small gold locket, half-hidden under a diamond-studded Maltese cross. The plain case, its worn surface nicked with age, looked very out of place among the sparkling baubles.

Curious, he clicked the cover open.

It might have been Sofia staring out at him, save that the painted features were a touch softer, a shade sadder.

Again, there was nothing terribly unusual in the fact that a young lady kept an heirloom locket with her mother's portrait tucked away among her valuables.

And yet . . .

Osborne sat back heavily on the chinoise chair. He had an excellent eye for art, and there was something about the faded image that drew a whisper from the depth of his throat.

"Bloody hell."

Fisting the filigree chain, he tucked the locket into his waistcoat pocket and quickly straightened up the tabletop. He had only a short walk to follow up on his hunch.

"You are looking very lovely, Contessa," said De Winton as he handed Sofia up to the seat of his high-perch phaeton.

"How very kind of you to say so. I was afraid you might be angry over my little indiscretion the other night." She deliberately settled her leg against his. "Osborne had been hounding me for some time. He wouldn't take no for an answer."

A flick of the whip set the horses into a brisk trot. "You did not look to be protesting too loudly," he replied.

"Oh, come now, Adam. I never pretended to be a nun. And I don't imagine that *you* are a monk."

His mouth relaxed slightly. "Hardly. A life of pious celibacy would not be at all to my taste."

"Exactly," teased Sofia. It required all of her mental discipline to play the role of jaded flirt. The man was a depraved dastard, a party to murder and fraud all because of personal greed. She would much rather have thrashed him to within an inch of his life.

Instead, she held her outrage in check, knowing that by fighting deception with deception she could help bring all the miscreants to justice. "And speaking of taste, it is far more fun to sample a variety of treats, don't you think, rather than stick to a steady diet of the same thing day after day?"

De Winton laughed at the innuendo. "Seeing as you had been absent from several parties, I thought that perhaps your appetite was satisfied by sweetness and sunshine."

"It was merely embarrassment that kept me away. I was afraid I had given you the wrong impression."

"You might have saved the first bite for me." He eyed her with a wolfish leer. "So, you are still interested in finding out what special pleasures your key gives entrée to here in London?"

"Oh, yes." Sofia leaned in, close enough for her feathers to tickle his jaw. There was a softness to its shape—the pale skin reminded her of the underbelly of a cod—and the scent of his cologne had a decadent sweetness that nearly made her gag. "Very much so."

Manuevering his team through a tight turn, De Winton seemed to be taking a malicious satisfaction in drawing out the silence.

Did he wish for her to beg? Some men found it exhilarating to wield such power over a woman.

Summoning all her strength, Sofia edged her body a touch closer to his. The fight was no longer just a matter of principle. It was now personal. Among the victims of

De Winton's crimes could well have been her own cousin. She would consort with the devil himself to see justice done.

"Do say I am forgiven, Adam," she pleaded. "I am simply dying to know what you and your friends do behind locked doors."

"Osborne won't be invited." His flash of teeth was likely meant as a smile. "Is that a problem?"

"None whatsoever," she said.

"Good. The meeting is not yet set. I will let you know in a day or two when and where."

"I can hardly wait." Sofia stroked the folds of her skirts as she gave him a coy look. "Will I have a good time?"

De Winton laughed. "I promise it will be an experience that you won't soon forget."

Chapter Eighteen

$\mathcal{T}$he Duke of Sterling was at home, and in response to Osborne's calling card, he sent a servant to escort him to the library.

"Thank you for giving me reason to set aside my steward's report." Sterling removed his spectacles and pinched the bridge of his nose. "I trust him to make the decision about sowing wheat or rye, but the fellow's feelings are hurt if I don't read over his reasonings."

"Duty is often tedious," murmured Osborne politely.

The duke sighed. "Yes. I confess that I find much more pleasure in translating Cicero than the current technical data on farming. But I'm sure you did not come here for a lecture on ancient Rome."

"Actually, I did." Osborne was quick to smile. "I was wondering if I might see the display of Roman coins in your South Gallery. Lady Hentman asked me for some ideas for a decorative frieze in her morning room, and I was thinking of suggesting a motif of classical portraits."

"I am always delighted to show my collection to someone who appreciates art." Sterling rose. "Come this way."

As Osborne remembered, the glass case was filled with burnished bronzes and gleaming golds. He took his time over the display, pretending to study the nuances of the different faces. "Magnificent," he finally murmured. "Would you mind if I made a few quick sketches?"

"Why, not at all, not at all," replied the duke.

"The thing is, I seem to have forgotten my copybook." Osborne gave an apologetic smile. "Might I trouble you for pencil and paper?"

As he had hoped, Sterling waved off the problem. "It's no trouble. There are writing supplies in the desk next door. I shall just be a moment."

As soon as the duke was out of view, Osborne hurried over to the wall of family portraits. Stopping before the gilt-framed canvas of the duke's daughter, he drew out the locket and thumbed the case open. Just as he suspected, the miniature was an exact copy of the painting.

His breath caught in his throat. Seeing the larger image, Osborne was struck by the subtle resemblances to Sofia. The same winged brows, the same slant of the cheekbones, the same determined set of the mouth. Rather than shed any light on the subject, the painting only deepened the mystery surrounding her and Lynsley's strange request.

If Sofia was the duke's granddaughter, why was there a secrecy surrounding the family connection? And even more puzzling, what was she doing stealing valuables from the *ton*?

The more he thought about it, the more it made no sense at all. And he doubted that the marquess would answer any questions. . . .

"Good God, where did you get that?" For a large man, Sterling was surprisingly light on his feet.

Osborne made no effort to prevent the duke from snatching up the locket. "I am very sorry, Your Grace. But at the moment, I am not at liberty to say."

Sterling fingered the worn case, then traced the delicate brushstrokes with a trembling hand. "I had this made as a keepsake for Elizabeth on her eighteenth birthday." A tear rolled down his cheek.

"I thought I recognized the face," said Osborne softly. "And so I borrowed it from the owner to see if my hunch was correct."

"Please tell your acquaintance that I will pay any price to have it, especially if I can learn how it was obtained." Sterling wiped at his cheek. "I was estranged from my daughter, you know. On account of her eloping with a man I considered beneath her. How I paid for my pride and my prejudice! It took months for me to learn of her death. His voice turned ragged. "It was an epidemic of influenza, which also struck down her husband and newborn child. By the time I journeyed to their village, all mementos of her had disappeared from the cottage where they lived."

So, the duke didn't know about Sofia?

"The current owner is not offering it for sale, Your Grace," replied Osborne. "I'm afraid I must take it back. But now that I know its provenance for sure, I promise to see what I can do to reunite you with your lost . . . heirloom."

Sterling let the filigree chain slide slowly through his fingers. "You have always struck me as an honorable man, Osborne. I will trust you to keep your word."

Sofia untied the strings of her bonnet and tossed it on the entrance table. Shopping was more tiring than fencing drills, but at least the appointment on Bond Street had allowed her to cut short her ride with De Winton.

Things had gone well enough with the Scarlet Knight, she decided, though his touch now made her skin crawl. Compared to Osborne . . .

No, she would not allow her thoughts to go there. Thankfully, De Winton had made no effort to offer his escort to the mantua maker. *Out of sight, out of mind.*

Shrugging off her shawl, Sofia entered the side parlor. She had been neglecting her study on ancient Rome, and if she was to keep up appearances for the duke, she ought to finish reading—

She stopped short on seeing Osborne sitting by the window. Legs outstretched, cravat loosened, he was perusing her book. But the tension in his shoulders belied the casual pose.

Masking her surprise with a curt nod, Sofia asked, "To what do I owe the pleasure of this unexpected visit?"

In answer, he held up the locket.

Sofia felt the color drain from her face. Taking a quick stride toward him, she tried to snatch it away.

He yanked it back out of reach. "Another gold bauble you have stolen?" he said sarcastically, a dangerous edge to his voice.

"No!" she said shrilly. "Damn you, Osborne. You have no right to riffle through my personal things."

"Where did you get it?" he demanded.

"None of your bloody business," she cried.

"Not mine, perhaps. But isn't the Duke of Sterling entitled to know that his granddaughter is masquerading as an Italian contessa?"

Sofia tried to speak but found her lips refused to form any words.

"Or perhaps it is the other way around," he added.

"*What?*" She didn't have to feign her confusion. He already had her off balance. Somehow she must regain her equilibrium.

"I've been sitting here for some time, trying to work out just what it is that you are up to." Osborne's eyes were cold as ice. "I cannot quite see Lord Lynsley being part of a scheme to deceive Sterling. So perhaps you are just taking advantage of a resemblance to the duke's daughter. Did you simply steal the locket? Or did you do away with Elizabeth Woolsey's daughter so that you could take her place and claim a rich inheritance?"

Sofia couldn't hold back a twitch of her lips. "And perhaps you are a long-lost relative of Anne Radcliffe—your imagination certainly rivals hers when it comes to the plot of a horrid novel."

"Have I got the story wrong?" he retorted. "Is the real motif theft? Given your skills at stealing, it wouldn't surprise me to hear you were planning to rob the duke of his priceless antiquities."

Her quirk of humor quickly faded. "In all seriousness, Osborne, do you really think I am capable of murder and such duplicity for the sake of greed? Just a few days ago, you did not believe it so."

He threw up his hands. "I don't know what to believe anymore."

"It's nothing like that," she replied.

"Then for God's sake, tell me what is going on! Why doesn't the duke know he has a granddaughter?"

Turning away, she moved to the sideboard and poured herself a sherry. Her hands were trembling badly. "There is no proof that I am of the duke's flesh and blood," she whispered.

Osborne drew a deep breath. "I've seen the original portrait, Sofia. The family resemblance is unmistakable."

She shook her head. "I happen to have black hair and green eyes. So do any number of orphans in St. Giles." As soon as the words were out of her mouth, she knew she had made a tactical blunder.

"Orphan?" Osborne narrowed his eyes. "Is this another one of your absurd lies? Lynsley himself told me that he had arranged for your riding master." His fist smacked against his palm. "Bloody hell, stop playing me for a fool, Sofia."

She sighed. "Would that I could."

His expression softened. "Trust me."

"This isn't about you, Deverill, or me. It's about . . ."

"*What?*"

As Osborne's demand echoed in her ears, it was joined by the whisper of Lynsley's earlier words. *I would prefer to keep this a secret.*

Torn between her heart and her sense of duty, she tried to put him off. "I—I can't tell you that either."

His hand was suddenly on her shoulder. If he had shouted, or shaken her, she could have fought back. But instead he simply stroked the ridge of her collarbone, then touched the pulse point at her throat. His fingertips thrummed with warmth, and she could feel the beat of his heart—strong, steady—in harmony with hers.

"I am so very sorry that you cannot bring yourself to share your secrets with me," he said. "I've tried to show myself worthy of your trust. But if heart is not enough, there's naught more I can do. I will leave you to your task."

A fleeting caress to her cheek and he stepped away. "The duke is an old man. He doesn't know the truth and deserves to. I hope you will have the compassion to tell him at some point."

"Wait!" she cried.

Osborne turned, a crooked smile on his face. His wind-blown hair fell in gilded curls around his collar.

"I will tell you what I can—"

He stopped her with a small shake of his head. "No more half-truths, Sofia. No more conundrums and innuendos. You either trust me wholeheartedly or not at all."

She hesitated.

He waited a fraction longer, then let himself out of the room.

Out of her life.

"Osborne." It was more of a murmur than a shout. Did she dare add force to it? Once the step was taken, there was no going back.

"Osborne!"

The silence seemed a mocking echo of her hesitation. He was gone for good, and who could blame him for turning a deaf ear to her call?

Then, as if by magic, the door reopened.

"Yes?"

She released a pent-up sigh, suddenly sure she was making the right decision. "It's true—Lynsley did arrange for my riding master. In fact, he arranged for all my schooling. There is an academy outside of London for . . . girls like me."

"A school for charity cases?" he asked after closing the door behind him.

"I suppose you could call it that," she said.

Osborne frowned. "Why the marquess, and not your real family?"

"I had no idea who my mother was. Not until a few days ago. The only family I ever knew was an aging whore in a run-down bawdy house in St. Giles," replied Sofia. "She told me that her sister appeared one night, weak with influenza and bearing a mysterious infant and the locket. But that was all she knew—her sibling died before dawn."

Osborne's expression softened, yet there was still suspicion in his eyes. "I don't understand about Lynsley, and why he would involve himself with the schooling of orphans, given all his other duties."

"No, I don't imagine you would. He keeps it very hush-hush."

"Why?" Exasperated, he threw up his hands. "Is it a state secret?"

A smile stole to her lips. "As a matter of fact, it is."

Seeing he was on the verge of another explosive outburst, she went on quickly. "Mrs. Merlin's Academy for Select Young Ladies is located outside of London. But it might as well be on the moon for all that the public knows of the place. You see, I was not joking about a school for spies."

"Damn it, Sofia," he began.

"Wait, hear me out."

His jaw clenched. "Go on."

"According to our headmistress, Lord Lynsley founded the Academy after reading a book on Hasan-I-Sabah, a Muslim caliph who raised a secret society of warriors at his mountain citadels. His men were known for their deadly skills and fanatic loyalty. The caliph used them only in times of dire danger to his rule. And legend has it they never failed on a mission. The very name *Hashishim*—or Assassins—was enough to strike terror in the heart of the Master's enemy."

"Assassins," repeated Osborne. "You don't mean to say you are trained to—"

"Kill? But of course," said Sofia calmly. "However, we prefer to use bloodshed as a last resort."

To his credit, he didn't blink. It was, however, an uncomfortably long silence before he asked, "How does the marquess recruit you?"

"I was not lying about the orphans either."

His expression still hovered between doubt and trust.

She wished she could gloss over the details. But Deverill Osborne had earned the right to know everything about her. Even the parts of her life that she was not terribly proud of.

"Lord Lynsley handpicks the students from the legion of children running wild in the stews," she went on. "I have been told he looks for courage and cleverness." It was not easy to speak so dispassionately about her past, but Sofia forced herself to go on. "He saw me fighting off a pimp who was trying to take away one of my friends, a smaller girl who was not tough enough to stand up for herself. Evidently I was quick enough and good enough with a blade to catch his eye."

Osborne was regarding her through the fringe of his lashes. Blurred by the sun-kissed flecks of gold, his expression was impossible to read.

"How old were you?"

Sofia lifted her shoulders. "Eleven or twelve—I cannot say for sure."

"And then what?"

"When we first come to the Academy, Mrs. Merlin shows us the large ornate globe that stands in her office and has us choose a name from the myriad of cities lettered on its surface. A new name for the new world we are about to enter." Sofia paused for a moment, thinking about her little muddy finger running at random over the varnished surface. "From there, we enter a program of rigorous training—learning proper speech and etiquette as well as traditional schoolroom subjects. And, of course, the martial arts."

"It sounds demanding," said Osborne. "I would imagine that not everyone achieves a passing grade."

"Competition for the Master Class is fierce. Those who don't make it are trained for other useful purposes, such as maids, tavernkeepers, or governesses. The marquess has eyes and ears in most every city from here to Peking."

"And you?"

Her mouth curled up at the corners. "I suppose you could say that my fellow Merlins and I are England's secret weapon."

He began to pace, and the slanting shadows hid his face. "How many of these warrior women are there?"

"Our number varies," answered Sofia. "Right now, the ranks of full-fledged Merlins are somewhat depleted, due to . . . circumstances beyond Lord Lynsley's control."

"Death?" he asked through gritted teeth.

"That is always a possibility," she said softly. "However, in this case, I was referring to matrimony."

"Good Lord." He turned slowly. "Perchance is one of your comrades named Siena?"

Sofia countered with her own question. "W-what do you know of Siena?"

"Only that she recently married one of my closest friends." He raked a hand through his hair. "It seems that . . . Well, it's rather a long story. And we have our own tale to sort out."

That was putting it mildly. However, before changing the subject, Sofia explained, "Siena was one of my roommates. I have not yet had a chance to meet the Earl of

Kirtland. Neither Shannon nor I were able to attend the wedding ceremony, for Academy rules forbid any public appearances where someone might wonder about our identity." The thought of her friends was another sharp reminder of how alone she was in the world. "I was not aware of your friendship with Lord Kirtland. But then, I suppose it is not surprising—you are friends with most everyone in Society."

"Julian is special," replied Osborne. "He and I have been through a lot together. On the field of battle, you quickly learn which comrades you would trust with your life."

She nodded. "Yes, I know what you mean."

His face pinched to an odd expression. His voice was equally enigmatic. "Yes, I imagine you do."

Was he shocked by her profession? Disgusted? The females of his world were all genteel, well-bred ladies, trained to excel in the social graces, rather than the sordid arts of war.

Despite the ache in her chest, Sofia gave a careless shrug. "No doubt you think me a hardscrabble hellion, unworthy to rub shoulders with the proper ladies of the *ton*. However, there are times when a female is best suited to root out the enemy, and I don't mind getting my hands dirty."

"I think . . ." Osborne turned, the sunlight from the window suffusing his features. "I think that you are, without question, the most admirable individual I have ever met. You make me ashamed of my own lily-white hands. We lords and ladies live in a world of pomp and splendor because you are willing to fight to defend our privileges."

Her cheeks were suddenly hot as molten steel, and to her surprise, Sofia realized she was blushing. *Damn*. She was acting like a giddy schoolgirl rather than a trained soldier.

"I fight to defend all of England, from the highborn patrician to the lowborn laborer."

His step was hesitant, halting. Reaching out through the shadows, Osborne framed her face with his hands. *Strong, sure.* There was nothing of the pampered aristocrat in his touch.

"Which makes you even more noble."

"Please, don't make me out to be a saint, Deverill. I have all too many flaws." She gave a rueful grimace. "Just ask Lord Lynsley. He'll assure you I am far from perfect."

"When next I speak to Lynsley, it will be on a different topic." He drew in a long breath and let his hands fall away. "But to return to you, and your reasons for being in London, does this mean your interest in De Winton is purely professional?"

"Yes. The marquess sent me here to see if I could uncover evidence of government corruption. He had reason to suspect that a ring of conspirators was manipulating military contracts and that the Duke of Sterling's grandson suspected the illegal activities. . . ."

Sofia went on to explain her mission as best she could, along with a brief summary of what she had learned so far. "There is much that is still conjecture. And the personal complication with the duke was, of course, completely unexpected. For the time being, it cannot interfere with my work."

"Have you made progress?"

"I have some ideas," she replied somewhat evasively. It was one thing to tell the truth—it was another to draw Osborne into danger. He had already risked enough on her account. "And some leads that are worth following up on."

"How can I help?" he demanded.

It was not really meant as a question. She saw in his eyes that he wouldn't take no for an answer.

"Your contacts among the *ton* could be very useful," she said slowly, careful not to give in too quickly.

"If I don't know the person in question, I will likely be acquainted with a close friend. In any case, I can get access to most anyone, and I am rather good at establishing myself as a trusted confidante."

"You could charm the scales off a snake," agreed Sofia with a small smile. However, she had no intention of letting him anywhere near the nest of vipers she had uncovered. "Though I would rather convince you to stay away from possible trouble—"

"Not a chance."

"I had a feeling you would say that." She exaggerated a sigh. "Very well, if you really wish to help, I would be grateful if you could approach Lord Coxe and see what you can find out about how he acquires his antiquities."

Osborne's well-shaped brows quirked in question. "Coxe? The man is over seventy years old! Surely you don't suspect him of being a criminal mastermind?"

"Not wittingly," replied Sofia. "But I have reason to suspect that messages between the conspirators, as well as valuable contraband, are being passed along inside cargos of expensive art." One of the lessons she had learned at the Academy was that the best lies always had a grain of truth to them. "If we knew what shipping firm handles his business and who arranges the deliveries, it could help shed light on the whole operation."

Coxe, a fellow member of her Roman society, was a noted collector who frequently received deliveries from all over Italy. That he was also a sweet old man, without an evil bone in his body, would ensure that Osborne would be off digging through harmless information.

His initial look of skepticism sharpened to a speculative stare. "I see what you mean. Clever of the bastards."

"Quite," she murmured.

Osborne pursed his lips. "Come to think of it, isn't that fellow Sforza involved in shipping?"

Damn, he was quick. Too quick. "Don't bother with Sforza or Familligi. Marco is already investigating their businesses."

"Marco?" Osborne's voice took on an odd edge. "You trusted him before me?"

"Marco is one of Lynsley's operatives," she murmured.

"So, the fellow is more than a braggart and a buffoon?"

"In fact, he was one of my instructors at the Academy."

"Dear God," growled Osborne. "I shudder to think what he teaches."

"Fencing, among other things." She grinned, hoping to further distract him from thoughts of the Scarlet Knights. "He is very good with a blade."

The force of his oath surprised her. "He had better keep it sheathed around me—and you. Else he'll be fishing his cods out of the Thames."

Surely Osborne wasn't . . . jealous? Though he was known for his even temperament and adroit avoidance of emotional entanglements, she knew that deep down he was a man who cared passionately about certain principles. *Honor. Friendship.*

She must not confuse his feelings for her as anything more than the concerns of a true gentleman.

"Marco is far too fond of his *gioelli de famiglia* to risk offending either of us, Deverill." Her teasing softened Osborne's scowl just a touch. "Besides, despite his braggadocio, he is a consummate professional. He won't leave a stone unturned in seeking to uncover what his fellow countrymen are up to here in London."

"Which is your way of tactfully telling me not to muck things up by getting in his way." He made a wry face. "I can't help but feel you have given me the easiest of all the assignments. I am to spend a comfortable evening drinking brandy and discussing art, while you expose yourself to God knows what sort of dangers."

"All of our roles are important," she said softly. "As for my next move, right now I do not anticipate any real danger. Aside from engaging in a bit more flirtation with De Winton, I have no other immediate plans."

Osborne didn't look completely convinced. "Promise me you will not take any rash steps without telling me. I have been thinking . . . The alley attack might well have been a warning that someone suspects you are not what you seem."

"Let us not imagine phantom dangers. We have enough real conundrums to contend with." Sofia saw his jaw tighten and quickly went on. "The chances that someone has discovered my real mission are very slim. Lynsley and his operatives are very good at what they do. As am I."

"Nonetheless . . ." His movements were like a quicksilver wink of sunlight. Before she quite realized what had happened, she was in his arms and the warmth of his lips grazed her cheek. "Promise me you will not take any untoward risks."

"I—I will do my best, Deverill."

"I suppose I must be satisfied with that." His mouth was no longer so gentle as it took her in a hard, possessive kiss. There was an oddly vulnerable note of longing to his whisper that left her slightly weak in the knees. "For now, at least."

A soft rap on the door interrupted his words. Reluctantly, he released his hold and allowed her to step back.

"Your pardon, milady."

Sofia noted with wry amusement that her maid did not wait for any reply before entering the room.

"If we do not begin dressing for the evening, you will be late for Countess of Wright's card party."

"Thank you, Rose," she said. "Lord Osborne was just taking his leave. I shall be up in a moment."

"Very good, milady." The maid's basilisk gaze lingered for a moment on Osborne before she took her leave.

"My fears are put slightly to rest by knowing that such a woman is standing guard over you," he murmured. "I, for one, would not care to risk her ire."

"I can't say that I blame you. I have reason to believe that Rose possesses a number of formidable skills, aside from her talents with hairpins and a crimping iron."

"Another of Lynsley's agents?" he asked.

"Yes."

"In that, at least, I have no quarrel with him." He cleared his throat. "As to this evening—"

"It is purely a social engagement. The countess has invited a group of her lady friends for a quiet evening of whist and supper. I am attending merely to keep up the appearance of seeking entrée into Society."

"Then I shall start in on making myself agreeable to Lord Coxe," said Osborne. "He often stops by at White's for a cigar and brandy before retiring for the night." A pause hovered between them, heavy with unspoken questions. But when he spoke again, it was simply to ask, "What about your plans for tomorrow?"

"I believe my schedule calls for a lecture at the Literary Ladies of Mayfair."

"If things change, you will let me know?"

"Please don't worry, Deverill." Sofia sidestepped an outright lie as she moved for the doorway.

He wasn't fooled by the manuever. "Sofia—"

"I had better go, before I incur Rose's wrath."

"Have a care, sweeting." His voice was as soft as the rustle of her silks. "May Luck watch over you like a hawk."

"And you, *cara*," she whispered as she hurried up the stairs.

But in truth, she sensed they would need more than luck to beat the Scarlet Knights at their own game.

Chapter Nineteen

*L*eaving the puzzled shipping clerk a generous payment for his efforts, Osborne tucked the copy of the manifest into his pocket and returned to the waiting hackney. He was no expert in the criminal underworld, but if the firm of Hillhouse and Brewster was hiding any nefarious activities, he would eat his hat, grosgrain ribbon and all.

Like Coxe, the two elderly proprietors of the business could not have been more happy to talk about the logistics of transporting valuables from abroad. Pretending an interest in assembling a private collection of his own, Osborne had asked a number of detailed questions, all of which had been answered with great openness. Files had been retrieved from the storerooms, and the recent records reviewed. He had even been invited to visit one of the ships docked in Greenwich.

Frowning, he took another look at the latest shipping bill. It only confirmed what he had seen for himself at the earl's town house. The items were naught but a rather boring assortment of marble fragments. Sculpted of solid stone, they were all of modest shape and size. Not a one offered a sliver of space in which to hide contraband goods or communication. Either Sofia's hunch was way off the mark.

Or she had deliberately sent him astray.

Had he been a fool to accept her story about the school for spies? A cadre of swashbuckling females headed by that paragon of propriety, Lord Lynsley? Osborne rubbed at his temples, admitting that were he to repeat a quarter of what he had heard the previous afternoon, he would be laughed out of his club. If not hauled off to Bedlam.

But however outrageous the details might sound, he did not really doubt Sofia's veracity. She cared—and passionately—about justice. It came through in any number of subtle ways. It was in her voice, her eyes, her body. The very texture of her being. A good many things could be faked, but not courage, not conviction.

And besides, Lynsley's odd reaction to the reports of Sofia's behavior corroborated her claims. A proper guardian, especially one as supposedly straightlaced as the marquess, would have had a fit of apoplexy on hearing of her exploits around Town.

Oh, yes, she was telling him the truth. Though not all of it.

Osborne sat in a brooding silence as the simple brick business buildings gave way to the elegant mansions of Mayfair. It didn't take much mental effort to come to the conclusion that she had made her decision for one of two reasons—either she didn't trust him to keep silent about her strategy, or she didn't think him capable enough to outwit or outfight the enemy.

He wasn't sure which was worse.

After another stretch of melancholy musing, he rejected the first possibility. She knew him better than to think he would spill her secrets in some unguarded moment of bluster. Which left him facing the fact that she must consider him a bumbling ox.

Any gentleman worth his salt would find that thought rather irritating, decided Osborne. He did not consider himself to be a conceited coxcomb, but he *was* a battle-hardened veteran of the Peninsular War. His steadiness under fire had been tested time and time again, and though he didn't have as many medals as his friend Kirtland, he had saved his share of lives.

Come to think of it, he hadn't done too badly in defending *her* neck from attack.

That the lady considered his skills somehow lacking piqued his pride. If Sofia would not allow him to prove his worth, he would simply have to take matters into his own hands.

Osborne expelled a breath, then rubbed the fog from the windowpane. *Deception and diversion.* She would soon find that such tactics could be a two-edged sword.

Sofia stared at the card on the silver tray, then set aside her notebooks and followed the butler to the drawing room.

"Adam, what a pleasant surprise," she exclaimed, approaching her guest. "May I offer you some brandy?"

De Winton still had his gloves and hat in his hands. "Regretfully, I am in somewhat of a hurry and cannot stay." He looked a little on edge. "I just wanted to inform you that the special meeting of the Golden Key members has been set. It's tonight."

"Tonight?" echoed Sofia.

"A special celebration, in honor of the arrival of a new

shipment of . . . but, of course, you know what is arriving from Venice. I'm sure you will not want to miss it."

Though his gaze was hooded, she could tell he was watching her intently. She knew that she could not refuse. Not that she wanted to. "I wouldn't dream of it."

"I hoped you would say as much." His eyes had an over-bright glitter, leading her to wonder whether he had already been indulging in opium. His wits still seemed sharp enough, though. "It is to take place at the Puff of Paradise, a special establishment hidden in the stews of Southwark. A carriage will call for you at eight."

"No need," she replied. "I'll come in my own conveyance."

De Winton shook his head. "Trust me, it's better this way. Your man does not know the streets, or the procedure. We prefer not to draw attention to our gatherings."

Sofia didn't dare argue. "At eight, then. I will be ready."

"One last thing." He smoothed at the scarlet silk of his waistcoat. "It goes without saying, but be sure to bring your key. We go by the same rituals here in London as in Venice."

"Yes. Of course."

"Excellent. Then I shall take my leave." De Winton left off toying with his watch fobs to flourish a farewell. "*Ciao*, Contessa."

Again, Sofia was struck by his mood, which seemed an odd mix of anticipation and apprehension. The celebrations planned for the evening must be even more dissolute than usual, she decided. But De Winton's appetites were not of primary concern.

Turning her gaze from the mantel, Sofia hurried for the stairs. He hadn't given her much time. For a moment, she thought about sending word to Osborne. But only for an instant. Aside from the fact that De Winton had been very clear that the meeting was only for keyholders, this was *her* responsibility, *her* risk. Osborne would be a dangerous distraction. His valor was unquestioned—it was her own heart that might waver. She couldn't take the chance of being weakened by the worry that some harm would befall him.

She was a Merlin, and her wings were strong enough to lift her over any challenge.

A tiny sigh fluttered from her lips. Though she had no qualms about flying into the unknown, she would not have minded having Marco around to watch her back. However, he had sent word this morning that he had been asked to join Familligi at a gaming hell in Seven Dials. There was no point in changing plans now.

She would go well-armed, of course. A small Italian pocket pistol in her skirt pocket and a stiletto strapped to her leg, along with an Indian throwing star disguised as a hair ornament. *Silk and steel.* Between the two, she should have no trouble getting the job done.

From the shadows of the garden wall, Osborne watched De Winton hurry down the steps of Sofia's town house and set off on foot in the direction of the park. A prickling of foreboding ran down his spine. The Scarlet Knight did not often appear in the light of day. *Coincidence?* He doubted it. His suspicions that Sofia had misled him seemed confirmed.

However, he was ready to get back on track.

Moving out from his hiding place, he edged into the alleyway between the mews and slipped a knife blade into the gate lock of Sofia's garden. A twist turned the tumblers, allowing the iron-banded oak to open a crack. He followed along the line of the privet hedge to the back of the town house terrace, where thick vines of ivy rose up to the slate gables.

His earlier surveillance of her bedchambers and its surroundings had revealed the thin ledge of Portland stone running the length of the building just below the window casements. He flexed his hands. It had been a while since he had scaled the cliffs around Badajoz, but he was not yet in his dotage. Slowly, silently, he worked his way up through the curling greenery, giving thanks that the angle of the setting sun wreathed the gardens in shade.

The day was still warm, and with any luck, Sofia's window would be open to the breeze . . .

"The crimson silk, milady?" The maid's question floated out clear as a bell. "Are you sure? If things go wrong, it won't provide much camouflage."

Osborne heard Sofia laugh. "If things go wrong, I'll likely not make it out to the streets. But let us look at the brighter side—red is far more alluring than indigo, and as I mean to draw the enemy into making a fatal mistake, I'll take the chance."

So, he had been right about her plans.

"Very well, milady. But as a precaution, I ought to know where you are going, in order to pass on the information to Lord Lynsley."

"Agreed," replied Sofia. "De Winton named a place called the Puff of Paradise, in Southwark. As for information, the marquess can find all of my notes, locked in the secret compartment of my escritoire drawer. The key is hidden beneath the velvet cushion of my jewel case."

The Puff of Paradise. Osborne had heard rumors of the exotic opium den. It would not be too hard to find.

"I will inform him, if necessary," said the maid. "Do

stop fidgeting, milady. As it is, we have our work cut out for us to have you ready to leave at eight."

"Forgive me, Rose. I find it hard to sit still, now that the time for action is finally near."

"I understand." Osborne heard the click of metal on metal. "You are taking your pistol, I presume?"

"Along with several blades," said Sofia. "I shall have a choice of weapons at my fingertips . . ."

Having heard enough, Osborne started to inch away from the mullioned glass.

"What was that?" Sofia's voice rose a notch. "I heard something stirring outside."

"A dove, no doubt," said Rose. "Don't move—I'm using the forged steel hairpins, in case you have need to pick a lock."

"I've my key," quipped Sofia. "Let us hope it will open the way to shutting down this evil operation."

Osborne heard no more as he made his way to the far end of the building before slipping back down to earth. He had now a time and a place. Come hell or high water, Sofia was not going into the night alone.

"How very interesting." Sofia regarded the arched door. Screened from the main room of the opium den by a line of potted palms, the oiled teakwood was an intricately carved panel of eye-popping erotic scenes. Men with ruby-tipped phalluses. Women with pink diamonds between their legs. Sexual positions that must have required years of yoga training . . .

"It's designed to put everyone in the mood for what pleasures lie inside," leered Sforza.

"The patrons seem to need little added encouragement to enjoy themselves," observed Sofia. Squinting through the haze of smoke and fizzled light, she saw that a goodly number of gentlemen were already occupying the velvet-cushioned banquettes. Scrims of colored silks hung from the ceiling, their sinuous shapes dancing in the flickering flames of brass braziers and latticed lanterns. "Do you turn a good profit?"

Sforza snickered. "They pay an arm and a leg for admittance."

Those were not the only appendages involved, noted Sofia. The barmaids serving drinks were all as naked as newborns, and some of the men had already followed suit.

"The place makes an obscene amount of money—like all our ventures," the Italian went on. "Our leader is a genius when it comes to—"

"Upstairs is by invitation only," interrupted De Winton, signaling the hulking porter to undo the latch. "For special guests. We have our own private room. Come, let us show you. The others will be along shortly."

Sofia stepped into the dark stairwell. Inside her glove, the gold key pressed hard against her palm. What did it unlock? She still didn't have a clue and would have to go on very carefully. A stumble at this stage of the game could put the whole mission in jeopardy.

"Turn to the left at the top of the stairs." De Winton's voice had an otherworldy quality to it. Was the potent perfume and exotic incense already affecting her head? Sofia covered her nose and tried to draw in a breath of fresh air.

The stairwell opened up to a large octagonal entrance hall. A velvet curtain cloaked each of the corners, but from the sounds of gurgled laughter floating through the air, she guessed that there were a number of pleasure rooms hidden behind the draperies.

"In here." De Winton beckoned for her to pass through the folds of shimmering scarlet.

Candlelight cast a reddish glow over the tasseled floor cushions and thick Persian carpets. A glance around showed that the walls were hung with iridescent silks in jewel-tone shades of topaz and amethyst. A matching pair of gilded wood screens angled out from the back corners, and set in the very center of the room was a low divan, covered in sumptuous Moroccan leather.

A pleasure palace, indeed, thought Sofia, half expecting a genie to pop out of the ornate oil lamp hanging overhead.

"Here is your change of clothing." De Winton handed her a set of folded garments. "You may change behind the far screen, while we use this one."

Sofia stared down at the gauzy garments in dismay. *Damn.* She doubted the flimsy material would hide her weapons.

"Yes, relax and get comfortable, Contessa," added Sforza. "We want to make sure you enjoy your experience with us."

She would have to change plans along with her attire. A wry twist came to her lips as she shook out the set of harem pantaloons and sleeveless blouson. It looked as if she would have no choice but to fight with her bare hands if it came down to a struggle. Given the sheerness of the silk, she might as well be donning nothing at all.

Smoothing the folds into some semblance of modesty, she stepped out from behind the shelter of the screen, leaving her own clothing and weapons wrapped together in a neat roll.

"You look ravishing, Contessa," said Sforza with a broad

wink at De Winton. Both men had slipped into flowing Bedouin robes tied at the waist with a scarlet sash.

"Good enough to eat," he agreed. "Have a seat. I'll call for the refreshments to be brought in." He punctuated his words with a loud clap. "Gulmesh!"

Sofia eyed the empty cushions as she sat down. "Should we not wait for the others?"

De Winton waved off the question. "There's been a delay. We are to start without them."

"They will be coming, won't they?" she probed. "My friends in Venice speak so highly of your organization. I am anxious to meet everyone. Especially the man in charge."

Sforza laughed. "What makes you think our head is a man? A clever little hussy like you is proof enough that females can possess the cunning of a Machiavelli."

Sofia felt her mouth go a bit dry. Was he merely playing games with her? Or was there a possibility she had missed a key clue? Feeling their eyes upon her, she covered her confusion with a show of bravado. "Of course we are clever and cunning—we have to be, in order to get anywhere in a man's world."

"A toast to the feminine mind." De Winton uncorked one of the bottles that the servant had brought in. "You must try our special blend of brandy and cognac." A splash of amber spirits filled her glass.

"I brought along a rare vintage from Tuscany," said Sforza. "Have a taste, Adam, and tell me what you think." He poured two portions of the red wine. *"Cin cin."*

The fortified brandy was cloyingly sweet. Sofia choked down a swallow as she regrouped her thoughts. "Let me take a guess. Lady Guilford seems to possess some talent."

"Only in the boudoir. Her mind is not nearly as dexterous as her hands," replied Sforza. "Guess again."

Before she could speak, the servant reappeared, this time bearing a tray of Oriental water pipes. The inlaid brass took on a coppery glow in the lamplight, and the coiled hoses, with their carved amber mouthpieces, looked like cobras rising out of the shadows.

With a slow flourish, DeWinton reached into his robes and withdrew three gold boxes. "You are, of course, familiar with the ritual from Venice. Each of the keys unlocks an individual box, and inside it is a share of the monthly profits, divided according to how many shares each member owns." He set them on the divan. "But seeing as this is your first meeting, and your share of the London operations has yet to be worked out, we decided to prepare a special treat for you. An initiation, if you will, into our Society."

"It is an honor to be admitted to your company," murmured Sofia, trying to think of a way to keep the guessing game alive. "But—"

De Winton pushed one of the boxes her way. "But, of course, you must show us that your key fits and is not a well-made fake. There is only one craftsman who knows the secret of cutting in the correct grooves to open the locking mechanisms."

Holding her breath, Sofia inserted her key and gave it a turn.

Snick.

The lid popped open. Inside, lying on a bed of rose petals, was a sticky substance rolled in the rough shape of a ball. Its color was a deep cinnamon, speckled with poppy-red flecks.

"Opium of the highest grade," said De Winton softly. "Mixed with our little secret additions to give it an added punch."

"Let me show you how to use it." Sforza took up the

razor-sharp knife from the tray and shaved off a few thick curls into the bowl of her pipe. Next to it was a small bowl filled with glowing coals. "You take the tongs and hold a coal like so."

De Winton polished the pipe's mouthpiece on his sleeve, then handed it to her. "Abracadabra. Now, you simply take a puff of pleasure."

With a languid laugh, Sofia drew in a mouthful of the pungent smoke, trying to use her yoga training to inhale as little of it as possible. *Concentration. Control.* She must keep her wits about her.

"Sweet," she said, expelling her breath with a soft sigh. "Won't you join me in a taste?"

Both men had already fired up their own pipes. "No, your portion is a very rare and costly blend." It was De Winton who answered. "It's for you to savor, compliments of our leader."

Ah, finally the chance to turn the tables in her favor. Reaching across the divan, Sofia teased a caress to De Winton's hand. "My dear Adam, I am beginning to fear that I have fallen out of your good graces. Have you decided to favor your mystery lady over me?" She pursed a provocative pout. "Tell me the name of my rival so that I may know whose charms I must compete with."

"You still haven't figured it out?"

The opium had to be a powerful narcotic, for even with exercising extreme care, Sofia felt a wave of dizziness wash over her. "Give me another hint," she coaxed.

Perhaps it was the sweetness of the perfumed smoke, but the only female who came to mind was the young widow. *Serena Sommers?* Surely not. Despite her slightly naughty parties, Lady Serena had a certain air of innocence about her. A daughter of privilege, she had been pampered, protected all of her life. The idea of her as the mastermind of a criminal organization seemed crazy.

"I'll do more than that," said De Winton. The candles flickered in a sudden swirl of air, setting off a strange flare in his gaze.

No doubt her own eyes looked filled with fire.

"We owe this all to Lady Serena," he went on.

"I confess, I wouldn't have guessed her capable of putting together such a complex organization," answered Sofia. "I see I underestimated her."

"Many people do." Through a puff of smoke gleamed a pearly flash of teeth. "She looks so dainty and demure, doesn't she? But then, we all know that looks can be deceiving."

"Indeed," she agreed, ignoring De Winton's veiled innuendo. When in doubt, it was best to brazen out any suspicions. "Most people see Roxbury as a glorified clerk and Andover as a mere shopkeeper, but they obviously have brains and a bold imagination. Concord has connections with influential politicians, while Neville has made friends with many of the wealthy peers in Town. And with your Italian friends supplying the ships and the banking connections . . ."

"So you figured that out for yourself?" said De Winton. "I commend you, Contessa. You are very clever too."

His answer was final confirmation of her surmises. She now knew all the names for sure. The hard part was over. From here, it was simply a matter of getting back to Lynsley, as soon as she found an excuse to absent herself.

If only she didn't feel so lethargic . . .

"Yesshhh. I hope to play a large role in your future plansshh." Sofia realized she was slurring.

"We'll see." De Winton added more of the special opium to her pipe and fanned its burn to a red hot glow.

"I . . . I . . . ," she stuttered. Her words dissolved in a fit of giggles. Somehow the inability to speak seemed funny. The room began to spin. Things were suddenly blurry . . .

The last thing Sofia heard as she slumped to the floor was De Winton's throaty laughter joining with hers.

Chapter Twenty

*D*amn.

Osborne was growing more and more uneasy with each passing minute. Sofia had passed through the guarded portal some time ago. He couldn't imagine why she would be up there so long with De Winton and Sforza . . .

Yes, actually he could.

Thinking of her indulging in any intimacies with the dastards drew another low oath from his lips.

"Care fer another drink, luv?" One of the barmaids sidled up to him, flashing a saucy wink. "Or a pipe? I got a cozy little booth in the corner, where we can be private."

"Thank you, but I haven't yet decided what I want." Waving her away, Osborne edged closer to the screen of palms. The low light and hazy shadows hid his movements from the guard. And if spotted, he could always feign a drunken disorientation. He slanted another look around, but no one seemed to take any notice of his shuffling steps or bizarre dress. The other patrons were all in various states of undress, so the fact that he had tied a scarf around his head, pirate style, to hide his blond locks and had left his coat and cravat in the alleyway did not look a hair out of place.

Indeed, compared to the hulking Sikh guard, with his towering turban and sashed robes bristling with weaponry, Osborne felt that he blended right into the woodwork.

Slipping deeper into the overlapping fronds, he moved in for a closer look at the carved door. He had been told that admittance to the top floor was by invitation only. But it seemed very odd that a walking arsenal was necessary to enforce the policy. Something was not quite right here—he was sure of it. His hands clenched. He should have thought to bring something more menacing than a penknife with him.

However, if Sofia did not reappear soon, he would force the hinges open with his bare hands.

As the brass latch gave a loud click, Osborne crouched down among the terra-cotta pots. A moment later, De Winton and Sforza emerged from the stairwell. Both men were laughing, and their scimitar smiles sent a stab of fear through his chest.

Where the devil was Sofia? Inching as close as he dared, Osborne strained to overhear their words.

"You go see that Roxbury has the coach ready. I'll check on the warehouse," said De Winton, brushing a bit of ash from his sleeve. "We'll meet back here in a half hour and finish the contessa off, if need be."

Sforza laughed. "She will not be waking from that dose. I mixed it myself. A pity—I was looking forward to swiving the bitch before we got rid of her."

"Both our pricks will be on the chopping block if we don't take care of business before pleasure," replied De Winton grimly. "After we dispose of the contessa, we will head to Lady Serena's town house. Understood? After to-night, there will be no loose ends left to tie up."

Osborne felt sick. Both ladies knew too much.

"*Si,*" said the Italian.

De Winton signaled to the swarthy Sikh. "I'll have Arjun make one last check on things upstairs, then remain on guard here to ensure that she does not leave."

Osborne inched forward, grateful for the haze of smoke and wildly flickering patterns of the latticed lamps.

Framed in the open doorway, the guard bowed and listened intently to the whispered instructions.

"Yes, *memsahib.* It shall be done," he growled as the two conspirators turned and hurried away.

Osborne allowed the door to fall nearly closed before darting out from the greenery and sticking his penknife between the moldings to keep it from locking. He waited a moment, then slipped inside.

Blinking lights, dancing smoke, whirling colors. Sofia blinked, trying to bring the room into focus. How odd, but her head felt swathed in silk.

"Mmmmmmmm." Her own voice was weirdly altered as well. It sounded as if she were purring like a cat.

She had a feeling that she should be fighting the sensation, yet couldn't quite put her finger on why. Struggle seemed far too much of an effort. It was very pleasant lying on the pillows, listening to the laughter from outside and the lazy rasp of her own breathing.

As she gave a feline stretch, a languid, liquid laziness took possession of her limbs. Sleep beckoned. Why resist?

Sweet dreams.

Whatever the reason she was here, it could wait until later.

*   *   *

The only light in the stairwell was the guard's glass-globed lantern. Praying that the Sikh would not look back, Osborne kept close to the man's heels. At the top of the landing, the guard headed to the right, allowing him to duck into the opposite room—where he quickly discovered that he wasn't alone. Lolling on the thick Persian carpet were two middle-aged gentlemen, naked save for their garters and stockings. The low light of the brass brazier showed they were surrounded by a bevy of exotic courtesans, ranging from a creamy-skinned Swede to an ebony African.

A redheaded Celtic beauty rose and with an inviting shimmy of her hips sidled up next to him. "Care to join in?"

Shaking his head, Osborne pointed across the way. "I'm here to meet a friend," he mouthed. "But thank you."

She made a moue of disappointment and sought to twine her arms around his neck.

He slipped away, leaving only his pirate headscarf in her grasp. Would that he could extract himself—and Sofia—as easily from this hellhole. *Where was she?* Taking shelter in the next doorway, he waited for the Sikh to reappear. There were six other rooms, but for the moment, discretion still seemed the better part of valor. Until he knew what all he was facing, he dared not risk a confrontation.

Yet every excruciating second counted. Time was ticking away.

A flutter of velvet and the guard finally emerged from behind the scarlet drape. Padding on bare feet, the man did not glance up as he tugged at his *kirpan* and headed back down the stairs.

One, two three . . . Osborne counted to ten before crossing the hall and fisting aside the folds of fabric.

Lying spreadeagle on a stack of silken pillows, Sofia appeared dead to the world. Her eyes were closed, and her hair had come loose from its pins. As he came closer, he saw she was dressed in Eastern garb rather than her own English clothing. The gauzy Turkish trousers were cinched at the waist with a sash of embroidered silk, and the top was a sleeveless scrim of linen, so sheer that the dark areolae of her breasts were plainly visible.

"Sofia." His voice was barely more than a whisper. In the smoke-smudged light, he couldn't tell whether or not she was breathing.

"Sofia." He managed to say it louder, and to his relief, her lashes stirred ever so slightly.

He lifted her gently into his arms.

One lid lifted, showing a peek of glassy green.

"Can you stand, sweeting?" he asked.

A giggle slipped from her lips. Her legs were still unresponsive, but her hands came suddenly alive with amorous intent, caressing at his crotch and trying to work free the fastenings of his trousers.

"Mmmmmmm." Her kiss missed the mark by several inches. "Y' smell good 'nough to eat."

Osborne steadied her sway. There was indeed a cloying scent of sweetness in the air. Clove, cinnamon, and some earthier spices that threatened to suffocate his senses. The effect was unsettling, unpleasant.

Realizing how deeply she was drugged, he slapped her face. "Sofia. Wake up."

She laughed, then frowned. "That hurt. Kiz me instead, Dev."

He evaded her lips. "Yes, sweeting, I'll kiss you, but later. Let's get some air."

Sofia slumped, her body going slack against his.

"Mmmmm. Too tired t' move. Let's lie down." Her speech was growing more slurred.

Tilting her chin, Osborne saw that her pupils were dilated. He slapped her again, harder.

The sting drew a flutter of life. She tried to lift her hands and push him away. "Yes, that's it—fight back," he whispered.

Her groan was more of a slurred mewl. And after a moment, Sofia was once again limp as a kitten.

Pushing through the red curtain, he moved into the foyer and looked around for a way out. The Sikh guard was watching the stairs, and even if he managed to slip past the man, the two hulking porters posted at the main entrance were certainly in De Winton's pay. There must be another route of escape. He tried to think, but the sickening scent of the smoke was making him light-headed.

"Sunshine!" Sofia's head rolled back, and she stared at him with glazed eyes. Her pupils were nearly as big as saucers as her gaze drifted to the flaming wall sconces. Her face lit in a beatific smile. "Sunshine."

Keep moving, keep moving. There wasn't a moment to lose. He had to prevent her from falling unconscious.

A side door opened, and a naked man stumbled out, weaving a path for the Pipe Parlor. Following right behind him, a woman wearing only a leather thong crawled out on her hands and knees.

"Any brandy left around here, luv?" she asked.

He nudged a half-empty bottle over with his foot.

"Yer an angel." Grabbing the amber glass, the harlot looked up with a grin. "The great Golden Gabriel."

"Take it with my blessings," he murmured. Craning his neck, he peered into the shadowed room. In the light of the single lamp, he could just make out a mattress on the floor, a tangle of silken sheets . . . and a window.

Osborne forced a leering smile. "What say you to spreading your wings with me and m' friend."

"The three of us?"

He nodded, already angling Sofia through the narrow door.

The harlot shrugged. "Why not? As long as I get to ride on top."

"Oh, I've got something even more fun in mind." Propping Sofia against the wall, he began to knot the bedsheets together. "Here, give me a hand," he said, tossing several to their new companion. "Tie them tight."

Comprehension dawned, along with a low titter. "We're making a rope? Whattya got in mind, Gabriel? Tying us up?"

"Something like that." Osborne slid up the frosted glass and drew in a gulp of the fresh air. It wasn't much more than a thirty-foot drop. The silk should be just long enough.

Taking Sofia by the shoulders, he stuck her head outside. "Breathe deeply. In and out, like in your yoga classes," he ordered, punctuating the command with a sharp slap to her derriere.

The harlot giggled. "Me next."

"In a moment. But first, hand me your section." He knotted the two lengths together. "Now hold this end." Satisfied that the silk would hold, he smiled. "That should do."

She clapped and turned with a saucy wiggle of her bare bum. "Ye gonna spank me now, Gabriel?"

"Yes. Lie facedown on the mattress."

The harlot did a swan dive atop the eiderdown duvet. "Ready when you are, luv," she cooed.

His first smack drew a delighted giggle.

"Sorry," he muttered under his breath, his hovering hand moving up to her throat. Her laugh gurgled to a snuffled sigh as he pressed hard at a point just behind her ear. "You'll awake in several hours with nothing worse than a slight headache," he added.

Stepping over the harlot's prostrate form, Osborne hurried to the window.

"Sofia." He slid the window up a notch.

"C-cold," she muttered through chattering teeth. Her arms were pebbled with goose bumps.

"It's good for you." He snugged the silken sheet beneath her arms. "Try to stand, sweeting," he coaxed.

His words drew only a querulous mutter.

"Damn it, Sofia. Snap to attention!"

The martial command seemed to penetrate her fuzzed brain. Slipping, sliding, she mustered a modicum of control over her treacly limbs.

"Hold tight," he barked. After knotting the makeshift rope under her armpits, Osborne fisted her hands around the tail end. "Don't let go until I say so." He would be doing all the work in lowering her to the ground, but a flapping arm might smash a windowpane or draw unwanted attention.

Adding a silent prayer that the porters did not keep a close eye on back of the building, Osborne maneuvered her out onto the narrow ledge. Once he braced himself against the stone, lowering her down took only a few moments. *So far, so good*. As soon as her feet touched the ground, he turned and took up a steel-handled whip from the collection of sex toys arrayed on the wall. The shaft was wider than the window, and once wedged inside the casement, it looked sturdy enough to hold his weight.

Not that he had much choice. The great golden Gabriel was not about to sprout wings.

After tying the end of the sheet to the shaft, he slithered out the window. Boots rasping over bricks, he slid down the wall as fast as he dared. Though the silk was soft, the friction burned and blistered his palms. Ignoring the pain, he wrenched Sofia free of the knots and shoved her forward.

"March!" He mouthed a whispered shout. The fog was thick with the smells of the river, yet somehow the scent of rot and decay was not as noxious as the perfumed lies within the opium house.

Sofia soldiered on a few steps, then stopped and gagged. Her eyes were going opaque.

Fighting down a sense of panic, Osborne looked around. There was no time to make their way through the rookeries on foot. He needed to purge the poison from inside her. Already it might be too late. They would have to chance finding a hackney in the narrow street and hope they did not encounter De Winton or one of his henchmen.

Lady Serena might also be in danger. The sudden thought caused his throat to tighten in frustration. He would try to send a warning, but until Sofia was safe, he could do nothing.

Bloody hell. Why did the ladies he cared for seem drawn to danger? Osborne gave a harried sigh, admitting in the same breath that he couldn't really blame the young widow for being seduced by the Scarlet Knights. Curiosity was a potent drug in its own right, and a lady of sharp intelligence had so little opportunity to explore the world outside the narrow boundaries set by Society. He, too, would have chafed at the rules and restrictions.

"Oy, stay clear o' me rig, nancy boy."

In the fog, Osborne had stumbled up against the wheels

of a glossy black landau. The driver flicked his lash, the leather cutting a sting across his cheek.

Before he quite realized what he was doing, Osborne set Sofia against the side of the cab and vaulted up to the perch. His fist smashed into the driver's jaw before the man could wield the whip as a weapon. A second blow knocked him out cold. Cursing under his breath, Osborne dumped the limp body on the ground beside a stack of broken wine crates.

"Next time, keep a civil tongue in your head," he muttered. "Come, Sofia, we are almost there."

She didn't make a sound as he lifted her to the seat. The silence sent a shiver down his spine. Grabbing the reins, he set the horses into motion, mindless of the pain shooting through his bleeding hands. Mayfair was much too far away, he thought as he guided the team through the twisting turns. Yet where in the godforsaken slums of Southwark could he look for help?

His thoughts were spinning furiously as the carriage careened around the corner. Just ahead, he would have to choose which way to go. Left or right. *Salvation or damnation.* If Sofia died, he wasn't sure he could ever live with himself.

There was one place . . . It was a gamble, but he would have to roll the dice.

Chapter Twenty-one

*P*raying he could recall the way through the squalid rookeries and broken-down gin shops, Osborne turned the horses toward the river. A stretch of warehouses loomed, dark and deserted in the ghostly mists. He counted the passing buildings. *One, two, three . . .* At the fourth, he turned sharply and pulled to a halt in front of a narrow brick house tucked between the stone structures. The ornate iron gate was slightly ajar, and he took the marble steps two at a time, despite the dead weight of Sofia in his arms.

"Stop, sirrah! You cannot bring your own doxy in here." A middle-aged matron hustled out from behind a velvet curtain. She was dressed in peacock blue, and the iridescent feathers in her graying hair fluttered wildly in the glow of the oil lamps. Her frown grew more pronounced on surveying his rumpled shirt and muddied trousers. "Indeed, you cannot bring yourself in here. This establishment caters exclusively to *gentlemen*—"

"Harkness—I need to know if Lord Harkness is here." Osborne fought to catch his breath.

"We don't discuss our patrons," came the cold reply. "If you—"

"Please! I need his help. This lady is going to die if I can't purge the poison from her stomach. Harkness knows about such things." He must have been shouting, for a pair of female faces suddenly peered out from behind the curtain, and several doors opened along the length of a dimly lit corridor.

"She don't look good, Mistress Mavis," murmured one of the girls. "Best we get her te shoot the cat."

Osborne swayed slightly, feeling he was trapped inside some horrible nightmare. "Damn it, I don't want *any* living thing to die!"

"What Rosie meant, sir, is we got to get yer friend to cast up her accounts," offered the girl's companion.

The matron's stern face softened slightly. But before she could speak, the thud of steps sounded on the staircase.

Osborne looked up. "Nick!" Relief welled in his eyes— to hell if tears were considered unmanly.

His friend was barefoot and still trying to stuff his shirt-tails into his trousers. "Dev. Good Lord, what—"

"I remember back in school you had a trick for making the other boys puke," he cried. "Can you do it now?"

Harkness blinked, then to his credit did not waste any time hemming and hawing. "Yes, the ingredients are all common enough." Turning to the matron, he rattled off a list.

She nodded. "They should all be among our medicinal supplies. Fanny, go fetch them from the cabinet. And bring a basin as well." She pushed up the sleeves of her gown. "There is a sofa in the parlor. Let us lie her down there."

"My room is empty," piped up Rosie. "A bed will be a mite more comfortable."

"Don't just stand there, gentlemen." The matron pointed the way. "First door on the right."

"Thank you," said Osborne, his voice still unsteady.

"What did she eat or drink?" asked Nick as they laid Sofia on the counterpane.

"I—I'm not sure. Opium and brandy. Maybe some other drug."

"How long ago?"

Osborne tried to think. It felt like an eternity since he had passed through the doors of the Puff of Paradise. But in actual time?

"A little less than an hour." A glance at the mantel clock confirmed the guess.

Harkness frowned. "We need to work fast. By the look of it, whatever she ingested was meant to cause a violent reaction. Her pulse is weak, and her breathing is shallow."

"Sit her up," said Mistress Mavis. "I've seen drug overdoses before. Rosie, run and get a cold compress. And fetch a funnel from the kitchen."

Osborne cradled Sofia in his arms and brushed the tangled strands of hair from her cheek. Her skin was deathly cool to the touch. "Don't you dare leave me, love," he whispered. "We've not yet settled our wager on who is the best shot, and honor demands that you not renege on a bet."

He felt a slight stirring of air against his jaw.

Harkness squeezed his shoulder before moving to the bedside table. "I'll need a candle and a measuring spoon."

"Keep talking to her, sir." Despite the outward show of gruffness, Mistress Mavis took a seat on the bed and set to chafing Sofia's hands. "Rosie, hand the gentleman that compress," she directed, seeing the girl return with a dampened flannel. "Place it on her brow, sir. And keep talking."

Osborne wasn't sure what he was saying. The words

were simply babbling out of their own accord, as if they were a lifeline that could hold Sofia from slipping into darkness.

"Hurry, Nick," he added as he dabbed the cooling cloth to Sofia's brow. Her earlier chill had turned feverish. Her face was now sheened in sweat.

His friend held the spoon over the candle flame a moment longer. "Almost done," he answered. Adding the heated liquid to the glass on the table, he stirred furiously. "How did such an accident happen?"

"It was no accident," answered Osborne through gritted teeth. "She uncovered some secrets that will send several gentlemen to the gallows, once the evidence becomes known to the authorities."

"Good Lord." Harkness gave a last swirl of the liquid. "Open her mouth, Dev."

The matron slid his trembling fingers aside and helped insert the funnel. "Like this, sir. She mustn't choke on her own tongue."

Harkness tipped the potion down her throat. "Be ready to move quickly, Dev. Where is the basin?"

"Here, sir." Rosie and Fanny took hold of each handle.

Osborne felt his chest constrict. There was no sign of life from Sofia. She still lay pale and unmoving in his arms. "It's not working, Nick." His voice sounded unnaturally calm, as if it were detached from his own body.

"Give it a moment more," whispered his friend. Harkness was sweating, too, the muscles of his clenched jaw standing out in sharp relief in the flickering shadows.

"Thank you for trying—"

There was a sound from Sofia, a zephyr of a groan. Her eyelids fluttered open. "Arrrggh." She shuddered, then was suddenly violently sick.

A laugh welled up in his throat.

"It's *not* funny," she gasped between retches. "Ooooh, I feel sick."

Sick, but alive. Gloriously alive.

Sofia lifted her chin. Her eyes were slitted in shadow, and her hair was hanging in snarls. Never had she looked so lovely.

"W-what happened?" she asked.

"De Winton tried to kill you with an overdose of narcotics."

"Damn." She blinked and tried to focus her gaze. "I . . . I have to—"

He hugged her tighter and pressed the cloth to her lips. "Rest easy. You aren't going anywhere tonight. I will find Lynsley and inform him of all that has happened. Let him clean out that nest of vipers."

She looked about to argue, but her strength sagged and she slumped back against his shoulder.

Looking up at the circle of faces, he managed a wan smile. "Thank you—all of you."

"I've got a clean nightrail in me chest o' drawers," volunteered Rosie. "If ye gents will give us a few moments, we'll see yer lady friend tucked in right and tight."

Harkness drew him into the corridor. Mistress Mavis followed along behind them and drew the door shut.

"Might I impose on your goodwill a while longer, madam?" Osborne turned. "I must go warn the authorities before the miscreants try to escape from the country." He raked back his hair from his brow. "But even before I do that, there is another lady who may be in danger. That will be my first stop."

The matron gave a curt nod. "Your friend is safe here for the nonce."

"Who?" began Harkness.

"Lady Sommers."

"You'll need a coat and a carriage," said Harkness. "Take mine."

"I've a fresh team right outside. But I'll accept the loan of clothing." His mouth twitched. "Sorry to leave you in the lurch, Nicky."

"I shall take care to see you pay me back. In spades." His friend grinned. "Wait here. I'll just be a moment."

There was a short silence, save for the patter of steps on the Oriental runner.

"If, perchance, your female friend is looking for future employment . . ." murmured Mistress Mavis.

Osborne smiled. "She has a job."

The matron sighed. "I do hope it is not with a competitor. Her beauty and body are quite unique."

"It's in a different line of work."

"Ah. Well, good luck to her. And to you, sir."

Harkness returned and thrust a clean shirt and coat into his arms. "Godspeed."

Osborne nodded, but he was not going to count on divine help. He would crush the devils who dared harm Sofia with his bare hands if need be.

"Ye best not try te move, miss."

Though still woozy from the effects of the narcotic, Sofia managed to sit up.

"Here, have some more tea." A pair of young women were hovering over her bedside, their kohl-rimmed eyes wide with concern.

"Thank you." Her throat was parched, and she gratefully sipped the sugared beverage. "I feel much better."

Both were blond and buxom, with rouged cheeks and

painted lips that quickly curled up in matching smiles. "Thought ye were a goner," said the one on the right.

"Aye, and so did Goldilocks." The one on the left winked. "Right handsome gent is that one. He your protector?"

Osborne her protector? Sofia quirked a small smile. "I suppose you could call him that. Though we are more like . . . friends."

"Oy, trust me, duckie, the gent has far more than friendly feelings fer ye. If I had a toff that said half the things he just did, I'd march him up the aisle afore ye could say 'Parson's Mousetrap.'"

"The gentleman is not about to make any offers of marriage." Sofia swallowed the last of the tea. The hazy recollection of strange, seductive whispers was likely just hallucinations brought on by the drugs. "However, I do need to speak to him without delay."

"Sorry, he's left."

"Left?" she echoed.

"Aye, he said something about having te go see Linsey. Ain't that right, Rosie?"

"Aye," agreed the other woman.

"I must go too. He doesn't know—" She nearly swooned as she tried to bolt up and swing her legs to the floor.

"Ye ain't in any shape te be gallivanting around Town."

"I will be in a moment." Drawing in a deep lungful of air, Sofia sought to clear her head and regain control of her senses. Her yoga teacher had stressed that the mind could master the body—it was simply a matter of willpower.

After several more slow, cleansing breaths, she managed to stand. "Where are my clothes?"

"Ye weren't wearing nothing but that nit o' rags when ye came in." Rosie pointed to the tangle of exotic silks draped over the dressing table chair.

"Damn." Combing her hair back from her face, she added, "Well, if I have to fashion a shift from these sheets, I am leaving."

A knock sounded on the door. "Is anything amiss in there?"

"I think ye better come in, Nicky, and see if ye can talk some sense into the lady," called Rosie. "She wants te run after Goldilocks."

The door opened.

Harkness mirrored her own surprised stare, his eyes widening in sudden recognition.

"Bloody hell," he muttered under his breath. "Girls, kindly step outside for a moment." He waited for the latch to click shut before letting out a harried sigh. "Lady Sofia! I'd no idea it was *you*." His gaze darted to the gauzy Turkish trousers and sleeveless blouson, then shot back to her face. "What the devil is going on? Deverill said that you were drugged, but how on earth did that happen?"

"It's a long story," she replied. "I need to speak with Osborne. It's imperative that he and Lord Lynsley hear about Lady Sommers."

His face relaxed. "Don't worry. Deverill is heading to her as we speak. He means to pass on a warning before going on to Lord Lynsley."

"No!" The last of the cobwebs cleared from her head. "I have to stop him!"

Harkness touched her arm. "Come, Contessa, you had better lie down. Your wits are still a trifle confused."

Sofia shook him off. "I promise you, it's not the narcotic. Deverill is in grave danger. The lady is part of the cabal that tried to kill me earlier this evening."

He still looked uncertain as to whether to believe her.

"Lord Harkness, I know I am asking you to make a leap of faith, but I am not delusional or dicked in the nob."

"Have you any idea how crazy your story sounds?"

Her lips curled up in a rueful quirk. "Yes. Which ought to assure you I am not making it up." Holding his gaze with unflinching resolve, she added, "Please, I need your help."

Silence stretched for one long moment. Then two. "Perhaps *I* belong in Bedlam." He pressed his palms to his brow. "What do you have in mind?"

"I'll explain during the drive—I take it you have a carriage here."

He nodded.

"Get it." Her steps were now sure and steady as she marched to the door. "Rosie," she called softly, only to find the two girls stumbling back from the keyhole.

"Er, yes, ma'am?" Beneath the face paint, there was hint of a faint blush. Her companion, however, showed no sign of shame.

"Oooooh," exclaimed Fanny. "This is ever so much more exciting than that book Mistress Mavis is reading te us—ye know, *The Damsel and the Dark Lord*." She tugged at her bodice, which was perilously close to exposing both her breasts. "Wot can we do te help?"

"Clothing." Sofia eyed the clinging fit and trailing ribbons of their frilly gowns. "Something practical. I may need to climb a few walls."

"We got plenty of gent's clothing in the storage room," offered Rosie. "They tend te forget a few items when they take their leave."

"Excellent. The darker the better, and throw in a pair of black gloves if you can," she replied. "Please hurry."

They pelted off in a swirl of silk, nearly knocking the matron down in their rush.

"Nicky," muttered Mistress Mavis as she drew Sofia back into the bedchamber and shut the door. "You do know that you and your friends are wreaking havoc with business this evening. My patrons come here expecting discretion and decorum."

"Start a tab for Osborne," replied Harkness. "He will be happy to make up for your losses."

"Assuming he survives the night," added Sofia.

Mistress Mavis brushed one of the drooping ostrich feathers from her cheek. "You are saying that he, too, is in danger?"

Sofia quickly gave the woman a terse explanation of the situation, omitting only the most sensitive information about Lynsley and the existence of the Merlins.

The matron's expression did not change a whit during the tale of drugs, debauchery, and government corruption. Given her profession, she had probably heard far wilder stories, thought Sofia.

"She's not mad," murmured Harkness.

Mistress Mavis maintained a measured silence as she looked back and forth between the two of them. No doubt trying to decide whether Harkness was also a stark, raving lunatic.

"Nor am I imagining the threat to Lord Osborne. As you have seen, these people will not hesitate to kill," said Sofia. "Have you any weapon in this establishment?"

To her credit, the matron did not bat an eye at the request. "Do you know how to load and handle one of the new Land-Pattern pistols?"

"I'm a crack shot with any firearm, be it a pocket pistol, a Baker rifle, or a Bundukh Torador," replied Sofia calmly.

"I had a feeling you might be. No pampered young lady

has muscles like yours." The matron smoothed at her skirts. "Would you care for a poniard as well?"

"All the better."

"I will be back in a moment." As she turned for the door, Mistress Mavis nudged Harkness into action. "Come, Nicky, what are you waiting for? Have your carriage out front in five minutes."

"I will be there in four."

Sofia had already tied back her hair in a simple plait. Flexing her shoulders, she spun in perfect balance and cut an imaginary sword stroke through the air.

"Make that three."

Chapter Twenty-two

*O*sborne reined the lathered horses to halt outside the red brick town house. Not a flicker of light shone at any of the windows. *Was he too late*? De Winton and his henchmen would have had plenty of time to make their murderous way from Southwark to Mayfair.

His hands fisted as he slipped down from the driver's box and edged through the open entrance gate. He had not thought to ask for a weapon at the Rake's Retreat. He would have to rely on stealth and speed rather than steel.

So far, there was no sign of the Scarlet Knights.

Making his way around to the back of the house, Osborne found the gap in the boxwood bushes and crept across the garden terrace to the stretch of mullioned doors. They were all locked, but after wrapping his hand in his handkerchief, he punched out one of the windowpanes and drew back the bolt.

Still no sign of life. The crackle of broken glass did not appear to have roused any of the household. After waiting a fraction longer, Osborne stepped over the shards and crossed through the Garden Room into the corridor. He turned into the entrance hall and was about to start up the staircase when a metallic click sounded right behind him.

"Stop where you are."

He froze in his tracks. Given the darkness and the up-turned collar of the caped driving coat, it was no wonder the lady did not recognize him.

"Now turn slowly. And be warned—one false move and I'll blow a hole through your heart."

He did as she ordered. "Please hold your fire, Lady Serena."

"Osborne?"

Relief flooded through him on seeing her unharmed. "In the flesh," he quipped, a crooked smile coming to his lips.

Her pistol was still aimed at his chest. "What are *you* doing here?"

"I came to warn you. I don't mean to alarm you, but you are in grave danger."

"Danger?" she repeated.

"Yes, I . . ." Osborne hesitated, unsure of how to explain the web of intrigue that had caught both of them in its design. "The story is a long one, and we haven't much time. Please trust me when I tell you that De Winton and his friends are spawns of Satan. They tried to murder the contessa earlier this evening, and as we speak, they may be on the way here."

Lady Serena's face looked ghostly pale in the light of her lone candle. "Lady Sofia—"

"Is safe for the moment," he said quickly. "I have her hidden in an exclusive bordello near De Winton's Puff of Paradise."

"Forgive me, but what you are saying defies the imagination."

"I know, I know." Aware that his disheveled appearance was not helping to inspire much confidence, he tucked his hands into his pockets. Despite the handkerchief, he had cut himself on the jagged glass. The sight of blood might frighten her into pulling the trigger. "However, I assure you that it's all true."

"Those are very serious allegations, Osborne." She bit at her lower lip. "I'm sorry. But before I can believe you, I'll have to hear more of what proof you have."

"I can't say I blame you." He darted a look out the rosette window. The street still looked to be deserted. But for how long? By now, De Winton and Sforza must have discovered that Sofia was not lying dead in one of the opium den's boudoirs. "However, might I suggest that we find a more secure spot?"

"Let us go up to my private study." Lady Serena gestured for him to continue up the stairs. "The door is quite thick, and the lock is sturdy."

He waited until she had lit the colza lamp on her desk before speaking again. "Lady Serena, I am not drunk or deranged. Adam De Winton has reason to be seeking my demise—and yours."

"Why?" She was maintaining a remarkably cool composure considering the circumstances.

"Because we both know too much about his activities here in Town." The pistol was still pointed at him, but he couldn't fault her for being cautious.

"He is not the only gentleman to dabble in drugs," she replied. "I can't see him trying to kill any of us over a bit of opium."

"Be assured, it's far more than a bit. But even so, that's the least of his wrongdoings. His real operations involve a complex web of corruption and collusion that stretches from London to Bombay. You see, by substituting inferior goods or faking phantom shipments to our armies abroad, he and his friends make an obscene profit on a number of large military contracts. That our soldiers go into battle with gunpowder that won't fire or boots that fall apart in the dead of winter doesn't bother him in the least."

"H-how did you discover all this?"

"I didn't," he admitted. "It was Lady Sofia who opened my eyes to what was going on."

Lady Serena frowned slightly. "How and why did *she* come to have an interest in De Winton's affairs?" she mused.

He shook his head. "I'm sorry, but I am not at liberty to reveal Lady Sofia's secrets. Suffice it to say, there is more to her than meets the eye." He allowed a fleeting smile. "Indeed, her courage and cleverness are even more striking than her beauty."

A spark of emotion seemed to flare in Lady Serena's eyes. *Jealousy?* He recalled with some guilt how his flirtations with her had become rather heated of late. Perhaps she had mistaken his attentions for a deeper, more serious sentiment on his part.

Or perhaps he had merely mistaken the flicker of lamplight on her golden lashes. For when she replied, her voice held no hint of hurt feelings. "So it seems. I take it she has proof of all this? Otherwise it will be only her word against De Winton's. And as you point out, he has a number of influential friends."

"So does Sofia," he answered. "But, yes, she has enough incriminating evidence to send certain men to the gallows. And once the evidence is turned over to the authorities, I'm sure the miscreants will quickly finger the leader of the group."

"She has not yet handed over the proof?" Lady Serena moved to the window and peeked out through the draperies.

"I was just on my way to alert her . . . contact in the government. However, I thought it vital to stop here first and warn you."

"How fortunate I am that you are a true gentleman." But rather than reassure her, his words seemed to put her more on edge. He saw her grip tighten on the pistol. "Who else have the two of you discovered to be working with De Winton?"

"I'm afraid a number of your friends are part of the sordid scheme. Andover, Roxbury, and Concord for sure. Others will undoubtedly be implicated by the documents." He flashed an encouraging smile. "Don't worry—they all will get the punishment they deserve."

A noise from downstairs caused her to start.

"Damn." Osborne went very still. It sounded as if someone was rattling the front door. "Can you see anything outside?"

Lady Serena took another look. "Yes," she replied flatly. "A carriage. It looks to be De Winton's."

He spun around for the door. "I'll go down and tell him that the game is over. He has no reason to do you harm. Let me have your pistol. Then lock the door—"

"Sit down, Osborne."

He turned to find that Lady Serena was once again drawing a bead on his chest. "I know how confusing this all must be," he exclaimed. "But you are making a terrible mistake. I swear, De Winton is the dangerous dastard, not me."

Light glinted off the gun barrel as she took a step toward

him. But the look of anger in her eyes was even more lethal as she suddenly swung the butt at his head.

Stunned by the blow, Osborne fell to the carpet.

"Adam," she called. "Up here."

He was dimly aware of more than one set of footsteps on the stairs.

Sure enough, De Winton was not alone.

"What's this sodding little prick doing here?" demanded Sforza. "The della Silveri bitch would be dead now if he hadn't interfered with our plans. He's ruined everything!"

"Calm down, Lorenzo," commanded Lady Serena. "All is not lost quite yet."

De Winton said nothing, but as Osborne raised his head, a vicious kick caught him flush on the jaw.

"Control yourself too, Adam. There is still a chance that we can emerge from this unscathed, but we will have to work quickly." She set down her pistol and opened the top drawer of her curio cabinet. "Get him up and into that chair." A wave of her hand indicated the slat-backed desk chair rather than one of the leather armchairs.

"Why not just kill him on the spot?" asked De Winton.

She tossed him a length of cording. "Because he knows where the contessa is right now. We find her, and we find the papers she's stolen from Concord's study. Apparently she's not yet turned any evidence over to the authorities." Lady Serena untied the fastenings around a slim roll of black velvet. "So, we may still be in business, gentlemen."

Though his face was still half numb from the force of De Winton's kick, Osborne managed a curl of his lip. "Hell will freeze over before I tell you anything about Sofia's whereabouts."

"Oh, you will talk far before that time comes, Osborne." She unrolled the cloth to reveal a set of exotic scalpels, each tucked into its own thin pocket. "And then you shall scream. And then you will beg for a bullet to the brain to put you out of your misery."

At Sofia's signal, Harkness drew his team to a halt in the shadows. "Trouble?" he asked when she returned from a quick look down the street.

"It appears that Osborne is not the only visitor to the lady's town house," she whispered. "I'm going in. You must go straight on to Lord Lynsley's residence—not the family mansion on Grosvenor Square but his private abode." She gave the directions. "Tell him about this place and the Puff of Paradise. He will know what to do."

Harkness shook his head. "I can't allow a lady to take all the risks while I trot off to get help," he murmured. "Code of honor and all that."

"I'm trained for this sort of thing, Lord Harkness."

He looked doubtful. "With all due respect, Lady Sofia, I can't imagine what sort of training would give you an edge over any man in a fight."

There was no time to argue the fine points of noblesse oblige. "See the sign on the door across the street?"

"Yes, but—"

She whipped out the knife that Mistress Mavis had given her and sent it flying through the air. "How about *that* sort of training, Lord Harkness?" she said as its point hit smack in the center of the lettering. "Unless you can do better, be on your way."

He hesitated, but only for an instant. "Godspeed, Lady Sofia."

"And you," she murmured before moving quickly across the cobblestones to retrieve her weapon. A last look around showed the phaeton disappearing into the mists.

She was on her own.

Keeping close to the low wall lining the street, she made her way to Lady Serena's residence. De Winton's carriage had drawn to a halt by the iron gates, and the coachman sat slouched on his perch, his collar turned up to ward off the rising breeze. It took only a moment to render him unconscious. After trussing his hands with the lash of his whip, Sofia turned her attention to the entrance.

The front door was slightly ajar. No light shone through the crack. Like the rest of the town house, the entrance hall was as dark as a tomb. Quelling the urge to draw her steel and plunge ahead, she forced herself to make a more measured approach. The Academy fencing master had often counseled that probing for a weakness was often a far more effective way to gain victory than trying to overpower an enemy with a slashing assault.

Ducking through the boxwood plantings, Sofia flattened herself to the brick and inched to the edge of the casement windows. From there, she angled a look inside. *Nothing.* She gave it another minute, watching for any shift of darkness within the darkness. Her patience was rewarded—a wink of movement caught her eye just as she was about to turn away.

The man's black beard and dusky skin made his face nearly invisible in the dappling of moonlight. His tunic and pantaloons were a deep indigo as well, which blended into the midnight shadows. It was the flicker of metal in his pointed turban that gave his presence away. Squinting, Sofia could just make out his shape. He was well over six feet tall and broad as a Brahmin bull. How Lady Serena had come to have a Sikh from Punjab in her employ was no doubt a question that would greatly interest Lord Lynsley.

But right now her only concern was putting him out of

action. No small feat, seeing that his sect was one of the most feared group of warriors in all of Asia.

Think. Sofia didn't need the quickening thud of her heart to remind her that Osborne's life depended on her strategy. She wouldn't get a second chance.

The man shifted his stance and blew out his breath. He looked to be growing bored and a bit restless. *Turn the enemy's strength into a weakness.* It was one of her fencing master's favorite exhortations. She drew in a calming breath and moved for the side of the house, giving thanks that her Academy instructors included not only the best blade in all of Europe but also an Indian guru and a Chinese tai chi expert.

Each discipline taught that flexibility, both physical and mental, was a weapon unto itself.

Locating the broken window latch on the parlor window—a detail she recalled from her earlier visit—Sofia slipped inside the room. She, too, had the advantage of clothing that helped mask her presence. Rosie had dug up a pair of slim black trousers abandoned by an Eton prefect while Fanny had located a pleated silk shirt left by a Prussian count who fancied himself the Lord of Midnight. Black satin slippers, courtesy of Mistress Mavis, allowed her to move noiselessly over the parquet floor of the corridor.

"Arrumph." The Sikh warrior shifted his weight and stretched. Hanging from his sash was a *kirpan*, the deadly sharp curved sword worn by all members of his sect.

The man was a walking arsenal, thought Sofia as she took cover in a recessed nook beneath the curved staircase. In hand-to-hand combat, the odds were not in her favor. But head-to-head . . .

The door behind her came slightly ajar, revealing a small storage closet used for coal and the cast-iron scuttles.

Stepping inside, she took up a tiny sliver and tossed it onto the polished wood.

For a big man, the Sikh moved quickly and quietly. Rounding the corner, knife in hand, he surveyed the empty stretch of space.

She rattled the iron and gave a tiny growl.

"Harrumph." He had to bend low to stick his head inside the cramped space.

Whooomph. The layers of his headcloth somewhat muffled the crack of metal against bone. A moment later, an echoing thud sounded as his bearded chin hit the sooty floor.

Sofia paused just long enough to pluck the quoits from his turban and lock the latch, then raced for the stairs.

Lady Serena touched her thumb to the edge of the first blade, a crescent sliver of steel topping a thin brass rod. The others laid out on the desk were equally unusual in shape, and all were decorated with intricate patterns of gold damascene.

"Have you ever seen a set of knives like these?" she asked, holding one of them uncomfortably close to Osborne's eyes. "They are used by the Sikh Akali sect, who are famous throughout India as religious fanatics and fearless fighters, to extract information from their enemies."

"Thank you for the anthropology lecture. But if you feel compelled to demonstrate one of Andover's little trinkets, I would rather see a demonstration of the techniques used to create his collection of Persian painted books."

She slapped him hard with the back of her hand, the faceted diamond ring raising a welt across his cheek. "Don't make this hard on yourself, my dear Deverill." Her voice was chillingly calm. "Tell me where she is now, and I'll promise to make your death a painless one."

Osborne swallowed hard, the sharp sting of bile mingling with the taste of his own blood. He was not ashamed to admit his hands were shaking and his shirt nearly soaked through with sweat. As he had told Sofia, he was no storybook hero, impervious to fear or pain. Harkness knew his intentions, but he would be long dead before his friend figured out that anything had gone wrong.

Things were not looking good.

As if reading his thoughts, Lady Serena gave a light laugh. "I wouldn't count on anyone riding to your rescue. Even if you left word on where you were going, an Akali warrior came along with our friends and is now stationed downstairs to greet any uninvited guests."

"He is quite a sight. All of the sect members wear a towering turban of indigo cloth, decorated with quoits of all different sizes," said De Winton.

Sforza drew a finger down the center of his chest. "The better to gut an opponent."

"Yes, I would rather like to see someone try to slip by Arjun's guard," snickered De Winton. "I saw him practicing his throwing technique the other day. He could split a man's skull in two at thirty paces."

Osborne felt sickened by their callous depravity. Suffering was a subject of mirth. Death was a matter of entertainment. Thinking of all the brave men who had died on account of the group's greed renewed his fighting spirit. He would go to the grave with Sofia's secrets.

"Indeed he could." Sforza rubbed his hands together. "I would guess that Lady Serena will be equally skillful in her own way."

"Make sure the curtain is drawn," she ordered.

Sforza wiped the leer from his face and hurried to do her bidding.

Bloody hell. Osborne swore a silent oath. Had his legs been free, he would have kicked himself. It had certainly taken him long enough to see the obvious—the leader of the cabal was not a *he* but a *she*.

"Very clever," he murmured. "I don't know why I didn't catch on any earlier."

"Because you are, like most men, blinded by your pride and your prejudices." Flexing her wrist, she cut through the front of his shirt with a silky slash. "You cannot conceive of a female having the brains or the boldness to oversee a business operation like this one."

She was right, of course, admitted Osborne. Though he, of all people, ought to have had an inkling of just how capable a woman could be in a man's world.

"Your talents are indeed extraordinary," he said aloud.

Lady Serena looked pleased by the compliment. Perhaps he could use her own pride and vanity to his advantage.

"How did you come up with the idea?" he asked.

The blade stilled just above his bare chest. "My husband was asked by a friend to invest in a shipment of opium," she replied. "A very small deal, though it proved profitable enough. I pointed out the potential of the business, but Freddie was too stupid to understand the opportunities that were opening up, what with Napoleon marching through Europe and the Mahratta fomenting trouble with the East India Company's trade."

"As I said, very clever," murmured Osborne. "So you convinced him to let you do all the thinking?"

Her laugh was devoid of emotion. "In a manner of speaking. You see, his drinking and gambling soon became a liability. His partners didn't want to deal with an unreliable investor. So, as with any liability, I took steps to eliminate the problem."

Osborne blinked. Good Lord, the lady was even more cold-blooded than he imagined. "Let me guess," he said softly. "An overdose of opium?"

"Freddie's excesses were well-known. No one was surprised when his heart simply could not keep pace with his depravities."

"His partners were willing to accept a female?"

"Unlike Freddie, I recognized genius when I saw it," said De Winton. "I had no objections to letting a lady give the orders. After all, one of England's greatest monarchs was a woman. And Lady Serena quickly proved she deserved the power."

De Winton would have taken orders from a snake if there was any profit in it, thought Osborne.

"*Si.* And as we Italians have a long tradition of females wielding their influence in business and politics, I was happy to go along with the arrangement," added Sforza with a shrug.

"Enough of the history lesson." Lady Serena's tone was once again brusque and all business. The knife pressed lightly against his flesh. "Where is Lady Sofia?"

"Just out of curiosity—what made you choose to become friendly with me?" he asked, stalling for time.

"Because with your connections in Society, you could have been extremely useful in opening up new doors. People like and respect you, Osborne. I could have made you very rich, had you been willing to bend your prudish principles just a bit." She made a face. "Most men are seduced by greed. Or sex. You proved to be an exception. A pity, really. We could have made a lovely couple."

The idea of any intimacy with her made his skin crawl.

His face must have betrayed his disgust, for her expression suddenly hardened. "You favored that slut Sofia over me. A bad investment, as you see now. But I shall give you one more chance to recoup some of your losses. Where is she?"

Osborne closed his eyes.

"My dear Deverill." He felt her fingertip caress the line of his jaw. "We can make this easy. You can have pleasure . . ." Her mouth touched his, her tongue teasing over his lower lip. "Or pain."

The scalpel bit into his flesh, cutting a razor-thin gash above his right breast. He clenched his teeth to keep from crying out.

She flicked a drop of blood from the steel tip. "Where is Lady Sofia? I won't ask again nicely."

"Sorry." Osborne mustered a smile. "A gentleman never discusses a lady in public. It's a matter of honor, you know."

"You won't be speaking so glibly when she reaches your testicles," said De Winton.

"And you won't be sneering so smugly when the Crown's hangman knots the noose around your neck," he retorted.

The reply earned him another cut. *Damn.* The pain was not so bad now, but he had no illusions about how quickly that would change. During his time in Portugal, he had seen the partisans torture an informant. He still had nightmares in which he heard the man's screams.

"This is your last chance, Deverill. Don't play the hero," said Lady Serena. "You think the contessa would sacrifice herself for you?" The sharpened blade kissed up against his throat. "Where is she? Speak up now, or I promise you will regret it."

Strange, but his only regret was that he had never told

Sofia that he loved her. He wished he had spoken from the heart, had expressed his admiration for her courage, her compassion, her convictions. His magnificent Merlin. Just thinking of her gave wings to his sinking spirit. His own sun might be setting, but she would live to see another day.

Brightened by the thought, he mustered a laugh. "Go to hell."

"Very well. If that is your answer, we will get down to business. First, I am going to flay a strip of skin from—"

"I think not."

Osborne's eyes flew open.

"Step away from the chair, Lady Serena." Sofia stood framed in the doorway, pistol in hand. "There is no need to ask Lord Osborne any more questions about my whereabouts. As you see, I'm right here."

Chapter Twenty-three

$\mathcal{A}$rjun!" cried De Winton.

"If you are looking for your guard, he is engaged in *Naam Japna*—the quiet meditation of God required of all good Sikhs each day," said Sofia. "He won't be waking anytime soon."

"A dramatic entrance, Contessa." The momentary shock on Lady Serena's face had smoothed to a look of cold calculation. "But one that shows how unschooled you are to match wits with real professionals. By charging in with weapons drawn, you've made a fatal mistake." Darting a look at her two henchmen, she gave a short laugh. "She has one bullet and there are three of us—shoot her."

The lady had nerve, thought Sofia. To go along with her utter ruthlessness. As for her own emotions, she didn't dare look at Osborne. She must remain disciplined, dispassionate.

Instead, she mimicked Lady Serena's air of icy indifference. "You are right. Simple arithmetic would seem to add up in your favor—that is, assuming I don't have a pocket pistol tucked in my trousers." Sofia flexed her finger on the trigger. "So, who wishes to be the sacrificial lamb?"

"Sforza, you do the honors," ordered Lady Serena. "Even if she manages to fire, she likely can't hit the broad side of a barn."

"Me?" The Italian wet his lips as he edged back. "Bloodshed was not part of our deal."

"Especially his own," said Sofia. Seeing Sforza's uncertainty mirrored in De Winton's eyes, she gave a curt laugh. "Your Scarlet Knight does not appear to be in any great rush to be a hero either. No doubt he prefers the coloring of his waistcoat not to come from his own veins."

"Shoot her, Sofia," said Osborne calmly. "It's what she deserves."

"Shut up," ordered Lady Serena. She was still standing next to him, her bloodied blade dangerously close to his throat.

Too close. Sofia had a clear shot, but a twitch of the razored steel might well sever his artery. And despite the other lady's murderous madness, she couldn't quite bring herself to kill in cold blood. "Step away from Lord Osborne, Lady Serena, and lay down your knife. Surely you are smart enough to see the game is over. The authorities are being alerted as we speak. There is no chance of escape."

"You are bluffing." For the first time, Lady Serena's voice betrayed a flicker of doubt.

"No, I am not." Sofia spoke with a measured calmness, though her heart was beating an erratic tattoo against her ribs. The opaque look in the widow's eye was frightening. It was beyond hatred, beyond reason. "Surrender now without further bloodshed and I will see that your cooperation will be taken into account with the government."

"Don't believe her." Lady Serena shot a sidelong glance

at her cohorts. "No one knows, other than these two." Her lip curled. "And do you really think that the government will show any mercy? Trust me, we will all hang if we are caught, so there's nothing to lose."

Sofia saw fear flare in De Winton's eyes. His hand jerked up.

Damn. She had no choice but to fire first.

"It seems that I underestimated you, Contessa." Lady Serena watched De Winton slump to the floor. "You *do* have nerve. But not brains." Her knife jabbed a mocking cut at Sofia. "Finish her off, Lorenzo."

The Italian fumbled for his pistol.

Sofia had the split second she needed. Spinning forward, she whipped the hidden quoits from her cuffs and sent them flying through the air. Her left-handed throw sliced across Lady Serena's wrist, knocking the knife from her grip. The other sliver of steel struck Sforza square in the chest.

He screamed and fell back, knocking the lamp to the floor. The glass shattered, spraying hot oil and sparks over the damask draperies. With a muffled *whoof*, the heavy fabric ignited in flames.

"Deverill!" Sofia lunged for the chair as Lady Serena swore and clawed the pistol from the Italian's limp grip. Grabbing the back slat, she knocked it over, covering Osborne's trussed form with her own body.

A shot exploded overhead as they hit the carpet, followed by another high-pitched oath.

"Damnation." Osborne's curse was considerably softer. "Stop taking such devilishly dangerous risks, Sofia."

"Not when you insist on riding to my rescue." She fumbled for her hidden knife and quickly set to work cutting away his bonds.

A second bullet whizzed past the overturned chair, missing them by a hair.

"Not much help, was I?" he said wryly. "What sort of hero bumbles right into the arms of the enemy?"

The blaze lit the bruises and gash on his cheek, and beneath her fingers, Sofia felt his shirt was sticky with blood. "Only the very bravest sort," she whispered, brushing a kiss to his brow.

"Only the most besotted sort." His mouth curled in a lopsided grin. "Have I told you how much I love . . . your bravado?"

"No—you've been too busy ringing a peal over my head." Her hands, which had gone very still, began moving again. For an instant, she had thought he was going to say something else. "Just one more twist." The last bit of rope snapped free.

"I've never met anyone quite like you."

"I don't doubt it. Your friends have all been raised to be ladies, not hellions." She ducked as a jade figure smashed against the hearth, sending a shower of shards over their heads. "Sorry to put you through such a dangerous ordeal."

The flames were licking higher. Dropping the spent pistols, Lady Serena ducked through the acrid clouds and darted out the door.

"Ordeal? I haven't had so much fun in years." Sofia saw that the flying stones had cut another ragged nick across his sweat-streaked flesh. And yet he was smiling.

Lord Sunshine. The light of her life.

"I would recite a sonnet or two to express my sentiments," he continued. "But we really ought to be moving."

The smoke was so thick she could hardly breathe.

"Wait," she gasped. "We can't leave these two here, much as they deserve to roast in hell."

"Are you sure they aren't dead?"

Sofia nodded grimly. "I didn't try for a mortal blow."

"Far be for me to question your aim." Osborne crawled over to De Winton and took hold of his coat collar. "Can you handle Sforza?"

Shielding her face from a fresh flare of flames, she nodded.

On hands and knees, they managed to work their way through the burning debris and maneuver the wounded men down the stairs. The top balusters were already alight, and Sofia heard the crack of a ceiling beam as it crumbled into cinders.

"Hurry," called Osborne, shouldering open the front door.

The rush of fresh air was blessedly cool on her face. Sofia drew in a deep gulp, then turned back. "The guard—"

He shoved her outside. "I'll get him." The muffled thumps from beneath the stairs gave ample indication of where the Sikh was trapped.

Both men emerged a few minutes later, coughing and sputtering. She did not ask how Osborne had come to be holding the *kirpan*.

Looking rather dazed, the Sikh collapsed on the ground next to his unconscious employers, moaning in Hindi and stroking his singed beard. Osborne bent over and braced his hands on his knees, expelling a whoosh of air. "I don't fancy the idea of attempting *that* again," he said through cracked lips.

Sofia had no intention of allowing him to risk his life in the inferno. She had already angled herself for a run at the open front door. "Keep an eye on these three," she called. "I'm going after Lady Serena."

"The devil you are!" Spinning around, Osborne tried to grab her arm, but she eluded his grasp. His words, however, followed her into the house.

"Damnation, wait for me."

Not bloody likely. Shoving the bolt into place from the inside, she headed up the stairs.

Mano a mano. This mission was no longer just about abstract ideals. Against all the rules, it had become intensely personal. Lady Serena had killed her cousin Robert and would have murdered the man she loved without batting an eye. Sofia dodged a falling timber. Come fire or brimstone, she would see to it that the lady did not escape justice.

Coals crackled beneath his boots as Osborne took the treads two at a time. The sword had proved useful in breaking the casement windows and cutting away the mullions. Still, the delay had cost him precious seconds. Squinting through the billowing clouds of soot and ash, he tried to make out which way Sofia had gone. Her dark clothing would make her difficult to spot in the swirling smoke.

A wall of flames drove him back from the study. There was no choice but to follow the corridor to the back of the town house.

"Sofia!" he shouted, trying to make himself heard above the roar of the fire.

A hiss of sparks seemed to mock his feeble effort. His throat was dry, and the heat was growing unbearable. Pressing a handkerchief over his mouth, he stumbled forward. For some reason, he had kept the *kirpan* in his hand, and though the brass pricked against his palm, he used it to steady his step.

"Stop!" The disembodied cry floated up from the back rooms. Silhouetted against a bank of arched windows, a quicksilver shape darted out from the doorway and ran for the servant stairwell. Following in hot pursuit was a sinuous smudge of black.

Osborne broke into a run, heedless of the falling plaster and spreading flames. He dared not imagine what filthy tricks Lady Serena might still have up her sleeve. And Sofia was armed with only her courage and her indomitable sense of honor.

Hardly a fair fight.

He paused for a moment at the stairwell entrance, listening for whether the chase had gone up or down. A flurry of footsteps sounded overhead. *The roof.* It made some sense, he decided, picking up his pace. The blaze had likely drawn a crowd around the town house entrance—including the authorities. Lady Serena must have figured that her best chance of escape was to cross to one of the neighboring rooftops. From there, under the cover of darkness and confusion, it would not be very hard to slip away unnoticed.

A narrow hatchway opened onto a flat stretch of tiles. A low railing of Portland stone rimmed the perimeter, and from there a short but steep pitch of slates fell off on all sides. The footing would be treacherous in the darkness, observed Osborne. But it could be done.

His gaze rose, searching among the hide-and-seek shadows for Sofia. And Lady Serena. Plumes of smoke rose up to meld with the mizzled moonlight, giving an eerie, otherworldy glow to the night. It was just bright enough to show them emerging from behind one of the large chimney pots.

As he feared, Sofia was unarmed. Lady Serena did not appear to have a pistol, but she had not come away from her rooms empty-handed. In her fist was a thick, braided bullwhip.

The lash snapped out, falling a hair short of Sofia's face.

She didn't flinch. "You might as well surrender, Lady Serena, and avoid any further bloodshed."

"What a naïve appeal. You really think I care about that?" replied Lady Serena as she recoiled the leather. "On the contrary, it would give me a good deal of pleasure to see your bones broken on the terrace stones below before I make my escape."

"There is no escape," said Sofia. "I won't let you get away."

The whip cracked again, forcing Sofia to cut back toward the chimney pot.

"Stand back, Sofia." Osborne had stayed silent so as not to distract her, but he could no longer hold back. If Lady Serena sidestepped another few feet, she would have Sofia trapped. "She isn't worth the risk. Let her go—she won't get far with General Burrand's men on her trail."

"Men." Lady Serena allowed a contemptuous curl of her lip. "I've outwitted all of them before." She, too, had seen her advantage and moved quickly to her right.

The lash could only strike at one of them. Osborne was about to make a rush when Sofia flexed her knees and sprang straight up. Her hand caught the top of the funnel, and in an shadowy blur of somersaulting limbs, she launched herself into a backflip and landed lightly on the other side of the chimney.

"H-how . . ." Lady Serena fell back a step in surprise. "One would need wings to fly like that!"

"I am a Merlin." Sofia reappeared as if by magic from the twisting tendrils of smoke.

"Sofia—" he began.

"It's all right, Deverill. Let me handle this on my own."

"You are a trained soldier," he counseled. "Don't make the mistake of allowing emotion to override the proper battlefield strategy."

"Who the devil *are* you?" demanded Lady Serena, her eyes darting back and forth between the two of them.

"Someone who is more than a match for your own Machiavellian mind," replied Osborne. He edged to the front parapet, hoping Sofia would see what he intended. "Like you, Sofia is not what she seems. She is a trained killer—and seeing that you murdered her cousin, Lord Robert Woolsey, she is not about to let you melt away into the night."

"You lie," said Serena. "The duke's sons have no female children."

"But the duke's daughter did," replied Osborne.

"Impossible!" whispered Lady Serena. "Elizabeth Woolsey died long ago, and she left no child behind."

"Then I must be an avenging angel," said Sofia.

As she spoke, she slipped to a position along the low stone railing. Her eyes met with his, and she gave a small nod. Lady Serena was now caught between them. She would have to turn one way or the other to wield her weapon, allowing one of them to pounce.

"Go to hell." Lady Serena raised the whip but realized her dilemma.

Shouts rang up from the street below. Osborne recognized Marco's voice among them.

"Give it up," said Sofia. "In another few minutes, the authorities will have the street surrounded."

"Admit defeat? Never. I *never* lose." Lady Serena looked around, icily calm despite the fire of fury in her eyes. "Ha!

I, too, can fly." The leather snaked across the gap between buildings and curled around a decorative iron railing.

"Damn." Osborne saw what she had in mind. Using the whip as a swing, Lady Serena could sail across to the lower terrace of the neighboring town house. From there, she just might have a chance to slip through the rear gardens before Lynsley's men could circle the area.

A parting smile, and then Lady Serena jumped from the ledge, her flapping skirts creating the illusion of a great malevolent crow silhouetted against the pale plumes of smoke.

There was only one way to stop her. Gauging the distance, Osborne raised the *kirpan*. Its razored blade would slice through the leather—

"No." Sofia caught his arm.

"But—" His words cut off as he watched the lash slowly slip from around the metal.

Lady Serena's low laugh turned to a shrill cry as she realized what had happened. Her spinning fall ended with a sickening thud upon the town house terrace.

Osborne did not look down. Sofia stood beside him, her profile as still and solemn as carved marble. "Why did you stop me?"

"Physics," she replied. "We trained countless hours in that trick, and if the leather is wet, there is no way it will hold." She turned to face him. "And a far more personal reason. You are a man of honor. You would have regretted killing a woman when it was not in self-defense."

"I had damn good reason to want revenge," he growled.

"Revenge is not a good motive for taking a life."

He touched her cheek. "You are right. There are far more compelling reasons for defending a life. Like—"

A lick of flames shot up from the trapdoor.

Sofia turned, an oddly tentative look on her face. "You were saying?" Her face was streaked with soot, and her hair fell in wind-snarled waves over her shoulders. No wonder firelight and the diamond-bright glitter of stars were considered romantic by poets and painters—she was the most beautiful sight he had ever seen.

However, now did not seem quite the time for artful speeches from the heart.

"It can wait," he murmured. "I would rather not go out in a blaze of glory." His fingers brushed an errant curl from her cheek. "I hope your Academy training has included how to outmaneuver a raging inferno."

Sofia smiled. "Follow me."

Chapter Twenty-four

*L*ynsley rose from examining the twisted corpse on the terrace tiles and dusted the ashes from his fingers. "It is not quite the ending I would have chosen for this affair. But in certain ways, it may be for the best. The lady's demise can be explained as an unfortunate accident, avoiding a sordid scandal for both the government and her family."

"If you live by the sword, you must be prepared to die by the sword." Osborne dropped the *kirpan* onto the ground.

Despite the tricky descent along the face of the adjoining town house, he had kept hold of the weapon. *Like a knight out of the Arthurian legends, ready to do battle with a fire-breathing dragon.* A slightly bedraggled knight, thought Sofia with an inward smile. No armor, no lance, no snow-white warhorse. Just himself—a flesh-and-blood hero, rather than a flight of fancy out of a storybook tale.

"Amen," murmured Lynsley.

"Yes, I suppose she got what she deserved." Sofia sighed, forcing her thoughts back down to earth. "And yet, I can't help feeling some pity for her. What a shame such talents went to waste. Society gives women so few choices in life. To exercise her creativity, a female is forced into the underworld of Society. She must be a criminal or . . . someone like me."

"You have a point," murmured Lynsley. As several of his men approached to cover the body with a canvas sheet, he motioned for Sofia and Osborne to follow him out through the mews. The fire brigade had the flames under control, and amid the clatter of axes and jostling of the bucket brigades, Sofia saw the wounded prisoners being carried out through the side alley.

The marquess's men would discreetly clean up, she thought grimly. By morning, the charred rubble would tell no tales of what had really happened.

"Bella!" Marco's voice rose above the cacaphony.

She turned to see him shoving his way through the crowd that had gathered to gawk. His claret evening coat was torn in several places, his cravat was missing, and his trousers were covered with mud. *"Grazie a Dio,"* he cried, clasping her to his chest. "You had me worried for a moment."

"Things were a little warm," she replied. "But thanks to Osborne—"

"Si! Prego, prego, amico!" Marco turned and gave Osborne a fierce hug as well. "Sorry," he added, seeing Osborne's expression. "I tend to forget my English manners when I get overwrought."

"No apologies necessary," said Osborne. "Indeed, I owe you one for thinking the worst of you."

Marco waved off the words with a cocky grin. *"Si,* I can be an insufferable prick, eh? But it was all for a good cause."

"Yes, it was." The look Osborne gave her sent a prickle of heat down her spine.

Don't be a fool, she chided herself. It was likely the residue of the drugs that had her imagining a spark of emotion in his eyes. A hallucination. Or simply the fleeting reflection of the burning building.

Deverill Osborne had acted out of duty, not devotion. He was a man of honor, of courage. A steadfast comrade, a gentle lover. He shared his strength with his friends. But as for his heart, she feared that it was wholly his own.

"Dev! Lady Sofia!"

Sofia looked up to see Harkness join them. "Damn, I'm glad to find both of you alive." English restraint prevented him from repeating Marco's exuberant display of emotion, but his clap to Osborne's shoulder held fast for an extra moment or two.

"Thank you, Nick. With your help and a little luck, we managed to dodge the devil."

"Not without getting a few scrapes," said Harkness, observing Osborne's lacerated cheek and bloodied shirt. "What in the name of Lucifer happened to you?"

Lynsley cut off the conversation with a brusque cough. "Sorry, gentlemen. Though I share your sentiments, I must cut short this touching scene in order to finish my official duties. Government questions must take precedence over personal ones." Looking to Sofia and Osborne, he indicated the gate across the carriage way. "Please follow me. The house next door has been commandeered in order to direct the firefighting efforts. My assistant has arranged private rooms for us in the back wing."

"What about De Winton and the others?" asked Sofia once they had gained the privacy of the garden.

"He and Sforza will stand trial for the murder of Lord Robert Woolsey," answered the marquess. "Marco convinced Familligi to testify against them in order to save his own neck. With your evidence, they will go to the gallows. Andover, Concord, and Roxbury will be spending a number of years in prison on embezzlement charges."

That she had helped root out the poisonous poppy conspiracy brought Sofia a measure of professional satisfaction. Their scarlet sins would soon be only a faded memory. As for her own performance, had she earned a passing grade? The marquess would have to be the judge of that, once he heard the full story. Mistakes had been made, and despite the hellfire heroics of the evening, there was still much left to be resolved.

"A messy business." Lynsley closed the door to his temporary war room. "But, thankfully, it is finally at an end." He sighed. "Well done. Both of you."

"Thank you, sir," began Sofia.

"Actually, it's not over," interrupted Osborne.

"Please, not just now, Deverill," she said, fearing she knew what he was about to say.

Ignoring her warning, he went on. "A complication has arisen, Lynsley. One that can't simply be swept under the rug, like the others."

The marquess arched a brow. "Yes?"

"Shall I tell him, Sofia? Or would you prefer to do it yourself?"

She bit her lip, uncertain about . . . about everything. But perhaps Osborne was right—it was best to get it over with.

"I'm sorry, sir, but I seem to be, er, that is, it may be possible . . ."

"Bloody hell, you don't have to apologize for who you are, Sofia." All of a sudden, Osborne seemed to explode in anger. Eyes ablaze, he turned on Lynsley, his tone taking on an edge of sharp sarcasm. "Congratulations on a successful mission. But perhaps you ought to do a bit more checking up on the backgrounds of the urchins you pluck from the streets and thrust into harm's way to do your dirty work."

The marquess's face darkened in a rare show of uncontrolled emotion. "You think me remiss in my duties? Do you imagine that I enjoy sending the Merlins into danger?" His voice rose to a pitch she had never heard before. "You have been quite vocal in your criticisms, Osborne. Now, damn it, I expect you to explain your scurrilous accusation—"

"Gentlemen." Sofia spoke softly, yet they both fell silent, looking a trifle embarrassed. "Really, there is no need to shout at each other."

"I suppose that was an unfair blow, Lynsley. Accept my apology." Osborne ran a hand through his disheveled hair. "Espionage is a nasty, dangerous business. However, Sofia has nothing but praise for your methods and motives."

The marquess nodded stiffly.

"Besides," he added with a wry grimace, "gentlemen ought not raise their voices in the presence of a *lady*."

Lynsley's brow pinched in question.

"Let us not make a Gothic tale of it," blurted Sofia. "What Osborne means to say is that during the course of my investigation, I discovered that I may well be the Duke of Sterling's granddaughter."

"Sofia has a locket. Inside is a portrait of her mother—or so she was led to believe by the prostitute who raised her," added Osborne. "It is an exact copy of the painting in Sterling's private study."

"Good Lord." Lynsley's expression mirrored her own initial shock. However, his surprise quickly turned into a rueful smile. "I confess, I try to plan for every contingency, but I never quite imagined this one. Though in truth, perhaps I should have expected that such a revelation might happen one day."

Forcing a nonchalant drawl, she replied, "Why ever would you think that one of your ugly ducklings might turn into a swan?"

"So, it seems that our charade had a grain of truth to it, milady." Lynsley pursed his lips. "Does Sterling know?"

She shook her head. "No, sir. I only just stumbled upon the possibility a few days ago. And to be fair, there is no real proof."

"You are living proof, Sofia," insisted Osborne. "The likeness is undeniable. Why fight it?"

Because the thought was more daunting than any danger she had faced. All of her training had stressed the importance of keeping an emotional distance between herself and everyone around her. She couldn't quite picture being part of a real family.

"A painting seems an awfully tenuous connection by which to claim a connection to a noble title." Sofia shot an appealing look at the marquess. "Don't you agree, sir?"

"I think that is something only you and the duke can decide," said Lynsley softly.

"But I am so used to being alone," she whispered. "Our worlds are so different. I fear I'll never quite fit in."

"You will find your own place, Sofia. Of that I am very sure." The marquess clasped his hands behind his back. "However, before you turn in your spurs for satin slippers, I will need to have a final report on the mission."

Osborne, who had stepped back into the shadows during the last exchange, suddenly turned and cleared his throat. "Before you two march off, might I have a private word with Sofia?"

"This is rather important, Osborne," said Lynsley dryly.

"I promised the minister a report within the hour. Can't it wait until morning?"

"So is this." Osborne stood his ground. "And, no, it cannot."

"Very well." The marquess hesitated, fixing Sofia with a fatherly smile. "It seems as if I'll be losing another of my best agents. Your roommates have found family by marriage, but you . . ."

Osborne coughed. "Sir."

"Ten minutes, Osborne." It might have been merely a quirk of the candlelight, but Sofia thought she saw him wink. "On second thought, I'll allow you fifteen."

"That doesn't leave me much time." Osborne winced as he tried to smile.

How his lip had come to be cut was not something he remembered. By now there were precious few parts of his anatomy that weren't covered with scrapes or bruises. He ached all over. But the sharpest stab was in his heart, as he recalled how close he had come to losing Sofia.

"First of all, I want to thank you for saving my skin," he said.

She didn't meet his gaze. "I was simply returning the favor."

Her tone—so cool, so casual—sent a shiver down his spine. Did she mean to say she was merely doing her job? This wasn't going to be easy. He wasn't sure he had the courage to make himself so vulnerable.

Coward. It was Sofia who possessed the indomitable spirit of a true warrior . . . not to speak of the sensual body of a woman. Brains and beauty—it was an irresistible combination. He had lost his heart and soul to her. He must somehow summon the strength to tell her how much he had come to admire her conviction, her courage.

How he had come to love her.

Love. It wasn't a word he had much practice in saying aloud. Most other phrases tripped so easily from his tongue. Be it art, poetry, politics, fashion, there wasn't a subject on which the *ton* did not seek his informed opinion. The charming, witty Deverill Osborne could always be counted on for a clever quip. A lighthearted laugh. But now he wished to be deadly serious. For so long he had wondered who he really was, what he really wanted. Suddenly the answer seemed right before his eyes.

"Sofia. Please look at me," he said.

Her face was a little lopsided, her lovely features streaked with soot and scratches. As Osborne leaned closer, a reflection in the silver epergne showed that he looked even worse. He couldn't help it—he started to chuckle. "Lord, what a pair we make."

That finally drew a ghost of a smile from her. "The *ton* would be horrified. We've broken every one of their rules on deportment and decorum. And then some, I suppose."

"But we got the job done."

"There is a difference," whispered Sofia. "It was my duty, while you . . . I should never have allowed you to risk your life." Her lip quivered as she spoke, the first sign she was not in complete command of her emotions.

The small sign gave him the heart to press on. "Should I not be allowed to choose for myself? You did. I may not have honed my skills to as sharp an edge as yours, but perhaps with a bit more practice . . ." Osborne paused for breath. "By the by, does every Merlin's man have to pass through a trial by fire to win her hand?"

The question seemed to catch her off guard. Staring

down at her muddied shoes, she mumbled a halting reply. "I . . . I am not sure. You would have to ask Lord Kirtland or Mr. Orlov."

"I have a good deal to say to my friend Julian when next I see him," he replied. "But right now, my most pressing question is for you, Sofia."

The case clock in the corner continued to tick off the time. Lynsley would soon be knocking, and if he allowed her to slip through his fingers, he might never have a chance at this moment again.

Do or die.

"Will you marry me, Sofia? Proper etiquette dictates that I should have some flowery speech, some precious jewelry to accompany the proposal." He took her face between his scraped palms and tilted it upward. "But at this moment, all I can offer is me and my heart."

The candlelight caught the flutter of her lashes. And then the shimmering spill of a tear. "You are," she whispered, "a gift beyond words."

"I love you," he murmured. "Or should I say, *ti amo.*"

Her lips touched the corner of his mouth. "Love has a language all its own."

"Does that mean . . ."

"That I love you too?" Sofia's caress feathered against his flesh. "Of all my secrets, that was the hardest to hide, Deverill. I think I have loved you since that first glimmer of sunshine cut through the shadows of the drawing room."

"You certainly had a strange way of showing it."

"I will likely never behave like a real lady." She drew back a touch. "Can you live with that?"

"Let me consider the question for a moment." His hug tightened, joining their bodies as one. "I think the answer is yes."

Osborne lost count of the time. All he knew was that the kiss ended far too soon. "What's the hurry?" he murmured, keeping hold as she tried to slip out of his arms. "Lynsley can cool his heels for another few minutes."

"I get demerits for dereliction of duty." She smiled, but he saw a shadow of doubt cloud her eyes. "But before he returns, we still have something to resolve. Are you sure about marriage? I can't promise to be a conventional wife. I doubt I shall ever be able to forget all the lessons I have learned at the Academy." Her mouth quirked. "As you have seen, docility and obedience are not among them."

"If I wanted a creature to obey my every command, I would get a dog."

"I'm very fond of animals," she murmured. "Could we consider a cat as well?"

"You may have a whole menagerie of beasts—dogs, cats, hawks, unicorns. Just so long as I am one of the creatures you care for."

"You are the *only* creature I care for, Deverill. Now and forever."

"Amen," he murmured. "May I take that as a yes?"

"Yes." There was a fraction of a pause. "But—"

He groaned. "Please, no buts."

"But this is quite serious," insisted Sofia. "Can you imagine what will happen if word gets out about who I really am? Society would be utterly scandalized by your making such a shocking match. A secret government operative—one who trained in a host of unladylike skills—is not at all the proper wife for one of London's most popular lords. Not that anyone will know the full truth, but still, I would not wish to make you the butt of vicious gossip."

"My love, if we can outwit a group of dangerous criminals, we can certainly deal with the *ton*. Trust me on this.

You forget—you are already a contessa in their eyes. That you are also the Duke of Sterling's long-lost granddaughter will be greeted as a wonderfully romantic tale." He grinned. "I can already think of the beginning—It was a dark and stormy night. . . ."

Sofia burst out laughing. "Perhaps Lynsley should think of recruiting you to our ranks. You *do* have a gift for duplicity and deception."

A knock on the door interrupted their embrace.

"Speak of the devil." Osborne sighed. "I suppose we had better report for duty."

"Right." He felt her hesitate. "I don't quite know how to break the news to him. Or to the duke. I'm far more skilled with weapons than with words."

He took her hand. "Follow me. From now on, whether we are marching into the jaws of death or a ducal drawing room, we will do it together."

"Osborne." Surprise deepened the lines on the duke's face as he looked up from the Roman coins he was studying.

"Forgive me for the unannounced intrusion. Your butler wished to stop me, but I wouldn't take no for an answer." A few hours of sleep and a change of clothing had improved his appearance to some degree, but Osborne did not doubt that his face still looked like hell. "I know I am not a very pretty picture at the moment. But I thought you would want to hear my news without delay."

Sterling's hand was trembling slightly as he set down his magnifying glass. "Has it something to do with Elizabeth's locket?"

"Yes," replied Osborne. "And with Robert's death."

"You mean to say the two are related?"

Osborne nodded.

"For the love of God, man, go on!"

"Actually, it is not for me to say more. The person you really wish to speak with is just outside the door. She, more than I, has been instrumental in seeing that the truth be brought to light." He glanced back at the polished panels of oak. "Shall I ask her to come in?"

Sterling scraped back his chair and rose. "Please," he whispered, his voice as unsteady as his legs.

Sofia took a tentative step into the room. She did not feel much like a Merlin at the moment. It was not confidence taking wing within her—it was a flock of nervous butterflies fluttering against her rib cage.

What to say? She felt tongue-tied. All her training seemed to desert her. She had never felt so awkward, so unsure.

"Don't be shy, Lady Sofia." Osborne came to her rescue, offering his arm and an encouraging wink in the same smooth motion. "Chin up, my dear," he murmured. "You've faced far more fearsome challenges than this."

"Hah," she breathed, but his humor helped her relax.

"Contessa." The duke held out his hands to greet her. "What a pleasant surprise." He smiled, but he turned a questioning look to Osborne.

Osborne in turn regarded her.

"Perhaps you had best be seated, sir," she said with a wry sigh. "My unexpected appearance here is likely to be the least of the surprises you will receive this afternoon."

Osborne began to retreat toward the door.

"Deverill," she said faintly, losing what little courage she had.

"I'll be right outside, in case you have need of me. But I am confident this is one battle you can fight on your own."

"Battle," echoed Sterling. He eyed her with a mixture of concern and confusion. "The two of you look as though you've faced off against Lucifer and his legions. But I confess, I am bewildered by how this is linked to me and my family."

Uncurling her fist, Sofia reached out and pressed the chain and locket into his unresisting hand.

The duke staggered slightly, as if the weight of the world had just been placed in his palm. "Where did you get this?"

"From the woman who looked after me as a young child. Who in turn received it—and me—from her sister . . ." She told the tale in a rush, watching the waves of conflicting emotion flood the duke's face. Shock, sorrow, regret. But most of all, love.

"Why, that means you are . . ."

"Maybe not," she said quickly. "We can never be truly sure, sir."

His gaze met hers, and lines etched around his eyes seemed softened by the shimmering trickle of tears. "Oh, my dear, there is not a shadow of a doubt in my mind, now that I look at you closely. I see Elizabeth in the shape of your smile, the curve of your cheek, the strength of your character." He opened his arms to her. "Welcome home, child."

It was some time before either of them could speak again.

When finally Sofia lifted her head from her grandfather's shoulder, she wasn't sure whether she was laughing or crying. "Dear me, I fear this may take a while to get used to. My past has not schooled me for a life of privilege and wealth."

Sterling sighed. "Which begs the question of how you came to be here in London, calling yourself Contessa della Silveri."

"That was a cover," admitted Sofia. She went on to give him a terse explanation of the Academy, Lord Lynsley's role as secret spymaster, and her recent mission. "And so, in the end," she summed up, "the miscreants have been caught and some measure of justice has been achieved for Lord Robert. Without his sacrifice, we would never have uncovered what was going on."

The duke leaned back rather heavily against his chair. "A school for spies? Why, I've known Lynsley for years, and he never gave a hint at being involved in such dashing dangers."

"He takes great care to hide his endeavors beneath a cloak of boring respectability."

"Indeed, indeed," mused Sterling. "Is Osborne also a part of your network?"

"Not officially," murmured Sofia. "But he played a crucial role in defeating the enemy."

"I will be sure to thank him and Lynsley. And you, my dear." The duke reached out to twine his fingers with hers. As if drawing strength from her closeness, he squared his shoulders. "Like a phoenix, you rise from the ashes of loss. It is a miracle."

"Merlins are said to have a bit of magic."

"I quite believe it." Sterling squeezed her hand. "I can't tell you how happy I am to have you here after all these years, taking your rightful place in the bosom of your family."

"It is only right to inform you that you are getting more than you bargained for, sir—"

"Please, you must call me Grandfather rather than sir, Sofia."

It felt very strange on her tongue. But then, there were a great many things she would need to learn. *Practice makes perfect*. Smiling, she began anew. "What I meant to say, Grandfather, was that I hope you will not mind making room for yet another new family member. You see, Lord Osborne has proposed, and I have accepted. I hope you will not feel too crowded."

Throwing back his head, the duke gave a hearty laugh. "The more, the merrier. Let us call in your betrothed, along with a bottle of champagne. This calls for a toast."

"Indeed it does," said Osborne, throwing open the door and signaling for the footman behind him to pop the cork. "To family."

Epilogue

*T*o family."

As the afternoon sun filled the duke's gallery with a soft glow, Sofia watched Lynsley raise a salute and take a sip of his wine. It must be hard to swallow the loss of a well-trained agent, she reflected, though the marquess's gentlemanly smile gave no hint of censure.

"Kind of you to stop by and offer your congratulations," said Osborne. He rose from the worktable, where he and the duke were sketching plans for the wedding decorations, and drank from his own glass. "Thank you for accepting the news with such good grace." A week had passed since the night of the fire, and the banns had just been posted.

The marquess sketched a polite bow. "I have learned in this business that one must be flexible. And pragmatic. All of the Merlins eventually leave the nest." He turned to Sofia. "I wish you joy."

"Thank you, sir." She had found love, she had found family, she had found herself. The only sense of loss was in parting ways with the Academy. She must leave the dirt and the dangers behind now that she was taking her proper place in Society. It seemed impossible to think that the two worlds could ever coexist.

Sterling came over to shake Lynsley's hand. "Forgive me, Thomas," he said, wiping away a tear. "I seem to have turned into a watering pot in my old age. However, allow me to thank you for redeeming the death of one grandchild. And for bringing a lost one back to life."

"I am not the Almighty, Henry. Merely a humble servant of the government. But I am happy to have been of some service to you." The marquess did dart an ironic look at Osborne. "In all truth, I ought to be angry—I can ill-afford to lose such a sterling agent with Napoleon marching on Moscow." He exaggerated a sigh. "But love conquers all."

The duke laughed.

Sofia turned away, feeling the sting of salt in her eyes. The marquess was in many ways like the father she had never known. She was sorry for letting him down.

Lynsley, to his credit, did not harp on his disappointment. Indeed, he sounded quite jovial as he asked about plans for the wedding trip.

Sterling cocked his head. "I thought I mentioned to you that we are all going to my estate in Scotland for an extended stay. The Highland heather and moors around Craigellachie are lovely this time of year. The young people will have a chance to relax and recover from their ordeal. And I shall have an opportunity to become better acquainted with my granddaughter."

"Ah, yes, you did mention something of the sort." The marquess coughed and turned to Sofia. "I don't suppose I could interest you in a small task while you are there? There are rumors of French agents infiltrating along the North Sea coast. I could use a pair of trained eyes to look around and report on the situation." He drew out a crumpled map. "But, of course, you likely have other things on your mind."

Sofia looked longingly at the weather-stained paper. "It *is* going to be awfully quiet there," she murmured.

"It wouldn't do to have a bored bride," drawled Osborne. "However, if you wish to accept the marquess's proposal, I will have to insist on an additional clause to be added to our marriage contract."

"Which is?" she asked softly.

"That any danger we face, we face together."

The duke clasped Lynsley's arm. "Come, let us have a celebratory sherry in the library and leave the two of them to negotiate the terms in private."

"An excellent suggestion," said the marquess. "I hear you have a cask of the '89 Amontillado in your cellar . . ."

Sofia waited for the door to close before letting out her breath. "This is no laughing matter, Deverill," she said, seeing the smile on his face. "I nearly got you killed on this last assignment. I don't want to force you into an arrangement you will come to resent."

"My love, I never felt so alive as in these last few weeks. Neither of us would be satisfied with a life of indolent indulgence. We would be bored to flinders."

"But you are the darling of Society. The *ton* looks up to you as a shining light of charm and wit. I . . ." Sofia looked around the room, taking in the sumptuous furnishings, the polished woods, the expensive art. "Your world is a comfortable one. I fear you will miss the accolades and attention."

His smile faded, replaced by a crooked uncertainty. "The *ton* will find a new Lord Sunshine. They always do. As for me, the clever quips, the glitter, and the gaiety have long since lost their allure. I was more alone than you can ever know until I found you, Sofia."

"Dev—"

Osborne's arms were suddenly around her, strong and sure as he drew her against his chest. "No, hear me out, sweeting. The bon mots may come effortlessly to my lips, but talk of true feelings is not so easy. It is hard to find words for how much I admire your strength, your honor, your sense of purpose." His lips were warm against her cheek. "So let me simply say again that I love you."

Through her tears, the blue of his gaze was a shimmering sapphire blur. Sofia blinked. "Merlins aren't meant to cry. We are trained to fly alone, but my heart is here with you. I know none of the fancy poetry of your world—"

Osborne silenced her halting words with a kiss. "We will make our own world, a balance between light and dark," he murmured.

"That sounds beautiful beyond words."

"Then let us go report for duty and get the details of our next mission from Lynsley." But rather than release her, he swept her up into his arms and carried her to the sofa. "But not quite yet."

It was some time before Sofia straightened her skirts and smoothed the errant curls from her cheeks. "We had better make an appearance. They will be wondering what became of us."

He chuckled. "No, they won't. However, I shall discipline my naughty desires for the moment and obey your command."

She gave a mischievous grin. "Get used to it."

His brow arched. "Now, just a moment! I must insist on equal rank. I would never live it down if my friends learned that my wife wore the trousers in the family."

"Speaking of trousers, it goes without saying that I will wear breeches and boots for riding."

Osborne flashed a wicked smile. "I've no objection to seeing your lovely legs—" As he opened the brass latch, a folded sheet of paper fell from between the door and the molding. It was sealed with a black wax wafer bearing the image of a hawk in flight.

"Hmmm." After a long look, he handed it over to Sofia. She cracked the seal and smoothed out the creases.

The towns to watch are Nairn, Fidhorn, Burghead, and Lossiemouth. I've arranged for a small yacht to be at your service. It will be anchored in the village of Spey Bay. Messages can be sent to me through the owner of The Gorse & Grouse.

Good hunting,

L.

One last thing—in consideration of his past services, tell Osborne he can consider himself a full-fledged Merlin.

He read it over her shoulder and laughed. "I have just one question."

"What's that, my love?"

"Do I get a tattoo?"

DON'T MISS
THE FIRST TWO NOVELS IN
ANDREA PICKENS'S
MERLIN SPY SERIES!

THE SPY WORE SILK
(Grand Central Publishing 0-446-61800-4)

They were once orphans from London's roughest slums. Now they are students of Mrs. Merlin's Academy for Select Young Ladies, learning the art of spying and seduction. Bold, beautiful, and oh-so-dangerous, they are England's ultimate secret weapons. . . .

A DUEL BETWEEN DUTY . . .

The most skilled of "Merlin's Maidens," Siena is assigned to unmask a traitor lurking among an exclusive club of book collectors. Armed with only her wits, her blades, and her sultry body, she joins the gentlemen at a country house party. But her prime suspect, disgraced ex-army officer Lord Kirtland, proves as enigmatic as he is suspicious—and sinfully sensuous.

AND DESIRE.

Kirtland's instincts tell him the enticing "Black Dove" is hiding more than a luscious body beneath her fancy silks. Yet, as he starts to plumb her secrets, a cunning adversary lays plans to destroy them both. To live, Siena must end her tantalizing dance of deception and desire—and decide whether to trust her head or her heart. . . .

AND ALSO FROM
ANDREA PICKENS'S
MERLIN SPY SERIES:

SEDUCED BY A SPY
(Grand Central Publishing 0-446-61799-7)

They are students of Mrs. Merlin's Academy for Select Young Ladies, learning the techniques of spying and seduction. . . .

ART OF DECEPTION

Hot-tempered and a warrior to the bone, Shannon is the most daring of "Merlin Maidens." Her assignment: Stop the fiendishly cruel assassin who is targeting a top British ballistic expert's family. Marshaling her intelligence, fighting skills, and weapons is easy. Being forced to work with the sinfully handsome Russian spy she loathes is something else.

GAME OF DESIRE

Witty, resourceful, and notorious for his rakish charm with women, Alexandr Orlov tempts Shannon's fierce reserve and lithe body to win her trust. But in the remote Scottish castle where they must protect the innocent, their games of parry and thrust could end in death. A ruthless enemy is watching . . . and planning to turn their passion into the most dangerous weapon of all.

THE DISH

Where authors give you the inside scoop!

From the desk of Andrea Pickens

Dear Reader,

As you can imagine, swashbuckling secret agents cannot be distracted by trifling matters, such as the state of their wardrobe. They have much more important things to think about—like swordplay, spying, and seduction. (It goes without saying that they are *lady* spies. Men would have no interest in discussing the cut of their trousers, would they?) However, there are exceptions to the rules of engagement, especially when the spies in question have known each other since childhood. So, when three best friends got together to discuss a recent mission—as documented in THE SCARLET SPY (on sale now)—the conversation went as follows:

Siena (*to her friend Sofia*): "Nice dress."

Shannon (*sounding a little jealous*): "I had to wear pink, rather than that luscious shade of scarlet." A *sigh.* "Pink is not my best shade."

Sofia (*with a sardonic smile*): "Well, it didn't matter overly much, seeing as how it seemed to come off you rather quickly. Mr. Orlov has very clever hands."

Shannon (*her face turning red*): Expletive deleted.

Siena (*tactfully changing the subject*): "Nice pistol. Is it one of the new turnoff Italian pocket models?"

Sofia (*flashing up the weapon*): "Yes, isn't it cute? And it matches the trim on my reticule."

Shannon (*to Siena*): "How come we only got daggers?"

Sofia (*with an airy wave of her hand*): "You two are dangerous enough without gunpowder. Lord Lynsley knew he could trust my ladylike restraint."

Shannon and Siena (*chortling in unison*): "You, a lady?" *The sounds of mirth grow louder.* "Ha, don't make us laugh."

Sofia (*arching a brow*): "I might surprise you."

Shannon (*narrowing her eyes*): "What's that supposed to mean? We are sisters-in-arms and have been for years. There are no secrets between us."

Siena (*after a slight pause*): "Are there, Fifi?"

Sofia (*fluttering her lashes*): "Sorry, girls, you will just have to read my story . . ."

No matter how hard they tried, her friends could pry out no further information. I, on the other hand, managed to learn a few more tidbits about Sofia's scarlet secrets. They involve a trip to London, where she encounters the sinfully sexy

Lord Osborne as well as a devilishly dangerous adversary, who . . .

Well, it's a long story, and I'm running out of space here. You will just have to visit www.andrea pickensonline.com for a more tantalizing peek at THE SCARLET SPY and her adventures.

Happy reading!

Andrea Pickens

♥ ♥ ♥ ♥ ♥ ♥ ♥ ♥ ♥ ♥ ♥ ♥ ♥ ♥

From the desk of Shannon K. Butcher

Dear Reader,

I'm a planner. I like to schedule things, make lists, and keep my life in nice, neat, organized bundles so I know what I'm going to be doing for the next two years or eighteen months, if I'm getting sloppy.

Needless to say, it doesn't always work.

For instance, as careful a planner as I am, I never planned for Grant, my hero in NO ESCAPE (on sale now). I never even saw him coming until he was there on the page, making me grin.

When I wrote NO REGRETS, Grant was just a buddy—a sidekick created to add a bit of comic relief. By the time I'd finished NO CONTROL, I knew Grant was destined for his very own book. He kept popping up in my head, demanding a happy ending of his own.

Even though I didn't realize it at the time, Grant was born years before I'd even decided to give writing a shot. It was the day my husband taught our then five-year-old son a lesson he called "drive-thru justice." The two of them had picked up fast food on the way home, and when they got back with our feast, the toy was missing from the kid's meal. It didn't matter that our son didn't really need the toy or that there were likely five more like it in his room. What mattered was that he'd been looking forward to that toy all day, he'd been really good in school, they'd ordered and paid for it, and it wasn't in the sack. That toy was important to our son, so my husband declared they would get drive-thru justice. They drove all the way back to the restaurant and demanded the toy. And got it.

In the end, I think my husband spent more time playing with the toy than our son, but that lesson of justice—of righting even a small wrong on the behalf of someone who couldn't—always stuck in my head. It came out in the form of Grant—a man who refused to let people smaller and more helpless than him be mistreated in any way.

That trait nearly landed Grant in prison when he was a teen. Now, years later, Grant is back in the last place on earth he wants to be—his hometown—to check on an old friend who left him an odd phone message he couldn't ignore. But he finds out that Isabelle is not okay. She's afraid, and Grant has never been able to ignore her fear. Not fourteen years ago when he killed the man who tried to rape her, and not now. It doesn't matter that she's a grown woman and perfectly capable of taking care of herself or that she never really intended for Grant to get caught up in this mess.

Of course, fixing it isn't going to be easy. Someone is killing people from their past and staging the deaths as suicides, and bodies are piling up fast. Grant and Isabelle must work together to convince the police that Isabelle's suspicion of murder is right before the next person falls victim.

This book was without question the hardest one I've ever written. Not only does it deal with some really tough issues, but also when I was outlining the story, it was nearly impossible to create a woman who was able to make Grant give up his womanizing ways. I mean, the man has it all—looks, brains, courage . . . stamina. Luckily, Isabelle is more than up to the task of taming Grant and giving him the life he so richly deserves.

Enjoy!

Shannon K. Butcher

www.shannonkbutcher.com

♥ ♥ ♥ ♥ ♥ ♥ ♥ ♥ ♥ ♥ ♥ ♥ ♥ ♥ ♥ ♥

From the desk of Lori Wilde

Dear Reader,

Starry-eyed Rachael Henderson from ADDICTED TO LOVE (on sale now) is mad as heck, and she's not going to take it anymore. After being stood up at the altar—*twice!*—on the very same day, she learns her parents are getting divorced after thirty years, and it's the last straw. Born on Valentine's Day in Valentine, Texas, she's convinced she's been fed a line of bull about love. She's a romanceaholic, but no more! She's drawing a line in the sand. Determined to stomp out unrealistic ideas about love, she starts Romanceaholics Anonymous.

Except she never counted on one very sexy sheriff with a heart as big as Texas.

Take Rachael's test to see if you, too, might be a romanceaholic. And visit Rachael's Web site at www.romanceaholicsanonymous.com.
You might be a romanceaholic if:

- You replace the heroine's name with yours when reading a romance novel;
- You knock down bridesmaids to catch the bouquet;
- You go to the rodeo just to watch the wranglers in their Wranglers;

- You wear nothing but a black silk teddy and stilettos while cooking dinner;
- You have a wedding planner on speed dial;
- Your everyday dishes are Royal Doulton's ALLURE bone China;
- You purchase rose-colored prescription eyeglasses;
- Your voice mail says, "Leave a message, hug, hug, kiss, kiss";
- You've placed your phone number inside fortune cookies and passed them out to handsome single men;
- And, last, but not least, you spray lavender on your sheets at night.

Hope you enjoy ADDICTED TO LOVE!

Lori Wilde

www.loriwilde.com

Author Andrea Pickens
loves to hear from her readers,
so visit her Web site at:
www.andreapickensonline.com

AND . . .

*Keep an eye out for the next,
new series of Regency novels
from Andrea Pickens,
filled with more rogues, rakehells,
and ROMANCE. . . .*
Coming soon from
Grand Central Publishing!